On To Richmond

Book # 2 in The Bregdan Chronicles

Sequel to Storm Clouds Rolling In

Ginny Dye

On To Richmond

Copyright © 2010 by Ginny Dye
Published by A Voice In The World Publishing
Bellingham, WA 98229

www.BregdanChronicles.net

www.GinnyDye.com

www.AVoiceInTheWorldPublishing.com

ISBN 1507884958

Printed in the United States of America.

*For Scarrie, my incredible little sister
who had the courage to
fight for her freedom, and who is now
using that same courage and spirit to
pursue her dreams.
I'm proud of you and I love you!*

A Note From the Author

There are times in the writing of history when we must use words we personally abhor. The use of the word "nigger" in *On To Richmond* is one of those times. Though I hate the word, its use is necessary to reveal and to challenge the prejudices of the time in order to bring change and healing. Stay with me until the end – I think you will agree.

My great hope is that *On To Richmond* will both entertain and challenge you. I hope you will learn as much as I did during the months of research it took to write this book. Though I now live in the Pacific Northwest, I grew up in the South and lived for 11 years in Richmond, VA. I spent countless hours exploring the plantations that still line the banks of the James River and became fascinated by the history.

But, you know, it's not the events that fascinate me so much – it's the people. That's all history is, you know. History is the story of people's lives. History reflects the consequences of their choice and actions – both good and bad. History is what has given you the world you live in today – both good and bad.

This truth is why I named this series The Bregdan Chronicles. Bregdan is a Gaelic term for weaving. Braiding. Every life that has been lived until today is a part of the woven braid of life. It takes every person's story to create history. Your life will help determine the course of history. You may think you don't have much of an impact. You do. Every action you take will reflect in someone else's life. Someone else's decisions. Someone else's future. Both good and bad. That is the **Bregdan Principle**...

**Every life that has been lived until today is a part
of the woven braid of life.
It takes every person's story to create history.
Your life will help determine the course of history.
You may think you don't have much of an impact.
You do.
Every action you take will reflect in
someone else's life.
Someone else's decisions.
Someone else's future.
Both good and bad.**

My great hope as you read this book, and all that will follow, is that you will acknowledge the power you have, every day, to change the world around you by your decisions and actions. Then I will know the research & writing were all worthwhile.

Oh, and I hope you enjoy every moment of it, and learn to love the characters as much as I do!

I'm already being asked how many books will be in this series. I guess that depends on how long I live! As of now, there are 8 books. My intention is to release 2-3 books a year, each covering 1 year – continuing to weave the lives of my characters into the times they lived. I hate to end a good book as much as anyone – always feeling so sad that I have to leave my friends. You shouldn't have to be sad for a long time!

If you like what you read, you'll want to make sure you're on our mailing list at www.BregdanChronicles.net. I'll let you know each time a new one comes out!

Sincerely,
Ginny Dye

Chapter One

May, 1861

Carrie Cromwell frowned as she stared out over the raging, turbulent waters of the James River. Four days of steady rain had transformed the usually placid river into a furious monster tearing at its confining banks. Torrents of water sweeping down from the western Appalachian Mountains would soon enable the river to succeed in its quest to top the banks and seek its claim on the surrounding farmland. Massive tree trunks swept by like weightless match sticks, their solid darkness almost matching the muddy swirl of the water.

Carrie lifted her eyes from the river to gaze up into the brilliant blue sky. The rain had ended just the night before, leaving the air crystal clear and deliciously fresh. She allowed herself to stare up into it for just a moment before she turned her eyes back to the river. It more closely matched her thoughts.

"Are you going to tell me about the letter you got from your father? Or are you just going to continue stewing about it?"

Carrie managed a slight smile as she turned to look at Rose. "How did you know?" She laughed. "Don't even bother to answer that question. I should know by now that you know me almost as well as I know myself."

Carrie lapsed into brooding silence again, knowing Rose would give her all the time she needed to answer her question. Granite, her towering gray Thoroughbred gelding, moved under her restlessly as the waters of the river won their fight with the muddy banks and began to edge slowly toward where the two friends watched astride their horses. Finally, Carrie reached deep into the pocket of the navy blue dress she wore and pulled out a thick envelope.

"This letter from Father came just this morning."

Rose nodded. "I saw the man who delivered it." She paused and then asked carefully, "Is it bad news?"

Carrie managed a slight laugh. "Is there anything *but* bad news in our country right now? Fort Sumter has fallen. Virginia has seceded. The war has begun." She shook her head. It would not do to let her thoughts go where they wanted to. She knew the thoughts would come later, when it was dark and there was no flurry of activity to block them out. But for now she would concentrate on what was at hand. She stuffed an errant, wavy black strand of hair back into her long braid. In a hurry to get to the river, she hadn't even bothered to shape it into a bun. Now the silky strands sought to escape the confines of the thick braid, as the breeze teased her hair into rebellion.

A frown creased her brow again as she stared down at the letter in her hand. "Father has been asked by Governor Letcher to take a high position in the Virginia state government."

"Surely you expected that. Your father has been working with the governor since he left in November."

Memories of her father's hopelessness after the death of his beloved wife, Abigail, swept through Carrie's mind. She missed her mother, too, but they had grown close only in the last month of her life, so her death hadn't left the same gaping hole. She nodded as Rose's words penetrated her thoughts. "Yes, of course I expected it..."

"Then what is troubling you so much?" Rose demanded.

Carrie almost smiled at the impatience in her friend's voice. The freedom they experienced in their friendship was wonderful. A year ago, things had been very different. Rose had still been her best friend, but the reality of Rose being her personal slave, while she lived the luxurious life of a wealthy plantation owner's daughter, had put an impenetrable barrier of protocol between them. The past year had blown those barriers away. Now they were like sisters.

Carrie struggled to express her feelings. "Everything is so different now," she began haltingly. "It was exciting to think of Father standing close to the helm of Virginia when we were still part of the Union and everyone was fighting so hard to keep it that way, but now..." She paused and stared out at the rampaging river as she tried to force her turbulent thoughts into some form of order. "Father believed so much in keeping the Union together. Now he has flung himself into the struggle for Southern independence. I guess that's what is hard. He is fighting just as hard to defend what he didn't believe in as he did to keep it from happening." She shook her head slowly. "I still can't believe it's true. Virginia is no longer a part of the United States. I am no longer a United States citizen."

"What else did your father say, Carrie?" Rose's voice was now gentle, as if she sensed the deep turmoil boiling in her friend.

Carrie shook her head more firmly. "I'm sorry." Her short laugh held no humor. "I realize I'm not being very communicative today. Let me try this again." She gazed down at the letter she held in her hand and searched for the right place. "Here it is." She straightened in the saddle to read her father's words, bracing herself to accept the truth of what she read.

> *Dearest Daughter,*
> *I have grand news for you. Our fair capital of Richmond is being chosen for a high honor. The decision is being made, even as I write this letter, to place the seat of our wonderful Confederacy right here in Richmond.*

Rose looked at Carrie in surprise. "I thought the Confederate capital was in Montgomery, Alabama?"

"It was." Carrie put down the letter and tried to explain what her father had written without having to decipher his handwriting again. "It seems Alexander Stephens, the vice president of the Confederacy, arrived in Richmond just a few days after the convention voted to secede. He was impressed by Richmond's beauty, but it was much more that caused him to make his recommendation for Richmond to become the capital. He is well aware of Richmond's economic wealth and the potential for growth."

Carrie paused as she tried to remember what else her father had said. "Tredegar Iron Works played a big role in his decision. That, along with the other iron companies in Richmond. Stephens said the Confederate government's war-waging capacity would have suffered a staggering blow if Virginia hadn't seceded. They're counting on Richmond for cannons, ammunitions, boats and other things." She looked out over the river again as she tried to erase the image of Southern cannons pointed toward her friends in the North. "My father said something about Richmond being strategic in a military sense, but I'm not sure what he meant. He may write more about it later."

"Do you want the South to win the war?" Rose asked bluntly.

Carrie turned to stare at her friend. "You do manage to cut through to the quick of an issue, don't you?"

Rose merely shrugged and returned Carrie's look.

Carrie swung her gaze back to the river. It matched her emotions now even more than it had a few moments ago—her feelings as tossed and jumbled as the muddy cauldron. Finally, she turned back to Rose. "I don't know," she stated flatly. "I think this whole war is stupid. I think people should have had enough sense to keep it from ever happening. But now that it's here? I just don't know, Rose. Does that make me bad?"

Rose sat quietly.

"You're not going to say anything are you?" Carrie asked.

Rose shook her head.

Carrie managed a brief laugh and forced herself to look deep into her heart. Rose's question had made her realize what was really eating at her heart and mind. She was living in a nation at war. Where was her allegiance? Did she have one? Did it make her a traitor to her beloved South if she couldn't enter the conflict wholeheartedly? How could she support a war that was being fought largely over the continuation of slavery—an institution she despised? But how could she *not* fight to keep her homeland from being destroyed? And what about Robert? The turbulence of her thoughts once again threatened to overwhelm her, just as the river was overwhelming the defeated banks it was now seeping over. "I don't know. I simply don't know." she murmured.

Her troubled thoughts demanded an outlet. She shook her head and cried, "Beat you back to the house!" Spinning Granite on his haunches, she launched him into a ground-swallowing gallop. She knew Rose, on the much smaller mare, Maple, wouldn't stand a chance, but she didn't care. She had to release her spinning thoughts. She leaned low over Granite's neck and allowed the fresh air to envelop her. Granite pulled at the reins, and she gave him what he wanted. The big Thoroughbred flattened himself to the ground as he flew down the road leading back to the Cromwell Plantation house.

Carrie moved as one with the horse she had owned since childhood. As they flashed through the afternoon sun, flying in and out of pockets of shade, she slowly felt herself relax. She could almost feel the cobwebs floating out of her mind. She didn't have to have any answers yet. Her heart was demanding one, but life wasn't yet demanding one. She knew that, for now, she was supposed to stay on the plantation, doing what she had been doing since her father had left to go to Richmond. When the time came that she needed to know her heart and mind more clearly, she would know what she was supposed to do. She would simply have to believe that.

As the realization of that truth sank in, she gave a glad laugh and pulled Granite down to a slow canter. Only then did she think of Rose. She glanced back but could catch no glimpse of her friend. She slowed Granite down to a walk and turned him around to stare in the direction she had come from. Nothing. Concern replaced the glad smile with deep lines of worry. Had Rose fallen off? Was something wrong? She had taught her friend how to ride several months ago, but Rose still wasn't entirely confident on a horse. Berating herself for dashing off in a wild run, Carrie urged Granite into a gallop and sped back down the road.

She was halfway to the river before she caught sight of Rose trotting Maple calmly down the road. "Are you all right?" she cried. "What happened?"

Rose laughed softly. "I'm fine. I didn't have any inside bombs to diffuse. Maple and I are simply enjoying the afternoon. She agreed with me that it was silly to go racing after a horse we could never catch."

Carrie laughed at the amused expression on Rose's face and swung Granite alongside to trot with them.

"Are you feeling better after your mad run?"

Carrie nodded. "It always helps," she said.

Rose smiled and fell into a short silence. "What did your father say about the plantation?"

Carrie frowned at her question. "I don't know how long we can keep up our little game. Father asked about Ike Adams again. He was concerned that Adams would have to leave the plantation as overseer."

"Why?"

"It seems Virginia is even more nervous about her slave population now that the war has started. They're afraid more and more slaves will try to escape and head north to join up with the Union. The Confederacy is already calling for huge numbers of volunteers to join the army. In addition to that, the Virginia government is calling for more men to join the state militia, to keep down any uprisings and to bring back slaves who are trying to escape. Father asked in his letter whether Adams was talking about joining the militia and leaving the plantation. He said something about the government making overseers exempt from military service."

"So they can keep all the slaves under control," Rose stated in a hard voice.

"There are a lot of people who are afraid the slaves are going to rebel more now that the war has started. They're frightened of losing control."

Rose merely nodded, her contemptuous look speaking her heart. Then she turned back to the subject they had started with. "He's going to find out sooner or later, Carrie."

Carrie nodded. "I know. I know." She couldn't believe they had pulled off their deception for this long. Her father was working in Richmond, secure in the supposed knowledge that Cromwell Plantation was being managed under the capable hands of his overseer, Ike Adams. He had no idea that Carrie had thrown him off the plantation seven months earlier for attempting to rape Rose. Since that time, Carrie had been running the plantation with only the aid of Rose's husband, Moses, whom she had appointed as the overseer.

"I still can't believe someone hasn't told him. It seems like everyone locally knows about it," Rose said.

"Father is so caught up in his work, he isn't aware of anything else." There was no bitterness in Carrie's voice. She had long ago accepted she was right where she was supposed to be. She hated the deception but believed it was necessary.

Yet, more and more, the necessity of lying to her father was eating at her. Their relationship had always been built on trust. Would he ever forgive her when he discovered the truth? Which, of course, he would someday. How much longer could she live with herself knowing she was lying to her beloved father? The plantation was still running smoothly. Wasn't that what really counted?

She shook her head to push away her disquieting thoughts. Pulling Granite back down to a walk, she reached into her pocket to dig out the letter again. "Let me read you what else he wrote."

Sunday morning, April 21, dawned warm and balmy. The churches of the city were unusually full. The final prayers were just being said by our minister when the bell on the square began to toll. In an instant, all was confusion. Soon the streets were full of shouting that the Yankee gunboat, Pawnee, was steaming up the James to shell the city. Military companies joined together, the artillery was called out, and women and children streamed to the river to watch the battle for the defense of our city.

I, of course, had to go rapidly to confer with the governor. Word reached us shortly that it had been nothing but a false alarm. Indeed, it was almost laughable. There was no boat coming up the river. Even if there had been, her heavy draught would not have permitted passage to the city. Richmond's citizens, relieved there was no attack, were able to laugh at their gullibility and resume their Sunday routine.

It was not treated so lightly in the capitol. We are all relieved that Colonel Robert E. Lee arrives tomorrow to take over the command of Virginia's troops. The Pawnee Scare, as we are all now calling it, simply demonstrated the chaotic unpreparedness of Richmond's defenses. It may have been a good joke on the city, but it also revealed a very un-comic state of unpreparedness. We have much work to do to be ready to defend our city from the attacks that will surely come from the North.

"When does he think the North will attack?" Rose asked.

Carrie shrugged, folded the letter, and stuffed it in her pocket. "I don't know. He ends the letter there with an apology that he can't write more because of time." Something in Rose's voice had caught her attention. She turned to look at her friend. "Who do *you* want to win the war, Rose?" She had been so busy thinking of her own answer to that question that she hadn't bothered to think how Rose would answer.

Rose met her eyes squarely. "The South is fighting to preserve its right to slavery, Carrie. I know there are many other issues at stake, but wouldn't you agree that is a major one?"

Carrie nodded, knowing where Rose was headed.

"I won't support a war that would leave my people even one second longer in bondage and misery. I have no idea what the outcome of all this will be, but I can only pray for freedom for my people. Freedom to learn without having to hide in the woods in a secret school. Freedom to live our lives the way we desire. Freedom to marry and never worry we will be sold away from each other. Freedom to know our children will not disappear one day, sold to the highest bidder." Rose paused. "I'm not sure what will happen to the slavery system if the North wins—maybe nothing—but I *am* sure what will happen if the South wins."

Carrie nodded. "I understand." She knew most of her friends and family were ardently opposed to the beliefs she now held, but she was comfortable with what she believed. There would be times when her position would cause her heartache, but she had to be true to herself.

The look Rose directed her way was a mixture of appreciation and compassion. Carrie knew what she was thinking. *Robert.* They had not talked about him since Carrie had returned from Richmond a month ago. Rose didn't know about... Carrie reined her thoughts back in. Now was not the time. "Tell me how your school is going," she said instead.

Rose played the game well, launching easily into a newer, safer subject. "The school is going wonderfully! Every child on this plantation can now read a little and write their name. There are some who struggle to do that, but others are going almost faster than I can keep up." Rose paused, her eyes glowing with excitement. "Oh, Carrie, there is nothing more exciting than seeing a child struggle to read and suddenly get it. It's just like a light goes on in their head. I can see it because it lights up their eyes. Suddenly all those shapes make sense, and a whole new world is open to them!"

Carrie smiled as she watched her friend's face. "Someday you'll have your own school, Rose. You'll be free. Then you can be the teacher you've always dreamed of being."

"That's all I've ever wanted." She paused. "I'm in no hurry, though. The only way I can have my dream is for Mama to die. I can't even stand to think that way."

Carrie nodded, unable to imagine Cromwell Plantation without Rose's mama, Sarah. Rose adored her and had vowed to never escape the plantation as long as she was alive. Sarah had been a part of Carrie's life, too, since she'd been born. She had been more like a mama to her than her own mother had been.

"I'm content for right now," Rose continued. "Moses and I have that wonderful new cabin you gave us. The plantation children are growing and learning, and I still get to teach the adults. So many of them, especially Opal, are learning so fast."

When Rose fell silent, Carrie knew she was thinking about the group of slaves she had helped escape through the Underground Railroad ten months earlier. Opal could have been part of that group, but she had chosen to stay on the plantation, too afraid to leave the security she had always known. It was many months later before Carrie discovered the whole story.

"She would make a different decision now, wouldn't she?" Carrie asked quietly.

Rose shrugged. "I think so. She knows she can leave, though. I just don't think she has anything to go to. And all the slaves are happy now. They have plenty of free time. They are working hard because they want to. You've given them land to plant their gardens, and their livestock is thriving. The ones who are left simply don't want to leave." She paused. "Freedom is more important to some of us than others. Some people can think of nothing but freedom, while others concentrate on security and safety because that's what is most important to them. I think all the slaves with a yearning for freedom are gone. The ones who are still here are here because they want to be."

Carrie nodded and then started in the saddle. A far-off call had caught her attention. Straining her eyes, she looked off to the west. It took a moment for her eyes to focus. "It's Moses," she said suddenly. "I wonder if something is wrong."

It took only a couple of minutes for Moses to canter up to where they waited for him on the road. The towering black man rode his large gelding easily. He had learned to ride when Rose did, but it had come naturally to him. Now he looked as if he had spent all of his life in the saddle.

Carrie admired his grace for a moment and then spoke quickly. "Is something wrong, Moses?"

"Not a thing," he grinned. "I just saw my beautiful wife and my favorite plantation owner's daughter and thought you might like to take a look at the fields. It's been a while since you've ridden the fields, Carrie."

"I trust what you're doing."

Moses nodded easily. "I know that. But you've been doing all your work inside lately. You haven't been doing what you love. I'd like to show you what we've been doing."

Carrie hesitated and then agreed with a smile. "You're right. I've been too chained to papers and reports lately. Not to mention nursing sick people down in the quarters. I certainly will be glad when this latest illness goes away. Two more of the children came down with it yesterday. It's not too serious, but they will be miserable for a few days." Her face creased with a frown as she thought about them.

Moses interpreted her look. "Sarah will take care of them till you get back, Carrie." His tone was gentle but firm.

Carrie gazed at him for a moment. "Lead the way, overseer. We're all yours."

Carrie allowed thoughts of everything else to flow from her mind as the three trotted easily down the road. She was thankful for the raised roads her father had so carefully built. The hot sun had already almost dried the well-drained surface, while the fields still had standing puddles from the massive rains. Stretched out on each side were luxuriant fields of green.

Moses pointed proudly to his right. "The tobacco is coming in fine. Even with fewer hands to work it, we're still on target with what they did last year. This last rain is going to help us a lot. The ground was getting pretty dry. These soaking rains will put all the moisture back in the soil. We should have a bumper crop this year."

Carrie smiled as she looked over the fields. She knew her father would be proud of the way they looked. She also knew he would be shocked to learn they had been completely supervised by one of his own slaves. Her father was convinced blacks were intellectually incapable of being in charge of themselves and of their destiny. If he could only see what Moses and the rest had done, maybe it would change his mind...not that she held much hope of that. She and her father had argued about slavery before. They stood on opposite sides of the fence. He and Robert were in agreement on that issue.

Robert...

Once again the thoughts she fought so hard to control flooded her mind. His handsome face and flashing dark eyes, surrounded by a shock of wavy dark hair, rose before her.

Granite, startled momentarily by a rabbit bolting from the brush lining the fields, shied and snorted his disdain for the furry little creature before he once again picked up his steady trot. It was enough to jolt Carrie from her errant thoughts.

The three friends rode in silence for a long while. It was Moses who broke the silence. "It doesn't seem possible there is a war going on. Life is going on around here just like always."

Once again a frown creased Carrie's face. "I hope the war doesn't touch us here." She paused. "I don't know how realistic that is, though." For just a moment she could see swarms of soldiers flooding the fields of Cromwell Plantation. She shook her head to push away the vision. "My father said in his letter that men from all over the South are pouring into Richmond to train as soldiers. Lee has started up a training camp at the fairgrounds. With Washington less than a hundred miles away, there are sure to be attempts to take Richmond. He said the people actually seem to be eager for a fight." She shuddered as she thought of the death and destruction on both sides. "They seem to think one good beating from the South will make the North tuck their tails between their legs and flee back to their homes."

"You disagree?" Rose asked.

"I think too many people are still seeing it as a game. When Southern boys are killed and the wounded start pouring in, I believe reality will set in. And no, I don't believe the North is full of cowards as they think it is. I know many of them. They, too, are going to fight for what they believe in."

Moses nodded. "It's going to be a long war, I think."

Something in his voice caused Carrie to turn and stare at him, questioning him with her eyes.

He met her gaze without flinching. He squared his shoulders and spoke evenly. "I don't have anything against you, Carrie. You're one of the finest women I know, but I got a big problem with all the folks who done been keepin' my people in bondage for so long. I done seen too much misery to forget it."

Carrie watched him with compassion. It was times like this that Moses slipped back into the slave dialect he had spoken all his life. He had learned to read and write quickly under Rose's tutelage, and he had worked hard to improve his speech so he would be ready to go out into the world when his opportunity for freedom came. But when his great heart became aroused about something he was passionate about, he could still slip back into his old speech.

"You know what we're doing with the tobacco right now, Carrie?"

Carrie was surprised by his sudden question. What did this have to do with what they were talking about? She furrowed her brow and tried to pull her thoughts back to the cultivation of tobacco. Finally she nodded. "You should be pruning and worming right now."

Moses nodded. "That's right." He paused for a long moment and then continued. "Raising tobacco is the same everywhere. You always got to do the worming or those big green worms will wipe out an entire crop."

Carrie watched him closely. Where was he going with this? He knew that she was as informed about farming techniques as he was. Her father, lacking a son to train on the plantation, had imparted all of his knowledge to her. She had even spent some time helping with the worming. She remembered her disgust at having to crush the worms one by one so their voracious appetites wouldn't obliterate a crop.

"My little sister was working the fields one day when the worming was being done." Moses' face had gone expressionless and his voice was flat.

Carrie's face softened. She knew he was reliving the pain of his life on the plantation he had come from the year before. She also knew how his heart ached for his family, which had been sold away from each other at the auction house in Richmond.

"June was just a little thing then. Not even six years old. She had been in the hot sun all day long, and she wasn't feeling too good. She finally got too tired to kill the worms. Instead of crushing them in her hands, she just dropped them in the field and moved on to the next one. She didn't have no idea she was being watched..." His voice trailed off and then picked up the story. "I turned around just in time to see the overseer grab her and spin her around. First he slapped her across the face..." Moses' voice roughened as he remembered. "Then he reached down and grabbed a whole handful of them worms and stuffed them in her mouth. June was a-gagging and a-choking while he stood there and laughed."

A deep silence fell on the three as they all experienced the humiliation and pain of Moses' story.

Finally he spoke again, his voice once more under control. "I don't know what will happen to slavery if the North wins this war, but I do know for sure what will happen if they don't." Moses took a deep breath and straightened his broad shoulders a little more. "I aim to do whatever I can to help the North if the opportunity ever comes. Right now, I ain't got no idea what that is..." He paused for a long moment. "I'll know when the time comes, though." His gaze swung out over the fields as his voice dropped to a rough whisper. "Yep. I'll know when the time comes."

Carrie watched him, not in surprise or shock, but in sorrow. Sorrow that it had come to this. Americans fighting Americans. Her heart grew heavy as she, too, allowed her eyes to roam the land that was her home.

The clouds that had descended upon America with the fall of Fort Sumter had intensified in their darkness.

Carrie shuddered. Brothers were preparing to fight brothers. Men everywhere were leaving their families and homes to fight in a war they little understood. Friends, divided by loyalties and geography, were taking up arms to destroy friends. Families were being ripped apart by differing allegiances. Carrie knew that dark angels of death waited in the wings, while the clouds moved ever lower to meet the darkness of men's hearts.

Cool air had moved in to claim the night. Carrie sighed with relief as a welcoming breeze flowed through her curtains and swept underneath the canopy of the bed where she lay. As usual, she was exhausted. The days began early and ended late, full of frenetic activity, as she worked to keep a huge plantation running smoothly.

She lay back against her mound of pillows and allowed the refreshing air to caress her tired body. Gradually, she felt herself begin to relax. She knew what would come next, but she also knew there was no way to fight it. She had tried for the last five weeks to control her thoughts to no avail. She would let them run their course, until she fell into a deep sleep of exhaustion.

Unbidden, thoughts of Robert Borden flooded her mind. His handsome face smiling down at her as they swirled and dipped around the dance floor. His enchanting laugh as they cruised up the James River on the packet boat *John Marshall*. His angry look when she tried to talk to him about slavery. And finally, the look of hatred on his face as he told her of watching his father die at the hand of a slave.

Carrie's emotions swirled with the pictures racing through her mind. She loved Robert Borden, she would not deny that, but the love brought her no joy. It brought nothing but pain.

The pictures in her mind faded away as the most vivid one took their place—the look of confusion, pain and anger on Robert's face the day she had told him, five weeks earlier in Richmond, that she could not marry him because they held such different views on slavery and on the value of a people God held as his own. Her heart had broken that day just as surely as his own. There had been a short note the day she left Richmond that had given her a brief flicker of hope, but nothing since then.

In the lucid light of day, Carrie knew she had done the right thing. She could never join her life with someone who held such hatred and anger in his heart, but at night... At night she remembered all the wonderful things about Robert. The way they laughed and talked so easily. The feel of his arms holding her. The memory of the one kiss they had shared. The kiss that held so much promise. A promise that had been swept away by the reality of their differences.

Once again the questions tortured her. Had she done the right thing? Had she thrown away her only love? Where was he? Would he be going into battle soon? Would she ever see him again? Carrie tossed and turned as the answerless questions stormed through her.

Gradually, fatigue won the battle over her mind. As a new moon lifted its shiny sliver to glimmer a faint light down on the roiling rampage of the James River, Carrie slipped into an exhausted slumber.

Chapter Two

Laughter rang out in the still evening air. Carrie smiled and walked faster in the direction of the quarters. She was ready to have some fun. Buried under mounds of papers and receipts all day, she had just a few minutes ago pushed herself back from her father's desk. There was still correspondence to take care of, but she had determinedly turned her back on it. There would always be too much to do. She was learning that she had to set limits somewhere. Sarah had invited her down for dinner a week ago, and nothing would make her miss it.

Carrie's smile widened as she broke out into the clearing surrounded by the slave cabins. It looked as if most of the plantation's children were there, playing a rousing game of chase. Shrieks of laughter and shouts of triumph or defeat filled the air as lithe bodies darted in and out of the shadows and around the trees bordering the edge of the clearing. Carrie paused for a long moment to watch the activity and listen to the happy sounds.

Suddenly one of the children, a young girl named Hannah, spied her and dashed over to where she was standing. As if remembering her manners, she came to an abrupt standstill. She quickly smoothed her faded red dress and patted at her tight braids before she grinned up at her. "Howdy, Miss Carrie."

"Hello, Hannah. Sounds like y'all are having a fine time."

"Oh, yessum! We be having a passel of fun!"

Carrie laughed at the excited pleasure in Hannah's eyes. This little girl with her glowing ebony skin and wide grin had always been one of her favorites. Her mama and daddy worked as field hands. Hannah had been born on the plantation.

Hannah's clear eyes suddenly clouded over. "Miss Carrie?"

"Yes, Hannah?" Carrie stooped down so that she would be more on the level of the small child. She knew what she was going to ask.

"How be Jubal? Is he going to be all right?"

Carrie patted Hannah reassuringly on the shoulder. "Jubal is going to be just fine," she said. "I checked on him this morning. His fever is going down, and he is starting to eat a little bit of food. I predict he'll be playing with you again in a few days."

Hannah looked up into her eyes for a few moments and then nodded as if satisfied. "That be good," she said shortly. Then she turned and dashed back into the wild game.

Carrie laughed and watched her for a few minutes. Jubal was Hannah's older brother. Somehow the little girl had missed the latest sickness being passed around among the quarters' children. They weren't sick very often, but when something hit, they all seemed to share it.

"Miss Carrie!"

Glancing up at the sound of her name, Carrie moved toward the cabin at the far end of the clearing. It was small, but it was much larger than the other cabins that housed the Cromwell Plantation slaves. Carrie had asked Moses to build it during the month of December, not telling him the purpose for it. He and Rose had been shocked to discover it was Carrie's wedding gift to them. "Hello, Sarah. How are you tonight?"

"Ain't got no reason to be complainin', and I done got me a heap of reasons to be thankful. I reckon that makes me be doin' just fine, Miss Carrie. It sure be good to see you, girl. I was afraid you weren't goin' to make it here."

Carrie leaned down to give the tiny, wrinkled woman a gentle hug. "I wouldn't miss one of your dinners for anything, Sarah."

She could feel her spirits lifting as she entered the cabin Rose and Moses called home. Sarah had insisted she fix dinner there tonight so all of them would have more room. Carrie sniffed appreciatively as she entered the room. "Sweet potato pie! My favorite. I was hoping we would have some tonight."

Sarah smiled and settled down in the rocker next to the front door. "It will be ready right soon. I picked fresh greens today and found a mess of new potatoes that be roasting on the coals. I even had Moses bring me a slab of ham."

Carrie glanced over at the table. "Are those biscuits I see there?" she asked hopefully, feeling like a small girl again. There was never a week that had passed by without her coming down to the quarters for some of Sarah's biscuits slathered with butter.

Sarah snorted. "You know without askin' what them be, chile. You think ole Sarah gonna be fixin' you a meal without biscuits?"

Carrie smiled and settled back in another chair. "How are my patients?"

"They goin' to be right as rain in a few days, Miss Carrie."

"Do I have time to check in on them?"

"You down here to eat, not play doctor." Sarah's voice was stern, but her bright eyes glowed with approval.

Carrie stood and leaned down to kiss her leathery ebony forehead. "It won't take me long. I'll be able to relax better when I see how they're doing for myself."

Sarah smiled. "You gonna be one crackerjack doctor one o' these days, girl. You mark my words."

Carrie tried to push down the feelings of frustration at Sarah's words. She really was content here on the plantation—at least most of the time. She knew she was where she was supposed to be, but her dream continued to dance before her almost daily. More than anything in the world, she wanted to be a doctor. Her mother's death and the beginning of the war seemed to have dashed all hopes of it ever happening, but still she dreamed. Still she hoped. Still she clung to the belief that she would someday be able to leave the plantation. There had to be a chance for her to follow her dreams.

The sun was dipping below the tops of the towering oaks surrounding the clearing when she approached the tiny cabin she used as an infirmary. Having Sarah always in the quarters was a wonderful blessing. For several years she had been the quarters' mammy.

Someone had to be responsible for the children who were too young to work in the fields. They all adored the tiny old woman with the big heart who gave them so many hugs.

"Good evening, Jubal," Carrie said as she entered the darkening cabin. "How are you feeling?"

Jubal, a strapping lad of eleven with an easy grin, lifted himself up on one arm and looked at her. "I be feelin' right much better, Miss Carrie. That stuff you done gave me was like some kind of magic."

"I feel that way about it sometimes myself, Jubal," she laughingly agreed. "That magic is called yarrow."

Jubal nodded. "Miss Sarah was tellin' me 'bout it. Said y'all fetched it from out in the woods." He shook his head in wonder. "'Magine that! An old weed keepin' me from bein' sick."

Carrie laughed again. "I used to think they were old weeds myself. That is, until Sarah taught me how to use their magic. There are still regular medicines I use, but sometimes the *magical herbs*—that's what I call them— work better than anything else. Yarrow works well at bringing down fevers. That, combined with the ice baths Sarah gave you this morning, seemed to have done the trick." She looked with satisfaction at the renewed shine in his eyes as she placed a hand on his forehead.

She turned to the other bed. "And how is our other patient doing tonight, Adam?" She reached her hand out and laid it on his forehead. "Still fighting with that fever are you?" His thin face was hot and drawn.

Adam, a wiry little seven-year-old, nodded wearily. His attempt at a smile failed miserably. "I reckon so, Miss Carrie," he whispered.

Smiling gently, she sat down on the edge of his rough bed. "You've only been sick for today, Adam. It seems to take a couple of days for the worst part of this to pass. I predict you'll be feeling better tomorrow."

Adam nodded again but watched her with his dark eyes. It was obvious it took too much effort to say anything. Carrie moved over to the table she had set up next to the window and reached for the bottle of dried leaves she had left there earlier in the morning. Taking a precise amount, she mixed two small glasses with the water Moses had drawn for her from the well and handed them to her two young patients. "Drink all of this down. It will make you feel better."

Jubal and Adam drained the liquid without a murmur of complaint. Carrie patted them both on their heads and moved toward the door. "I have to go now. Jubal, your mama will be over in just a little while to spend the night with you two. She knows to come get me if I'm needed." She fixed a warm smile on her littlest patient. "Adam, try to get a good night's sleep. You'll feel much better in the morning."

"Yessum, Miss Carrie."

Rose was just walking up to the cabin when Carrie emerged into the waning light. "Mama sent me over to get you. She said if you want hot biscuits, you better stop doctoring and start thinking about eating."

Carrie laughed and lengthened her stride. "I'm ready to think about nothing *but* eating."

Sarah was just setting her pan full of biscuits on the table when Rose and Carrie burst through the door laughing and out of breath.

Sarah looked at them with a smile of satisfaction. "That's the way life's done meant to be lived. The good Lord done made us to laugh. There be plenty of times when the heart be too heavy to laugh, so's you got to take advantage of them times when you *can* laugh. It done makes the soul strong for dem times when you can't."

Carrie took her place at the table next to the window that overlooked the quarters. All of the children had been called in to eat their own suppers, so for a few minutes, peace reigned. A chorus of frogs and crickets had come out to herald the arrival of night. The first fireflies were flashing their magical lights through the thick underbrush of the surrounding woods, an occasional one darting into the clearing as if it dared one of the children to try and capture its mystic incandescence. Carrie could feel herself relaxing.

Sarah had just turned toward the table with the first plateful of food when Moses strode through the door, his massive body blocking all light from the waning dusk. A single candle flickering on the table cast a tiny circle of light. Rose stood to meet him with a kiss and then moved over to light the lantern. Soon the room was filled with a warm glow that turned the rustic cabin into a warm, comforting place.

Moses gave a sigh of contentment as he settled down in front of the huge plate of food Sarah placed in front of him. "Looks great. And I already know how it's going to taste."

Sarah smiled and moved back to fill the next plate. Within moments, the table was groaning under the weight of the plates she had placed in front of all of them. Carrie had learned long ago not to complain at the amount of food put in front of her. She always managed to clean it up. And she always felt like she was waddling home. But she was always happy.

After a brief blessing, there was silence for a long while. Finally, Moses pushed back from the table and patted his stomach. "You outdid yourself that time, Sarah. Thank you."

Sarah smiled at her son-in-law. "Does a heart good to see her cookin' eaten. I hope you done saved room for some sweet potato pie."

"Since when do I need room for your sweet potato pie? There will never be a time in my life that I won't find some extra space for that." Moses laughed.

Just then there was a timid knock at the door.

"It's open," Moses called.

No one was surprised that someone was at the door. Moses had become the undisputed leader of the quarters, Rose was revered by all as the teacher, and Sarah was who everyone came to when there was a need. There was hardly a night they got through dinner without someone coming by.

The door opened to admit a dark-skinned woman of average height. Her dress, which had once fit her loosely, now seemed to clutch at her mid-section.

"Opal, you're here just in time to have some pie," Sarah said warmly.

"Oh, no," Opal protested. "I didn't come to disturb your dinner." She clutched tighter at a piece of paper she held in her hand. "I can come back later."

"Nonsense," Rose said, rising to pull another ladder-back chair forward. "We were just finishing. And you will too have a piece of pie," she added firmly. "You know how much you love it."

Opal smiled then. "Well, if you insist. Sarah, you do make the best pie in Virginia."

Sarah snorted but smiled with pleasure. She stood and moved toward the table where the pie waited. "Get on with you, girl!"

Rose turned to Opal again. "What do you have there, Opal?"

Carrie was surprised when Opal turned to her eagerly.

"It was you I came to see, Miss Carrie."

"What can I do for you?" Carrie asked. She had never seen Opal so agitated. Or maybe she was just excited. There was a light in her eyes Carrie had never seen and her ample body seemed to be trying to control a quiver.

Opal looked down at the paper she had in her hand. "My cousin up in Richmond sent me this letter. Sam done brung it to me today. She gave it to him when he was there last week."

"Sam *brought* it to me today," Rose corrected. She was always the teacher.

"What did the letter say?" Carrie asked.

Opal took a deep breath as if she were gathering all her courage. Then she looked Carrie straight in the eye. "You remember telling us slaves that if we wanted to be free, we could be?"

"I do."

"Did you mean it?"

"Of course she meant it," Moses interrupted. "You know that. You know that twelve of the Cromwell people have left in the past few months. What are you asking a question like that for?"

Opal looked down at the ground. "I'm sorry. I didn't mean to say it like that."

Carrie hastened to ease her embarrassment. "That's all right, Opal. I can tell you're very excited about something. What is it?" she asked gently.

Opal seemed to gain renewed courage from her words. "Like I said, I got this letter from my cousin. She's free and living in Richmond. Seems like they need extra people at the Tredegar Iron Works and at the State Armory. She told me slaves are coming in from the country, hired out by their owners to work there." Opal paused and looked at Carrie. "I want to go to Richmond to work, Miss Carrie. I'll send you back the money I make. And maybe"—she hesitated—"maybe I can earn enough extra to pay for my freedom."

"You don't have to pay for your freedom," Carrie protested. "I've already promised you can go free when you want."

"Your father know he's losing a lot of his slaves?"

"Well..." Carrie decided to be honest. "No, he doesn't."

"What's he gonna do when he finds out?"

"I have no idea," Carrie confessed. "I'm sure he won't be happy, however. That's not what's important, though. I don't believe slavery is right, and I happen to be the one in charge of Cromwell Plantation. How my father reacts is my problem, not yours."

Opal shook her head. "I don't aim to be causing no problems for you, Miss Carrie. I done already know that your father don't know about what you're doing." She smiled. "I think it's wonderful. But my running away to freedom won't help anyone, 'cause it's to Richmond I intend to run. Somebody there will see me and maybe say something to your daddy. That would ruin everything here for everyone else. I ain't gonna do that."

What she said made sense. It was obvious Opal had thought through this. "Let me get this straight. You want me to hire you out to work at the armory or the iron works? Where are you planning on living?"

"My cousin has a place down at the bottom of Shockoe Hill. She said they have room for me. She and her husband have four children, but they want me to come."

"And you want to go?"

"Yes, Miss Carrie. I want to go." There was a set look of determination on her face and a shine in her eyes that spoke of something more than Opal was saying.

Carrie opened her mouth to press further but thought better of it. She had offered all of her slaves freedom. If Opal was turning down freedom to protect the rest of the slaves, Carrie would agree to let her be hired out. Slowly she nodded. "I will arrange for you to be taken to Richmond, Opal. Sam is going into town next week. You can go with him then."

Opal's face lit with a glorious smile as a sigh of relief exploded from her lips. "Oh, thank you, Miss Carrie."

"You're welcome," Carrie said. "And just remember, Opal, your freedom is yours when you want it."

Carrie sighed as she ran the ivory-handled brush repeatedly through her long black hair. It still felt better when it was done for her, but she had determined months ago to take care of herself. It was hard to even imagine that she had once had everything done for her— her baths drawn, her clothes selected and laid out, her hair brushed and arranged. At one time, Rose had done it all for her. Carrie's time in Philadelphia with Aunt Abby had changed all of that. Wealthy enough to pay for any services she desired, Aunt Abby chose to care for herself.

Carrie's face grew sad at the thought of Aunt Abby. She missed her terribly. Most of the time it seemed as if she actually were *her* aunt, and not the aunt of one of her close friends. The month she had spent in her home the summer before was one of the most special memories of her life. The two had connected on a deep level, attracted by the honesty and independence they found in each other. The age difference between them had melted away as they spent hours in heart-to-heart conversation.

Carrie allowed herself to imagine what she would be doing right now if she had been free to accept Aunt Abby's invitation to come and spend several months with her, pursuing her dream of becoming a doctor. Her mother's illness and subsequent death had aborted all those plans. Carrie had become the mistress of Cromwell Plantation. How many times she had longed to walk away from her responsibility and follow her dream. There had been time before the war started to simply tell her father he must hire a new overseer, and then she could have moved to Philadelphia and started her education. Knowing she was where she was supposed to be sometimes did nothing to ease the pain of her situation.

She had struggled earlier when she had walked home from the quarters. She was excited Opal was going to have a new beginning in Richmond. She had had to fight a creeping bitterness that nothing new was on the horizon for her. Only laughing at herself had finally helped her to gain perspective. How could she be jealous of a slave? Opal, no matter what she did in Richmond, would know she was a slave. Carrie had to keep reminding herself she had options. She could leave the plantation any time she wanted to. She knew her father would understand. It was her choice that kept her here. She could either make the best of it, or continue to grumble.

Reaching into her dressing table drawer, Carrie pulled out a thick sheaf of letters. Turning the lantern up a little brighter, she flipped through page after page of letters Aunt Abby had sent. Their correspondence had been a saving grace for Carrie as she struggled to fulfill her responsibilities and duties on the plantation. Now even that had been taken away. Lincoln had ordered all mail service halted between the warring states.

More than ever, Carrie yearned for a good long talk with her friend. Was she making the right decisions? Carrie knew Aunt Abby would give her no answers, but she would ask all the right questions so that Carrie could examine her heart clearly and know what she really believed, what she really wanted, and what would be the best course of action. Sometimes it was so difficult to see a situation clearly when you were immersed in it. You could so easily lose sight of the goal when the surrounding problems pressed in so tightly that they obscured the view.

Oh, God...

It was sometime later when Carrie lifted her head, sensing the peace that she could find only in talking with God. Her reflection in the huge, ornately gilded mirror on her wall flickered back at her. She began to run the brush through her hair once again. She would take one day at a time. She would do the best she could. She could do no more, and no more was expected of her.

Carrie's heart nearly failed her at times when she tried to look far into the future, but, one day at a time. Most of the time she was sure she could make it through just one more day.

Gazing more deeply into the mirror, Carrie smiled at her reflection. As the soft breeze swirled around her, once more she tried to fathom the secrets and mysteries hidden in the mirror. She had sensed them there ever since she was a young girl. She would spend hours staring into its clear depths, trying to imagine what secrets her great-great-grandmother had bestowed upon the mirror, and whether she, her great-great-granddaughter, would be found worthy to know the secrets.

Carrie knew the heritage the mirror had bequeathed to her. She knew that it stood as a six-foot-tall, gilded symbol of courage and determination and the will to carve the life you wanted out of impossible circumstances. It stood as a challenge before her all of her life. Each night it spoke to her, urging her on to be all she could be and to not give in to the circumstances of life.

Tonight it spoke to her once again, but in a different way. The mirror issued the same challenge as always, but as she stared into it, it seemed to offer back the courage she would need to meet those challenges. The flickering lantern light, tossed about the room by the billowing of her long drapes, seemed to sink deep into the mirror and come shooting back out at her, offering more radiance on its way out than on its way into the depths. Carrie sat quietly, absorbing the strength and courage it was offering her tonight.

She felt awed, sensing that she had discovered one of the secrets of the mirror. If she could see herself reflected, and feel comfortable and confident about the condition of her heart, the mirror would reach out and give her the strength necessary to follow the dictates of her heart.

Carrie reached over to lower the wick on the lantern. Moving over to her bed, she slid gratefully under the covers. She sighed as the soft warmth of the bed welcomed and cradled her tired body. Just as she rolled over to bury her head in her pillows, a burst of song reached across the night and crept through her window. Carrie sat up to hear more clearly. She knew it was from the quarters.

On certain nights, when the breeze blew just right, the sounds of the Cromwell Plantation people singing would rise to her window. Closing her eyes, she listened closely.

> *Swing low, sweet chariot*
> *Coming for to carry me home*
> *Swing low, sweet chariot*
> *Coming for to carry me home.*
> *I looked over Jordan and what did I see*
> *Coming for to carry me home*
> *A band of angels coming after me*
> *Coming for to carry me home.*

Carrie smiled and snuggled deep into her covers. No unbidden thoughts would bother her tonight.

Chapter Three

Robert Borden had a smile on his face as he trotted his gelding away from the bustling area of the Richmond fairgrounds. *What had been the fairgrounds*, he said to himself. The citizens of Richmond could hardly recognize their city anymore. In a matter of weeks, its ordinary population of forty thousand had exploded. What had been a peaceful town was now suddenly an armed camp. Soldiers were everywhere—walking the streets, filling the taverns, marching with drums and fifes, arriving in swarms at the train station. It was both exhilarating and disconcerting.

Robert had reason to smile. For the first time in three weeks, he had been given permission to leave the camp of instruction—now referred to as Camp Lee—and go into town. A message sent to him earlier that day as he was leading his unit in drills had confirmed his dinner engagement with Thomas Cromwell. He was looking forward to seeing his friend and welcomed the possibility of hearing news of Carrie. At the thought of Carrie, the smile left his face. In its place was a mixture of pain, exasperation and anger. He could only hope her father could give him some understanding. Shaking his head, he tried to force thoughts of the beautiful girl he loved out of his mind. There were other things he needed to think about. He knew Thomas would have many questions for him.

As Robert rode on toward the middle of town, he barely noticed the cloud of dogwoods that fairly blanketed the gentle slopes of the city. He could hardly believe it had been a month since Virginia had seceded from the Union. He'd had barely a moment to himself since that fateful day. His return to the city after gathering military information in Charleston during the battle of Fort Sumter had resulted in the rank of lieutenant in the Confederate Army. He knew the amount of work to be done before Virginia would be able to defend herself against the enemy perched on her northern border. He had thrown himself, heart and soul, into the effort.

His mind traveled back now to the units he had left for the evening. Every aspect of the transformed fairgrounds stood crystal clear in his mind. He could see the tents rising in long lines around the permanent buildings. Endless tables and racks for food stretched out beside them. Many a man had nothing but a bedroll and the ground, and still they poured in.

He could still faintly hear the shouted commands of the Virginia Military Institute cadets who had been brought in to establish some semblance of order and discipline in the swelling ranks of volunteer soldiers. Both days and nights had become an endless siege of drills, marches and orders. Some of the new soldiers complained, but most of them had thrown their hearts into forming an army able to repel the Northern troops of aggression.

As the sounds faded into the distance, Robert was able to focus on the city unfolding before him. Though his heart remained entrenched in his beloved plantation, Oak Meadows, he had a genuine love for the city. He also knew he was preparing to fight to defend everything he held dear. On a daily basis, he pushed away his longing for home and concentrated on what it would take to make it *remain* his home.

As he rode up the street leading past Capitol Square, he smiled as the Capitol building came into view. Stunning from the river, it lost a little of its glamour as you drew nearer. The columned front was commanding, but the dirtiness of its rather drab stucco exterior stole some of its allure. Tonight, though, it seemed magical. The setting sun, slipping down behind the forested slopes of the turbulent James River, cast a pinkish glow that turned it into a splendid palace. Spreading dogwoods changed from white to rose-colored as the departing sun kissed them gently. For just a moment, if he focused on nothing but the verdant park surrounding the Capitol, Robert could pretend nothing had changed. His fantasy had no hope of lasting, however.

Into the brief flicker of peace the setting sun offered exploded the cacophonous sounds of a city gearing for war. Carriages rattled down the brick and cobblestone streets of the city. Swarms of people—gaily dressed ladies out to catch a glimpse of the soldiers, businessmen hawking their wares to a burgeoning city, children running everywhere, eager not to miss one single thing—filled the streets to capacity. And everywhere were the troops.

By train, horseback, or on foot, they had poured into the city. At first it was only the volunteers eager to defend the state they loved, but they had been joined by soldiers from every state in the Confederacy once word spread that Richmond was the new capital of their splendid nation. They came armed with shotguns, bowie knives, muskets or squirrel guns. They came in fancy militia uniforms or dressed in the homespun muslin of the hills. All of them came with the confidence that soon they would be home again, laughing all the way about how the North had tucked its tail between its legs and run home when it realized what it was up against.

Robert had agreed with them, until...

Looking up, he realized he was almost to the door of the Spotswood Hotel. Thomas Cromwell now owned a home on Church Hill, but they had arranged to meet here so both of them would be closer to their work. Robert dismounted, handed the reins over to a servant and strode eagerly into the hotel. Once inside, he stopped short in surprise.

"Doesn't look quite the same as it did a couple of months ago, does it?"

Robert spun around to meet his friend. "Mr. Cromwell! How are you, sir?"

Thomas gave Robert a warm handshake. "Fine, fine. We have a table waiting for us. That's a rare commodity these days, so we'd best claim it before it disappears." He turned and led the way into the well-appointed dining room.

Robert followed, genuinely glad to see the older man. He was also relieved to see how well he looked. His wife's death had almost destroyed him, seeming to rob from him any caring for life. Being in Richmond, far from the memories of the plantation, had been good for him. Thomas looked once more like the vital man Robert had met the year before.

Thomas led the way to a small table in the far corner. Nestled between two twelve-foot windows, it gave the feeling of being out in the midst of Main Street while affording a sense of privacy. Once again Robert looked around.

"Like I said, it doesn't look much like it did a couple of months ago, eh?"

Robert chuckled. "I should say not."

The Spotswood had long coveted its reputation as one of the focal points of Richmond society. It was a sign of prestige to be listed among its clientele. Even when it was full, it had managed to maintain an aura of elegance and decorum. The coming of war had changed all of that. Richmond was not prepared for the influx of people pouring into its confines. The dining room was a mass of people, with harried waiters dashing around trying to meet their needs. Bedrolls leaning against the far walls gave credence to the rumors that when the dining room was empty it became a bedroom for those not lucky enough to find regular boarding in the city.

Thomas looked around for a long moment and then turned back to Robert. "This one is pretty mild. There are hotels where every chair in the lobby has become a bed, as well as the surrounding floor and even the pool tables. The Spotswood has set some limits, especially upon learning that President Davis and his family will be residing here until they have a home ready for him."

"You sound rather excited about it, sir."

"About President Davis being here? Of course I am."

"No, sir. That's not what I meant. You sound rather excited about the crowded condition of our cities. I understand most Richmonders are doing their best to adjust, but they do feel a sense of intrusion."

Thomas shook his head. "There are those in Richmond who still doubt the wisdom of all that has happened, but mark my words, young man, the vast majority of our fair city is solidly behind the crusade we have embarked upon. And those who are lagging behind will stand with us soon, when they understand the treacherous plans of the North to subjugate us."

Thomas stared off into the dining room, deep in thought, before he turned back to Robert. "Making Richmond the capital was the best decision our new government could have made."

Robert nodded. "I agree. At first I thought it was foolish to put the capital of the Confederacy so close to Washington—"

"I know what you mean," Thomas said, interrupting. His eyes snapping, he continued. "In the final analysis, Richmond was the best choice. The security of our industrial potential is essential to the Confederacy."

"And Lee convinced me that the five-day march between Washington and Richmond could be extremely costly to Northern troops trying to invade us," Robert added.

"Very costly," Thomas said. "We are counting on our shore batteries and the Navy to keep Union gunboats out of our rivers. If they can hold the line on the coast, the distance and terrain between here and Washington favors a determined defense. Our dense forests, rivers and swampland are a tremendous benefit."

Robert nodded, his face intense as he thought through the strategy that had been discussed so much in the previous weeks. "Our troops can choose their battlefield and strike the North anywhere in the hundred-mile corridor between the Blue Ridge Mountains and the Chesapeake Bay."

"The Union's cry of 'On to Richmond' may very well prove to be a siren's call luring them onto a killing ground." Thomas' deep voice sounded very satisfied.

Robert gazed at the older man for a long moment. Finally he said, "You have come full circle, sir."

Thomas frowned fleetingly. "Yes, I suppose I have." He paused and looked at Robert. "I, too, remember the first day we met. Our dreams for keeping the Union together. Our insistence that secession would be disastrous for the South." Ruefully he shook his head. "In the end, union was no longer an option. Lincoln was foolish to believe Virginians would take up arms against their fellow Southerners. He pushed us into a position many of us had resisted for a long time."

"Do you have doubts, sir?"

"Doubts? Perhaps doubts that the action we have taken is in all ways the wisest one. Doubts as to whether there was any recourse left open to us? None," he said firmly. "Virginia has been pushed into a corner. I learned a long time ago that people can be most dangerous when that happens. They feel trapped, and with nothing to lose they might as well give their all."

He took a breath and spoke briskly to the waiter who appeared with his whiskey. "This will be all for now. We will order our meal shortly."

Thomas took a long drink of his spirits and turned back to Robert. "Mark my words, my boy. Virginia is prepared to give its all." His eyes flushed with excitement. "And I will stand with my state. The North will rue the day they tried to subjugate the people of Virginia—the people of the South." Then his exuberance dimmed and the careful caution Robert had grown to know so well reasserted itself. "I meant what I said last year, Robert. The South will be victorious in this war, but it will not be without great loss and suffering on both sides. There will be a high price to pay for our independence and the right to live our lives the way we choose. People don't want to believe that, but the time will come when reality will have to be faced."

Robert nodded. "I believe that too, sir. After the ease of taking Fort Sumter, I'm afraid I jumped on the bandwagon with those certain that the war would be little more than a scuffle, and that the North would elect to let us go in peace."

"You've changed your mind?"

"I would say General Lee changed it for me."

Thomas nodded his agreement. "Lee is a fine man—a real gentleman. He is a man all of Virginia can rally behind. Besides being a fine man, he is an excellent soldier. Virginia can be proud that he chose to take his stand with her."

"As far as Lee is concerned, sir, he had no choice. He has no use for slavery and hoped fervently that secession would not be the result of the last years of conflict. Once the decision was made, however, he knew he could never take up arms against his native state and the people of the South. His resignation from the US Army broke his heart, sir."

"Yes, I've heard it was very difficult."

"He has family fighting for the Union. He has left his home overlooking the city of Washington. He is aware he may never go back."

"Surely he does not think the South will lose?" Thomas' voice was suddenly sharp as he leaned forward to stare at Robert.

Robert shrugged. "Lee is going to give the South the best he has, but he shares none of the disillusions I carried for a while." He paused and took a long swallow of his drink, staring out over streets bustling with activity even as night had settled in. He fought to contain the emotion his own words created. "Lee has told me this is going to be a long war. There will be much pain and suffering on both sides. He does not believe for a minute that the North will turn away from its quest to preserve the Union. He has served alongside many of the men who are now considered his enemy. He insists the Northern people will never yield in the contest, except at the conclusion of a long and desperate struggle."

Both men fell silent as they envisioned the results of a long conflict.

Finally Thomas spoke. "You have spent time with Lee. What kind of man do you think he really is?"

"None finer," Robert responded. "He is a leader well worthy of the state and of our cause." He reached into his back pocket, pulled out a folded piece of paper, and carefully smoothed it on the table. "I believe the *Richmond Dispatch* says it best."

A more heroic Christian, noble soldier, and gentleman could not be found. Of him it was said before his appointment, and of him it may be well said, no man is superior in all that constitutes the soldier and the gentleman—no man more worthy to head our forces and lead our army. There is no one who would command more of the confidence of the people of Virginia than this distinguished officer, and no one under whom the volunteers and militia would more gladly rally. His reputation, his acknowledged ability, his chivalric character, his probity, honor, and—may we add to his eternal praise—his Christian life and conduct make his very name a tower of strength.

"He sounds a little like God," Thomas said dryly, "and yet I find I agree with all of it. I recently read a report that General Winfield Scott said he would rather have received the resignation of every general than that of Lee." Thomas smiled again, even more broadly. "Let the battle be long. Victory will certainly be ours. The price will be high, but it will be worth it."

His attention was drawn away by the waiter once more appearing at the edge of the table. "Ready to order now, sir?"

Thomas nodded. "Robert?"

Robert had barely scanned the menu while they were talking but already knew what he wanted. Camp food was adequate, but he was ready for a good meal. "I'll have the roast duck, please." Quickly he added to his order potatoes, green beans, biscuits and fresh strawberry pie. Then he leaned back to continue talking, his stomach growling in anticipation.

"One more question, Robert?"

"Only one, sir?" Robert asked smiling. "I had anticipated many more."

Thomas chuckled. "You're right. Just one more about Lee."

"Ask what you'd like. I'll do my best to answer."

"Lee has no affection for slavery. He was not in support of secession. Yet, just a few days after he resigned from the United States Army, he agreed to command the Southern troops. Why?"

Robert took another long draught of his drink and sat back. "It's rather simple, at least in Lee's mind. His first thoughts and considerations have always been of Virginia. It's true he resented the attitudes of many of the secession leaders. He felt they were trying to force the involvement of the border states in their struggle. He refused to be pulled in. Virginia's secession changed all that. He is well aware of the vulnerable position of our state in relation to Washington and the North. Quite frankly, he knows we stand no chance without the assistance of the rest of the South. It was Virginia's welfare that put him on the side of alliance and common effort."

Thomas nodded. "He is quite a remarkable man."

"That he is." Robert was ready to change the subject. "You seem to be doing well. Are you happy in your new position with the Virginia government?"

Thomas nodded thoughtfully. "My heart is with General Lee. I will give my all for Virginia. For my home," he added fiercely. "I suppose all this has done me something of a favor."

Robert was fairly sure he knew what the older man was getting at. He was not disappointed.

"I couldn't seem to find a reason to live after Abigail died." Thomas paused to collect himself. "She meant everything to me, you know."

Robert nodded, his mind traveling back to the gracious and beautiful woman who had made him feel so much at home the first night he met the Cromwells. "She was indeed a special woman."

Thomas shook himself as if to bring his thoughts back to the present. "That she was," he said. "I floundered for quite a while, trying to find something to live for. Leaving Carrie with the plantation..." Again, he paused. "Well, it wasn't fair to her."

"Carrie is content on the plantation, sir."

Thomas leaned back in his chair. "That's enough of that, young man."

"Excuse me?" Robert asked in confusion. "Enough of what?" Did Carrie's father not even want him mentioning her name? What had he been told? Suddenly the blood began to roar in his ears. He had had such hopes.

"Enough of calling me sir. You are a lieutenant in the Confederate Army. You are not a boy. I would appreciate it if you would call me Thomas from now on."

Robert leaned back with a rush of relief. "Whatever you say...Thomas."

Thomas nodded, not seeming to have noticed Robert's momentary panic. "And I know Carrie says she is content. I also know the depth of my daughter's ability to dream. She is on the plantation because it is her duty, not her love. When duty no longer demands her presence, she will move on to follow her dreams."

Robert merely nodded, knowing Thomas was right. Carrie's shining green eyes and glistening black hair rose up to taunt him. It was her aliveness that had drawn him from the moment he first laid eyes on her. She radiated a life and exuberance that seemed to explode from within. Her independence and strong will had proven to be a magnet for him. Until...

"Why the frown, my boy?"

Robert flushed. He wasn't sure he was ready to talk about his feelings. He looked up and saw the genuine look of caring and warmth shining from Thomas' eyes. Thomas knew how Robert felt about his daughter, and he had told Robert *the secret*. Robert still harbored a hope that Thomas could help him see a way out of this mess. He managed to shrug, knowing Thomas would see right through it. "I'm hoping you can help me understand your daughter."

Thomas gave a short laugh and leaned back again. "Understanding most women is a difficult thing. I think Carrie stands in a class of her own." He hastened to add, "That's what makes her so special."

Just then the waiter arrived with their meal. Robert waited until the food had been set on the table before he responded. "Carrie is special indeed."

"Then what's the problem?"

"I asked her to marry me. The night before I left for Charleston."

"I didn't know that." Thomas waited for Robert to continue.

"She wouldn't have me."

"But I know Carrie loves you," Thomas protested.

Robert shrugged. "Yes, she told me she loves me. She said she couldn't marry me because of slavery."

Thomas took a deep breath and leaned back. "Maybe you should explain a little more." He looked down at his plate heaped with food. "While we eat, of course. I suspect you haven't had a meal like this for a while. Letting it get cold would border on criminal."

Robert forced a smile, along with several forkfuls of food, while he allowed his mind to carry him back to the night he had sat so hopeful on the steps of St. John's Church. "Carrie is quite adamant in her belief that slavery is wrong. She doesn't believe marriage would work between us because we cannot stand united on the subject." Hesitating, he wondered if he should tell Thomas about his father's death—about watching him be killed by a runaway slave when he was just a boy. Carrie was the only person he had ever told. She had been sympathetic, but still... Now she was telling him she could not marry him because of the hatred in his heart. He swallowed his words and shook his head. "I don't know what to do."

"Did you tell her it is our divine destiny to be slave owners?"

"She doesn't believe that, Thomas." Robert paused, pulling his thoughts together. Why did Carrie's words still haunt him? "I told her the Bible sanctions slavery."

"Yes."

"She wanted to know where it says that."

"What did you tell her?" Thomas' eyes bored into him.

Robert shrugged helplessly. "That I didn't know the answer. I told her it wasn't my job to know—it was a minister's."

Thomas nodded. "That's true," he said firmly.

"She doesn't agree," Robert continued. "She told me the Bible didn't sanction slavery, but that people can find a way to justify anything they want to believe. She said she had sought God's heart, and that she could no longer condone slavery."

"Yet, she is running the plantation with our slaves," Thomas said.

Again, Robert shook his head. "She says she owns not a single slave—that they belong to you. If she had her way, she would let them all go free."

Thomas looked startled. "That would mean the end of all we've ever known. Surely she can't mean that." He paused for a moment. "It's a good thing Cromwell Plantation isn't completely in her hands. At least I have the comfort of knowing Ike Adams is doing his job to keep the slaves in line."

Robert shrugged, wondering if he had said too much already. He had kept Carrie's secret about Adams since Christmas. There were many times he had wondered at the wisdom of his promise, but still...a promise was a promise. It was also obvious Thomas was going to offer him no way to change his daughter's mind. For weeks now, Carrie's words had haunted him. "Where does the Bible say slavery is sanctioned by God, Thomas?"

Thomas looked at him sharply and spoke in a stern voice. "You need to be asking a minister those questions. It is their job to interpret the scriptures for us."

Robert sensed he should drop it, but somehow he couldn't. "Carrie believes she has received answers from God..." His voice trailed off, his mind full of Carrie's challenge to him. *Ask God to show you the truth, Robert. If you're right, there is nothing to be afraid of.*

Those words, when he wasn't completely occupied with military matters, had haunted him since the night she had uttered them. It was easy to shove them away when he was busy planning the defense of all he had ever believed in, but in the few quiet moments he had, her voice and her face rose up to taunt him.

Robert could read the frustration on Thomas' face. He could also tell Thomas was trying to think of something to say. His words, when he finally spoke, were half-hearted.

"My daughter will come to accept the truth eventually. She loves you. I don't believe she will let this issue keep you apart."

Robert nodded, knowing that Thomas was wrong, and knowing Thomas knew he was wrong. He could remember the pain and determination on Carrie's face when she had turned down his marriage proposal. On the long trip to Charleston, he had toyed with the idea of returning and telling Carrie he had changed his mind about slavery. His love for her was like a burning coal sinking into his heart. No matter how hard he tried, he couldn't envision life without her.

Two things kept him from doing that. One was the reality that he couldn't imagine life on Oak Meadows without the labor and income from his slaves. It was the only way he had ever known. The other was honesty. Carrie, in spite of the pain it had caused, had been courageous enough to be totally honest. In his more lucid moments, he realized how much her position was costing her as well. He could do nothing less than respond with the same honesty.

The silence between the two men deepened as each sat absorbed in their own thoughts.

"Mr. Cromwell?"

Robert started and turned to gaze at the young man standing behind him. He couldn't help but notice the anxious note in his voice.

Thomas rose to meet him. "Peter." He looked at Robert. "Peter is an aide at the Capitol." Then he turned back to the blond young man, barely out of his teens. "What is it?"

"I hate to bother you, sir. Governor Letcher has called an emergency meeting of the legislature."

"Is something wrong?" Thomas asked.

Peter shook his head. "I wouldn't know, sir. I was simply dispatched to find you."

Thomas looked anxious for a moment and then shook his head, laughing lightly. "There has been no ringing of the Capitol bell, so there is no threat of an invasion. I'm sure it has to do with little more than figuring out better ways to handle the pressures our fair city has come under now that Richmond is the capital. We find new challenges thrown our way almost daily."

Robert nodded. "I'm sure you're right, Thomas." He hid the disappointment he felt about the older man being called away, although Thomas seemed to have no answers about his beautiful daughter. Robert flinched when he realized how much he had been counting on Thomas to give him hope concerning his love for Carrie. One look at Thomas told him his friend's mind was already behind the columned walls of the Capitol building.

Extending his hand, Robert stood up. "It was wonderful to see you, Thomas."

Thomas looked up from laying his napkin next to his plate. "Good to see you as well, Robert. Keep up the good work, son."

"Yes, sir. I will."

Thomas turned to leave and then, as if realizing the condition of Robert's heart, turned back around. "Don't worry too much about Carrie. Things will work out. And right now, all of us have plenty to keep our thoughts busy. She will come around."

Robert watched him walk away and turned back to finish his meal. He knew Thomas was wrong.

Chapter Four

Carrie looked up from where she was sitting behind her father's massive oak desk. Hazy sunlight poured in through the tall window, but there was no movement in the still, hot air. "Are you sure this is what you want to do, Opal?"

"Yes, Miss Carrie." Opal's voice was firm without a trace of hesitation.

Carrie looked the woman over carefully. Not too many years older than her own nineteen, Opal appeared much older. Already the hard labor in the fields had creased her dark face with tiny lines. Her jet black hair still had a sheen to it, but her shoulders had taken on the familiar stoop of a tobacco worker. In spite of the hard work, she had also begun to develop a bulge that tightened the waistline of her light blue dress. Her eyes, normally too tired for one her age, had an unusual brightness to them.

Carrie looked back down at the pass she was carefully forging with her father's name. "I don't want you to send any of your wages back."

"Why, Miss Carrie, I've got to do that!" Opal gasped. "What if somebody was to find out I wasn't sending my wages? There could be trouble for sure."

Carrie was amused at the panic in the woman's voice, but it caused her to reconsider. Finally she nodded. "You may be right." She grabbed another sheet of paper and wrote quickly, stopping every few minutes to think about what she was doing. Her father had always taken care of hiring out the slaves. Hopefully she wasn't making any grave errors in procedure or protocol that would serve as a red flag to those on the lookout for runaway slaves.

Finally she looked back up. "Here, take this with you. It is instructions to the manager of the Federal Armory.

He is to send home fifty percent of your income. The other half will be yours."

Opal gasped again, her eyes widening as she reached out to take the paper with trembling hands. "I'm actually going to be making money of my own?" she whispered disbelievingly.

Carrie nodded. "Do what you want with it, but I urge you to use wisdom. I have heard of slaves using their money to buy alcohol. Alcohol brings nothing but trouble, Opal."

"Oh, yes, ma'am. I know that for sure. Ain't I seen it in Mr. Adams?" She paused, her dark eyes growing even darker when she thought about the vengeful overseer. "I'm going to save all my money." At the thought of it, her eyes began to glow brighter. "I'm going to pay my way in the city, and the rest I'm going to put aside to buy my freedom when the time comes."

Carrie shook her head in protest. "I've already told you. You can have your freedom any time you want it."

Opal seemed to have thought everything through, however. "That's all fine and good when you're the one in charge, Miss Carrie. Might not always be that way, though. Your daddy come home, or send a new overseer, and things could change. And what if the South wins this war? Only the slaves who are way up north gonna still have their freedom. I aim to be sure I can buy mine if it looks like I got to."

Carrie watched with admiration. "You're a very brave woman."

"Nonsense," Opal snorted. "If I was a very brave woman, I would be in Canada now instead of going to work in Richmond."

When she grew silent, Carrie knew she was thinking about her friends who had escaped with the first group of Cromwell slaves to use the Underground Railroad.

"Miss Sarah tells me everything always works for the good, though. I reckon God let me be a chicken and get left behind for a reason. I aim to find out what that reason is."

Once again a look of determination filled Opal's face, but there was something else, too. Carrie was tempted to find out what the woman was hiding, but she smiled and handed Opal the pass. "This will get you into the city. Keep it with you all the time." She heard her voice becoming sterner, but she did nothing to soften it. "And I mean *all* the time," she added. She knew what the city could do to blacks. All Opal had ever known was the plantation.

Opal reached out to take the papers Carrie had prepared for her. "Yes, ma'am," she said. "I know I ain't never been away from Cromwell Plantation before, but I done heard the stories about Richmond. I'll be real careful."

"You'd better be," Carrie said. Her smile faded as she watched another one of her father's people walk through the door and out of her life. "Do me a favor," she called after the disappearing form.

"Yes, ma'am," Opal said, turning to face her again.

"If you run into my father, don't tell him who you are."

Laughter rang through the house as Opal turned and left.

Sam was waiting for Opal in the carriage when she emerged from the house. She took a long moment to stand on the porch and look over the beautiful fields of Cromwell Plantation. June had always been one of her favorite months of the year. The fields, bursting with the beginning of new life just weeks ago, were now covered in fertile growth, the green shoots and stalks straining to see which could reach closest to the sky. Everything was still a luxuriant green. There was no strained look to the plants like there would be in another couple of months, when they would have to spend too much of their energy sucking available moisture from the late-summer ground.

"You comin', girl?" Sam asked as he picked up the reins. The horses, a matching pair of bays, snorted and shifted in anticipation.

Opal nodded but still didn't move from where she was standing. She could still hear the sounds of the children playing in the quarters. Her mind traveled back to the carefree days before she began work as a field hand. Unexpectedly, her eyes glazed over with tears. She was leaving all she had ever known. To go to what?

"Opal, we's got to get goin'." Sam's voice was a little kinder this time. He seemed to know she was struggling with her feelings.

Opal walked slowly down the stairs. She turned for one final glimpse of the house and saw Carrie watching her from the office window. Taking courage from her warm smile, she waved and stepped into the waiting carriage. Sam gave a gentle cluck, and the carriage rolled down the drive.

Opal was glad she had said goodbye to everyone in the quarters earlier that day. She didn't want them to see the tears rolling down her face as the carriage moved through the tall hedges of boxwoods and out of sight of the three-storied, columned house. Taking a deep breath, she sat straighter in her seat. As she faced Richmond, she felt her first twinge of excitement. Her emotions up to this point had included fear, doubt and determination. Not once had she felt excitement, simply a resignation that she was doing the right thing and a determination to see it through. She had let fear keep her from going to Canada. She wasn't going to let fear stop her now.

"You okay?"

Opal started at the sound of Sam's soft voice. Immersed in her own thoughts, she had almost forgotten he was there. "I'm okay, thanks." She was relieved to find the tremor was gone from her voice. Taking a deep breath, she settled back and let the warm wind blow across her face.

Sam nodded and kept driving, content to let silence reign between them.

Opal was glad to be left to her thoughts. It hadn't seemed real until last night when she had been packing her meager belongings for the trip. Somewhere around midnight, it had struck her that she may never see

Cromwell Plantation again. She may never see Old Sarah again. Never see the little children that called her Auntie Opal. Never enjoy another Christmas dance in the old barn. That's when the tears had come. Protected by the darkness of her cabin, she had sobbed until there had been no more tears. Then she had straightened her shoulders and faced the future—whatever may come.

"What you be knowin' 'bout Richmond, girl?"

"What do you mean, Sam?"

"Just what I said. What you be knowin' 'bout Richmond?"

Opal hesitated. "Not very much, I guess. My cousin told me she has a small house down at the bottom of one of the hills. She's going to help me get a job in one of the iron works, and I got this letter from Miss Carrie that handles my pay. I guess that's all I need to know for now." In truth, she had spent a lot of time thinking about Richmond and realizing how little she knew. The reality had done nothing but fuel her fear.

Sam barked a laugh and turned to stare at her from his seat. "Come up here next to me, girl," he ordered, pulling the horses to a stop. "We got a passel of talkin' to do. You go into the city like that, and they's gonna chew you up."

Opal climbed up on the seat next to Sam.

He started right in on her, anxious to make sure she knew what she needed to know before she reached her destination. "What you be knowin' bout the Black Code?"

"The Black Code?" Opal echoed. The sound of it did nothing to reassure her. It couldn't be anything good.

"I thought as much," Sam snorted. "Now you listen and you listen good, black girl. You's got to know this stuff so's you can stay out o' trouble."

Opal nodded. He had her complete attention.

"You got to make sure you ain't out after dark. For sure not two hours after the sun done gone down. Leastways not without a pass. The Black Code says they can whip you for dat. A pass don't always make no difference. Some people's got mean in their bones and just wait to find a nigger to whip."

Opal shuddered and resolved to confine her activities to daylight hours if at all possible. She wondered what kind of danger she was walking into. She gripped the wagon seat to control her shaking hands and tried to remember her earlier courage.

Sam continued. "Can't no slave ride in a carriage or nothin' without a written pass sayin' he can. They find you doin' that, they'll whip you. They call it punishin' with stripes." His tone was scornful.

"Does it happen very much?" Opal was horrified. She had thought it would be different in the city, away from overseers who took their anger out with the whip.

"Happens plenty," Sam said. "You gots to watch where you walk, too. If you be on the sidewalk and you see a white person comin' at you, or you be passin' one, you got to pass to the outside. If there ain't be 'nuff room to do that, you's got to get off the sidewalk and down in the street."

Opal listened intently. She was deathly afraid of the whip. She also didn't want to draw undue attention to herself. It could put everything in jeopardy.

"Your cousin... Miss Carrie say in dat letter dat she gives her permission for you to be livin' dere?"

Opal nodded. "I read it myself and had Rose read it with me, too."

"That's good," Sam said. "I'd hate to see your cousin get a beatin' 'cause she was puttin' you up."

"Miss Carrie said she was going to make sure there was no trouble."

"I'm sure Miss Carrie did the best she could, but trouble seems to follow us no matter how careful you be."

Opal could feel her fear threatening to overwhelm her. She stifled the impulse to tell Sam to turn the carriage around and take her back home. Nothing was worth this.

Sam, oblivious to her feelings, continued on. "You's got to watch how you talk to a white person. All the time, you's got to watch it. You say something wrong, or maybe just something they think is wrong..."

"And you get the whip."

Sam nodded, his satisfied look saying he was relieved she was getting it.

Oh, she was getting it all right. She was going to go to Richmond, stay in her house, and not say a word to anyone. Not that it would do the cause any good. Silently, she willed Sam to stop talking. All he was doing was making her more fearful. "I thought the city was going to be different from the plantation? Why, Sam, there be blacks there who are free!"

Sam nodded. "They be free. In some ways, that be. All them laws—the people don't care whether them niggers be free or slave. All they care 'bout is keeping them under control." Sam shook his head. "As much as they do to us to keep us afraid of them, they still got a whole passel of fears 'bout us."

"Is that why you haven't run away, Sam?" Opal had always wondered about that. She knew Sam had free family up north. Why had he never joined them?

Sam looked at her for a long moment and then turned back toward the road. A long silence stretched between them. Finally he spoke. "My mama and daddy were born on Cromwell Plantation. They used to talk to me 'bout leavin'. Told me 'bout my kin up north. Used to dream 'bout goin' up dere. I done known 'bout the Underground Railroad for a long time."

When he fell silent, Opal resisted the urge to say something. She could tell he was lost in his thoughts. He would talk when he was ready. Sam had always been like that.

"I'd planned on leavin'..." Another long pause passed as the horses trotted down the road. "Then John done give me a job to do. I done been doin' that job ever since."

Opal was confused. "John?" She could tell by the look on Sam's face that he wasn't going to say any more. She cast in her head for a solution. "Do you mean Sarah's John?"

Sam shrugged. "Don't know none other."

"But what job did he give you to do?"

"That don't matter none," Sam said. "I've did my job the best I could. Dat's all that matters." He turned his head and clucked to the horses to speed up. As the wheels turned faster in their pursuit of Richmond, Opal knew the old butler had said all he was going to say. Many miles passed as she tried to figure out what he could have been talking about.

Opal gazed around in awe as the carriage rattled down the road leading into Richmond. Nothing she had ever experienced had prepared her for this.

"Look up dere on the hill," Sam said, pointing his finger.

Opal gasped as the building came into view. "Why, it's bigger than the plantation house!" She leaned forward and allowed herself to drink in the sight of the huge columned building on the hill. "What is it?"

"That be the Capitol. It be where Marse Cromwell work now."

Suddenly Opal was nervous. What if she ran into her owner while they were riding through town? Sam was here on business for Miss Carrie. If the marse saw her with him, it would mess everything up. Marse Cromwell hadn't seen her enough to recognize her away from the plantation, but he would know Sam instantly. Instinctively, she shrank down into her seat and ducked her head.

Sam laughed heartily. "Ain't no reason to be nervous, girl. We ain't goin' up dere. The part of town we be headed to, I guarantee he ain't gonna be dere."

Sam's words comforted her. Soon she was looking around again, trying to drink in all the sights. The hills of the city were enough to amaze her. They were beautiful in their lush, green growth. She had never known anything but the flat land along the James. Sam was silent as he navigated the crowded streets.

Her attention was caught by something else as they rounded a curve. "Is that our river, Sam?"

Sam laughed again. "That be the James, for sho."

Opal could only shake her head as she stared. All she had ever seen were the wide-open expanses of a calm river as it moved to join the sea she had been told about. Here, the James looked like a stranger. She watched, fascinated, as it boiled over rocks and crashed down falls. The swirling waters churned into foamy rapids and then glided smoothly around little dots of islands. Her amazement increased even more as she noticed a large black object moving toward them on an expanse spanning the entire river. "Sam!" she exclaimed. "Is that thing a train?"

Sam looked at her almost in sympathy. "You sure got a heap o' learnin' to do." He chuckled. "Yep, that be a train. That bridge be the only thin' keeping that train out o' the river. I allus been glad I didn't have no reason to go on dat train. Don't know as how I'd trust that wooden thing."

Opal shuddered at the very thought of getting on that metal monster, but she felt a surge of excitement. Who was to say that someday she wouldn't be free and headed somewhere on that train? She almost laughed at the idea but decided to hang on to it. The rest of the trip passed in a haze of discovery and astonishment.

"Here we be, Opal."

Opal started as Sam pulled the wagon to a halt. She had been staring at the rows of simple wooden houses they had been passing. Were all the black faces peering at her really free? How had that happened? Why had she been born a slave—spent all of her life in slavery—when they got to live free?

She pushed down the resentment that tried to choke her. Miss Carrie had told her she could go free. Right this moment, she could be on her way north if she had chosen, but it had been her decision to come to Richmond. She knew what she was doing. The day may come when she could be free, but until then she would follow Old Sarah's advice. She would bloom where she was planted.

"Opal!"

Opal gave a glad cry and jumped from the carriage to meet the woman running toward her with outstretched arms. "Fannie!"

Within seconds she felt herself wrapped in a warm embrace. For long moments she stood there, reveling in the feel of a hug from someone who was family. There were tears in her eyes when she stepped away. "Fannie," she whispered. She could think of nothing else to say.

Fannie had tears in her eyes as well. "Come inside. The rest of the family is waiting to meet you."

Opal nodded and reached for her bag.

"I'll take it inside for you," Sam said. Not giving her time to reply, he gripped the small bag and strode through the dirt yard toward the front door.

Opal turned and gazed at Fannie. Her cousin was tiny—almost as tiny as Old Sarah. She hadn't expected that. The strong letters that occasionally reached her through the slave grapevine had made her envision a much bigger, imposing woman. Her short ebony hair was already taking on a salt and pepper effect, but Opal saw her strength. The eyes gazing at her with so much warmth were eyes that had seen much suffering and come through victorious. They were Sarah's eyes. Opal sighed, knowing she had come to a good place.

"Look the way you expected me to look?"

Opal shook her head and laughed. "You look ten times better." Feeling a burst of confidence and excitement, she reached out and tucked her arm through her cousin's. "Let's go meet the family."

Fannie smiled and turned to lead the way. Opal gazed at the house. Compared to some of the houses they had passed on the way here, Fannie's home was small and run-down. But compared to the tiny cabin in the quarters that had been her home all her life, Fannie's home was like a mansion. Fitting snugly against the surrounding two structures, the wood was gray and weathered, rising up two stories. The small porch with three sagging steps leading up to it looked like it had seen much better days. The yard was small and barren of any growth. Opal had just a moment to absorb her new surroundings before she stepped through the doorway.

Instantly she felt at home. Warmth and love seemed to be a living thing, reaching out to embrace her. She saw Sam smiling as Fannie's husband and their four children rushed forward to envelop her in big hugs. All was wild confusion and talk, until they heard Fannie banging a big spoon against a large cast iron skillet.

"I didn't stand in a hot kitchen cookin' all day so's that y'all could talk away the supper hour. Y'alls can talk whilst you eat."

In seconds, all were seated around the huge plank table, laughing as Fannie passed big platters of cornbread, cabbage and beans. There was even fresh squash and tomatoes.

Opal stared at the feast set before her. "Do y'all eat like this all the time?" Visions of wanting fled from her mind.

Fannie laughed. "As long as the garden produces, we do." She jumped up from the table to walk over and open the door leading outside.

Opal smiled in delight. The front yard may be barren dirt, but the back yard resembled the Garden of Eden. Every square inch was taken up with growing things. Large clumps of squash plants sported bright yellow blossoms. Green beans climbed stakes Eddie, Fannie's husband, had pushed into the ground to support them. Tomato plants vied for the center of attention. Fannie let the door swoosh shut before she could identify more.

After that, silence reigned as the food was consumed. In the distance, Opal could hear children yelling and the steady chug of a train climbing the steep tracks to the main station on Broad Street. Dogs were barking and roosters were crowing. Opal relaxed as the familiar sounds of the country mingled with the new sounds of the city.

Finally, she set her fork down and looked around the table. Eddie, seated next to Sam, was almost as tall as Moses, just not nearly as big. He looked like he hardly ate. The four kids were watching her closely. Carl, the youngest at six, eyed her with the delight of finding a new toy. Amber, the next oldest at nine, was merely watching her carefully—not unfriendly, but careful. Her large brown eyes promised friendship if she felt it was due. Sadie, budding into womanhood at thirteen, was going to be a real beauty. It was Susie who held her attention, though. At sixteen, she gave off a confidence that was beyond her years. Holding herself straight and tall, she ate slowly, all the time watching their newest house member. Aware that Opal was watching her, she smiled, a warm smile that said she was her mother's child. Opal knew they would be friends.

Fannie was the first to break the silence. "Did you have a good trip here?"

Opal nodded. "Sam was trying to train me how to stay out of trouble in Richmond." She laughed as she told them of Sam's warnings. Now that she was here, she was sure Sam had been exaggerating. The warmth of their welcome had erased her fears.

Eddie was the first to respond. "Don't be thinking Sam was joking, Opal," he said somberly. "Things in Richmond used to be pretty easy. There's been a lot of changin', though. The comin' of war done made a lot of people nervous. They especially nervous 'bout us blacks. When people get nervous, they try to get things back under control. That can mean some rough times for us."

"Some people were real mean to my daddy!" Amber burst out.

Opal's heart pounded as she waited for Eddie to explain. The fear that had disappeared during their meal had come back even stronger. Eddie shrugged and kept his voice light. "Seems I didn't get off the sidewalk fast enough when some white folks were coming down it. They took offense."

That's all he said, but the worried look that sprang into Fannie's eyes, and the grim tightening of Eddie's mouth, spoke more than his words did.

Fannie changed the subject. "The children been doin' nothing but talking 'bout your coming. They've made me tell the story over and over about why we've never met.

Sadie spoke up them. "I think it was real mean of y'alls old owner to sell family away from each other."

Opal shrugged. "It happens." She had been only two when she and her mama had been bought by Thomas Cromwell. Her mama and Fannie's mama had been sisters. When the plantation they had grown up on was sold, all the slaves went to the auction block. The sisters had been separated but knew where the other was going.

In less than six months, Opal's mom had taken sick and died in an outbreak of scarlet fever. Other women at Cromwell had raised the little girl. When she had gotten older, they gave her the stack of letters that had arrived sporadically over the years since her mama had died. Rose read them to her. Opal cried the whole time. It had been so wonderful to know that somewhere she had real family.

Shaking her thoughts back, she said, "It's now that counts. Now we can be together as family." It seemed too good to be true.

Fannie's mama had been hired out to someone in the city. While she was working, she had met and fallen in love with a freed slave who was a bricklayer. Determined they would be together, he had saved all his money until he could buy the freedom of his love and her little girl. Fannie had been only five when she had come to live in Richmond as a free black.

The next hour passed quickly as stories flowed around the table. So little living can be crammed into letters. Fannie and her family knew virtually nothing about Opal's life. She had learned to read and write only months ago and had only been able to get two short letters to them.

Finally, Eddie settled back in his chair and fixed his kindly gaze on his children. "Why don't you young'uns go outside and play for a while?"

A chorus of protests rose, but one look from Eddie ended it. In just minutes, there were only adults sitting around the table—adults, and Susie. She hadn't moved. Obviously she knew she was no longer considered a young'un.

"We're glad you're here, Opal," Fannie said softly.

Opal knew what she meant this time. "I want to help in any way I can."

Eddie spoke softly as well. "We probably shouldn't be talkin' now, but I wanted Sam to be here."

Sam? Opal looked around in confusion. She thought they had just met Sam. Why would Eddie want him to be there?

Sam chuckled. "There's a lot you don't be knowin' 'bout me, girl. I been knowin' your family here for a long time."

When Opal stared at him blankly, he continued. "I made my decision to stay on the plantation and do the job I had to do. That didn't mean I quit helping my people. It didn't mean I quit dreamin'."

Chapter Five

Carrie rubbed a hand across her weary eyes and stretched to loosen her stiffened muscles. A glance at the clock told her it was long past her dinner hour. She turned back to the desk, made a final entry, and snapped the records book shut. It was her fault. They should have been done weeks ago, but it was a job she hated and always found a reason to avoid doing. She needed to send a report to her father soon, however, so she couldn't put it off any longer. She had ridden the fields with Moses earlier that day and then locked herself away in the office. Pushing back from the desk with a satisfied sigh, she rose to her feet and smoothed down her dark green gown.

When she pushed open the door to the office, Sam was standing near the front door, peering out the window. "I'm starving, Sam." Her stomach growled in agreement. "Would you please have Annie bring me lunch in the parlor? I'm going to relax for a little while."

"Don't know 'bout no relaxing," Sam said. "It looks like you be gettin' comp'ny."

"Company?" Carrie echoed in a surprised voice. "I wasn't expecting anyone." She moved to join Sam by the window. What she saw caused her heart to sink. "It's Louisa Blackwell," she said in a dismayed voice.

"Looks that way. Want me to tell her you're out?"

Carrie looked at him in surprise. Her heart screamed for her to say yes, but she felt herself shaking her head. The hospitality code of the South wouldn't allow her to do that, nor would her integrity. "Show her to the parlor," she said.

Determined to make the best of what was sure would be a difficult situation, Carrie escaped to the kitchen, drank down a frothing glass of milk, and hurriedly ate a biscuit. Whatever she had to face, it would be faced more easily with some food in her stomach. She lingered just long enough for the warm familiarity and delicious smells of the kitchen to calm her heart as she gazed out over the pastures and finished her small meal. Finally, fortified and ready, she patted stray hairs into place and walked slowly to the parlor.

"Why, Louisa, what a surprise to see you. Welcome to Cromwell Plantation." She would at least begin this visit in a cordial manner. It was really too bad. She and Louisa had never been good friends, but the proximity of their fathers' plantations had created a relationship that went back to their childhoods. Carrie looked at her neighbor carefully. She had not seen her since the Christmas ball six months earlier. Their encounter then had not been pleasant. The hardness in Louisa's eyes warned her not to expect anything different today.

Louisa stood up to greet her. Her petite body was encased in a charming blue gown, her blond curls and blue eyes creating a stunning touch to the picture she made. She hurried forward and gathered Carrie's hand in a warm clasp. "My dear! It is so wonderful to see you."

Carrie wanted to laugh at the feigned affection gushing from the other girl's lips. She knew Louisa had no love lost for her. Their differences seem to hold them constantly in conflict. "Thank you," she murmured, and then moved away to perch herself on the rose loveseat positioned by the massive fireplace that was the focal point of the parlor. What was Louisa up to?

"I don't normally call on people without an announcement or an invitation...but I found I just couldn't wait to tell you my news."

Carrie managed to control her snort at Louisa's drawn out version of *invitation*. She was as much as saying that Carrie had been remiss in her duties as a neighbor not to have invited her over. Carrie supposed it would have been the proper thing to do, but quite frankly she hadn't been interested in the proper thing. She had been too busy nursing her mother and running the plantation. Louisa knew that.

Louisa broke into her thoughts. "Aren't you even going to ask me what my news is?" she asked in a petulant voice, her eyes becoming harder.

"Of course," Carrie responded in an even voice. "What is your news?"

Louisa leaned forward in excitement. "I have just returned from two glorious weeks in the capital of the Confederacy," she said triumphantly. She sat back and took a sip from the tea Sam had delivered while she was waiting.

Carrie nodded. "That's nice." When Louisa sat watching her expectantly, Carrie knew she was expected to ask more, but she simply wasn't in the mood for any games today. If Louisa had something to say, she could just say it.

Louisa finally tossed her head and laughed a brittle laugh. "I was sure you would be dying to hear all about what is going on where your dear daddy is."

Carrie bit her lip. This was typical Louisa—trying to manipulate her by insinuating her father wasn't important to her. Carrie stifled the impulse to throw something at her. She was really too tired to deal with Louisa today. It didn't look as if she had a choice, however. She thought longingly of Sam's offer to tell Louisa she was out. She should have taken him up on it, but when a neighbor traveled more than two hours to visit, you couldn't exactly turn her away. Forcing her voice to remain pleasant, she responded. "Of course I'm interested. Did you see my father?"

"No," Louisa said, waving her hand dismissively. "I was much too busy to do that." She leaned forward eagerly, her eyes snapping.

Carrie refrained from shaking her head in disgust. Louisa had the floor for now. She wouldn't give it up until she was ready. Carrie settled back on the loveseat, thinking of the hot meal she should be consuming in peace right now.

Louisa tilted her head and smiled brightly. "Being in the center of the social whirl of Richmond kept me much too busy to do ordinary things. I do believe this war is going to do wonderful things for our city."

"Such as being the target of Union attacks?" Carrie asked.

"Oh, poo. It will never come to that. And besides, let them come if they are foolish enough to try such a thing. Our brave boys will send them running back to the North."

Carrie looked at her sharply but didn't say anything.

Louisa rattled on, mindless of Carrie's silence. "This war is doing extraordinary things for the social life of our capital. Choosing Richmond to be the capital of our whole wonderful new nation was simply a precious move. Why, do you realize the increased number of parties and dances going on there?" She glanced at Carrie but didn't wait for her to speak. "The teas are simply marvelous, and I, along with some other girls, were out at the camp of instruction three different times taking cakes and other goodies to our dear boys. Why, I was even fortunate enough to be there for one of the horse races they stage for entertainment. It was simply a glorious time."

Louisa smiled and batted her blue eyes, seeming to forget for a moment there were no handsome young men to impress. "I do believe I attended a social function every day I was there. There is no end to the eligible bachelors to escort you and dance with you. It is any girl's dream come true."

Not *any girl*, Carrie said to herself. Her mind strayed to the things she still had to do that day. When Louisa prattled like this, it wasn't necessary to really listen. If you simply nodded your head when she took a breath, she would be content she had your undivided attention.

Louisa took a breath, watched for Carrie's nod, and hurried on. "I don't believe I have ever seen anything so noble as the masses of soldiers coming to protect our city. Some of them are really quite plain young men, but many of them are the finest Virginia has to offer. They have laid aside their riches and position to perform their duty in this, our time of need." Louisa paused, her voice becoming reflective. "Why, many of them have come with only a servant or two. Of course, it is ridiculous to expect them to do the work of a regular soldier. A group of us girls talked with several of them while they directed their servants in cleaning the military grounds they were supposed to clean themselves. Don't you think they're terribly clever?"

Carrie spoke carefully. "I think they may be surprised when they are forced to take care of themselves on the battlefield." Her mind was full of the struggles she had faced in learning to care for herself and not rely on another person.

Louisa shot her a cross look. "Why must you always be so negative, Carrie Cromwell? All this talk of battlefields is so depressing and really quite unnecessary. I have talked to many people who believe there won't be any real fights in this war."

Carrie's mind flashed back to the letter she had received from her father just the day before. In it he had talked about the surety that the battle to win Southern independence would be long and hard-fought. She knew it would do no good to say anything, so she remained silent on the matter. "I find I rest better facing reality, rather than imagining fantasy," was all she allowed herself to say, knowing the result it would have, but finding she didn't really care.

Louisa flushed with anger and opened her mouth, but quickly shut it again. She looked down at her hands for a long moment as if regaining control and then looked back up with her simpering smile. "You really should go to Richmond yourself, Carrie. Your position as a government man's daughter would open many doors for you. There is no end of young men who would eagerly pursue you."

I'm only interested in one. Instantly, Carrie pushed the errant thought aside. It had been her decision to end the relationship. Still, she couldn't control the yearning of her heart—just the actions.

"Of course, I've noticed you don't always wait for young men to pursue you."

Carrie's head shot up as Louisa's voice took on a calculating tone. She had a feeling she was about to discover the real reason for Louisa's visit. The cold look in her neighbor's eyes shot out a warning. "Whatever are you talking about?" Carrie asked.

Louisa shrugged. "You had no trouble pursuing Robert Borden last year."

Carrie's eyes flashed, but she managed to control her temper. Louisa was still angry about not having her way at her ball a year ago. She had wanted Robert to choose her as queen of the event, not Carrie.

Louisa didn't wait for her to reply. "Of course you put the dear boy in a horrible situation, hanging on him and making him feel it was his duty to choose you as queen."

Carrie moved to demand that Louisa leave the house. She didn't have to sit and listen to such nonsense. Louisa's next words kept her where she was.

"I tried to assure him he had nothing to be responsible for or feel badly about when I saw him at one of the dances last week." Louisa's tone was gloating.

Carrie settled back in the loveseat, feeling as if she had received a blow. Louisa had danced with Robert? They had discussed her? She could do nothing but stare at her tormenter, all the while knowing she was playing into Louisa's hands.

Louisa laughed again, this time a triumphant laugh. "I wouldn't feel too badly about losing Robert Borden, Carrie. You never could have been what he needed." She continued, each word spoken carefully. "He needs someone more suited to his position in life. Not someone who throws overseers off her plantation and then becomes a nigger lover." Her last words were delivered with angry, cutting precision.

Carrie gasped and stood up. "That will be enough, Louisa Blackwell. I hardly think it is your place to come into my home and insult me. I will have Sam show you to the door." She struggled to control the angry tremor in her voice.

"Oh, sit down." Louisa said in a sharp voice. "Do you really think everyone around here doesn't know what you are doing? Someone had to come over to try to talk some sense into you. Don't you realize what you are doing to all of our reputations? Especially your father's?"

Carrie remained standing where she was, but her face whitened at the mention of her father.

Louisa peered even closer. "He still has no idea what you're doing, does he?"

Carrie didn't respond, her fists clenching at her sides. She considered attacking Louisa, as she had once when they were much younger. The girl deserved it then, and she certainly deserved it now.

Louisa laughed again, this time in disbelief. "How in the world have you managed to deceive him for so long? It must be true. The poor man is in his own little world. I almost feel sorry for you, Carrie, being left behind to manage this plantation while your father runs away to Richmond."

Carrie had heard all she intended to listen to. She walked over to stand directly in front of Louisa. "That will be all, Louisa. You have insulted me. Now you insult my father. It is time for you to leave."

"Oh, poo, why let such little things disturb you?" Louisa made no move to leave, merely sitting back in her chair and reaching for her tea. "Surely you aren't afraid of a little truth?"

"When the truth becomes a distorted pack of lies, it is indeed disturbing. I will have Sam show you out." Carrie turned sharply and headed for the parlor door.

"Don't you even want to know that Robert asked after you?"

Even when angry, Louisa could be simpering. Carrie hesitated the merest second and continued to move toward the door. "Sam?" He appeared at her side instantly. "Miss Blackwell is leaving now. Would you please show her to the door?"

Carrie heard Louisa's angry gasp and then the rustle of her skirts as she jumped up from the chair where she had been sitting. Carrie knew she was safe for the moment from her acid tongue. Louisa would never consider talking about personal things in front of a slave.

Carrie watched her stalk to the door and stop just long enough to throw an angry glare over her shoulder.

"I'm sorry I ever came all the way over here to see you. I told them it would do no good," was her parting shot.

"I'm sorry you came all the way over here, too," Carrie replied. "I hope you have a good trip home." With those words, she turned and walked back into the parlor. She stood at the window and watched as Louisa flounced down the stairs and settled herself stiffly into her carriage. A sharp word from her, a raise of the driver's hands, and the carriage rolled down the drive.

Carrie watched for just a moment before she sank into the chair next to the fire and lowered her head into her hands. Her head was pounding and her face burned with anger and embarrassment. It was bad enough that Louisa had insulted both her and her father. To know that she had been discussing her with Robert made her feel sick inside. *You don't know how much of what she said is true*, a voice cautioned.

"Can I bring you some food, Miss Carrie? That might make you feel some better."

Carrie looked up at the sound of Sam's deep voice and managed a wavering smile. She didn't feel like eating, but he was right—it might make her feel better. "That would be nice, Sam. Thank you."

He nodded but didn't move away from the door. She looked up to see him regarding her thoughtfully.

"The best thing to do with folks like that is to ignore them. They ain't be worth the worry and heartache."

Carrie knew he had probably heard every word that had passed between them. Voices carried easily from the parlor. "I know. You're right," she said halfheartedly. "Do you think she'll tell my father?"

Sam shrugged his shoulders. "Your daddy gonna find out what's goin' on 'round here sooner or later, but I don't reckon he'll be findin' out from her. People like that girl...well, they like to cause trouble and make other people squirm. They's too busy takin' care of themselves, though, to think much 'bout other people when they ain't close enough to pester."

Carrie managed to smile. "I'll take that food now, Sam."

Louisa was furious as she rolled away from the Cromwell Plantation. Her cheeks were flushed red and her blue eyes were shooting sparks. "You'll be sorry for that, Carrie Cromwell," she muttered under her breath. She would never think of talking loud enough for her driver to hear. She was still mortified that Carrie had as much as ordered her out of her home within hearing distance of her butler.

She was busily calculating her revenge, a mile or so from the house, when a lone figure on horseback moved into the road from the surrounding woods. The man looked up as the carriage drew nearer, and moved over to the side of the road to let them pass easily. Louisa barely glanced at him as her driver slowed. She was far more interested in her own thoughts than in a strange man.

"Miss Blackwell."

Louisa looked up as the slight, wiry man lifted his hat in greeting. There was something familiar about him, but she couldn't place him.

"Ike Adams, ma'am."

Still she couldn't place him. She moved forward to tell her driver to continue on. His next words erased her thoughts.

"The old overseer at Cromwell Plantation, ma'am."

"Stop the carriage," she ordered quickly.

She looked at him with new interest as the carriage rolled to a halt under the spreading arms of an oak tree. She didn't particularly like what she saw. Something about him was rather unsettling. Maybe it was the cruel slant of his eyes, or the cocky bearing as he looked down at her.

"Mr. Adams," she murmured, slightly uneasy but angry enough at Carrie to pursue the conversation.

"I see you've been to visit our Miss Cromwell," Adams observed.

Louisa's face flushed with renewed anger as she thought of Carrie. "She is certainly not *my* Miss Cromwell," she said sharply.

Adams seemed to eye her with greater interest, and then he moved his horse closer to the carriage.

"I take it the visit wasn't pleasant?" he said, an oily smile on his face.

Louisa didn't usually lower herself to conversing with strange overseers, but she was eager to vent her frustration to anyone who would listen. "Carrie Cromwell can be quite unreasonable." She sighed heavily and cast her eyes down. She was quite experienced with the effect she could have on men.

"So I have seen," Adams remarked.

"Of course," Louisa said, even though she had no idea why Carrie had thrown the man off her plantation. It would be best to be cautious. "I have heard you are no longer employed by Cromwell Plantation."

Adams barked a laugh. "I imagine you've heard a lot more than that. I reckon I'm the talk of the area. It ain't everyone that gets tossed out on their ear by a girl," he said bitterly.

"No, I suppose not," Louisa agreed. She was intrigued to see where this conversation would lead. She waited for him to continue.

Adams was happy to oblige. "She was wrong, you know. I was just doing my job. If her daddy knew what she had done, I'd have my job back in a heartbeat."

Something in the man's face said he was lying, but Louisa didn't really care. She was feeling no sense of loyalty to her old friend.

"How's everything going on the plantation now, Miss Blackwell?" Adams' voice had taken on a wheedling, yet vulnerable tone. "I sure do miss that place."

"I suppose everything is going all right. I wasn't there for very long. The house was certainly in fine shape." When Adams flushed in anger, she sensed she had not given him the answer he wanted. An idea began to take shape. "What are you doing now, Mr. Adams?" Her voice was more pleasant.

"Trying to help slave owners like yourself hold onto their valuable property. I am at anyone's service any time of the day or night."

"You're a slave hunter," Louisa commented flatly. She could not imagine a more repulsive life than one spent hunting down runaway slaves, but she knew someone had to do it.

"That's right, Miss Blackwell, I'm a slave hunter," Adams said coldly, as if he detected the disdain in her voice.

Louisa realized that she had not responded in the best way. Obviously the man's pride had been battered by Carrie's actions. She batted her eyes at him as she gazed up. "You misunderstand," she said. "I think it's wonderful what you do. I'm sure many people appreciate your services."

Adams appeared somewhat mollified. A half-smile formed on his lips as he looked at her.

Louisa's plan had taken form while they talked. She was ready. "I've heard some of the Cromwell slaves are missing from the plantation again," she said casually. When Adams' face tightened, she knew he was thinking about the slaves that had escaped when he was still overseer. "Not the ones who ran away last summer. I'm talking about more recently."

Adams' eyes narrowed as he shifted in his saddle. "Miss Cromwell tell you that?" he asked.

"No," Louisa admitted, "but talk gets around you know."

Adams' lips tightened, but he didn't say anything.

Louisa knew she was getting somewhere by the bright, calculating gleam in his eye. She had him thinking. "I imagine those slaves are worth a lot of money."

"All Cromwell slaves are worth a lot of money," he stated. "Worth more every day now that the war is going on. Their value keeps going up. People know niggers are gonna be harder to come by."

Good, Louisa thought. She tried to keep her voice nonchalant. "I imagine Mr. Cromwell would be extremely eager to recoup his investment."

"Possibly."

She knew Adams was watching her more closely, wondering where she was headed. Taking a deep breath, she laid her cards on the table. "I imagine Mr. Cromwell would be very appreciative to the man who told him about his missing slaves and then recaptured them. Probably he would want to see that man as overseer, even if his darling daughter didn't."

Adams peered even harder at her. "What you got against Carrie Cromwell, ma'am?"

Louisa shrugged. "I'm merely suggesting that Thomas Cromwell might appreciate your services. You can do with that information what you want." She knew by the cold gleam in his eyes that she had planted an idea he would at least think about. As she looked at the cruel twist to his lips, she felt a twinge of remorse but shoved it aside. Carrie could act high and mighty if she wanted to, but at some point she would have to learn that her actions were simply unacceptable. She had tried going in friendship to warn her, but it had done no good. It was time her father knew the truth about what was really going on at Cromwell Plantation.

Adams lifted his hat and smiled briefly. "Thank you for the information, Miss Blackwell. Have a nice day." Touching his hand to his hat, he broke into a gentle canter and moved down the road away from the carriage.

Louisa looked after him with a satisfied smile and then spoke sharply to her driver. "Move ahead."

Carrie's heart was still pounding when Granite broke out of the woods into the small clearing along the James. She had been so upset by Louisa's visit that all she could think to do was come to her place. Swinging down from Granite, she strode over to her log and settled onto it. Her mind raced as she looked out over the placid water of the river. She almost resented its serene surface. She would have liked it better if it was being rolled and tossed by a savage wind. Then it would more closely match her emotions.

She didn't know how long she sat there before she took any notice of her surroundings. The tiny clearing was like a green palace. Low hanging limbs of oak and maple reached down to embrace the flower-bordered grass. The water lapped gently at the bank a few feet from where she sat. It bore no evidence of the flood that had covered it weeks earlier. Mother Nature had reclaimed it as soon as the water had receded.

It had been months since she had had time to escape to her haven. She longed for the carefree days of youth when she spent endless hours hidden away from the world in her secret place. She had only brought one other person here.

At the thought of Robert, her cheeks burned anew. She could imagine him and Louisa laughing about her, talking about her, making fun of her.

You don't know how much of what she said was the truth. The thought that had flitted through her mind earlier came back to her as she stared out over the river. Carrie knew Louisa was capable of saying anything. For all she knew, the girl had never even seen Robert. She could have made it all up to make Carrie angry.

For a long while, Carrie allowed her thoughts to be occupied by Robert. Here, protected by the trees that had watched her grow up, she allowed the memories and special moments to spill through her mind. She felt relieved when tears rolled and spilled down her cheeks. She knew she was nearing the breaking point, or Louisa's visit and caustic words wouldn't have bothered her so much. She would have simply gotten rid of the troublesome girl and then laughed about it. There was no laughter in her now.

Gradually, the peace of her sanctuary worked its magic. As the sun began to sink beyond the horizon, she could think clearly again. Louisa might very well have seen Robert. They might have laughed about her together. Their actions now had nothing to do with the action she had taken two months ago. She would do the same thing again.

Carrie sighed as she settled back against the log and let the soft breeze blow over her hot face. She knew she had done the right thing. She could only be responsible for her own actions. She couldn't mandate what other people did or how they perceived her. Once she came to that conclusion, she regained her sense of peace.

She was able now to think through Louisa's other caustic remarks. *Nigger lover.* Carrie smiled at that one. Louisa meant it as an insult. Carrie considered it a compliment. Yes, she loved all her black friends and was determined to do what she could for them. Let other people think what they wanted. She had made a decision she could live with. She knew hardly anyone in her sphere of friends would agree with her decision, but it was all right. She had to live with herself.

She could not deny the concern of what would happen if Louisa told her father about Adams being gone. She was sure she could convince him that Adams should never set another foot on Cromwell Plantation, but she wasn't as sure that she could keep him from appointing another overseer in his place.

As she pondered everything in her mind, she felt the worry connected with it slip away. Finally, with a sigh, she let it all go. She would take one day at a time. That was all she could do.

Chapter Six

July 10, 1861

"We'll take care of everything, Carrie. Don't worry about things back here."

Carrie smiled. "I trust you, Moses. I know I'm leaving the plantation in good hands. It's not you I'm worried about." She paused for a moment. When she spoke again, her smile had been replaced by a worried frown. "I can't get Louisa Blackwell's visit out of my mind. She seemed to think the neighbors were upset by what is going on here—or what they *think* is going on, anyway. They're bound to know I'm leaving the plantation for a while. What if they come over here trying to start trouble?"

She could tell by the worried flicker in his eyes that Moses had thought the same thing, but his voice was strong and confident when he answered.

"Don't be worrying none about things here. People have their own lives to worry about. They might be talking, but I reckon they have enough of their own problems to take care of without trying to make problems for us."

Carrie tried to take comfort in his words. Sarah had tried to reassure her the night before with similar words. Why couldn't she let it go? "Oh, I wish Father hadn't called me to the city!" she burst out. "I should have told him I was too busy to come right now."

Rose walked out onto the porch just then. "You know your daddy, Carrie. He's worried sick that something will happen and he won't be able to take care of you. Sounds like from his letter that the first real fight of the war is about to take place right here on Virginia soil. He's not going to be able to rest until he knows you are safe in Richmond with him. You can come back when the danger is over."

Carrie nodded but didn't say what she was thinking. When would she be able to return? When would her father think it was safe? That wasn't really what was bothering her, however. She had faced her feelings in the long hours of darkness last night when she had lain sleepless. The truth was, she was obeying her father's anxious plea to come to Richmond because she hoped for one last glimpse of Robert before he headed into battle.

That knowledge had filled her with both sorrow and self-contempt. It was she who had ended their relationship. She should just let it go.

Carrie gave Rose and Moses a final hug and settled herself into the carriage. "I'm ready, Sam. We should be on our way."

"Yessum, Miss Carrie." Sam raised his hands and urged the team of horses down the driveway. Once they were past the protective hedge of boxwoods, he turned and said, "I think you gonna be mighty surprised when you get to the city, ma'am."

Carrie thought to ask him what he meant, but she was too absorbed in her own thoughts. She would find out soon enough anyway. She did have another question, though. "Sam, do you like being a driver?"

Sam shrugged and smiled a half-smile. "I don't mind it none, Miss Carrie."

Carrie watched him handle the team expertly and thought with sadness of her friend Miles. He had been a slave on Cromwell Plantation long before she was born. The wise old man had taught her everything she knew about horses and had instilled in her his deep love for them. He had disappeared the year before with the first group of slaves who had escaped from the plantation. She still missed him.

"Do you think Charles found him?" She knew Sam would understand that she was asking about Miles.

Sam shrugged again. "I reckon if anybody could, Charles could."

Carrie waited for him to say more, but the large man fell silent again. Why did she always feel like Sam knew more than he was saying? She pushed that thought aside as her thoughts returned to Charles. He had been Miles' assistant and had taken over the stables when he disappeared. What he lacked in experience he made up for in commitment, but he had been one of the first to take her up on her offer to leave. She was glad to think he was free somewhere, possibly reconnected with the old man who had been like a father to him, but it had left a gaping hole on the plantation.

Sam glanced back to look at her. "What's that worried look on your face for, Miss Carrie?"

Carrie answered honestly. "I'm wondering how long I'm going to be able to keep plugging holes. So far, Father isn't suspicious because everything continues to run smoothly, but what happens when it doesn't anymore? I don't regret letting the people go," she said hastily, "but—"

"But you decidin' to borrow trouble 'fore it be here."

"I guess you're right." She couldn't let it go, though. "What do you think Father is going to say when you come driving up with me, instead of Charles?"

Sam shrugged. "He'll probably thank me for stepping in when Charles is so sick on the plantation and plan to give me an extra gift at Christmas time."

Carrie looked up at his words, caught the amused twinkle in his eyes, and broke out into a hearty laugh. "You always could make me laugh, Sam. Thank you." The laughter seemed to ease the weight of her heart.

Feeling suddenly weary, Carrie leaned back against the carriage seat. She closed her eyes and allowed herself to drift into a deep sleep.

The sound of a train whistle woke her. Opening her eyes slowly, she suddenly jerked to attention. "We're in Richmond, already?" she gasped.

"I'd say you needed to sleep," Sam chuckled. "Yessum, we be here in Richmond."

Carrie looked around her in astonishment. They had just entered the outskirts of the city. A quick look at the sky told her they had probably gotten here just in time. The sky that beamed hazy sunshine this morning had now taken on a yellow-gray tone, and the air was stagnant with humidity. As they slowed to maneuver the traffic in the streets, the breeze that had been stirred by their movement died. The sultry air seemed to reach out clasping fingers to grasp at her. She immediately felt the unwelcome sensation of sweat trickling down her brow and back, and reached under the seat to pull out a parasol. It would at least offer some protection from the midday heat.

"Do you think we'll get to Father's house before the storm hits?" she asked anxiously. She was not adverse to a little rain, but the threatening sky promised a severe storm. She had no desire to dodge lightning bolts.

Sam cast a practiced eye to the sky. After a few moments, he nodded. "I think we'll get there. Leastways, if the traffic don't stop up completely."

Carrie stared around her and saw that Sam's concern was justified. "This is what you meant earlier when you said I would be surprised when we got here," she guessed.

Sam, focused on navigating the bustling street, merely nodded. Carrie had never seen Richmond like this. There were people and carriages everywhere. She had expected, after Louisa's report, to see soldiers everywhere, but though they were in evidence, there didn't seem to be a preponderance of them. She quickly realized they must have all gone north to prepare for the battle her father predicted. Suddenly, she was very anxious to get to her father's house. He would know whether Robert had gone to battle yet or not.

As they inched down Broad Street, she craned to catch a glimpse of someone she knew. Not that she really expected to see anyone, but the sight of a familiar face would make her at least *feel* she was in her favorite city. Richmond seemed to have become a different world since she had been here last, less than three months ago.

Just as they drove past the train depot on Broad Street, an engine pulling its load of cars puffed up to the station. A great horde of people swarmed off the train, but very few people got on. The cries of carriage drivers vying for passengers filled the air as the rattle of wheels and the yells of people eager to reach their destination filled her ears. Carrie leaned forward to absorb it all, even though it frightened her a little. She had expected and grown accustomed to such madness in Philadelphia the summer before, but Richmond? The quiet, prosperous city on the James had exploded over night.

Rumblings of thunder over the cacophonous sounds of the city seemed to heighten the anxiety she felt in the air. Indeed, the whole city seemed to be gripped by a sultry spirit of fear and waiting that left no one the luxury of simply relaxing and living. Now that war had indeed come, it was all business, preparation and waiting—no matter what your position in life.

As Sam continued to inch down the road, Carrie realized what it was about the crowd of people that was bothering her. It was almost totally comprised of women, children and older men. The men were either quite old or dressed in the impeccable attire that spoke of a high government official. Other than the occasional soldier she saw moving down the street, the town seemed to be devoid of young men. That, more than anything, brought home the sharp realization of what this war really meant. The young men of the South had marched off to do battle with friends and family from the North.

Now, each face became a story. Each woman was the mother, wife, sweetheart or sister of a soldier preparing to fight the first big battle. Children had brothers and fathers off at war. The older men had the responsibility of these young lives resting squarely on their shoulders. Carrie shuddered and sank back against the cushion. The excitement had lost its appeal for her.

It seemed hours before their carriage reached the bottom of Broad Street and headed up Church Hill to her father's house. She turned her head away from the sight of St. John's steeple reaching for the sky. It brought too many painful memories.

A jagged streak of lightning bolted across the now leaden gray sky. The wind was blowing fiercely, causing dust to fly through the air and laundry to dance on the lines. As she watched, one door on a house banged open as a plainly dressed woman dashed outside to scoop the dried laundry into her arms. Thunder rumbled, and the first raindrops splashed onto the carriage as they made the final turn onto Twenty-Sixth Street.

"Hang on, Miss Carrie!"

Carrie gripped the sides of the carriage and smiled as Sam urged the horses into a quick sprint. It was a good thing the storm had driven everyone inside. A wild dash like this could hurt someone, but Sam was just trying to keep her dry. Now that she knew they would make it to the house, she was able to enjoy nature's fireworks show. The wind felt wonderful after the cloying heat of the day.

Sam had just pulled the blowing team to a halt when the sky opened up. Huge raindrops descended on them in a downpour. "Run for it, Miss Carrie!"

Laughing, Carrie jumped from the carriage and dashed toward the house. As soon as she reached the porch, she turned to watch Sam maneuver the carriage down the drive next to the house. He would be safe and dry with the horses in the small barn behind the house in just minutes. Content to watch the furious lashing of the storm, she leaned against the porch railing of the three-story brick house. She ignored her drenched condition as she watched the trees bend and sway in harmony with the wind.

"Miss Cromwell!"

She turned at the sound of the startled voice and smiled at the anxious black face peering out at her. "Hello, Micah."

"I'se didn't know you was here, ma'am." Her father's butler opened the door wider. "Come in, come in!"

Carrie cast one last wistful look at the storm and moved inside. Sam was just coming in the backdoor with her luggage. "Is Father here, Micah?"

"No, ma'am. He done sent a messenger a while back. Said he done got to be in a meetin'. He'll be home 'round dinner time."

Carrie glanced at the large grandfather clock that was just striking three. That gave her a couple of hours. She was anxious to see her father, but she was glad for the opportunity to take a bath. The long, dusty drive had left her feeling grimy.

Carrie, freshly attired in a stunning yellow gown, was waiting for her father on the porch when his carriage rolled up. The storm had vented its fury and then blown further down the river. She imagined the plantation would be getting it soon. The storm had left in its wake a gloriously blue sky, swept clear of all haze and humidity. The disappearing thunder clouds contrasted vividly with green trees outlined by bright sunshine. Carrie took a deep breath of fragrant air and hurried down the walk to meet her father.

"Carrie! It's wonderful to see you. You look as beautiful as ever." Thomas wrapped her in a hug and held her for a long moment. When he stepped back, his face was wreathed in smiles. He looked at her more closely. "No, I believe I was wrong. You're *more* beautiful than ever. You're growing up my girl, and I'm missing too much of it."

Carrie looked beyond the smile to the strained look in his eyes. "Nonsense, Father. You are doing exactly what you are supposed to be doing. Virginia needs you. When all this unpleasantness is over, we can talk about leading a normal life again."

"A normal life..." Thomas mused, almost as if he wasn't sure such a thing could happen again. He shook his head. "We don't need to stand out here talking. Let's go inside. Dinner should be just about ready."

Carrie was pleasantly full when she pushed away from the table and followed her father into the parlor. The curtains billowed as a steady breeze washed in over them. The air, fragrant from the afternoon rain, felt wonderful. She could feel herself relaxing as she sank back into the deep armchair. There had been little conversation during dinner as her father took the time to unwind after working all day. Now she wanted answers to all the questions swarming around in her mind.

"Is there really a danger to Richmond, Father?"

Thomas nodded. "If there wasn't, I wouldn't have brought you here. Our forces in northern Virginia are strong, but our intelligence says that the North's General McDowell has created a strong army."

"And you believe there will be a showdown soon?" Her father's letter hadn't said much other than urging her to come to Richmond as soon as possible.

Thomas' voice was tight. "I believe there will be a battle in little more than a week. Several advances have been made, but the main force of the Union Army is still encamped in Washington. Our sources tell us there will be definite movement soon."

"Your sources?" Carrie echoed.

Her father smiled grimly. "We need information. We get it any way we can."

Carrie looked at him in wonder as she realized he was talking about spies. She couldn't believe the United States had come to this. She was also reminded how utterly removed she was from what was going on in the country. The plantation had become her whole life. Oh, she got occasional newspapers, but fatigue kept her from staying abreast of all that was occurring.

"Why Manassas?" she asked, suddenly desperate to know more. "Didn't you say that's where you believe the battle will be fought?" She could remember passing through Manassas Junction on the train last summer on her way to Philadelphia. Her vague memories were of a pleasant little town. It was impossible to envision it as a battlefield.

"Virginia's railroads are our lifeline. We have long known the strategic value of the Manassas Gap line. It very neatly connects the two major avenues by which we may be invaded." Thomas' face took on an intense look. It was obvious that much time and energy had been spent on determining where the first great battle would happen. "It is also the answer to rapid deployment of our troops. If Johnston is attacked in Harpers Ferry, Beauregard's troops can be quickly moved to reinforce him. The same is true should Beauregard be the one to receive the first onslaught."

"I've heard people say there won't really be a battle. That the North is bluffing and will back off when they see the South is serious." Carrie didn't really believe it herself, but, for just a moment, she was choosing fantasy over reality.

Her father's grim words destroyed all such fantasizing. "There will be a fight, Carrie," he stated flatly. "We have over thirty-five thousand men prepared to fight an enemy we believe to be of about equal size."

Carrie shuddered at the thought of what such forces could do.

Thomas continued. "We can win this battle," he said with a glimmer in his eyes. "Beauregard is an excellent general. He has wonderful support. It has been hard work to transform thousands of farmers, shopkeepers and laborers into an army, but we have done the best we could in the time afforded us. Only time will tell if we have done a good enough job."

Carrie didn't know what to say. She felt no excitement over what was about to happen—only repulsion. And she could think of only one thing. Finally, she could stand it no longer. "Where is Robert?"

"Robert leaves tomorrow with the last batch of troops. He has been working hard to train the newest recruits. They are the greenest of the green, but they are eager to do battle."

Carrie whitened and nodded.

Thomas looked at her for a long moment. "You love him," he stated simply.

Carrie nodded again. "Yes, I do." She didn't even bother to deny it. Her father knew her too well. He would know she was lying, and it was time she told him the truth anyway. She had known this time was coming. It might as well be now rather than later.

"But you refuse to marry him."

"You've talked to Robert?"

"I had dinner with him a few weeks ago," Thomas admitted.

"Did he tell you why?"

"He told me you couldn't marry him because you two stood so far apart on the slavery issue." When Carrie merely nodded, he continued, his voice a little sharper. "I thought we had talked about that." He paused. "I'm disappointed in you. It's not like you to take a stand against something God so clearly sanctions."

"I don't believe that," Carrie whispered. It hurt to know that he was disappointed in her, though. Fighting tears that wanted to spring to the surface, she tried to explain. "I don't expect you to agree with me, Father. I struggled long and hard to come to this decision."

"How did you reach it?"

This time her father's voice was quieter, more like the man she loved and knew so well. Obviously, he was trying to be fair, trying to listen to her. His earlier sharp voice had probably been the result of too many long, strained days. She hated to add more weight to the burden he already carried, but she knew it was time to be honest.

"Why do you feel God sanctions slavery, Father?"

"The Bible states it clearly."

"Where?"

"You asked Robert the same ridiculous question."

Carrie struggled to keep her voice even. "Why is it a ridiculous question?"

"Because you are trying to put us in the place of a minister. It is their job to interpret scripture, not ours."

"But what if they're interpreting scripture wrongly?"

"You think you know the scripture better than a minister?" Thomas' voice had an edge now.

"I think I can read and understand as well as they can. Isn't that why you had me educated? So that I can think clearly?"

"And now it comes back to haunt me!"

Carrie's heart lightened as she heard the hint of humor in her father's voice. They would not agree on this, but in the end, they would love and respect each other. "I guess that's the price you pay," she said with a smile.

Thomas chuckled. "You always were different from everyone around you. Okay, daughter, let's tear into this issue."

The lanterns burned low as Carrie shared with her father the experiences and thoughts of the past year. She struggled to relay how she had felt that day she faced her beliefs in the clearing. She had already decided not to tell him about the current condition of the slaves on the plantation, nor about Ike Adams—especially now that she was here in Richmond. If he took it in his head to send an overseer while she was still here, there was no telling what would happen. She wasn't willing to take that risk. She was ready, though, when her father asked the question she had been expecting.

"How do you handle managing our slaves on Cromwell Plantation? Surely you know the plantation could not run without them?"

"They are not my slaves. They are yours. If they belonged to me, I would have already set every one of them free." Her voice was soft but firm.

Thomas stared at her. "How can you say that? Would you honestly throw away everything you've ever known?"

"I don't believe I would have to throw things away. I think things would have to be managed differently, however. The North manages to have a thriving economy without slavery."

"The North is an industrial wasteland!" Thomas snorted.

"There are quite a lot of farms in the North."

"Farms—not our glorious plantations."

Carrie spoke carefully. "Glorious at the cost of stolen human lives."

Thomas' eyes flared with anger as he swung around in his chair and stared out the window. When he turned back, his face was calm once more. "I have only one thing to say," he stated with somewhat forced amusement in his voice. "I'm very glad the slaves at Cromwell belong to me and not you."

Carrie managed to laugh, wondering what would happen if her father knew that a number of his slaves were now free. She wanted to tell him how wonderfully the plantation was running with those slaves who had chosen to stay and who were being given incentives and freedom. Surely it would help him to see he might be wrong about the necessity of slavery.

Not yet, her heart cautioned. *It's too soon.*

Chapter Seven

Carrie was up bright and early the next morning, but her father had risen even earlier. He was already seated at the table, running his eye over the newspaper as he sipped a cup of coffee.

"Good morning, dear," Thomas said. "I hate to leave you so early this morning, but I'm afraid my presence is demanded at the Capitol. There is still much work to be done to make sure Richmond is secure."

Carrie looked up from the cup of tea Micah had placed in front of her. "You think the Union forces will make it all the way to Richmond?" She hated the frightened tone in her voice.

"I think no such thing," Thomas said. "Our army will send them running back to Washington. But we have to be ready for anything. General Lee has labored long and hard to prepare the defenses of the city, all the while making sure we are ready to face the threat from the North. Ever since our grand city became the capital of the Confederacy, the cry from the Union has been *On to Richmond!*" He took another gulp of coffee and smiled. "If I really thought Richmond was in danger, I wouldn't have brought you here. You're here because I want to know you are safe."

"You don't think I'm safe on the plantation?"

"I don't know *what* you are when you're on the plantation. I'm simply too far away to know what is going on. That's what drives me crazy, and that's what prompted the letter pleading with you to come here."

Carrie jumped up and gave her father a big hug. "I love you."

"And I love you," Thomas said fiercely.

Carrie hugged him again and moved back to her place at the table. It was better to deal with this now. "I intend to return when the danger has passed."

Thomas simply shook his head. "I know it's no good to argue, but I'm going to hold you to your promise," he said hoarsely. "You promised me—"

"I would leave the plantation if it became too dangerous," Carrie finished for him. "You have my word, Father."

"Can't you go any faster, Sam?" Carrie asked impatiently.

"Ain't never learned how to fly one 'o these things like a bird, Miss Carrie." Sam's voice was amused but kind.

Carrie groaned with exasperation but knew he was right. There was no quick way to get the carriage through the mass of humanity thronging the streets that led to the railroad depot. But she had to be there! She had to at least catch a glimpse of Robert before he headed off to battle.

Her father had said Robert would leave from the station at 11:00. She had left the house at 9:30 for what was usually a twenty-minute trip. Thirty minutes later, they had not yet even started up the long hill more than a mile from the station. They had not moved an inch in more than ten minutes.

Carrie bit her lip in frustration. "I'm walking," she announced and jumped from the carriage.

Sam turned in protest. "Your daddy ain't gonna like that, Miss Carrie. He done told me—and you, too—that this city done got right dangerous since so many people done been pouring in. Said it ain't the same city you wandered around in before." He shook his head firmly. "No sirree! I can't let you be walking to the station. You best be gettin' back in this carriage. I'll get you there. You see if I don't."

"I don't plan on seeing that you don't, Sam. I'm sorry to upset you, but I simply have to be at the railroad station." She hadn't told him why it was so important.

Sam's eyes narrowed, and he stared at her intently. "This got somethin' to do with that Mr. Borden?"

Carrie chose not to reply.

Sam's eyes softened with understanding and something akin to pity. Sam knew what Robert had done that day to his slaves. He knew no more letters came for her. Struggling to control her sudden desire to cry, Carrie spoke abruptly. "I'll wait for you at the station."

"Yes, ma'am. You be careful. I don't want to have to face yo' daddy if somethin' done happens to you."

Carrie began to walk up the steep hill. It was impossible to move fast because of the crush of people, but at least she was moving. Ducking her head, she wove in and out of the crowd as fast as she could.

Suddenly, she was bumped hard from behind and almost lost her balance. Stumbling, she managed to grab onto a lamppost at the last moment to keep herself from falling. Indignant, she whirled around to speak to whomever had been so rude. Richmond may have changed, but there must be some limits.

She opened her mouth, but before she could say anything, a well-dressed man of middle age grabbed her arm and pulled her back. "Let it be, ma'am."

Carrie stared up into his blue eyes and tried to yank her arm free. "Did you see what he did?"

Just then voices caught her attention.

"What did you say, buddy?" came a voice was tight with anger.

Carrie quickly scanned the crowd and located the speaker. He was a young man, barely out of his teens, clad in the buckskin garb of the western Virginia Mountains. He had taken a defensive stance, his legs spread wide, his hands loose at his sides.

A man of similar age, with a haughty face and an expensive air, answered his question. "I said I would rather be home than here fighting Virginia's battle for her!" His tone was both refined and hostile. His accent identified him as a South Carolinian.

"I should say you have some nerve, rich boy," the buckskin man retaliated coldly. "It was you South Carolinians who started all this trouble. Now it's being left to Virginia to settle it for you."

"You calling us cowards, mountain boy?" The words were delivered with deadly quiet.

Carrie gasped as the Carolinian reached for his waistline and pulled out a sharp knife.

"You care to back up that fancy talk with some action, mountain boy?"

"Have it your way, rich boy!" With a quick movement, the buckskin man produced his own wicked-looking knife.

Carrie slowly backed away, unable to take her eyes from the scene in front of her. She had never seen such a thing in Richmond. The city had its fair share of violence, but it didn't usually happen in broad daylight, and it certainly didn't take place in the middle of a crowded street. Angry men usually took their arguments to the dueling fields located on the outskirts of town.

The two men began to circle cautiously, all other pedestrians giving them a wide berth. Some stopped to stare and watch, but most pushed their way on by. That fascinated and horrified Carrie even more than the fight. Had Richmond actually become immune to violence?

Just as the buckskin man pulled back his arm, the fight was over.

"That will be all, boys." A tall policeman appeared to tower over the two men. "Y'all got some fighting to do, but it ain't here in the streets of Richmond. Where you two boys headed?" His firm, no-nonsense voice did the job of cooling off the two men.

The Carolinian was the first to speak. "You're right, officer. I am due to ship out in less than an hour. I was on my way to the station."

The policeman scowled. "I think you should be anywhere other than where you are right now. Why aren't you with your unit?"

Both men, without answering, edged away and melted into the crowd.

Shaking his head and muttering under his voice, the policeman continued on his rounds.

Carrie stared after them and then turned to thank the kind man who was still standing by her side. Now that she had time for a good look, she was instantly drawn to the warm blue eyes that spoke of a deep capacity for caring. He reminded her of her father.

"You're welcome, ma'am. You need to be careful. It's not a real good idea for ladies to be roaming the streets alone right now."

"Why, I've walked the streets of Richmond ever since I was a child," she protested.

"Live here now?" he asked.

"I'm from a plantation west of the city," Carrie admitted.

"You'll find your city has changed a lot," he observed. "Being the capital of a nation at war can do that."

Carrie stared at him. "Does that happen often?"

"Fights? Not as much now that the troops are on the front. You got to give the boys a little break, though." He hesitated before answering her questioning look. "These boys been pulled away from home, brought down here to drill and march till they drop, and now they're being shipped off to fight. A lot of them don't really know what the war is all about, they're just doing their patriotic duty and thinking it will all be over soon." The disdain in his voice was obvious, but the tone was still kind.

Carrie liked him even more. "Who are you, sir?" She astonished her own self at her directness, but suddenly it was important that she know who he was.

"Pastor Marcus Anthony," he replied, bowing slightly.

"You're a pastor?"

"You're surprised?" he asked in an amused tone.

Carrie struggled to recover. "You just don't...I mean, you don't..."

"Look like one? Thank you," he replied with a smile.

"No. I mean, yes..." Firmly Carrie pulled herself together. "Excuse me for sounding like a schoolgirl. No, you don't look like a pastor, but I find I like that. I'm sorry for sounding so flustered. I guess the recent encounter left me a little shaken."

Suddenly, she remembered why she had been hurrying up the sidewalk. "Excuse me, Pastor Anthony, I must be going." Not waiting for a reply, she turned and continued her rapid stride, praying she still had time to make it.

She had just arrived at the train station when she heard the band began to play. Her father had told her that departing troops were sent off with great fanfare. Not caring who glared at her, she edged and shoved her way to the front of the mass of people surrounding the platform. She had just gotten situated when the first troops moved into sight.

Carrie's heart caught at the young faces, so serious above their smart gray uniforms. Why, some of them were hardly more than boys! Their mothers must be frantic with worry for them, but it was impossible not to see the determination and bravery shining in their eyes. Many of them searched the crowd eagerly for a familiar face, pulling their shoulders back further when they found one.

"Halt!" A strong voice rose above the crowd to direct the troops.

Carrie recognized the voice at once. Her eyes flew to the erect figure bringing up the rear of the column. As his men clicked to a standstill, Lieutenant Robert Borden strode to the front of the line.

Carrie's heart beat faster as she looked at him. His tall, muscular frame had taken on an erect military bearing. Every line of his face was set with determination. He had always been handsome, and now he had become distinguished as well. His dark eyes snapped as he reviewed his men.

As the troops remained at attention, the band began to play again. The crowd sang along as the familiar strains of "Dixie" filled the air. The sense of pride and expectancy was a palpable thing you could feel and almost see. Carrie could not help but feel it herself as she gazed at Robert. That he believed in what he was doing, no one could doubt. His eyes were filled with pride and courage as he looked out over the men he would be leading in battle.

Battle.

The word surged to the front of her brain, and Carrie was gripped with a sense of fear and urgency. She looked around the crowd and noticed the tear-stained faces full of pride and love—families, come to see their loved ones off.

"Go get them, old man!" a strong voice sang out.

Robert's face lighted with a grin that twisted Carrie's heart. Following his gaze, she saw another young man standing on the sidelines. The familiar lines of his face said he could only be Robert's brother, Daniel. She was glad Robert had someone there to see him off.

"*All aboard!*"

The troops began to file into the train cars as the crowd cheered and the band blared its music. Only when the last one was aboard did Carrie look toward Robert.

Across the span on the loading platform, their eyes locked. She had no idea how long he had been watching her. She drew her breath in sharply and felt the color rise in her cheeks. Still, she did not look away. As she watched, the boyish bravado that he had forged into courage flickered for just a moment. Once again she saw the look only she had ever seen—the flash of vulnerability that lit his eyes and twisted her heart.

"*All aboard!*"

A shrill whistle accompanied the stern reminder that in moments this train would be heading for the front.

As she thought of Robert in battle, Carrie's heart conquered her mind. She could not marry him, but that did not mean he had to leave without knowing she loved him. She quickly turned to the man next to her. "Do you have a knife?" she asked urgently.

"A knife, ma'am?"

"Please, I don't have time to explain. Do you have a knife?"

He looked at her oddly, but the desperate tone of her voice must have won him over. Reaching to his waistline, he pulled one out.

Carrie slipped a lock of her hair out of her tightly coiled braid and cut it off. Handing the knife back to the astonished man, she lifted her skirts and ran across the platform.

Robert was standing with one foot on the step, watching her run to him. The train began to pull away just as she reached him.

"Goodbye, Robert!"

His dark eyes gazed down into hers, but there was not time for more. The train was picking up speed and pulling away, and Robert was forced to swing up onto the next step. Carrie rushed alongside and pressed her hair into his hand. "I'm counting on you to win this one," she said in a tremulous voice.

Her mind flashed back to the first time she had presented him with a lock of her hair on the day of the Blackwell Tournament. He had told her he fell in love with her that day—that moment. The tournament had been child's play, but war was not a game. It was deadly.

"I love you, Robert."

She had just uttered the words before the train pulled him out of the range of hearing. The crowds continued to cheer and wave as Carrie stood and watched Robert grow smaller. Only when he was out of sight did she finally turn away.

Chapter Eight

Robert twisted and squirmed, trying to find a comfortable position on the hard ground. This night, more than any of the nine that had passed since he had left the train at Manassas Junction, sleep eluded him. His heart and mind refused to be stilled. The moon was high in the sky when he finally gave up the effort and pulled himself into a sitting position against a tree that might mean the difference between life and death to a soldier in the coming hours.

Robert gazed out over the bright landscape as he tried to envision what the day would bring. If a man had a good enough imagination, he could believe that all was right in the world. The sky was crystal clear, the moon bright and full. Its brightness cast shadows from the towering trees that were sheltering the position of their regiment. He peered around the big oak and watched the moonlight glisten off the waters of Bull Run. Sparkling particles in the stone bridge that spanned the river caught the brightness and caused the bridge to stand in stark contrast. Was it possible that in just a few hours the beauty of the scene before him would be destroyed by the roar of cannon fire and the shouts of contending men?

"Lieutenant?"

The voice sounding beside Robert was little more than a whisper. "Yes, Hobbs?" he whispered back. Robert had grown fond of the sixteen-year-old who had shown up from the hills of western Virginia, eager to do battle for the South.

"You reckon it's true, Lieutenant? That all the waiting will be over soon?"

Robert nodded grimly. "I reckon it's true. All the stalling and waiting is past. I believe we will face the enemy tomorrow."

There was a long pause. Robert could envision Hobbs' young, freckled face screwed up in intense thought, his brown eyes flashing thoughtfully under the thatch of rust-colored hair. The youth had worked harder than anyone to be ready for what would happen the next day. He had never once complained during the long, hot drills and had always been willing to do more.

"You reckon we'll see much action? Seems kinda like we're stuck up out of the way here."

Robert smiled. He knew how Hobbs felt. He, too, had been keenly disappointed when his regiment had been attached to Colonel Evans' brigade. He would have preferred to be in the thick of the battle. Everyone was sure General McDowell would focus his attack on Mitchell's Ford.

"We will all play an important role, Hobbs. We have to be ready when the time comes." He fervently hoped he was right. He hated the thought that they would stand watch in their woods the next day, simply listening to the sounds of what many thought would be the only battle of the war. Robert didn't share that sentiment with them. He simply wanted to be a part of this first great fight.

The silence grew even longer, until Robert wondered if Hobbs had drifted off to sleep.

"You scared, Lieutenant?" Hobbs' whisper broke the night once again.

Robert opened his mouth to speak and then stopped. He supposed he should be the strong, commanding leader and say he had no fear—that he was confident all would go well. Unbidden, Carrie's face, with her direct eyes and open honesty, flashed before him. *Tell him the truth.*

"Sure, I'm scared, Hobbs. Who wouldn't be?"

"Really?" the young voice gasped.

"Really," Robert said. "We've done all we can to get ready for this battle, but nothing ever goes the way you plan it. And one thing is for sure." He paused for emphasis. "Not everyone is going to get out of this alive. That's just a sad fact of war. How do I know it's not going to be me? How do I know it's not going to be someone I care about?"

He could almost feel Hobbs' brown eyes boring into him as he continued. "There isn't anything wrong with fear. Every great person has to face fear. The important thing is not to let it win out over you. You have to face your fears and not back down. Fear can actually be a good thing."

"How's that?" Hobbs' voice was skeptical.

"Fear can make you sharp. It can keep you from relaxing and taking things for granted. It can make you strive to be the best you can so that the thing you fear won't beat you. Fear can make you stronger when you realize you have conquered it."

There was a short silence before Hobbs' voice broke in again. "And fear can make you turn to God. That's what my grandma said before I left home. She told me if I was ever afraid, to talk to God." Another long pause. "I been talking to God tonight, Lieutenant."

"Got that right."

"Me, too."

"Amen!"

The soft chorus of whispers sounding from the night was the first evidence that anyone else was listening in on their conversation. It also meant Robert didn't need to respond to what Hobbs had said. He realized the anxiety that was keeping him awake was doing the same to the others. The thought gave him comfort.

One man's rough voice broke into his thoughts. "I don't think I realized until tonight what all this drilling and marching was about. It's right scary to know there are thousands of men on the other side of that river who are ready to kill us. I been trying to get things right." The voice paused and then continued a little softer. "I've done said the Lord's Prayer to myself seventy-five times. My mama always told me that was a good thing to do. I figure the more I say it, the holier I will get. Maybe the Lord will try a little harder to keep me safe."

Hobbs laughed softly. "Tell the lieutenant what else you done, Pickins."

The darkness proved to be a confessional.

Pickins continued in an embarrassed and slightly defiant tone. "I done threw away my deck of cards. I promised God I'd be a good moral man, I did. Told him I wouldn't grumble about menial duties again, that I'd go to church and even quit smoking. Why, I told him if I survived the war, that I would become a minister and preach the gospel!"

Robert smiled as low chuckles surrounded him. These were good men. "Good for you, Pickins."

Silence fell again as each man lost himself in his own thoughts. The moon was slowly gliding westward. Katydids and tree frogs kept up a steady chorus as if trying to serenade the tired men into a few hours of sleep. Robert took advantage of the quiet to let his thoughts return to Carrie. How wonderful it had been to see her at the train station. Memories of her filled his quiet moments. The look on her face when she had told him she loved him. The feel of her palm when she had pressed her hair into his hand. The sight of her watching him until he was gone.

Had it all been because he was going to battle? The images that flashed through his mind thrilled and tormented him. She loved him, but she wouldn't marry him. His fists clenched in frustration.

Startled by a hooting owl, Robert peered around his tree. Was that the beginning of dawn starting to creep over the horizon?

Trying to control the nervous twisting of his stomach, he tried to turn his mind back to Carrie. Instead, his thoughts returned to his men's comments about God—about giving their fear to him. Robert had wanted to tell them they were wasting their time, but the knowledge that he was responsible for keeping their morale up had stilled his tongue. His stomach twisted again, but this time in anger.

Robert rested his head back against the tree and tried to relax. He knew his anger was eating at him, but he had no idea what to do about it. He was angry at God for letting that slave kill his father. He was angry at God because slaves were keeping him and Carrie apart. He was angry at God for letting him love someone who would prove to be nothing but a torment to him all his life. Resisting the impulse to smash his fist into the tree, he buried his head in his hands. Was there to be no relief?

Just then, the sharp report of a gun in the distance broke the early morning stillness.

Robert reached over to grab his weapon and threw himself on his stomach to peer around the tree. His surveillance revealed nothing. The dark expanse of woods that bordered the field running alongside Bull Run was still. Who had fired that shot?

"Lieutenant?"

"Pass the word down, Hobbs," Robert said quickly. "Tell everyone to be at attention. To hold their position until Colonel Evans tells them differently. There is to be no movement to give away our position. It's better to leave them guessing how many of us are here."

"Yes, sir."

Robert continued to scan the woods as the word passed down the line of men hiding behind the trees and the crest of the hill facing the river. A movement to his left caught his attention. Close inspection revealed two companies of Confederate troops. He watched as the men took up positions on either side of the bridge. Colonel Evans had sent them down as skirmishers to distract whatever Union troops were advancing, and to sound a warning to the waiting brigade. General McDowell must be sending a few troops their way to keep them busy while the bulk of the battle happened downstream.

Robert could feel the tension in every part of his body. As he waited, each minute feeling like an eternity, he repeated to himself over and over the orders he had received the night before. This was his first battle. He wanted to make sure he handled himself, and his men, well.

The sound of hoofbeats broke into his thoughts. Moments later, Colonel Evans rode into view behind him. Robert liked this rude brawler of an officer— insubordinate, gruff and roughhewn. His full beard, high forehead and piercing eyes lent him a deceptively patriarchal air. His bravery and commitment to the cause were not to be questioned. He would give his all. Robert could respect that.

"Lieutenant!"

"Yes, sir!" Robert snapped.

"Move your men to the crest of the hill overlooking the bridge. I don't want anyone to see any movement, so keep everyone down. Only if the enemy crosses the bridge are you to open fire. I want to keep them guessing at how many we are."

"Yes, sir!"

Evans turned abruptly and moved away. Robert raised one arm to gain the attention of his troops. Moving swiftly, staying close to the ground, it took them less than ten minutes to reach their new position.

Robert glanced at his watch as he settled low to the ground. Five forty-five. The sun was still below the horizon but was casting its rosy hue across the sky. The morning air was cool, but the day promised to be scorching.

A sudden movement on the far side of the river caught his attention. A lone rider broke from the woods and moved toward the water, holding what looked to be a flag of some sort. As Robert watched, the rider moved to within a couple hundred yards of the bridge, evidently attempting to plant his flag.

Sharp gunfire from Confederate riflemen broke the morning stillness. After a long moment, the lone rider turned and disappeared back into the woods.

Robert chuckled. If that was the best they could do, this wasn't going to be much of a battle.

Boom!

Robert jumped as a thunderous report from the north side of the stream exploded onto the morning. Once again he glanced at his watch. Six a.m. The time would be forever etched in his memory.

The battle was joined. The bombardment had begun.

The next hour and a half passed slower than any of Robert's life. From their place of concealment behind the hill, they listened to the steady report of guns from the Union troops and from the two brigades down by the river. It chafed that he could not send forth a response from his hidden troops, but he had received his orders, and he would fulfill them—even if it meant he never got to fire a single shot during this battle.

As he listened to the steady firing, he wondered what was going on downstream. Were Union troops even now battering the better-prepared positions? It was so hard not knowing what was going on anywhere but in his own little sphere.

"Prepare to move out!"

Robert, unable to hear Evans approach because of the gunfire, spun around to look up at his commanding officer.

"All of this has been nothing but a ploy to hold our attention. I have just received word that an undetermined number of Federals are marching on our exposed left flank. Get ready to march to meet them."

Robert stared after him for a moment. Now, their brigade were not only faced with the enemy troops in front of them, but they had more coming at them from the side. Robert knew their small number would not be enough to hold back what seemed to be heading their way. In all of the Confederate defense, theirs was the weakest link. General McDowell had chosen to strike at the Confederacy's Achilles' heel.

Robert's concern was mixed with admiration for Colonel Evans. A man of less resolution would have withdrawn from his position in fear of being overwhelmed. No one would have blamed him. Hopelessly outnumbered, he had chosen to attack.

Robert looked at his men with a grim smile. "I guess we're going to get that action we were wanting." Pushing down his fear, he gripped his rifle and led his men in the direction Evans had indicated.

Sweat was pouring from his body as he double-quicked down the road. The sun was rising in the sky, fulfilling its earlier promise. Dust kicked up from the road, coating his face and clothes. Breathing hard, he kept up a steady pace for his men. He could hear gasping and an occasional curse behind him, but no one complained.

"Behind those trees!"

Robert flashed up Matthews Hill and moved his troops behind a grove of trees that would offer them good protection. They had a clear field of fire down the slope toward the open road down which the Union troops would have to advance. Only when all of his men were in position did Robert sink against a tree for just a moment and take a deep breath. Then he was up scanning the road in front of him.

He had done the best he could to encourage his men. Somehow they knew this battle wasn't going the way anyone had expected. The Union forces were taking unanticipated action. Everyone had thought the men skirmishing them this morning would eventually head east in an effort to give backup to the Union troops lined up along Mitchell's Ford. Now, all any of them could do was to hope their own Confederate troops would reach *them* in time with backup.

Colonel Evans had done all he could to give the impression of much greater strength than they actually possessed by stretching his men out along a long line.

Robert stared down at the road. Minutes after they had taken their position, a surge of Federals erupted from the woods.

"Fire!" Robert yelled.

He got off the first round and turned to reload.

Gunfire erupted as his order split the air. The Federals responded by plunging into the open in an all-out assault. Rifle after rifle exploded along the Confederate line in an attempt to halt them.

"Got that one!"

"Come on, you cowards!"

For now at least, the Confederates strongly outnumbered the Federals. It seemed like it took only minutes for them to pin the Union infantry down. The artillery ceased its fire.

Robert knew the Federals were calling for help. Hastily, he swiped at the sweat streaming down his face and reloaded his gun. They were being given a brief respite, but what was sure to follow would be worse than anything they had yet experienced.

Boom! Boom!

In what seemed like moments, more Union troops, complete with heavy guns, had swarmed from the woods to join in the battle. Once again, steady gunfire mixed with the shouts and the screams of wounded and dying men.

"Attack!"

Robert heard the shouted command off to his left, and watched as the First Louisiana Battalion swarmed from the woods and hit the center of the Federal Line. Looking back down the scope of his rifle, he pulled the trigger and gave a grimace of satisfaction as he watched an advancing blue uniform fall to the ground. Keeping up steady fire, he tried to keep tabs on the assault going on beside him.

He had grown fond of Major Roberdeau Wheat, who was leading the Louisiana Battalion. As the men surged forward, yelling, shouting and waving knives, the stout Wheat led the way. Robert knew Wheat's men had no hope of driving back the line, but they did seem to be delaying the advance. It would buy them time. That was all they could hope for.

Robert had just reloaded his gun and gotten another Federal in his sights, when he saw Wheat go down. Many of the major's men lay scattered on the hill, cut down by Union fire.

"No!" Robert refocused on the scope and pulled the trigger. He felt no satisfaction as he saw another man fall. "Hold them, boys!" He would do all he could to give the Louisiana Battalion time to pull their wounded leader behind the lines to the field surgeons. He loaded and fired as fast as possible, feeling a flush of satisfaction when Wheat was pulled behind the lines. Robert had no way to know if he was still alive, but he'd done his part.

Finally, the Louisiana Battalion pulled back and returned to the line. They had done their job, but Robert was aware it probably hadn't been enough. They had bought the Confederates some time, but there were no reinforcements in sight. Already the Union troops overreached both flanks of Evans' thinly spread position. Federal artillery had nearly silenced their guns. They could hold the line for only a few more minutes.

"Lieutenant?"

In the brief lull of gunfire, Robert heard Hobbs' young voice. He turned and gazed into his bloodshot eyes and dirty, grimy face.

"We gonna make it, Lieutenant?"

Robert swallowed hard. "It's not looking good, Hobbs," he said. He saw no other choice but honesty.

Hobbs' determined gaze never wavered. He simply nodded and clinched his rifle tighter. "I can maybe get me one or two more." His lips began to move in wordless prayer.

Suddenly, a shout caught Robert's attention. Glancing back over his shoulder, he gave a gasp of relief. *Reinforcements!*

"Hold on there, Hobbs. Looks like General Bee's boys are getting here just in time."

Robert and his regiment cheered as Bee's men surged through their line and moved to the front, giving them a brief rest. Never had they seen a more blessed sight than that wave of gray uniforms moving toward them. The sound of gunfire exploded around them once more.

Reaching for his canteen, Robert took his first sip of liquid in nearly three hours. He shook his head when he looked at his watch. Could it really be only ten o'clock? He felt like he had spent a lifetime on the battlefield already. He gulped the water down, trying to relax. He knew the respite would be over soon.

Looking out over the scene, in spite of the reinforcements surrounding him, Robert felt despair. They were easily outnumbered two to one. There seemed to be a veritable sea of blue coats facing them.

"Take your positions, men!"

Robert heaved himself up from the ground and quickly moved his troops back onto the battle line. Shells from the line of artillery facing them continued to pound their positions, seeming almost alive as they shrieked overhead, their whistle growing shriller as they approached. Huge clumps of dirt erupted around them as the shells impacted with the earth. He had a brief vision of Carrie's lovely, fresh face, before he sighted down his rifle scope and pulled the trigger. Then all thoughts of anything but survival fled his mind.

"Lieutenant Borden!"

Robert pushed himself back from his position and sprinted over to Evans. "Yes, sir." He listened intently for several minutes and then returned to his men.

Hobbs was watching him come. The look on the boy's face made him realize how grim the one on his own must be. He tried to force a smile. "Here's our chance to make history, boys," his voice rang out.

Long minutes passed as orders were given down the line. Then came the command.

"Charge!"

Robert leapt up from the ground and took off at a dead run down the slope of the hill. His men were all around him, beside and behind. They were able to fire off only one shot as they crossed the clearing, aiming for a thicket of trees that flanked the Federal guns. The musket balls poured like rain around them, striking their own muskets, their hats, and their bodies.

Robert ran as fast as he could, his eyes fastened on the sanctuary of the thicket of trees. It was only moments before he realized how deceptive his thinking was.

"Reload men!" he cried as soon as they reached cover.

"Fire!"

Their guns cracked in unison as they opened on the enemy batteries and companies of infantry stationed nearby. Almost at the same time, considerable bodies of the Union moved forward against them, overlapping their exposed right and part of their left as well.

The protective thicket turned into a place of slaughter as a whirlwind of bullets descended upon their position. The deadly missives rained like hail among the boughs and trees. Robert watched as man after man fell around him.

Chapter Nine

Carrie looked up, shocked by the drawn, haggard look on her father's face as he strode into the house. She watched him for a moment from the shadows of her chair next to the window. She had been sitting there for hours, waiting for him, waiting for some word. There had been rumors...

"Father?" she asked, afraid to hear what he had to say, but having to know.

Thomas turned slowly from where he was putting up his hat. "Hello, Carrie," he said somberly.

Carrie's heart sank. "Father, what is it?"

Thomas attempted a smile. "I'm sorry. I didn't mean to scare you." He moved in the direction of the fireplace. "Come, sit down here with me."

She followed him, and when they were both seated in the soft, blue, high-backed chairs, he turned to her.

"A telegram came through this afternoon. Beauregard is confident the battle will be tomorrow. His troops are all in position."

"Did Johnston make it in time?"

Thomas nodded. "Trains of his troops were still arriving when the telegram reached us."

Carrie sighed with relief. General Johnston and all of his men had been positioned near Harpers Ferry in western Virginia. Once Davis and Lee had been assured that McDowell was going to focus his attack on Manassas and that General Patterson would not be a threat to the Confederate troops, they had ordered Johnston and his men to join Beauregard for the battle soon to take place.

"That is just one more proof of how important the railroad is to us in that part of the state," Thomas continued. "Without it, there would be no hope of Johnston getting his men there in time to be of any use." He paused. "He is sure there are Union sympathizers in the railroad though."

"What?" Carrie asked in surprise.

Thomas nodded grimly. "He said the transport of his troops is taking way too long. The trains sometimes move at barely more than four or five miles per hour, and there have been suspicious breakdowns. He is sure it is deliberate."

"But most of them are there?"

"There will be some that may not see the battle, but the bulk of them have arrived," Thomas said with satisfaction.

"Then why the haggard look, Father? It would seem all is going well." She knew the answer, but she sensed her father needed to talk about it.

Thomas allowed the pain to show on his face. "No matter how well prepared we are, there will be many men who die tomorrow—many men who will not return to their families." He paused. "I know what it's like to lose someone your heart is intertwined with. I wish that on no one."

Carrie watched him sympathetically but felt the clutch of fear in her own heart. What about Robert? Where was he? Would he make it through the battle tomorrow? Would she ever see him again?

"I'm not sure we're ready here," he said after a long silence.

"I thought Lee felt better about the fortifications for the defense of the city?" Carrie asked quietly. She didn't add anything about the outrage she had felt when she discovered the means by which this had been accomplished. When it had become evident the work on the defense of Richmond was going much too slow due to lack of manpower, Governor Letcher had ordered the militia and the police to round up and commandeer unemployed free blacks to do the needed work. The city was paying them eleven dollars a month, but Carrie knew the pay was inadequate for the degradation attached to the work.

Thomas shrugged his shoulders again and his face took on the weary look she had become familiar with. "We have done all we can do. It will have to be enough. The truth is, though, that it's *not* enough. If a strong force were to come against the city, I don't think we could withstand it." He smacked his fist against his open palm. "Beauregard must stop them. The Union battle cry is *On to Richmond!* They must be stopped!"

Carrie wanted to rush forward and comfort her father; however, there was nothing she could say. There were no words of assurance she could give him. All their hopes were resting on an army of men perched on the edge of a battlefield.

The two sat in silence for a long while, only the occasional shrill whistle of a train breaking the quiet. The streets of Church Hill were unusually still that night. People had retired to their houses early to wait, and to pray.

"Father, could you kill a friend?"

"What?" Thomas asked vaguely, his thoughts jerked back from a long distance.

"Could you kill a friend?" Carrie repeated. Her father's face asked for more. "I've been thinking about it a lot lately. So many of the men who are fighting were once part of the United States Army. Now some fight for the North, others fight for the South. Men who once fought side by side are now going to be fighting each other. How can men plan to kill and destroy other men they once depended on for their own life?"

Carrie's voice broke as she struggled to explain the feelings that had kept her awake for endless nights. "General Lee has a nephew who is fighting for the Union. Will he one day look down the barrel of a gun and have to kill him?" She rushed on. "Matthew is most likely fighting for the North. What if he and Robert meet tomorrow? Will they—" She couldn't finish. The idea of Robert having to shoot at tall, red-headed Matthew, his closest friend from college, was more than she could bear.

She choked back tears and looked at her father. She didn't really think he would have an answer. It was more that, on the eve of this battle, she needed to express her feelings. She was half afraid her father would be angry— think she was being disloyal to the cause—but instead, he was looking at her with understanding.

"In spite of the pressures of being in the government," he said, "I have been very thankful I am not on the front having to make those decisions. There are many men my age in the army, and I think the number will grow daily if this war drags on. I am sure I have friends and business associates who would be across the lines from me. That question has haunted me as well."

"Do you think there is an answer?" Carrie asked, somehow reassured by the mute pain on his face.

Thomas winced. "I think that may be one of the questions of life for which there *is* no answer," he said. "At least, not one that can be answered by someone not in that situation. But I do have a theory," he continued. "I think it's possible that in the midst of a battle, men cease to see other men as men. They simply become part of the tactical strategy of war. They are an obstacle that must be overcome." He paused for a long moment and continued slowly. "Maybe that is what enables men to fight—the ignoring of individual humanity behind each gun."

The sound of a train pulling out of the station on Broad Street seemed to pull Thomas from his reflective mood. His eyes lost their faraway look and his face hardened. "That, and the knowledge that the cause they fight for is just and right."

Carrie merely looked at him. The idea that Robert was fighting for a cause he perceived as just and right did nothing to abate her deep concern for him.

Micah appeared at the door to the parlor. "I've had the cook keep dinner hot, Marse Cromwell. Wills you be wantin' to eat?"

Thomas looked up as the clock struck eight. "I suppose I should," he sighed. "Carrie, have you eaten?"

"I was waiting for you. You need to eat, Father. May's chicken is wonderful tonight."

They were halfway through dinner when Thomas looked up with a smile on his face. "I heard about a very unusual woman today."

"Oh?" Carrie pulled her thoughts back to the dining room with difficulty. She supposed she should be interested in anything that could put a smile on her father's face. "Who is she?"

"I think you would like her," he said as he settled back in his chair and lit his pipe. When the smoke was curling toward the ceiling, he continued. "She is the wife of Bradley T. Johnson, a Confederate officer from Maryland. She decided she didn't want to be left behind while her husband was on the battlefield, so she joined him in Harpers Ferry."

"They let her?" Carrie asked in amazement.

"I think she didn't really give them the option," Thomas chuckled. "Anyway, the first thing she saw when she got there was that his regiment had no arms. Now, this was back in May," he hastened to add. "Anyway, she left right away, bound for North Carolina and some influential friends she believed could raise the money they needed for the guns. She didn't have to ask, however. She presented her case to the governor, who then presented her with five hundred rifles, ten thousand rounds of ammunition and thirty-five hundred musket caps. Once she had those, she came here to Richmond. Governor Letcher provided her with blankets, tents and other camp equipment. It took her less than a week and a half to accomplish her goal."

Carrie listened, smiling reluctantly. "She sounds like a remarkable woman."

"Remarkable, indeed," her father replied. "One of the men she met in North Carolina paid her quite a tribute. He told her that if great events produce great men, then what she had done was proof that great events also produce great women."

As Carrie listened, she was filled with a sudden desire that the same would be said of her one day. It was a feeling she had felt before but never with quite this same intensity and determination. She fought to control the sigh of frustration that wanted to escape through her lips. She didn't know how anything like that was going to happen while she was here in Richmond, forced to wait for the outcome of a battle in a war she didn't believe in.

The last week and a half in Richmond had been very difficult for her. She had watched as the city had grown more and more crowded. Most of the military had moved out to reinforce Beauregard at Manassas. The steady stream of humanity pouring into the city had not ceased, however. More troops were coming in for training and assignment. As the new government became firmly established, there was a continual flow of politicians and civil servants. And then there were what her father called the hangers-on—people who had come to Richmond looking for opportunity in the burgeoning city.

The people of Richmond were adjusting now that the initial shock had worn off. They were searching for ways to deal with the rising crime rate, the horrendous overcrowding, and the struggle to provide for so many people. Food, which had always been such a plentiful commodity, was now causing hardship for many people.

"A penny for your thoughts."

Carrie looked up at her father and tried to smile. "I want to go home."

Thomas frowned. "I thought we had talked about that. I thought you understood my feelings."

Carrie nodded. "I do, Father. I know you would be worried sick with me on the plantation right now. I will stay until the threat is over." *Please let it be over soon.* "But then I am going back home." Her father's face took on a mutinous look. "I have to be able to make a difference," she pleaded. "I am going crazy here. I know the sewing the city women are doing is much needed, but that's not me. If I have to wrap one more bandage or put stitches in one more shirt, I will scream."

Her desperate tone forced a smile to her father's face. "Sewing was never one of your strong suits," he admitted. He looked at her more closely. "What will you do back on the plantation, Carrie?"

It was a fair question, and one she had an answer for. She had thought about it long and hard. "I will plant food," she said. "Governor Letcher has let it be known how scarce food is becoming—that fresh produce has become a luxury in our city. It never used to be that way, Father. I want to do what I can to help."

"But our garden is not that large," Thomas protested. "It will help, but it will just be a drop in the bucket."

Carrie chose her words carefully. "Isn't it true that the value of tobacco has dropped drastically because of the river port blockade? Didn't you tell me that huge stacks of tobacco are in danger of rotting because they cannot be moved?"

Thomas frowned and nodded. "I did." Understanding dawned on his face, and he began to shake his head.

Carrie hurried on before he had time to launch his protest. "I can plow up some of the tobacco fields. Just a couple would mean space for an incredible amount of produce crops." She hurried on. "Think what it would mean for Richmond. Think what it would mean for the cause." She paused, almost ready to laugh as her father's protest died before her eyes. How could he fight her on this? "I need to make a difference, and this is one way I can help. I can feed people. When the war is over, you can plant the land in tobacco again."

"It's late in the year to plant produce," Thomas observed.

Carrie controlled her triumphant smile. "I know," she agreed. "I've thought about that. The Almanac is promising a mild fall. I'll only plant crops that have a short maturation—potatoes, squash, carrots, beans, lettuce. The fields at Cromwell can help make a huge difference."

Thomas nodded slowly. "I will send a letter back to Adams telling him I agree with your plan."

Carrie said nothing. How long would she be able to pull off this deception?

The mention of Adams' name sent Thomas off onto another tangent. "I don't know how long Adams will be able to stay on the plantation. There may be times when he will have to be away."

"Why?"

"Right now overseers are exempt from having to serve in the army. There is concern over what would happen if they weren't there to control the slaves, but there is a continuing need for men to serve in the Virginia militia. They are needed to protect our own state, but they are also needed to keep a handle on the slaves and round up runaways."

"I see," Carrie murmured.

"I'm not sure you do," her father said sharply.

Carrie looked at him in shock. They had not spoken of slavery again since her first night there, but he had seemed to accept what she felt, even though he didn't agree with it.

"I'm sorry," Thomas said. "I didn't mean to sound that way. In addition to getting the news about the battle tomorrow, we also received a report today that the number of runaway slaves is escalating. They seem to think that war with the North means their freedom is imminent."

Carrie listened, hearing both anger and a twinge of fear in her father's voice.

"Carrie, we could have chaos if the slave situation gets out of hand. Governor Letcher is assigning more men to keep a handle on things. Adams will not be taken from the plantation yet, but there may be times he will be pulled away to help in a crisis situation. Do you think you will be able to take care of things?"

At least this was something she could answer honestly. "Father, you don't have a thing to worry about. I will keep everything under control. Why," she continued with a confident smile, "if Adams was pulled away right now, I believe the plantation would run as smoothly as it has been."

Thomas studied her. "I believe you mean that." He shook his head and laughed. "I hope you don't have to find out. Or me, either," he added. "It does my heart good to get reports as fine as the one you brought me from Adams when you first got here. It gives me a great deal of peace to know that all I've worked for is continuing in my absence."

Carrie nodded, wondering what in the world her father's reaction was going to be when he discovered the truth. Maybe she should have been honest with him from the beginning. The longer she played this game, the tighter the web she seemed to be weaving for herself. But when she tried to envision the plantation with another overseer, she couldn't do it. Her father had said himself that things were running wonderfully. She would continue on until necessity changed the path she was walking.

Unbidden, Aunt Abby's face floated into her mind. What she wouldn't give to sit down for a good talk with her friend. The woman had a way of helping Carrie see things clearly. She had received no mail from her since April, though, and there was no way of knowing when she would.

Thomas pushed away from the table. "I have some paperwork I need to take care of before I call it a night. Will you please excuse me?"

"Of course," Carrie said, rising also. She watched her father as he disappeared into his office, and then she turned toward the front porch. She needed some time alone outside. She longed to be on the plantation right now. How she needed a good ride on Granite. A long ride would surely help clear the cobwebs from her head.

There was a light breeze blowing as she settled down onto the porch swing. She could hear the occasional murmur of a voice from surrounding porches, but other than that, the night was silent. Even the crickets seemed to be quiet tonight. As she looked up at the brilliant full moon, she wondered if Robert was looking at the same sight.

A slight movement from the shadows caused her to jump. She leaned forward to peer into the darkness. "Who's there?" she called.

"It be me, Miss Carrie," came the quiet whisper from the shadows.

"Micah?" Why was her father's butler skulking in the shadows?

His dark form materialized in front of her. "I'se got somethin' for you, ma'am."

Carrie reached for the letter he was holding out to her. There was no return address on the thick envelope. "Why didn't you give this to me when the mail came, Micah?" Her voice was not angry, just puzzled.

"This here didn't come through the mail, Miss Carrie."

"But..." Carrie paused, looking at the handwriting in the dim light from the window. Could it really be? "How did it get here?" she asked breathlessly.

"Let's just say a friend brought it, Miss Carrie." With those whispered words, Micah melted into the shadows and disappeared.

Carrie stared at the envelope for a long moment and then carefully stuffed it in her dress pocket, making sure no edge of it betrayed its presence. She didn't want her father asking questions. Confident it was hidden, she turned and hurried into the house. She paused for a moment by the office door. "I'm going up to bed now, Father. I'll see you in the morning."

Thomas looked up absently and gave her an affectionate smile. "Goodnight, dear."

Once in her room, Carrie turned up the lantern next to her bed and more closely examined the handwriting. She tore into the envelope and pulled out the thick sheaf of pages.

The first words from Aunt Abby were enough to cause tears to begin coursing down her face. She had no idea how this letter had reached her hands. All she knew was that it was a gift from heaven. She read on eagerly.

Dearest Carrie,

What we have dreaded has really come to pass. Our beloved United States is at war—brother and friend fighting brother and friend. The ache in my heart has become a constant presence. I find myself thankful that my dear husband died before he could see such a thing come to pass.

I am sure you are wondering just how you are receiving this letter. My heart has been so troubled that our correspondence has been cut off. I find myself reading the same letters over.

Carrie laughed and brushed the tears away. She could almost see Aunt Abby's eyes light with laughter as she made her admission. She was so glad to know her friend was doing the same thing she had been doing.

I have grand news for you, Carrie. Miles, Sadie, Jasmine, and the rest of the Cromwell slaves have safely reached Canada.

"Oh, God, thank you." Carrie bowed her head for a long moment before she raised her shining eyes to continue reading.

> *All of them have found employment and are doing well. Miles was able to smuggle a letter to me via the Underground Railroad. That's when I discovered their usefulness as a mail service. Miles and the rest asked me to send a letter on to Rose. When I realized the possibilities, I asked my contact if it would be possible to send a letter to you in the same way. I have no way of knowing how long this letter will take to get to you, but I have confidence it will indeed get there.*

Carrie stopped reading and looked at the date at the top of the letter. June 10, 1861. Aunt Abby's letter had taken almost six weeks to make its way to her.

> *My dear, I think of you so often. How I wish we could sit down for a long talk. You've told me before that I help you think clearly. You do the same for me. How easy it would be to get caught up in the war fever that is sweeping the North, especially my beloved Philadelphia. Everywhere the cry is rising, On to Richmond! How my heart fails me to think of harm coming to you or your loved ones.*
>
> *My heart seems to stay in a quandary of confusion when I think of this war. I hold hopes that one of the end results will be the abolition of slavery, yet my heart knows there was a better way to accomplish that goal than this horrible task of fighting. All around me, I see people gearing for war, and yet Lincoln makes no move toward announcing the abolition of slavery. He insists that if the South sees the errors of their ways, he will not tamper with their "property." Yet the South insists they are fighting this war over the rights to their property.*
>
> *Is this war not really being fought because men allowed their passions, instead of their heads, to*

rule them? Is it not really being fought because once more men are being guided by the narrowness of their humanity, instead of allowing God to guide them? I shudder to think of the death and pain that will result from this latest fall of mankind.

Carrie nodded as she read. As usual, she and Aunt Abby were on the same track. Oh, how good it was to communicate, even in this limited way, with someone who shared her heart.

I find myself constantly questioning the will of God in all this. Is it God's will for the North to win the war? The South? I have finally decided I am not wise enough to know the mind of God in this. He has instead shown me that it will be best to simply ask what his will is for me. If I can determine the answer to that on a daily basis, then, no matter what is going on around me, I can be at peace and know I am being all I can be.

There are so many times I feel intense anger in my heart towards the people who have caused this awful war we must now suffer through. But then I must ask myself: Where do I place the blame? I have come to believe that most people, seeing life from their own perspective, think they are doing the very best thing they can. Others, including myself, may think they have the ability to see things more clearly, and maybe we can, but a person can only act from their own perceptions. I find myself more able to find understanding and acceptance of people when I remember that.

Once again, the tears flowed down Carrie's face. How had Aunt Abby known her heart so well? How was it possible that an answer to her inner struggle could arrive at just the right time? Carrie knew the answer and her heart was thankful.

How I wish I could sit across from you and ask you all the questions I long to. I wonder if you are still on the plantation. I wonder if your father has discovered your little deception yet. I wonder what you have done with your love for Robert Borden. So many questions and no answers. I find myself giving you to God on a daily basis. It is all I can do.

I thought you might wonder what has happened with Matthew. His heart has been so torn by the coming of war. I'm sure you have heard of the talk of western Virginia and their desire to pull away and be a separate state from the rest of Virginia. Matthew firmly believes that the diverse opinions are irreconcilable. Though his roots are in Virginia, he cannot bring himself to fight against the North he has grown to love. Neither can he stand the thought of bearing arms against family and friends. Matthew is one of the lucky ones. So many are not being given a choice in the matter. They are expected to fight. Matthew, however, has been assigned as a war correspondent for the Philadelphia Enquirer. He feels it is the best solution for him in the midst of an impossible situation. He is gone much of the time, but he is still kind enough to stop in occasionally. He has become like a son to me.

Carrie smiled as she thought of Matthew. She had liked him the minute she laid eyes on him. His ready smile and friendly, open nature had made him many friends. He and Robert had been college roommates in Philadelphia. Their friendship had remained strong, even though they had stood on separate sides of the issue now dividing the country. It relieved her to know Robert would not have to battle against his friend.

I find myself looking back with such longing for the carefree days of last summer when you arrived on my doorstep with Natalie and Sally. It seems like another lifetime now. Speaking of my niece, Natalie brings up another point of sorrow for me. My family simply cannot understand why I have not returned home to stand with Virginia. It horrifies them that I have chosen to remain in Philadelphia. Explanations of the necessity of being here to run my business have fallen on deaf ears. It infuriates them even further that I have not taken sides in this horrible war. Of course, I am no longer able to have communication with them. I hardly think they would welcome a mail carrier from the Underground Railroad.

Once again Carrie laughed. Aunt Abby still had her sense of humor intact. Or at least she had six weeks ago. How was she feeling now that the first major battle was about to take place?

I would love to ramble on, but I must have this letter ready to go in just a few minutes. My contact is waiting for me to bring it to him. Business continues to go well—the best it has been in years. It seems war can be a boon for the economy. I think it is not worth the cost of lives, but no one is asking my opinion.

I love you, Carrie. I long for the day when we can be together again, whether in a united country or a divided country at peace. My prayers and thoughts will remain with you always.

Love,

Aunt Abby

Carrie sighed and laid aside the last page of Aunt Abby's letter. Turning down the wick in her lantern, she laid back against her pillows, allowing the warm darkness to envelop her. She would read this letter over and over, but for now, she would simply allow the words to flow through her, content with the knowledge that God had answered the cry of her heart and given her contact with her friend.

Tomorrow, she would write a reply. She was sure Micah would find a way to send it on for her. It didn't matter how long it would take—it was simply good to know it would get there someday.

Just before her eyes closed in sleep, her thoughts returned to Robert. Would he make it through the battle tomorrow? Her last waking thought was a prayer.

Chapter Ten

"Down! Everybody down!" Robert shouted. He dropped to the ground, rolled over onto his back, and frantically reloaded his rifle. All around him his men were doing the same thing, their curses filling the air.

Robert rose up on one knee, took quick aim, and fired. He wouldn't go down without a fight. With his shot off, he dropped once more to the ground and reloaded. He also took a moment to look around the thicket. How many of his men had he lost? He could count at least twenty down.

How many were dead? How many wounded, in need of the surgeons up the hill and behind the lines?

A fierce surge of anger engulfed his body, but his mind was calm as he considered all his options. The best he could do was try and get as many of his men out alive as possible. And take out a few Union soldiers along the way.

Robert rose on his knee again and fired. He could feel his men's eyes on him. "Got me another one, boys! Let's do some damage and get the devil out of here." His voice was strong and confident.

One quick look told him his act was doing the job. Gone was the look of panic on his men's faces. With grim determination, they rolled onto their backs and reloaded.

"Got one!"

"We're not licked yet!"

Robert winced as another barrage of gunfire assaulted their position. As the bullets whizzed over their heads, he could almost hear the attending song of death they carried with them.

"We'll get them, Lieutenant!"

Fifty feet from him, Robert heard Hobbs' triumphant yell. Having reloaded his gun, the youth raised onto one knee and took aim. With a scream of agony, Hobbs fell backward, his rifle landing yards away.

"Hobbs!" Robert crawled toward him. He now hardly noticed the rain of bullets flying around him. Keeping his face to the ground, he crawled as fast as he could. It took only minutes to reach him.

"Keep up your fire, men! Prepare to retreat!"

Robert was relieved to see Hobbs' chest was still moving, but there was a widening red spot on the right side of his uniform. Robert quickly ripped away his jacket. The bullet had entered his chest, just below the left breastbone.

"They got me, Lieutenant," Hobbs gasped. His eyes glittered with fear, but he managed to force a smile through the layers of grime covering his face.

Robert squeezed his arm. "Hang in there, Hobbs. We're going to get you out of here."

Hobbs shook his head. "Leave me. You'll have a better chance of getting away." His voice trembled with the effort of speaking.

Robert didn't even bother to reply. He reached into his back pocket, pulled out a strip of cloth, and stuffed it into the hole the bullet had made. It would at least help stop the bleeding.

He looked around him. All of his men were on their backs reloading and watching him. Just then there was a brief lull in the action. Above him, he could hear a louder roar from the Confederate guns. More reinforcements must have arrived. This may be their only chance.

"Retreat!"

Robert gathered Hobbs up and tossed him over one shoulder. The boy gave a single gasp of pain and then went limp. He had passed out. *It's best,* Robert thought grimly. If they didn't make it, Hobbs wouldn't even know.

Within a few yards, Robert was gasping for breath in the dusty heat. The long morning had already drained him, and Hobbs' extra weight made every stride a fight. Ducking his head, Robert ran as fast as he could.

His men ran with him, several of them carrying other wounded comrades. They were only part way up Henry Hill when the barrage began again. Once more, bullets rained around them. An answering roar from the Confederate forces added to the fracas.

Run, Robert! Don't look! Just run! Each step was an agony as Robert lurched up the hill, Hobbs' head banging against his back. The man in front fell with a cry. Summoning all his strength, Robert jumped over him and continued his wild dash. He could not help that man now.

He finally reached the crest of the hill, gasping for breath as the line behind him closed ranks once more.

"Retreat!" Colonel Evans' voice boomed out.

Robert looked around him quickly, taking in the grim situation. Union forces were streaming in on the left, threatening to completely envelop their flank. That was bad enough. But off to the right, he could see a considerable body of troops approaching, completely enfilading their position and threatening their rear.

All around him, men began to pull back. He suppressed a groan, shifted Hobbs' weight, and continued to move. "Let's go! Double-quick time." Robert knew his men were exhausted. He also knew if they quit moving, it would all be over. Gritting his teeth, he continued to press on. He would have to set the pace for them.

A quick glance to the east gave him a glimmer of hope. He could see what appeared to be clouds of dust off toward Manassas. It could only mean more reinforcements. They just had to hang on.

Reaching the cover of the woods, Robert finally handed Hobbs over to the medics reaching out to help him. He had done all he could. The field surgeons would have to take over now. "His name is Hobbs. Take good care of him," he said gruffly. Then he turned back to his men.

"We're done for, Lieutenant," one gasped. His voice echoed the looks of despair surrounding him.

"We got to get out of here while we can," another cried.

Robert wanted to nod and agree with them.

Pickins was more vocal than the rest. "I can't believe we made it outta that slaughter hole alive." His eyes were burning. "I felt like I was in the very presence of death." He turned to Robert. "This is unfair, Lieutenant. Somebody is to blame for getting us all killed, but who?" His voice was as bewildered as it was angry. "I didn't come out here to fight this way. I just wish the earth would crack open and let me drop in."

Others from his regiment were nodding in assent.

Robert looked around. What was going on? Was the battle over? Were the Confederate troops really in hopeless retreat? Would they at least be able to retreat fast enough to keep the Union forces from cutting off Richmond? Where was Colonel Evans? What about General Bee? He had not seen a single officer since he and his men had escaped the thicket. What could he say to keep them going? Was there even anywhere to go? His head pounded as the questions swarmed in his mind.

"Reinforcements!"

The cry rose from the rear. Robert could have cheered when he saw Colonel Hampton and his legion of South Carolinians. Minutes later, he saw what appeared to be a full brigade—fresh and ready for the battle. General Jackson had arrived.

Robert looked around at what was left of his men. They had been through hell, but it wasn't over yet. He had to do something to bolster their morale. "I'm proud of you, men. You fought well."

"While our friends got slaughtered!" one cried out rebelliously.

"That's war," Robert shouted. "The question is: Are we going to avenge their deaths or are we going to run?" His challenge hung in the air. Robert glared around at the panicked faces staring at him. "You boys said you wanted action. You said you wanted to make a difference. Well," he paused dramatically, "you have your chance. What choice are you going to make?"

There was a long silence as the exhausted men exchanged glances. In the distance, Robert could see men disappearing further into the back line, ignoring the rush moving forward to take their positions. Those men had made their decision.

Pickins was the first to speak. "Where you want us to go, Lieutenant? We're sticking with you."

Robert heaved an inward sigh of relief and flashed them an encouraging smile. "I knew I could count on you."

Just then he caught sight of General Beauregard and General Johnston moving toward them. A quick glance at his watch told him it was twelve thirty. After a morning of agonizing battle, the leading Confederate generals had finally arrived. Maybe things could turn around after all.

"Where are you supposed to be, Lieutenant?" Johnston's voice was not unkind as his sweeping gaze took in the tattered remains of Robert's troops.

"Wherever we can do the most good, General, sir."

"That's the way," Johnston replied with a grim smile. "Move to the left and reinforce the line where Colonel Bartow is. We have to hold that position. This day is not over yet. Victory can still be ours!" Then he turned and rode to the next scattering of men.

Robert moved his troops quickly to follow Johnston's orders. The general's words had breathed new life into his disheartened troops. As Robert positioned his men, the steady bombardment from the Union troops continued. Sensing their strong advantage, they were moving forward.

"Give it to them, boys!"

With faces set in determination, his men fired off their rounds. They were back in the battle.

Reinforcements rushed into the fray all around them. As Robert fired and rapidly reloaded, he noticed with grim satisfaction that the tide seemed to be turning. Less than an hour ago, the Confederate left was in a confused and hopelessly outnumbered retreat. Now, they were holding Henry Hill with a long line of strong troops. General Johnston had been right. They weren't out of this yet.

"Lieutenant, look at that!"

Robert looked toward where Pickins was pointing. All he saw was the same line of powerful Union batteries that had been moved out of the woods to bombard their position earlier. The whistle of their shells had been relentless since then. He looked back at Pickins with a shrug.

"No, look at that," he insisted, a smile appearing on his face.

Robert looked back again. He gasped at what he saw. Colonel Cummings of the Thirty-Third Virginia was just leading his men from the woods, less than a hundred yards from where the battery was firing away. What was he doing?

As Robert watched, his face spread into a broad smile. Not all the Confederate troops were dressed in gray. Some, including Cummings' men, were dressed in the only uniforms they could obtain at the time—blue ones. It was obvious to Robert that the Union troops were uncertain as to the identity of the men moving toward them. He watched as one of the Federals moved to turn the guns toward Cummings' men, only to have one of his own stop him from doing so. The confusion continued as Cummings moved closer.

"How far is that crazy man going to take them?" Pickins asked in disbelief. He fired his rifle and, this time, didn't turn around to reload. He did it facing the action.

Robert watched breathlessly as the drama unfolded before him. If Cummings could pull it off, it would be brilliant. If not, it would mean the certain death of all his men.

Down below, the confusion seemed to end. Robert watched, horrified, as the big guns of the battery swung to face the oncoming troops.

Just then Cummings gave the order to fire. Instantly, a deadly volley rang forth from his men's guns. The watching Confederate troops cheered wildly as Union men fell right and left, joined by dozens of horses littering the ground. Within minutes, the triumphant company of blue-clad Confederates swarmed jubilantly as the Federal gunners fled for their lives.

Robert joined in the cheering as he realized the Union Army had just suffered a major setback. From that point forth, the battle turned in their direction.

At around four o'clock, massive reinforcements marched in from the east. General Early had arrived with his men. It was more than the now beleaguered Union troops could take.

"We got them, boys!" Robert yelled.

As Early's men opened fire on what was already a retreating army, the retreat turned into a rout. Blue-clad men left their formations and began to run in panic, headed for the bridges and fords that would take them behind the lines.

Cheers erupted around him.

"Look at them run!"

"We did it!"

"They're ours now!"

"They should have known better than to mess with us Southerners!"

Robert smiled but said nothing. Only hours earlier they had been the ones in full retreat. It was indeed a heady moment, but if reinforcements had not arrived precisely when they did, they would be the ones running for their lives.

Just then another more commanding voice rose above the cries of victory. "After them!"

Robert turned to see General Beauregard astride his horse, watching the retreating troops. Delight was stamped on his face.

"Bring back prisoners!" he cried.

Pickins was the first to surge forward. "Now it's our turn!"

Robert moved to take the lead, but his heart wasn't in it. He was tired, hungry and sore. The Union Army was defeated. Maybe the optimists were right. Maybe this would be the only battle of the war. Why did they need prisoners? Why not rejoice in the victory and enjoy Southern freedom? And yet, he continued to press forward. He had been given an order.

Robert gazed around the scene before him in astonishment. By now the temperature was somewhere in the nineties. Combined with the humidity and the lingering smoke from the battle, the elements had created a hazy fog that infiltrated the woods and seeped onto the open fields. It only intensified the surreal picture before him. Abandoned rifles lay where they had been thrown or dropped. Overturned wagons were still full of ammunition. Riderless horses stood dazedly among their fallen friends. Artillery pieces waited to fall into Confederate hands. Clothes, backpacks, canteens and other equipment nearly blocked the way, they lay so thick.

But it was the bodies that turned Robert's stomach—that made him want to turn and run. He had lost all taste for the hunt. Men not gathered by the fleeing forces were already bloating and turning black from the intense heat. Some lay with their eyes wide in horror, others were missing limbs that had been blown away.

Robert looked for a long moment, struggling to control the nausea. He pressed on resolutely, his men silent behind him.

In the distance, they saw a flash of movement. Robert welcomed some action to take his mind off the horror around him.

"After them, men!"

With a whoop, his men charged forward.

Robert could see the shadows of men fleeing through the woods trying to lose themselves in the cloud of smoke. Running forward, he grabbed the reins of a sturdily built bay gelding and leapt into the saddle. Within moments, he was leading the charge into the woods.

He pulled back on the reins and brought his mount to an abrupt halt. "You there! Behind that tree. Come out!" he shouted.

Silence met his loud command. He waved his men into position. "If you don't come out now, I will order my men to shoot," he commanded. He didn't want any more death, but he wasn't going to put his men at risk. Several of the men behind him lowered to one knee and raised their rifles to their shoulders.

"Don't shoot," came a pleading voice from behind the tree. "We're coming out." Slowly, five men edged forward, their hands reaching for the sky. Their blue uniforms were tattered and torn. All of them were covered with filth and grime. One was clutching a bandage to his arm to control the flow of blood from an earlier wound.

"You are now prisoners of the Confederate Army," Robert said. "Fall in!"

Robert continued to move forward. In just minutes, they were out of the woods and once more on the road. As they moved along, the scene in front of them began to change. Scattered among the remnants of a fleeing army were the souvenirs of a panicked Northern citizenry. Loud laughter rang from his men as they held up picnic hampers, ladies slippers and colorful parasols. Further searching revealed men's top hats, elegant field glasses and baskets of sandwiches. There were more than a few overturned buggies.

Robert shook his head in amazement. The people of Washington, DC must have driven out to the battlefield for an afternoon of amusement, believing their troops would sorely defeat the Southern army on the other side of the river.

"If that don't beat all," Pickins muttered as he picked up yet another pink parasol. "Those folks must be plumb crazy."

A sudden movement in the woods to his left caught Robert's eye. He said nothing, just waved a few of his men in that direction. Moments later, he heard one of his men shout for him. What he saw caused him to rein his gelding in abruptly.

"Who are you?" he demanded.

The elegantly dressed man before him looked a little worse for wear. His top hat was missing, and his long-tailed coat was torn in several places. His white shirt was covered with stains, he was missing one shoe, and his face was covered with smudges. Fear glazed his eyes, but he stepped forward with confidence.

"My name is Edward Mullins," he said a bit pompously.

"Well, Mr. Edward Mullins, what the devil are you doing here in these woods?" Robert kept his voice cutting.

The pompous look disappeared from Mullins' face. "I came here to watch the battle. I am a banker in Washington. My horse and buggy ran off, though." The pompousness returned. "I happen to be a very important man."

"Good," Robert said with a grin. "That means I will be escorting a very important prisoner back to the South."

"Surely you don't mean to take me as a prisoner?" Mullins gasped. "What threat am I to you? I am not a soldier. I am a citizen of the United States."

"Then you should have had enough sense to stay off a battlefield," Robert retorted. "Add him to the rest of the prisoners," he said shortly, before turning to ride away.

It was after dark when Robert arrived back at Manassas Junction with his men and the twenty prisoners they had rounded up. All of them were caked with dust and so thirsty their tongues were swollen. Many of his men rode horses they had picked up on the way. His prisoners stumbled in exhaustion.

He had done the best he could, allowing them to stop at mud puddles and fill canteens with water to pass among themselves. It wasn't much, but at least it was humane. He had never been in charge of prisoners before.

The appearance of Confederate campfires casting yellow light across the field cheered him somewhat. They had bypassed a mountain of food on the road as they rounded up their prisoners, but none of it had been eaten. There had been strict orders not to touch any of it in case it had been deliberately poisoned before the army had fled.

Robert was dismounting when Edward Mullins moved over to him. "See here. This really is ridiculous. I demand that you take me to your commander at once. You simply cannot hold a citizen as a prisoner of war."

Robert had lost all patience. He glared at the indignant man in front of him and snapped, "You people thought you could finish us off in one battle. You were wrong. We have won. You happened to be on the wrong side, and now you are our prisoner." He smiled briefly. "Enjoy your stay in Virginia, Mr. Mullins." Touching his hand to his head, he moved away. All he wanted was a good meal and a night's sleep.

Sleep eluded him as he gazed up at the sky. A sudden thunderstorm had washed the caked dirt off his body and had driven the foggy smoke into the ground. A hot meal had restored some of his strength, but nothing had removed the stench and horror from his soul. He had never stared death in the face the way he had today. He had seen his father die, but he had not seen the bloated condition of a blackening body before. He had never climbed over abandoned bodies and carcasses of horses. He had never listened to the screams of wounded and dying men.

"Carrie..." he whispered into the dark night.

Even the image of her lovely face did nothing to release the agony of his heart. Yes, they had won, but at what cost? And what cost remained to be paid?

It was going to be a long war.

Chapter Eleven

Opal moved her feet in time to the music pouring from Eddie's fiddle. She'd been at her cousin's house for only a few weeks, but already she felt like one of the family. A wide smile lighted her face as little Sadie, her beautiful eyes snapping with delight, played a ditty with her spoons. *Spoonin'* had always been one of Opal's favorite things. She leaned back in her chair as Susie's clear soprano burst forth into song.

> *Swing low, sweet chariot*
> > *Coming for to carry me home*
> *Swing low, sweet chariot*
> > *Coming for to carry me home.*
> *I looked over Jordan and what did I see*
> > *Coming for to carry me home*
> *A band of angels coming after me*
> > *Coming for to carry me home.*

Tears sprang into Opal's eyes as Susie's voice transported her back to the small clearing in the quarters. Barely a night had gone by that voices had not been raised in song that would float over the treetops and give them all hope that someday things would be different. Opal could still hear it now. Moses' deep bass reaching for the stars. Old Sarah's sweet voice instilling hope where there was none.

She missed them. Oh, how she missed them. She was happy where she was, but never a day went by that she didn't think of her friends on Cromwell Plantation and wonder how they were doing.

"Funny ain't it? How white folks ain't got no idea what we're really saying?"

Opal brushed away the sparkle of tears and turned to smile at Fannie. "Good thing," she said fervently. "They talk about how good it is we darkies have our little songs to keep us happy. What they don't know can't hurt them," she added with a quiet laugh.

Once again Opal's thoughts transported her back to the quarters. The very song Susie was singing now had become a mainstay of the quarters the summer before—especially after Miles, Sadie, Jasmine and the rest had escaped. Humming along with Susie, she interpreted as she sang.

Swing low, sweet chariot

The Underground Railroad's wagon that had taken her friends to freedom had indeed been a *sweet chariot.*

Coming for to carry me home

Where but up north could a slave find the freedom that would give them a true home?

Swing low, sweet chariot

If the sweet chariot swung low it would come close to where a slave was waiting.

Coming for to carry me home.
I looked over Jordan and what did I see

The Jordan could mean many things, but it always stood for the border between the North and the South.

Coming for to carry me home
A band of angels coming after me

What better description of an angel than the conductors of the Underground Railroad who led slaves to freedom?

Coming for to carry me home.

Susie's captivating voice fell away to a whisper as her eyes closed in longing.

Opal knew what she was thinking. The two had become close friends since the day she had first walked into the house. Just then Susie opened her eyes, stared at Opal, and closed one in a long, slow wink.

Opal nodded and rose from her chair.

"Be careful," Fannie warned. Her warm eyes were concerned but full of an unspoken confidence.

Opal drew daily strength and courage from Fannie's confidence in her. As Susie broke out into song once again and Eddie resumed his loud playing, Opal slipped through the sagging backdoor and down the rickety steps. She shuddered as she glanced westward and saw the sun dip below the horizon. She had wanted to leave earlier, but the plans had called for her to be on the outskirts of town at precisely seven o'clock. If she had gotten there early, her loitering would have attracted unwelcome attention. But now she must move quickly. She knew the driver would wait no more than five minutes before moving on. Everything depended upon her being on time.

"How do, Opal."

Opal nodded to the thin black man lounging on the stairs of his back porch. "Hello, Abram. Beautiful afternoon isn't it?" she asked pleasantly, trying not to show any nervousness in her voice.

Nodding her head in farewell, she continued to walk. *Not too fast,* she warned herself. *And not too slow.* She must look as if she were simply out to do an errand. Shifting her basket on her arm, she balanced it carefully with her other hand. The cargo she carried was precious.

As she moved down the dusty road, the cries of children, the barking of dogs and the crowing of roosters went by unheeded while Opal's mind raced. The last few weeks had flown by. Her job at the state armory was boring and mundane, but at least it wasn't the backbreaking labor of working in the fields. It was hard work, and she reached the end of each twelve-hour day exhausted, but she had never experienced a thrill quite like the one when she was handed her first week's pay. She had stared at it in joy before hurrying home. A portion of her wages was sent back to Cromwell, but of the rest, she gave half to Fannie and Eddie for her keep. The other half she had carefully stashed under her mattress.

Today, Sunday, was her only day off. She had joined the family for church that morning and then laughed and talked her way through the sumptuous lunch that followed. When Eddie had broken out his fiddle, she had moved to her favorite chair to relax and think. And to get ready.

This was the second time she had been asked to meet the driver on the edge of town. The first time, she'd had no idea what was so important about the basket of eggs and vegetables she had been asked to deliver. There had been no talk at all. She had stepped down from the sidewalk just as he arrived, silently handed him the basket she carried, and taken the one full of tomatoes he offered in return. He had simply nodded and driven on. The whole escapade had taken less than ten seconds, and then Opal had retraced her footsteps. Eddie and Fannie had welcomed her back as a hero, but she was totally clueless as to what she had done.

Until this morning.

Susie's eyes had been shining when she had returned from her job the evening before.

Opal had stood it for as long as she could. When the two were walking home together from church, she finally could stand it no longer. "Why are you looking so happy, girl? You look like you just got the biggest piece of the pie."

Susie grinned widely before she grew somber. After a moment of gazing at Opal, she nodded her head slowly. "You need to know, Opal. Daddy said it would be better if you didn't, 'cause it might scare you and make you act nervous, but Mama and I think you ought to know."

Opal waited. She had been hoping that someday they would take her into their confidence. She was happy to do what they asked without knowing more than that she was helping the cause, but she must have proven herself if they were going to tell her more.

Susie dropped her voice to a whisper. "The lady I work for, Mrs. Hamilton, she ain't what she seems." She paused. "She been living here in Richmond all her life, but she be for the Union, and she hates slavery. She wants to see all the slaves go free. She's what they call an abolitionist."

Opal stared at her, too surprised to say anything.

Susie nodded her head. "I was mighty surprised when I found out, too. She be a spy is what she be."

"Mrs. Hamilton?" Opal asked in disbelief, keeping her voice low and looking around to make sure no one could overhear their conversation. She could easily picture the elegant woman who lived in a large house just blocks from where Marse Cromwell lived on Church Hill. She had been a respected part of Richmond society for years.

"Mrs. Hamilton." Susie repeated. Then, looking around carefully, she lowered her head even more and continued. "I didn't know what was so important in that basket until yesterday. She must be trusting me more, 'cause she let me help her. She came back from being at that Spotswood Hotel all day and disappeared into her room. When she came out, she had a single sheet of paper and asked me to get her a bunch of eggs out of the box. She seemed to be in an awful hurry." Susie looked off, remembering.

Opal fought the urge to shake the story out of her. Susie was mature for her age, but she still loved to accentuate the drama of whatever was going on in her young life. Still, she *was* telling her. Opal would be patient.

"Well, anyway, Mrs. Hamilton, she took out a real sharp pin and poked some holes in one of them eggs. Then, real careful like, she sucked the yolk right out of it. Once it was all out, she took that sheet of paper and tore it up into little strips. Real slow, she rolled them tiny pieces of paper up and stuffed 'em into them holes."

Stopping, she looked over for Opal's reaction. She must have been satisfied by the wide-eyed look, because she only paused long enough for a breath and then kept going. "Once all that paper was in there, she took some glue and filled them holes up till the egg almost looked good as new. Then she put it in the bottom of the basket with the other eggs and told me to make sure you did your delivery tonight."

Opal waited for more, but Susie was done. "But what was on that sheet of paper?"

"You expectin' her to tell me?" Susie snorted. "Mrs. Hamilton, she's got to be real careful. They done started putting people in jail for having Union sympathies around this town. She sure don't want to go to prison." She paused, a slightly fearful look in her eyes. "I don't want to be going to prison, neither. If any of us be found out, my daddy said we wouldn't never have even known the meaning of trouble till then."

Opal had been thinking about the story ever since. Now she knew why her errand was so important. It also made her afraid to think what would happen if someone knew she carried a secret message to the enemy on her arm. Swallowing hard, she maintained her steady pace and kept her eyes on the dusty road in front of her. Her walk passed without incident.

Several minutes passed before she ventured to look up the road. Nothing was moving toward her. She looked at the three carriages already stopped, but none matched the one she had gone to the week before. She recognized none of the faces beginning to stare at her questioningly.

She tried to maintain her casual pose as her heart began to beat faster. Where was the driver? What was she supposed to do with her basket? Glancing over her shoulder, she saw the disappearing glow of the sun. The thought of impending darkness made her heart race more. She well remembered Sam's warning about being out after dark. She had made sure to be safe inside her cousin's house every night. If she didn't hand off her delivery soon, she wasn't going to make it.

Anxiously now, she peered down the road again. The other drivers were being open about their curiosity. She glanced behind her at the horizon again. The driver should have been here. She was waiting too long. Something must have happened to thwart their careful plan. If she didn't leave now, she might not make it back in time. But what if he came and she wasn't there? Would the message do any good if it was received later?

Finally, she had no choice. Fighting to control her feelings of fear, Opal turned and began to walk back the way she had come. She had gone almost a hundred yards, when she heard the rattle of wheels. Jerking her head around, she gasped. The carriage was coming. The red coat the driver was wearing was her signal, and she recognized the carriage from the week before. She had to get back!

She turned and once more moved toward the meeting place, all the time aware of the darkening sky. She retraced her steps and tried to walk casually as she approached the carriage. Wordlessly, she held the basket out to him.

The man's dark face was impassive, but his eyes glowed with appreciation. "Sorry I'm late," he whispered between tight lips.

Opal nodded, the knowledge of his appreciation giving her a warm glow. She had done her job well. She allowed herself a brief smile and turned quickly away, clutching the basket of tomatoes he had handed her. She must hurry. Head down, so as not to draw attention to herself, Opal walked quickly up the road. *Not too fast,* she cautioned herself again. *You have time... You have time...* A glance at the sun told her she was wrong.

Resisting the impulse to break into a run, Opal extended her stride. She didn't care if she drew attention now. Maybe someone would see she was trying to get home as quickly as she could and decide not to punish her. The image of the whip Sam had been talking about rose to taunt her. *Run! Run! You must escape the whip.*

She walked on resolutely. Everything they did depended on secrecy. Eddie had warned her not to do anything to draw attention to herself or their family. If she did, it could ruin everything for everybody.

Sweat was pouring down her brow when she finally turned onto her street. Dusk had laid its heavy hand on the afternoon and the streets were almost empty. There were no more cries of children playing. Muted laughter could be heard coming from open windows, but even the dogs and roosters were quiet. She didn't have much further to go.

A sudden clatter of wheels caused her to look up. Who was coming? None of the blacks in the area owned carriages, and surely no one was coming to do business on a Sunday evening. It could only mean one thing. Opal looked around frantically just as the carriage rolled around the curve.

The two men inside were laughing loudly. Their eyes were in constant motion, searching for signs of movement in the shadows. One spoke sharply to his horse as they rolled along. The other called out to his partner. "This being a policeman ain't all it's cut out to be. Course, it's a lot better than being up there at Manassas being shot at. You've heard about the battle, haven't you?"

"Of course I have," the other said contemptuously. "Ain't no one been talking about much else. I reckon there will be some more news coming in soon."

The voices faded away as the carriage rolled on.

Slowly, Opal picked herself up from where she had dropped to the ground behind a sparse covering of shrubs. She couldn't believe they hadn't seen her. If they hadn't been so involved in their conversation, they would have. Her heart pounded with fear as she hastily brushed the dirt and twigs off her dress. Glancing back over her shoulder to make sure the carriage wasn't retracing its route, she fairly flew the rest of the way to the house. She slipped around the back, looked carefully to make sure no one was watching her, and then eased in the back door.

"Opal! Girl, I was worried sick about you. Where you been?"

Breathlessly, Opal told Fannie her story.

"You made the delivery okay, then?" Eddie asked.

Opal nodded her head, wanting nothing more than her bed.

"I'm proud of you, Opal," Eddie said. "It's up to all of us to do what we can. If the South done win this war, we ain't got nothing but years more of bondage for our folks to look forward to. If the North wins... Well, at least we done got a chance."

Freedom! Opal was buoyed by that thought as she trudged wearily up the stairs. She would continue to do whatever they asked. Then she remembered the question that had been niggling at her. "Eddie?"

"Yessum?"

"The streets are mighty empty. More so than usual. It almost seemed like people were hiding."

"They be hidin' for sure. Word came through about that big battle up in Manassas. The South done won that battle, and the white boys gonna be feeling right proud of themselves tonight. It be best we just stay out o' the way," Eddie said grimly.

Thomas Cromwell burst through the door of the house, shouting wildly. "We won! They did it! We won!"

Carrie jumped up from where she had been making a weak attempt to read a book. She had not been able to concentrate on anything all day long. The thought of Robert in battle had consumed every waking thought. Her father ran right by where she was sitting in the parlor. She had never seen him so excited.

"I'm here, Father! Tell me quickly. What has happened?"

Thomas' face was flushed, his eyes glowing. "A telegram came through from President Davis just a few minutes ago. I copied the whole thing." Fumbling in his pocket, he finally produced the single sheet of paper. "Listen to this," he said. "'*Night has closed on a hard fought field—our forces have won a glorious victory.*' "

He shoved the piece of paper at her. "Isn't that glorious news?"

Carrie didn't know yet if it was glorious news. It did register with her that if they had won the battle, the North must have had the worst part of it. "Do we know yet who is hurt?" she asked. "Who didn't make it?"

Her somber questions calmed her father's excitement just a little. He shook his head. "It's too soon to know. Those reports will come in later." The excitement reappeared. "Come with me, Carrie. I came to get you. The whole city is going wild with joy."

As he spoke, Carrie could hear the first sounds of the celebration. Church bells began to clang all over the city and gunshots exploded in the dark. She knew there would be no sleep tonight. Besides, she wanted to know as soon as the reports of the wounded and dead began to flow in. "All right," she said with a smile. "Let me get a hat."

Within a short time, they were moving down Broad Street, watching wide-eyed as the city erupted with life and excitement. Cavalry soldiers waiting to be transferred to the front raced up and down the streets on their horses, discharging their pistols as they went. Foot soldiers simply raised their rifles to the sky, adding to the clamor. Everywhere, people were dancing and yelling.

In spite of herself, Carrie smiled as she watched their joy.

Richmond was a city that had endured much. They had given their whole city to the cause and sent off thousands of their best into battle. They had suffered overcrowding and violence. They had bent and twisted endlessly to accommodate all the needs and demands of a fledgling government. It was to be understood that they would rejoice in the news of a glorious victory. All of their sacrifice was not for nothing. The Confederacy would stand, and Richmond would be its permanent capital.

"It was a complete victory!" one passing man yelled.

"We did it! They thought they would march through to Richmond, but we sent them running with their tails between their legs," a woman crowed.

"Those Yankees will leave us alone for sure now!" another yelled as he pounded a nearby man on the back.

"This is cause for celebration," one man yelled, before he pulled a passing woman close to kiss her soundly.

Carrie laughed as the indignant woman pulled away laughing herself. Her father was right. The city was wild with joy.

A swarm of children caught her attention.

"I got one!" a little dark-haired boy cried. Brandishing his make-believe pistol, he rushed forward to finish the job with an imaginary bayonet.

"Look at them run!" another cried as he rushed up to a nearby bench, pretending he was discharging a mighty cannon.

"Those yellow-bellied cowards won't dare come down here again," a little girl cried. "I hate those Yankees!" she screamed defiantly, raising her fist to the North.

Carrie's heart grew heavy as she watched the drama unfolding before her. The children were too young to even know what they were saying. Shallow-thinking adults had taught them to hate a whole population of people—people they didn't know anything about. They had ripped the humanity of Northerners from these children's minds and replaced it with a blind hatred of a whole people. The unthinking passions that had ignited this war were now being passed down to the children. When it was all over, would it really be over? How would the unreasoning hatred be erased?

As their carriage rolled slowly onward, the children were left behind. Once more they found themselves amid mobs of people who were celebrating their wonderful victory. Thousands of Richmonders had flocked to the streets in response to the summoning of the church bells and the now constantly tolling Capitol tower bell.

"Isn't it marvelous, Carrie?" Thomas shouted above the din.

Carrie was still too confused about her own feelings to know whether it was marvelous or not, but she was glad to see unrestrained joy take the place of worry and anxiety on her father's face. She tucked her hand through his arm. "Indeed it is, Father."

As they continued to inch forward, she finally thought to wonder where they were going.

"The Spotswood," Thomas yelled in response to her question. "We will get any breaking news there first."

Carrie leaned back against her seat in satisfaction. Maybe now she would find out if Robert was okay.

The Spotswood was a madhouse. Carrie was sure everyone connected with the government was confined in that one place. They knew it was to the Spotswood that Davis would send any more news. There was a steady flow of messengers to the telegraph office. There were no empty places in the dining room, but Carrie spotted an empty place on a sofa in the far corner.

"Go over with the other men," she urged her father. "I will be quite content to sit here for a while."

Her father nodded his head in assent. "Thank you," he said simply. He squeezed her hand and moved over to join one of the knots of men.

Carrie sank down on the sofa and looked around. Men were talking and waving their hands. Looks of victory and excitement were mixed with determination and resolve. It was a group of ladies in the far corner that kept drawing her attention, however. They stayed clustered in one area, only looking up occasionally. Their faces, in contrast to the men in the room, were drawn with worry and concern.

"Those are all officers' wives."

Carrie turned to identify the voice that had broken into her thoughts. "Excuse me?"

"I saw you watching those women. They are all officers' wives. They're waiting for news of their husbands. Several also have sons or brothers who fought at Manassas today."

"I see," Carrie murmured, wishing she could go over to join them. Then she remembered the woman beside her. "Thank you." She turned to smile at the rather plain woman with the pleasant smile and tired eyes. Her hair, though carefully done, was lackluster and dull. Her gray dress added to the drabness of her appearance even though Carrie could tell it was well made. "Are you waiting for news as well?"

"No. My husband and I moved here from Louisiana," she said with a soft accent. "My name is Victoria Lewis. My husband, Richard Lewis, is an aide to the president. He insisted I come with him tonight."

"You don't sound excited about it," Carrie commented.

"I'm not. And I feel free to say that because your face looks about like mine," she said.

Carrie laughed, liking the outspoken woman. "I am waiting for news as well. All I care about right now is finding out if someone I care deeply for is okay."

"I hope he is," Victoria said. "I wouldn't wish the same pain Mrs. Bartow is facing tonight." She made no attempt to hide the tears welling in her eyes.

"Mrs. Bartow? Do you mean Colonel Bartow...?"

Victoria nodded. "The news came through a while ago. Thankfully, Mrs. Bartow didn't have to hear it as an announcement. Some of her close friends went to break the news."

Tears swarmed in Carrie's eyes at the thought of the pain the woman must be bearing. She had never met Colonel Bartow, but he had been extremely popular with his men and the city alike.

"General Bee is another," Victoria said.

"General Bee is dead, too?" Carrie asked disbelievingly. "How many? How many died?" she asked slowly.

Victoria shook her head. "That will take a while to tell. They'll send lists of the officers first. Then the enlisted men." Her voice hardened. "Then the wounded will come in. Richmond thinks she has struggled getting used to being a capital so far. My friend, they haven't seen anything yet. This whole city will be a hospital before this is all over." She continued, this time in a softer voice. "Women who not so long ago talked freely of their willingness to sacrifice their loved ones for the cause are now terror-stricken they might be called upon."

Carrie stared out over the celebration as her new friend's words struck home. The South had won the Battle of Manassas. Now they would find out the cost.

Chapter Twelve

Clouds and rain blanketed the city when Carrie joined her father the next morning for breakfast. He was poring over his paper, absentmindedly sipping his coffee, obviously in a hurry to be off to the Capitol. They had not gotten home until the wee hours of the morning, but he looked refreshed and rested, eager to face his duties. The news of the Confederate victory had invigorated him.

"Listen to this," Thomas said as she slid into the chair across from him. Flipping back to the front page of the *Richmond Enquirer*, he read:

> *Night has closed on a hard fought field. Our forces have won a glorious victory. The enemy was routed and tired precipitately, abandoning a very large amount of arms, munitions, knapsacks and baggage. The ground was strewn with their killed for miles, and the farmhouses and grounds around filled with their wounded... We have captured several field batteries and regimental standards and one US flag. Many prisoners have been taken.*

Carrie watched her father. His eyes were glowing. She was doing her best to understand him. She knew that, to him, all of this was about maintaining the only way of life he had ever known. Each victory meant he was less likely to lose that.

"Father, are you glad you don't have a son right now?" she asked.

Thomas lowered his paper. "A son?" He looked at her blankly for a moment until understanding dawned. "Yes, I suppose I am," he admitted. "It gives me peace to know you are right here in Richmond with me. I don't have to wonder if you are dead or alive."

"Has there been any word of Robert?"

Thomas shook his head. "These things take time," he said soothingly. "Robert is a resourceful young man. I'm sure he is okay."

"I understand Colonel Bartow and General Bee were resourceful men as well," Carrie observed.

"Yes. Yes, they were... We knew there would be an awful price to pay, but it's worth it," he said firmly. "Here, listen to this," he continued, obviously not wanting her to ask more questions. Once again he turned to the *Enquirer*.

> *The importance of the victory cannot be overestimated. If the enemy had destroyed our army as we have destroyed his, who can picture the gloom that would this day have shrouded our prospects? We would have been, for the present, almost at the mercy of the invading host which has profaned our soil. We cannot be too grateful to Heaven for the glorious deliverance which has been granted us.*

Carrie thought it best not to comment on what her father had just read. She had lain awake for long hours the night before envisioning the pain and suffering the men on both sides must have endured, and must still be enduring. She had taken Aunt Abby's words as her own—she could not determine the will of God in who should be victor of this horrible conflict. All she could do was live each day asking God what his will for her was. "When will news of the casualties and wounded soldiers reach the city?" she asked quietly.

"Telegrams should start arriving today. When I talked with Governor Letcher last night, he seemed to think the wounded would not make their way into the city before tomorrow." He flipped open to another page of the paper. "Here. Mayor Mayo is calling for a meeting in Capitol Square to make arrangements for the care of the wounded."

"There must be a lot," Carrie commented, watching her father's face closely. She sensed he knew more than he was saying.

Thomas looked up and saw her watching him. His face was grim as he nodded. "All I know is that there are well over a thousand who will need medical attention."

Carrie groaned and once more fear engulfed her heart. Fear, and sorrow for the men who would soon return to the city they had left so gallantly and lightheartedly just days or weeks before. Sorrow for the family members whose greatest fear had become jarring reality. "Over a thousand..." she whispered. Her heart was torn with conflict.

"What is it?"

She struggled to find words to express what she was feeling. "I am so torn. All I want to do is help people who are sick—people who have been hurt. I find myself wanting to stay here in Richmond and help with the medical needs, but"—she paused for a long moment—"there are needs to be met on the plantation as well. Our soldiers need food. The people of Richmond need food. I can meet that need as well..." Her voice trailed off.

Thomas sat quietly.

Carrie finally looked up at him. "Thank you."

He merely nodded. "It is a decision only you can make. I may have my preference, but I know in the end you will make your decision yourself."

Carrie nodded. "I will return to the plantation. I still feel my place is there. But I will not leave for a few days," she added firmly.

"Not until you know if Robert is okay." It wasn't a question.

Carrie nodded again, grateful that her father understood, even though it wasn't at the level she wanted him to. She would have to be content with what she could have. "Yes. I have to know about Robert."

The dark clouds dumping rain on the city also seemed to have cast a pall over the previous night's feelings of celebration and jubilation. There were no telegrams coming in to ease anxious hearts and minds. The rain had disrupted the lines and made communication impossible. How long before they knew the price of victory? How long before each family knew if they had been called upon to make the ultimate sacrifice?

Carrie was near the front of the crowd swelling Capitol Square when Mayor Mayo took his place on the steps of the Capitol Building. She listened as he spoke of the need to care for the gallant soldiers returning wounded from the glorious victory that had been won.

"We need a committee to go up to Manassas and aid in bringing the soldiers home," he said.

It took just minutes for a group of people to step forward to heed his call. Then the mayor continued on. "Hospital accommodations here in Richmond are rather limited..."

Rather limited, Carrie thought. She would have substituted the word, *painfully*. No one had thought very much about medical care. In fact, it had been given hardly any thought at all. People had gone blissfully along thinking there would be no real war, and if there was, the South would be gloriously victorious with hardly anyone injured. Reality was becoming a bitter pill to swallow.

She swung her attention back to the mayor as he continued.

"...until we can provide facilities on a more permanent basis, we will need a committee to help secure temporary facilities. We will need rooms, supplies and nurses to take care of the men coming in."

Carrie looked around as an eager swell of voices rose. Richmond may not have known what was being requested of her when she became the capital of the Confederacy, but the city was certainly giving her all to rise to the occasion. Once more, Carrie struggled with her desire to stay in the city. She could make a difference here. She knew she could. In spite of the crowded congestion, this was where she wanted to be. Once more the mayor's voice broke into her thoughts.

"And we'll need a committee to go out into the surrounding countryside. We need donations of farm-fresh produce. The soldiers will need good food. There simply is not enough to meet the need."

His words once again settled the conflict in Carrie's heart. For now, her place was on the plantation. She would return as soon as there was news of Robert. As she listened to the swell of voices, her mind was busily planning how to manage the fields to produce the most food for the city. It wasn't the job she wanted to do, but it was the job she had been given to do. She would do it to the best of her ability.

"Here comes the first train!" someone standing next to Carrie shouted. "Here come our boys!"

Carrie strained to catch her first glimpse of the approaching train. Already she was dreading what she would see. The stream of broken humanity had begun that morning. She was riding with her father in the carriage when she had seen a group of men moving slowly down the road ahead of her. Tears had rolled down her face as she drew close enough to identify them.

Tattered gray uniforms, still covered with the dust of battle, clothed the first troops to reach the city. They called themselves the walking wounded, still able to laugh and talk about the victory they had won. Bloody bandages covered head wounds, arms were held with slings, and rough crutches supported broken or strained limbs. Tears had swollen in the eyes of some as they witnessed the hero's reception with which they were greeted.

Now, the first ambulance train was rolling slowly into the station. Rain was once more pelting the city as the engine ground to a halt in the deepening twilight. A hush fell over the crowd as the doors to one of the cars slid open. Men and women had come by the scores, either curious to see what the great battle had cost or to look for loved ones.

Carrie had come only to look for Robert. She could not return to the plantation until she knew in her heart he was all right. She didn't stop to question or examine her feelings. She simply knew she couldn't leave. Maybe in the quiet of her own room at home on the plantation she would analyze the deep love that held her in the city when she should be breaking ground for seed in one of the fields. But not now. She didn't have a need to understand her feelings. She just had to know Robert was alive and well.

The first stretcher was carried slowly from the train.

The soldier looked to be in his late teens. He was filthy, but the sickly pallor of his skin stood out against the darkening day. His eyes were open but staring seemingly at nothing. His grimy hands gripped the side of the stretcher tightly, as if he were trying to control his desire to scream in pain. His head was wrapped in a soiled bandage and his arm was held tightly against his chest in a sling, but it was his leg that drew everyone's attention. There was only one of them. The other had been blown away by a cannon shell or taken away by a surgeon's knife.

Carrie raised her hand and quickly stuffed her knuckles against her mouth to keep from crying out. How could anything be worth this? The stunned silence around her continued as dozens of men were pulled out of the cars lining the tracks. Scores of carriages were lined up to transport the soldiers to the homes waiting for them. She wanted to turn and run from the horrible scene before her, but she couldn't move. She had to know if Robert's strong, handsome face was among those being pulled from the trains.

Over one thousand men... The caravan of ambulance trains would continue for a long time.

Carrie clutched the piece of paper in her hands. Her father had given it to her this morning. It was a list of all the homes housing wounded soldiers. She would go to them one by one. Another list had come through the night before. It was a list of the wounded from the battle at Bull Run. She had almost cried with relief when she had not found Robert's name. Then her father, understanding her need to know, had gently reminded her the list might not be complete.

Carrie looked up at the gracious brownstone in front of her. The steep stairs, lined with graceful wrought iron, must have been quite a challenge to the men carrying stretchers. This was a home designed for entertaining and family fun. She could smell the hospital odor as she slowly approached the door. Open windows allowed all the smells to waft out on the streets. She knocked on the door quietly so as not to disturb anyone.

"May I help you?"

Carrie smiled at the woman who answered the door. "My name is Carrie Cromwell. I'm so sorry to disturb you, but I'm looking for someone. His name is Robert Borden. Is he here by any chance?" she asked, fervently hoping the answer was no.

"I'm sorry, but no, he's not here. Have you seen the list of wounded? They have posted it at the Capitol," she said kindly, looking as if she wanted to help.

"Yes, I've seen it, but it may not be complete. I just have to know..." Her voice trailed off as the sympathy in the other woman's eyes deepened.

"Is Robert Borden your husband?"

"No," Carrie said quickly. "He's..." Just what was he? "He's someone very special to me."

"I see," the woman said. "Well, good luck in your search." A hoarse voice cried out, and she backed quickly away from the door. "Excuse me, please. I must go to my patient."

The door closed and once more Carrie was alone on the porch. She listened for a moment as the woman's calming voice drifted through the open window. The moans of the wounded man ceased. Carrie looked at the next address on her list, walked down the steps, and continued along the street. The next house was just one block further.

By late afternoon, Carrie was exhausted. She didn't know whether to be happy or disappointed. She didn't want to find Robert wounded in one of these houses, but she yearned for some sure knowledge of how he was. There were only three addresses left on her list when she knocked at the door of a plain, yet well-built wooden frame house. Dutifully, she repeated her speech, then waited for the woman to shake her head like all the rest.

"Robert Borden? Did you say Robert Borden? A lieutenant?" the rather large woman with the lined face asked.

Carrie took a step forward. "Yes! Yes, I did. Is he here?"

The woman shook her head decisively. "No, Miss Cromwell. He isn't here, but someone is here I think you would like to meet." She held the door open and beckoned her inside.

Mystified, Carrie stepped inside the cool foyer. The afternoon had brought a cooling breeze that ruffled the heavy drapes at the tall windows. The woman started up the wide staircase and then turned around.

"My name is Jane Fenmore. I'm sorry, I should have introduced myself earlier."

Carrie smiled graciously. "It's nice to meet you, Mrs. Fenmore." She controlled the urge to dash up the stairs past her.

"You must have had quite a search today," Mrs. Fenmore observed.

Carrie nodded, knowing she must look exhausted. "I started at nine o'clock this morning."

"You poor dear," she clucked. They reached the open door of a room at the far end of the long hallway on the second floor of the home. "Hobbs, I have some company for you," she said gently.

Carrie followed her in the room and stared at the young boy lying on the bed, propped up by several pillows. A bandage across his chest spoke of a bullet wound. His brown eyes were tired, but there was still a hint of a sparkle in them.

"Miss Cromwell, this is Warren Hobbs. He has told me everyone just calls him Hobbs. He likes it better that way." Carrie nodded, wondering when she was going to discover why she had been brought up to visit this stranger.

"Hobbs, this is Carrie Cromwell. I don't know who she is, but she showed up at my door looking for Robert Borden."

Hobbs' eyes lit eagerly. "Robert Borden? You mean Lieutenant Borden, ma'am?"

Carrie moved forward to stand beside the bed. "You know Lieutenant Borden?" she asked breathlessly.

"Know him? Know him?" Hobbs exclaimed. "Why, he saved my life, ma'am."

Mrs. Fenmore laughed. "He has talked of little else besides his lieutenant since he arrived here a couple of days ago." She patted Hobbs' hand and moved away. "I'll leave you two to talk." She pulled up a chair for Carrie and left the room.

"How do you know the lieutenant?" Hobbs asked. "Are you his girl?"

Carrie shook her head. "He's just a special friend of mine."

Hobbs' look said it all.

"The Lieutenant is a prince of a man, Miss Cromwell. If it weren't for him, I wouldn't be alive right now. He risked his life for me, he did." Carrie's questioning look drove him on. "We were down in that thicket, with Union soldiers raining bullets on us. Some of the boys didn't make it out."

Carrie shuddered as his face darkened with the memory. She couldn't even imagine what it must have been like.

Hobbs continued. "One of those bullets caught me right in the chest. The doc said it was a wonder it didn't kill me. It probably would have if the lieutenant hadn't carried me out." His face darkened again. "The lieutenant picked me up and slung me over his shoulder when they yelled retreat. Hurt like the dickens, but I didn't say nothing. I sure didn't want to get left behind in that slaughter hole. Then the lieutenant took off running up the hill with bullets whizzing all around us and me slapping on his back." He paused, remembering. "I passed out at some point, I guess. The next thing I knew I was in a surgeon's tent, with them probing in my chest for a bullet. Then I think I passed out again." He gave her a weak grin.

Carrie reached out and grasped his hand. "I'm so sorry," she whispered.

"Heck, don't feel sorry for me. I'm one of the lucky ones. I'm still alive, and I still got all my arms and legs. Some of the others weren't so lucky."

Carrie nodded. "I know." Silence fell between them for a long minute and then Carrie leaned closer. "Lieutenant Borden. Is he all right?" She couldn't wait one more second to know.

Hobbs nodded. "The lieutenant came out without a scratch on him."

Carrie sagged against her chair in relief while Hobbs continued.

"He came to see me before I got put on the train. Said it took him three hours of hunting to find me." Hobbs' face filled with something like adoration. "He wanted to make sure I was okay. I told him I would be right as rain soon and be back to join him in the next battle if them Yankees got enough guts to try and take us on again."

"So he is still up at Manassas?"

"Yes, ma'am. Least he was a few days ago. Don't you be worrying none, Miss Cromwell. The lieutenant's just fine. And he's one prince of a man."

Carrie nodded gratefully, her heart swelling with thankfulness. "Thank you so much, Hobbs."

She could understand why Robert had been so taken with the boy. His sparkling eyes, topped with the rust-colored mop of hair, made him very appealing. He couldn't be that much younger than her, but he looked like he was barely in his teens. "Where are you from, Hobbs?"

"Out in western Virginia, ma'am. My family been farming up in those mountains for a long time."

"Does your mother know you're all right? Does she know you got hurt? Has she been to see you?"

Hobbs looked at her in astonishment. "Been to see me? Why, my family ain't been farther than a few miles from home ever since I been born. Takes a lot of money to go places, ma'am. I reckon I'm the first one to go very far away," he said proudly. "But my mama, she ought to know I'm all right. Mrs. Fenmore done wrote a letter for me and sent it off. My mama might not have got it yet, but she will sometime. I told her not to be worrying about me. That I made it through that battle just fine."

"Did you tell her you got shot?"

"Shucks no, ma'am. Why would I do a thing like that? It would just make her fret about me that much more. No, I told her I was back here in Richmond a little while after winning the big battle." He grinned at Carrie. "What she don't know can't hurt her, you know? She's got plenty to be worrying about with all them mouths at home to feed. I don't need to add another worry. Besides, I'll probably be home soon. I don't see those Yankees coming after more of what we gave them a few days ago. I reckon it will all be over soon, and then won't I have a story to tell!"

Carrie handed her bags to Micah and turned to her father. "I have everything now, Father. I guess I'm ready to go." She was suddenly reluctant to leave him.

The city was still rejoicing in its victory, but the somber realities of war had settled in with a vengeance as house after house filled with the wounded. There was hardly an hour went by that a funeral procession did not wind its way down to Oakwood Cemetery where land had been put aside for soldiers to be laid to rest. The city, already stretched beyond its limits, was being stretched even more. The people were rising valiantly to the effort, but the strain was seen on almost every face. Her father was no exception.

Thomas walked with her out onto the porch and engulfed her in a hug. "I'm going to miss you, Carrie."

Carrie's throat tightened as she heard the roughness in his voice. "I'm going to miss you, too." She pulled back to look into his face. "I love you," she whispered.

"I love you, too," Thomas said, forcing a smile to his face. He cleared his throat. "You tell Ike Adams to keep taking such good care of things. And tell him to do whatever you want about those fields. Of course, you shouldn't have to. I wrote him a long letter with all the details. You have that, don't you?"

Carrie nodded and patted her bag. "It's right here. You don't have anything to worry about. The overseer and I are taking care of things just fine," she said smoothly. Now that she was headed home, she could hardly wait to get back to Rose and Moses. Her heart longed to spend time with Sarah. She had been in the city almost three weeks, and her soul longed for the open expanses of the plantation again, even while a part of her still yearned to stay in the city.

"Take care of yourself," Thomas said for what seemed like the hundredth time.

Carrie nodded. "I will. You too," she added. She wished there was some way to reassure her father. She had never seen so much worry in his face. She knew he hated having her so far away and felt guilty depending on her to keep the plantation going. She also knew he was concerned about her safety if any more battles happened soon. He was confident there would be more, but he didn't know when, or where.

She reached up and gave him another hug. "I'm a big girl. I'm going to be just fine. You do your job. I promise I'll do mine."

Thomas managed another smile and stepped away. "If you want to be there by dark, you need to be going."

Carrie waved until she was out of sight and then turned her attention to home. Already her mind was full of plans for providing food for the city.

"Are you comfortable, Miss Cromwell?"

Carrie smiled up at the large, burly man her father had hired to take her home. "I'm fine, Spencer. Isn't it a lovely day?" Surprise showed on the black man's face. It was obvious he wasn't used to having casual conversation with a white person.

"Yes, ma'am. It is at that," he responded. Then he fell silent.

Carrie left him to his thoughts. She had plenty of her own to occupy her. They had only been moving down the road a few minutes when a mass of movement caught her attention. She looked more closely. What in the world were a group of people, including well-dressed men and women, doing walking around outside of one of the tobacco warehouses? Leaning forward in her seat, she tried to figure out what was causing so much interest. She could see nothing but the sturdy brick walls of one of the buildings. "What in the world is going on, Spencer?" He would certainly know.

Spencer looked back at her with a wide grin. "That be the new prison, Miss Cromwell."

"The new prison?" Carrie echoed.

Spencer nodded. "Yes, ma'am. The soldiers done brought in a lot of them Union men a couple of days ago. I heard tell the army marched right into one of them warehouses and told the manager they was taking it over. That it would be a prison from now on. The one everybody be walking around is the one for the officers. Folks been swarming around outside ever since they found out them Yankees were in there."

Carrie stared at the imposing walls. Now that Spencer had said something, she remembered her father talking about the prisoners who had been taken after the Battle of Bull Run.

Spencer must have sensed that she knew nothing, because he kept right on talking. "They brought them soldiers in late at night on the train. I done heard they didn't want them to see much of the city. So's they couldn't send back information. You can't talk about what you don't see, you know."

Carrie nodded and studied Spencer carefully. He seemed genuinely excited about the prospect of Union prisoners. "How do you feel about this war, Spencer?" she asked.

Spencer looked back at her for a moment as if deciding whether it was safe to answer. "I reckon as how I want to see the South win, ma'am," he said.

Carrie gazed at him in surprise. "You do?"

"Yes, ma'am," he repeated.

"Why?" Carrie couldn't think of anything else to say. Was he afraid to be honest with her? She knew people were being jailed for Northern sympathies, yet he seemed genuinely excited.

Spencer shrugged. "I ain't got no complaints about my life, ma'am. I got me steady work. Sure, most of my money goes to my owner, but I get me some on the side for my work, too. My family, we all eat good, and we ain't never been treated bad." He paused. "I got me some family up north. They work harder than me to make a living, and it be awful cold up there. I don't want to leave the South. It be my home. I don't gots no idea what to expect if them Yankees come down here to try to take things over. My mama used to tell me it was better to fight a devil you knew than to fight a devil you didn't know. I reckon black folks in this country always gonna be fighting some kind of devil. I reckon I'd rather fight the one I know."

Carrie stared at him. "Thank you for being so honest." His candor had left her slightly speechless.

Spencer shrugged. "I know you ain't like most white folks, Miss Cromwell."

"How in the world do you know that?" Carrie had never laid eyes on Spencer until today.

He shrugged again. "Word gets around, Miss Cromwell. Word gets around."

Just then Carrie's attention was jerked back to the new prison warehouse by loud yelling.

"There they are!"

"Look at the Yankees!"

"Hope you have a good time in Richmond!" another taunted.

Carrie willed the carriage to go faster. She wanted to get home. She had no desire to taunt prisoners and make their lives more miserable than they already were. The carriage was directly in front of the prison when a barrage of rocks being thrown against the brick walls by the spectators had her snapping her head up. For just a moment, she looked up and saw the row of faces staring down from the second and third floor windows.

One face had her grabbing both sides of the carriage. "Matthew Justin," she breathed in a shocked whisper.

She leaned forward and spoke urgently. "Turn the carriage around, Spencer. I want to go back to my father's house."

Chapter Thirteen

Carrie gazed up at the tall brick walls of the former Harwood Factory. The building on the southwest corner of Twenty-Sixth and Main Streets had been a tobacco factory until recently. The first commandeered tobacco warehouse had proven too small for the number of prisoners taken, so the adjacent building had been put into use for the Union officers. The scent of tobacco was still very strong. Carrie had gone into the warehouses with her father often. She knew the rooms were large and airy. She also knew the windows were open to the elements.

"Stop here, Micah," she ordered as they came even with the large doors. She jumped out of the carriage, clutching the papers that would grant her entrance to the prison. It had taken both her father and Governor Letcher to make this visit possible. Without their influence, she would have been laughed out of the prison if she had dared approach it.

Just as she stepped down, a long line of carriages made their way slowly up the street. A score of young ladies peered out and up at the windows of the prison. Carrie could hear them as they rode by.

"Why, wouldn't it be just awful if one of those Yankee officers were to look out the window right now?" one asked in a contrived voice of horror.

"Why, you know how improper it is for a Southern lady to look upon the face of one of those *foreign devils!*" another exclaimed in mock horror, just before she looked eagerly toward the windows. Her disappointment at not seeing any faces was obvious.

Most of the ladies were much more discreet, hiding their faces behind their fans as they cast sideways glances at the building. A couple of the women noticed Carrie stepping from her carriage. "Driver, stop!" one of them commanded. She spoke to Carrie. "Are you really going into that prison?" she asked.

"I am."

The fashionably dressed woman stared at her for a long moment. "Haven't I seen you before? Is your father involved in the government in some way? Surely I've seen you at one of the dances?"

"I suppose that's possible," Carrie said. It was obvious the other woman did not approve of her going into the prison. She smiled and began to move toward the door. "Have a nice day," she murmured as she edged away.

She could hear the woman's voice behind her. "Well really! You would hardly think one of our very own would be pandering to Union prisoners. What in the world is possessing you to go in with those Yankee devils?" Her high voice rose shrilly as she hurled her question after Carrie.

Carrie held her head high and continued to walk steadily toward the door. She had tried reasoning with prejudice and hatred before. If she had thought it would do one whit of good, she would have turned around and talked to the woman, but knowing that it wouldn't, she chose to ignore it.

A scowling young man opened the heavy wooden door in response to her knock. "What can I do for you, ma'am?" he asked in a gruff voice.

Carrie eyed the young man dressed in his Confederate uniform. "I have come to visit one of your prisoners."

The guard laughed. "Our prisoners ain't taking no visitors, ma'am."

"One of them is," Carrie responded. "I have a letter from General Winder giving me permission to come in."

The guard's attitude changed abruptly. "General Winder? Let me see that."

Carrie handed him the sheet of paper. Her father had told her no visitors were allowed with the prisoners, but somehow Letcher had talked the superintendent of the prisons into writing this letter. It certainly paid to know people in the right places.

"Right this way, ma'am. You'll need to meet Lieutenant Todd."

Carrie followed the man to a small office set off to the right of the hallway. As she entered, a tall, stringy man rose to his feet. Her eyes went at once to the garish tattoos on both arms. Obviously the man had at one time been a sailor.

"What's this woman doing in my prison?" he snapped.

"She has a letter from General Winder saying she can visit one of the prisoners, Lieutenant."

"Let me see that thing," he snapped again, reaching for the letter. He scanned it quickly and then looked up with a scowl. "Which one do you want to see, Miss Cromwell?" he asked, his voice reflecting a little more respect but still heavy with what Carrie could only identify as bitterness and anger. Immediately, she felt sorry for the prisoners in his care.

"I am here to see Matthew Justin."

"His commission, ma'am?"

"I don't believe he has a commission, Lieutenant Todd. He is not a soldier."

Todd scowled again. "Oh, you mean that journalist fellow, don't you?"

"Yes, I believe I do." She managed to keep her voice calm and pleasant.

Lieutenant Todd looked at her more closely and then jerked his head toward the guard. "Go get Justin. She can visit him in the room down the hall." He turned back to Carrie. "I'm afraid I'll have to take your bag, ma'am. I can't have you taking anything in to one of the prisoners."

"That's not a problem, Lieutenant." She handed it over with a smile and stood waiting.

Todd stared at her again before he spoke. "Do you mind me asking why you are here to visit a Yankee prisoner, Miss Cromwell? It is obvious your father is important in the government if you were able to get a letter from General Winder."

"Mr. Justin is a family friend. My father would have come as well if he could have gotten away from his duty."

Todd scowled. "Don't you mean he *was* a family friend? How can you possibly claim someone as a friend who is bent on invading the sacred soil of the South?"

"He is a very special friend, no matter what side of this conflict he is fighting on. May I remind you, Lieutenant, he is not a soldier—he is a journalist."

Todd stared at her with open suspicion. "There are people here in Richmond that would take your actions as evidence of sympathy amounting to an endorsement of the cause and conduct of these Northern vandals."

Carrie wanted to laugh, but she held her tongue. General Winder's letter would get her in whenever she wanted, but she didn't want to cause trouble for Matthew. She sensed Lieutenant Todd could make life very difficult for those he didn't like. She spoke carefully. "I assume you are a religious man, Lieutenant Todd?" Her question seemed to have caught him by surprise, because he didn't answer right away. Just as well. "Don't you agree with me that love is the fulfilling of the law of God?" she continued in a pleasant voice. "You know, Lieutenant, if we want our noble cause to succeed, we must begin with charity to the thankless and the unworthy. I am merely trying to do my duty toward God." She tried to keep her voice soft and gentle. It would not do for the laughter bubbling just below the surface to boil over. He would know she was merely pandering to him.

"Well..." Lieutenant Todd looked at her for a long moment.

"The prisoner is in the room now, sir," the guard announced from the door.

Lieutenant Todd snapped his lips shut as if he were glad not to have to answer. He moved to take his seat behind the desk. "Take Miss Cromwell to the room. You have thirty minutes, ma'am. That's all."

Matthew was sitting behind a long wooden table when Carrie entered the room. His clothes were dirty and rumpled, his long red hair lay limply on his shoulders, but his bright blue eyes still sparkled, and his face lit up with the same boyish grin when he saw her enter the room.

"Carrie Cromwell," he exclaimed as he jumped up from the table.

Carrie glanced up at the guard, who quickly read the look on her face.

"I will be just outside the door, ma'am. I wouldn't try anything tricky if I were you," he warned before he turned and left the room, pulling the heavy door shut behind him.

Only then did Carrie turn to Matthew. "Matthew Justin," she said warmly, reaching out with both hands. Matthew came from around the table, his body still as tall and muscular as usual. She was glad to see he had no injuries.

"Carrie, how did you find me here?" he asked immediately.

"I was on my way back to the plantation yesterday and had to drive by here. I happened to get caught up in the parade of people coming to see the prisoners," she said with a smile. "When I looked up and saw you peering out one of the windows, I almost fell from my carriage. I turned around immediately and went back to my father's house."

"Your father, how is he? I'm sure he is still grieving your mother." Matthew paused. "I think often of the wonderful Christmas I spent at Cromwell Plantation. It seems a lifetime ago. I find it impossible to believe it was only seven months ago."

Carrie nodded. "I couldn't agree more," she said, thinking back to that magical time before their world fell apart. "My father is doing well. He sends his greetings and says he will come visit as soon as he can. He was shocked to hear you are in prison."

"Your father... Can he...?"

Carrie shook her head regretfully. "I'm afraid there is nothing anyone can do right now. It seems as if no one was prepared to have prisoners. It is all so new that no one knows what is going to happen. My father talked to Governor Letcher on your behalf, but he was able to offer no help either. I'm sorry, Matthew."

Disappointment clouded his even features for a moment, but he forced a grin. "I got myself in this mess. I'll have to be patient, see what happens, and make the best of it."

"How *did* you get yourself in this mess? You're not a soldier. How were you captured?"

"The same way our dear Mr. Alfred Ely found himself a guest at this wonderful hotel."

"Alfred Ely?"

"A congressman from New York," Matthew explained.

"There is a congressman from New York here as a prisoner?" Carrie gasped in disbelief.

Matthew nodded with a wry expression on his face. "I believe there is one other civilian besides us—a banker from Washington. The rest of my roommates are all officers in the Union Army."

"So how did it happen?" Carrie asked again.

Matthew shrugged. "The paper sent me out to do a story." He stopped to look at her. "I couldn't fight, Carrie."

Carrie nodded. "I got a letter from Aunt Abby. She told me."

"You received a letter from Aunt Abby?" Matthew asked incredulously. "The mail is being delivered here?"

"Well, of a sort," Carrie said with a grin. She held her hand up in protest. "I asked my question first. I'll answer yours later."

Matthew grinned. "Fair enough." He leaned back in his chair. "Like I said, I was sent out by the *Enquirer* to cover the big battle. We had been assured the victory would be fast and easy. I thought it odd that so many spectators had come from Washington to watch, but it wasn't my place to say anything. They parked their carriages and spread out blankets to picnic on. Wine flowed freely and everyone was quite excited about the prospect of seeing the Union soundly beat the South."

"They must have been quite disappointed." When Matthew looked at her sharply, she knew he was wondering where she stood on everything. She was still too confused to know her own mind, but she knew Matthew would always be her friend.

"They were more than disappointed," Matthew replied. "In the end, they were absolutely terrified as our troops swarmed past and through them in an absolute panic. All anyone could think about was getting away, but the roads were clogged with traffic and overturned wagons. And still, fleeing soldiers kept racing by." He paused, remembering. "I was doing my best to cover the story, trying to talk to everyone I could. Finally, I knew I had to get out of there. About that time, a couple of soldiers racing by grabbed my horse and took off on him. Then I saw a group of soldiers stumbling toward me. Two of them were badly hurt. I couldn't just leave them." He shrugged his shoulders. "I was trying to help when the Confederate troops captured us. Now I'm here."

Carrie looked at him in sympathy. How like him to sacrifice himself to help others. "I'm sorry."

Matthew's eyes clouded for a moment and then his ever-present grin broke through. "I'm going to have one heck of a story when I get out of this place."

"I imagine you will." Carrie laughed. "Are they treating you well here?"

"It's not so bad, I guess. The floor gets hard at night, and I'm already tired of gristly meat and doughy bread, but at least we have a place to sleep and something to eat. I never really imagined being a prisoner would be a pleasant experience."

"Lieutenant Todd doesn't seem like a very likable fellow," Carrie commented, then told him some of what she had told Todd in his office.

Matthew roared with laughter before he sobered. "One of the saddest things about this war is how it divides family. I'd say Lieutenant Todd is one for the books, though."

"What do you mean?"

Matthew looked at her. "Don't you know who he is?" Her blank expression answered his question. "Doesn't the name Todd ring a bell with you? Like maybe the maiden name of President Lincoln's wife?"

"Lieutenant Todd is President Lincoln's brother-in-law?" Carrie gasped.

"The same," Matthew said with a grin. "It'll make a great story one of these days." He sobered. "Have you heard from Robert?"

Carrie shook her head. "Not directly." She told him the story of meeting with Hobbs. "I'm sure Robert will want to see you if he gets back into Richmond."

"Maybe," Matthew said dubiously. "This war seems to wreak havoc on old friendships. They don't seem to stand up to the strain of divided loyalty."

"This one will," Carrie declared. "Robert would never turn his back on your friendship."

"You seem awfully sure of your man, Carrie."

Carrie paused. "He's not *my man*, Matthew," she said softly, forcing the words around the lump in her throat.

Matthew sat staring at her. "He loves you, you know."

Carrie nodded. "And I love him, but I turned down his proposal of marriage in May."

Matthew whistled but didn't comment.

Carrie continued. "We stand too far apart on certain issues."

"Such as slavery?" Matthew guessed.

Carrie nodded, struggling to hold back the tears that sprang to her eyes at Matthew's obvious sympathy.

Matthew waited a long moment before he said anything. "Robert has only ever known one way of life. It's going to be hard for him to see things differently, but I trust his heart. I don't know what it will take, but I have a feeling you will be together one day."

Carrie longed to take hope from his words, but she also didn't want to hang on to a fantasy. "We'll see," she said finally.

The door cracked open. "You got five more minutes," the guard said.

Carrie pulled herself back to the present situation. "I'm going to try to get someone to bring you some things—fresh food, clean clothes." She quickly explained Opal's presence in Richmond. "I'll find her today and ask her to visit you. General Winder was kind enough to add her name to the letter. I have to get back to the plantation," she explained. "I wish I could stay longer, but timing is rather critical."

Matthew eyed her for a moment. "Are you as torn by this conflict as I am?" he asked.

Carrie nodded. "Yes, I am. I find my heart torn on almost a daily basis. The South is fighting a war I don't believe in, largely over an institution I don't believe in. Yet, my father has thrown his whole heart into it, and people I care about deeply are fighting and risking their lives for *the cause*. It is so confusing."

Matthew nodded. "Thank you for being honest. I imagine your position is not extremely popular around here."

Carrie grimaced. "I find I hold a lot of opinions that are not very popular."

Matthew laughed. "That's why you and Aunt Abby hit it off. You're too honest to let public opinion determine your own beliefs."

Carrie brightened at the idea of being like Aunt Abby. It helped to remember she wasn't alone. "I remember something Aunt Abby told me once. She said the world was too full of people willing to put out their thinking the way they do their washing—to be done by others."

Matthew nodded. "Aunt Abby is one in a million. I agree with her. I think every individual should feel they alone are responsible for their thoughts and actions."

"Time's up!" the guard's voice intoned.

Micah was waiting for Carrie when she left the prison. Carrie hurried over to him. "We have one more stop before I go back to my father's, Micah."

"Yes, ma'am. Where you want to go?"

She gave him the address.

"You sure that's where you be wanting to go, Miss Carrie?" He was looking at her with a strange expression on his face.

"That's the place."

He shook his head but picked up the reins and urged the horses forward.

Carrie settled back against her seat. She understood the strange look. She was quite sure he didn't take too many white people to this part of Richmond, and they didn't have far to go. Opal lived only a few blocks from the prison.

Carrie gazed around her as they entered the neighborhood where Opal lived with her cousin. It was certainly barren and drab, but she had to admit the two-story frame houses were an improvement over the quarters at home. When they turned onto Opal's street, she could hear the sounds of children playing in the street, and men and women calling to each other. As they rolled along, though, quiet seemed to spread in a wave before them. Children who looked up and saw her immediately quit playing and ran to their porches, where they perched and watched her, their small faces set like stone. Voices quit calling out to one another as men and women turned away and acted as if they were busy with a chore.

Finally the carriage pulled up in front of the address. She could see little faces peering out at her, but no one came out to meet her. She was not expecting them to. Carrie gathered her dress, stepped down onto the dusty road, and walked quickly to the door. It was several minutes before a face appeared.

"Yes, ma'am?"

Carrie smiled at the girl in front of her, trying to dispel the fear she saw in her eyes. Maybe it hadn't been such a good idea to come looking for Opal. She didn't want to cause trouble for the people here, but she was already here, so... "I am looking for Opal. I understand she lives here." She kept her voice gentle.

The girl became even more guarded, though she kept her voice even. "Yes, ma'am, she lives here, but she ain't here right now."

Carrie looked at the girl in admiration. She guessed her to be about sixteen, though her manner made her seem much older. Her voice was musical and her diction was clear. It was the intelligence in her eyes that drew Carrie the most, however. The girl reminded her of Rose.

"Do you know when I might find her here? It is really quite important that I see her." She watched as the shutters closed further over the girl's eyes. Then she realized what she was doing wrong. This girl had no idea who she was. "I'm sorry," she said suddenly. "I haven't even introduced myself. My name is Carrie Cromwell."

"You be Miss Cromwell?" the girl exclaimed. "Why didn't you say so? Come on in this house."

Carrie smiled with relief at the rapid change. "Thank you," she said as she stepped in the door. Suddenly she was surrounded by three more children.

The girl who had met her spoke as soon as she was inside. "My name is Susie. This here is Amber, Sadie and Carl." She looked back up at Carrie. "We've done heard lots about you, Miss Cromwell. Opal thinks the world of you."

"And I think the world of Opal. Is she doing well?"

"Oh, yes, ma'am. Opal be doing just fine. She should be back any minute now. She went to run some kind of errand. She works most every day, but she had today off. She's going to be right happy to see you."

Any minute turned into an hour, but it seemed to fly by. Carrie had fallen completely in love with the children by the time she heard footsteps on the porch.

"Miss Carrie, what are you doing here?" Opal asked with delight as soon as she saw her. Then her face clouded with anxiety. "There be something wrong back on the plantation? Are you coming to tell me I got to go back?"

Carrie hastened to reassure her. "No, nothing like that, Opal. I came to ask you a favor. Your cousins here have been taking very good care of me." She looked Opal over carefully. "You look as if you're doing well," she said warmly.

"Oh, yes, ma'am. I'm doing real good. How's everyone on the plantation?"

"I assume they're doing well. I've been here in the city for the last three weeks."

"Here in Richmond?" Opal asked in surprise.

Carrie nodded and explained that her father had asked her to come. "I deliberately stayed away because I didn't want my father asking too many questions. That has changed now, though. My father knows you are here."

Fear sprang into Opal's eyes. "Oh Lord." was all she could say.

"It's all right, Opal. Once I knew I needed you, I also knew I had to take the chance. My father was fine with you being here. I didn't know it, but all the plantation owners are being asked to send some of their slaves to Richmond to help with the war. They are working in the factories, building the defenses, things like that. I am going to have to send more when I get home." Her last statement had caused her to get very little sleep the night before, but she had decided not to worry about it until she was back on the plantation.

Opal still looked anxious, even though the fear was gone from her eyes. "What kind of help you be needing from me, Miss Carrie? I'll do whatever I can."

Carrie nodded. "I know you will, Opal. I didn't know anyone else I could trust." She smiled at the pride shining forth in Opal's eyes and explained about Matthew. "He's a very dear friend. I can't stand the thought of leaving him in that prison. I have some money for you to buy him fresh food and some more clothes. He's also going to need paper so he can continue writing. I would appreciate it if you could visit him every few days."

Opal laughed. "They're not going to let me get near that prison, Miss Carrie. I've heard the stories. They're not letting *anyone* in to see those men."

Carrie pulled out the piece of paper she had carefully folded in her pocket. "This letter will get you in, Opal. General Winder, the one in charge of all the prisons, wrote it this morning. It grants entrance to me and," she continued with a smile, "you."

Opal's eyes grew wide. "That letter says I can go into the officers' prison? Anytime I want?" Her voice was disbelieving. She reached for the letter. "Can I read that thing?"

Carrie handed it to her with a smile. Once again she thought of Rose and felt a pang of loneliness. If it weren't for Rose, Opal wouldn't know how to read and write. Suddenly, all she wanted was to be with her best friend again. She had taken an extra day to make sure Matthew was provided for, but now she was anxious to get home. Spencer would arrive early the next morning to take her. "Will you do it, Opal?"

"'Course I'll do it, Miss Carrie. I'm glad there's something I can do for you seeing as you've done so much for me."

Carrie watched the pleasure shining in her eyes and thought how much she'd changed. There was strength and a confidence that wasn't there before. "You're different, Opal."

Opal looked up from the letter she had been reading and smiled shyly. "Yes, ma'am, I reckon I am."

"Why?"

Opal's voice was suddenly intense. "It changes a person to be able to decide things for yourself. I still ain't really free, but I get to decide things for myself now. There ain't so much to care about when you're a slave. It doesn't do you any good to think for yourself, because you can't do nothing with them thoughts. You're always told what to do and when to do it." She paused and looked Carrie straight in the eye. "I got dreams and hopes just like any white person, Miss Carrie. I'm going to work hard to make them dreams come true."

"What is your dream, Opal?"

Opal looked at her hard as if trying to figure out if she really cared. "I want to have my own eatin' place, Miss Carrie. I always thought I would love to cook, but I was always on the other end of a hoe or a tobacco worm. There wasn't much time left for cooking. I've been cooking some since I been here. I like it a lot, and the people who are eating my cooking say it's pretty good."

Carl spoke from where he was standing to the side. "Opal be as good a cook as my mama," he said proudly.

Everyone laughed as Carl rubbed his stomach and smacked his lips together.

"I've been going to church here, too, Miss Carrie."

Carrie nodded. "You went to church on the plantation, Opal."

"Yes, ma'am, but it be different when the preacher isn't saying only the things the plantation owner says he can say. This preacher is different. He talks about God like he's really real. And he's white to boot!"

Carrie laughed at her expression but was not surprised the preacher was white. It was against the law for a black congregation to have a black preacher. They could meet together, but their preacher had to be white. It was another way for the white people not to lose control. "I'm glad you're going to church, Opal. And I'm glad you're finding out God is real."

"Yes, ma'am. Pastor Anthony, he's a fine preacher, and he's a good man," she declared.

"Pastor Anthony?" Carrie thought for a moment. Why was that name familiar? Suddenly her mind flew back to the morning she had rushed to see Robert off on the train. "Is it Pastor Marcus Anthony?"

It was Opal's turn to stare. "You know Pastor Anthony, Miss Carrie?"

"We've met," she said. "I liked him right away, Opal. I'm glad he's your pastor."

Carrie stayed for just a little while longer and then left. She was having one last dinner with her father at the Spotswood before she returned to the plantation in the morning.

Opal turned and stared at Susie as soon as Carrie rolled off in the carriage. "If that don't beat all," she exclaimed.

Susie turned to the other three children. "Why don't y'all go back out and play now? Me and Opal need to talk."

Once the children were out in the yard, Susie joined Opal on the sofa next to the window. "A letter to get into the officers' prison. I can't believe it," Opal whispered, almost as if saying it out loud would make it untrue. Opal clutched the letter in her hand and stared at it. Just yesterday, Susie's employer, Mrs. Hamilton, had talked to her about how much she wanted to get into the officers' prison.

"Come on, girl. We're going to Mrs. Hamilton's," Susie said, springing up from the sofa.

"Right now?"

"Right now."

Opal smiled at the look of awe and delight on Mrs. Hamilton's face as she gazed at the letter.

"It's a miracle," the woman said in a whisper. She stared at it for a minute more and then turned her eyes to Opal. "Are you willing to help me?" she asked.

Opal nodded. "Just tell me what to do."

"Wait right here," Mrs. Hamilton said, disappearing from the room. She returned moments later with a large serving platter. "I want you to use this to take food to Mr. Justin."

Opal stared at it. What was so special about that dish?

Mrs. Hamilton smiled, then with a quick movement of her hand slid back the false bottom of the plate.

Opal and Susie gasped at the same time.

"We're going to take the officers things no one will know about," Mrs. Hamilton said coyly. "I hope we'll get little gifts in return."

Chapter Fourteen

Carrie stared out over the fields, satisfied with the progress being made. She had been home only two weeks, but already fifty of her father's acres had been plowed under and reseeded with food crops. She would have done more, but that was all they could handle. It had been a tremendous amount of work to pull up the maturing tobacco plants and haul them into the woods where they were now rotting in the August heat. They wouldn't go to waste, however. Next year, the compost would be worked back into the soil to nourish another generation of plants, whether it be a cash crop of tobacco, or more food. They had done all they could do. Now they could only hope for a long, warm fall. Food production would end with the first frost.

Carrie rode out into the fields every morning to check on the growth of her plants. She knew it was silly. It was too soon to expect anything more than barren dirt. Still, this had become her new passion, and she was pouring her heart into it. And she loved being out in the fields on Granite. The early morning rides rejuvenated her and gave her time to think. Every other minute of the day was filled with work.

This morning, however, she didn't even want to think. A cool wind had blown in the night before, and she wanted to enjoy the soft breeze on her body and take deep breaths of the recently turned earth. She couldn't really explain her feeling of peace right now. She had been so torn about leaving Richmond. So much of her had felt she should stay there—that she was needed in the city. All it had taken was having the carriage wheels roll onto Cromwell Plantation. Once more she had been at peace, confident she was where she was supposed to be for now. There was something more, though. Something she didn't quite know how to express. A feeling that she should make all she could of this time.

"Carrie!"

Carrie looked up and saw Rose riding toward her. She urged Granite into a canter and rushed to meet her. "Rose! Is something wrong?"

"No," Rose said, smiling. "I'm just coming out to deliver a message from my mama. She wants you to come for lunch."

"She sent you all the way out here to invite me for lunch?"

"Yes. She insisted I come so that you wouldn't make other plans. I didn't mind."

Carrie thought it odd that Sarah had sent Rose all the way out to the fields, but she didn't say anything. "Ride with me for a while," she said suddenly. She knew there was work to be done, but she felt it was important just to be with Rose. It was another of those feelings she was learning not to analyze. She interpreted the hesitant look on Rose's face. "We won't be out that much longer. The work isn't going anywhere, and we've had hardly any time together since I got back."

"Where to?"

Carrie surprised even herself with what she did next. "Follow me," she called, swinging Granite around and breaking into a gentle canter. They weren't that far away.

Carrie pulled Granite to a stop on the bank of the river and turned to Rose.

"This is your special place, isn't it?" she asked softly.

Carrie nodded. A long, comfortable silence stretched between them as they gazed out over the water. The breeze rustled the leaves overhead, creating its own background music. "Do you like it?" she asked.

Rose nodded.

Carrie looked at her more closely. She was startled to see tears shimmering in Rose's eyes. "Why are you crying?"

Rose smiled through her tears and answered the question with one of her own. "Why have you brought me here?"

Carrie thought before she spoke. At first it had been pure impulse, but now she knew it wasn't. "When I was younger, it was important to me to have my secret special place. I didn't want to share it with anyone. It was my place to come and be whomever I wanted to be. Now I don't need a secret place for that. I'm strong enough to be me wherever I am. My secret place has now become just my special place."

She paused, picking her words carefully as the thoughts firmed in her mind. "I think when you get older, special places become more special when you can share them with the most special people in your life. It adds to the memories." She reached out and touched Rose's arm. "You are one of the most special people in my life. You are my best friend. You are like a sister to me." Tears sprang to her own eyes. "I don't know how much longer we will be together. We both have dreams that are going to take us in different directions. I don't really know," she said a little helplessly. "I just knew I wanted to bring you here."

Rose gazed at her for a long moment. "Thank you," she said in a trembling voice. She paused as if struggling for words and then continued. "You've told me before that I'm your best friend. It's been hard for me to believe that sometimes. I mean... I think of you as *my* best friend, but it's hard to get over the slave-owner thing sometimes." She put up her hand when Carrie opened her mouth to protest. "It's impossible for you to understand how I feel. You've never been a slave."

Carrie closed her mouth. She couldn't argue with that. She could try to understand, but she would never fully comprehend what Rose had felt over the years.

Rose looked her squarely in the eyes. "I love you, Carrie Cromwell."

Carrie wasn't embarrassed by the tears pouring down her cheeks. "I love you too, Rose." A long moment passed, and then she asked, "Do you mind not having your own last name?"

"What?"

Carrie laughed. "I'm sorry. I guess I spoiled the moment, but I just thought of it all of a sudden. I mean, my name is Carrie Elizabeth Cromwell. Your name is Rose. I know you are supposed to take on the name of Cromwell since my father owns you, but doesn't that seem strange to you? Wouldn't you like to have your own last name?"

"You can change subjects and moods faster than anyone I know," she declared. "But yes," she said thoughtfully, "I'd like to have my own last name someday. Moses and I talk about it sometimes—what we will call ourselves when we are free. What name we will give our children." Her eyes shone as she talked. "We haven't decided."

Carrie smiled. "Make sure I know what it is so that I can find you if I ever need to."

Rose nodded. "I wonder what Miles calls himself now."

"Or Jasmine," Carrie added.

She smiled as she thought of the wild jubilation that erupted in Sarah's cabin when she had read them the part of Aunt Abby's letter that spoke of Miles and the rest reaching freedom in Canada.

"Do you like growing up?" Rose asked.

"Talk about changing moods and subjects," Carrie teased. She sobered as she thought about the question. "I don't know. Sometimes I think I still want to be a little girl with all of my problems taken care of for me. Then I think I wouldn't give up my new freedom for anything. I like making my own decisions," she said. "I guess I don't always like living with the consequences, though."

She thought again before she spoke. "I'm not sure I like growing up right now. The whole country seems to have gone crazy. Your mama told me something the last time I talked to her, though."

"What's that?"

"She told me every generation of people thinks they are growing up into a harder time. She thinks maybe it makes them feel better about the struggle they have leaving their childhood behind. I've thought about it, and I think she's right. Right now, we have this war going on. Not so many years ago, we were fighting the War of 1812. Before that was the fight for independence. The generation before that was trying to carve a life out of a wilderness. The one before that was fighting oppression in England. I guess there's always something hard going on."

Rose nodded. "That makes sense."

"Your mama told me something else. She said folks can blame bad decisions on the times being hard, or they can admit they made a stupid mistake and fix it. She said that's the real sign of growing up—when you don't blame your mistakes on other people or circumstances."

"That sounds like my mama," Rose said with a laugh.

Long moments passed while they stared out over the river, both lost in their own private thoughts. Finally, Carrie roused herself. "We'd better get back or they're going to send out a search party." She reached over to squeeze Rose's hand, but she spoke no more words. She had said everything there was to say.

Carrie was whistling as she strode down the path to Sarah's cabin. It had been a good morning. When she returned from her ride, she headed straight into the office. It had taken her the last two weeks to get the books caught up, snatching little morsels of time when she could find them. When she snapped them shut just minutes ago, everything was up to date.

Sarah was watching for her when she rounded the curve that led to the quarters. Carrie smiled at the sight of the tiny woman standing on her cabin step. As usual, her face was wreathed in smiles.

"Howdy, Miss Carrie. I'm real proud you could join me for somethin' to eat."

Carrie leaned down to give her a hug. "Hello, Sarah. Thank you so much for inviting me." She looked around the cabin and was surprised to find it empty. "I thought Moses and Rose were joining us."

"No," Sarah said shortly. "I just invited you. I got some thin's I be wantin' to say to you."

Carrie tried to discern the look in her eyes. It was a look she had never seen before and could not interpret now. She knew better than to ask questions, though. Sarah would tell her when she was good and ready. "What are we having for lunch?" she asked instead.

"Just got done bakin' some sweet taters. I'd reckon you'd get mighty tired of them things after a while, but I learned a long while back that you wouldn't be happy without some o' my taters."

"Nobody cooks them like you, Sarah."

"Nonsense! Taters be taters, but you can believe whatever you want to believe. Always did anyway."

Carrie laughed and sat down at the tiny table. She lifted the edge of a rough napkin and sniffed appreciatively at the biscuits staying warm underneath. Then she looked in surprise at the fire. Sarah was the only one in the quarters that didn't cook over the community fire in the heat of summer. "Is that a chicken you're cooking, Sarah?"

"Looks like a chicken to me."

Carrie couldn't hide her surprise. "A chicken in the middle of the day? Is there some special occasion I'm not aware of."

"I'd say you're pretty special, Miss Carrie."

Carrie looked at Sarah sharply. Her voice had grown softer when she made the last comment. What was going on? A feeling of uneasiness crept into Carrie, though for the life of her she couldn't identify why.

Sarah laughed then. "You gots too many questions, Miss Carrie. Can't an old woman do somethin' nice for somebody she cares about without havin' to be pestered with so many questions?" The teasing was back in her voice.

"Sure you can, Sarah." She patted her stomach. "I'm starving!"

"That's more like it," Sarah said with satisfaction.

Within moments, they were seated in front of a feast. Carrie moaned in delight as she took a bite of her tender, piping hot sweet potato, savoring the taste as it melted in her mouth. Her long ride had indeed made her hungry. She didn't care about talking anymore until her stomach was full.

When she finished, she looked up to see Sarah staring at her. "Is there something wrong with the way I look?" she asked teasingly.

"What you doin' bout your dreams, Miss Carrie?" Sarah asked.

Carrie wondered what had prompted that question, but she knew by looking at Sarah that she had something she wanted to say. Whatever it was, Carrie knew it would be worth hearing. "My dreams are there, Sarah. I'm just waiting for the right time to make them come true. I know I'm supposed to be here for right now."

"You gettin' scared to leave this plantation, girl?"

Carrie thought for a moment, then shook her head. "I don't think so. I'm content for now because I'm where I need to be, but I dream about the day I can leave. I dream about going to school to be a doctor."

"You make sure of that." Sarah paused. "Sometimes people can think they have dreams. They can ponder on those dreams and make them seem like the most important thin' in the world. But then they wait too long to make them dreams come true. *Thinkin'* bout them dreams becomes more important, and safer, than actually *livin'* them dreams. When their time comes, the dream don't have 'nuff power to get past their fears." She looked long and hard at Carrie. "Then they spend the rest o' their life regretting them dreams passed them by. I don't want that for you, girl."

"I don't want that either, Sarah," Carrie said softly, still wondering why Sarah had picked today to tell her all this.

"You been studyin' them books yo' Aunt Abby sent you?"

Carrie flushed and shook her head. Sarah was talking about the large package of medical books Aunt Abby had sent her just before the mail had stopped. She had sent a note saying the books would give her a head start until she could leave the plantation.

"Why not?" Sarah snapped.

"I've been so busy," Carrie protested. "I barely have time to do the things I have to do."

"Nonsense." Sarah leaned forward and fixed Carrie with her eyes. "You listen to me good, girl. You done got the healin' gift, and you got it good. It ain't nothin' you done. It be a gift from God. But you better not let that gift go to waste. You got to stretch it. You got to work it. Dreams are like that, too. You got to stretch 'em. You got to work 'em. Most of the people in this world have dreams, but they too lazy to make 'em come true. They want it to be easy. Big dreams don't come easy, you hear me?"

Carrie nodded, listening with all her heart. She had seldom seen Sarah so intense.

Sarah continued. "I don't want to hear nothin' 'bout being too tired to work on your dream. You go's ahead and do the thin's you got to do, and then you work on that dream. God'll give you the strength to do it when you think you don't got none. And another thin'," she added in a stern voice. "Make sure you ain't fillin' up yo' days with dream killers."

"Dream killers?"

"Dream killers," Sarah repeated, nodding her head. "They be all those thin's you think be so infernal important. You step back and take a look. Them thin's may not be all that important. Not if they be robbin' you of yo' time to follow yo' dream. This here plantation will suck you dry if you let it. There always be one more thin' that need to be done. You can one-more-thin' yo' way right into the death of yo' dream." She paused again. "You got what I'm sayin' to you, Miss Carrie?"

"I've got it." Carrie nodded. "You're right as usual. I've been letting other things take up my time. I've been waiting until I could leave, rather than making the most of my time here to prepare." All the wasted hours raised their heads to taunt her. "I'll start studying tonight, Miss Sarah. I'll do all I can to make sure I'm ready for my dream," she promised.

Sarah nodded her head, obviously satisfied with what she saw and heard. "I believe you," she said. "Just you remember one more thin'. God be the one that plants dreams in yo' heart. Them thin's you think be sent yo' way to kill yo' dream? They really be thin's sent to make you stronger—better able to live that dream. Don't you be runnin' away from the hard times. Embrace them and suck all you can out of 'em." She closed her eyes briefly. "I'm tired. I think I'm going to lie down for a little while."

Carrie had never in her life heard Sarah say she was going to lie down in the middle of the day. "Are you all right?" she asked anxiously.

Sarah opened her eyes and barked a laugh. "I'm right as rain," she said. "Can't an old lady get some rest if she needs it?"

Carrie nodded, trying to ignore the uneasiness she felt deep inside.

Chapter Fifteen

Rose looked up in surprise as she heard the sound of hoofbeats behind her. "You going riding again, Carrie?"

Carrie pulled back on the reins and brought Granite to a halt. "I've got some thinking to do. As usual, your mama gave me a lot to ponder. I always listen..." She paused for a long minute. "This time somehow felt different, though. Like she was trying to open my heart so she could pour her words and feelings right into it." She shook her head. "There was something about her intensity... Anyway, I'm going to take a ride and let what she said sift around in my head." Raising her hand, she moved Granite into a trot. "See you later," she called over her shoulder.

Rose watched her for a moment and then continued walking. She was on her way to her mama's. One of the children had come running up to her at the big house and told her that her mama wanted her. There had been nothing about the child's face to alarm her, but Rose had noticed her mama wasn't as strong lately. She probably just needed something done.

"Hello, Mama," she said cheerfully as she walked through the door. "Hannah said you wanted to see me."

Sarah, from where she was seated in her rocking chair next to the crude window, nodded.

Rose walked over and took the chair across from her. "You look tired, Mama," she said with a sudden anxiety as she noticed how hot and still the cabin was. The only sound was the buzzing of flies. "Why don't we go sit outside? There is more of a breeze there."

Sarah shook her head. "I be all right, girl. And what I gots to be sayin' be best said without listenin' ears pokin' in."

Rose sat back in surprise. "What do you want to tell me, Mama?" Now she felt even more anxious.

Sarah gazed at her tenderly for a long moment, her hands resting easily in her lap. "You been the best daughter a body could ever hope to have, Rose."

Rose didn't know what to say. "Thank you," she finally murmured. She knew without a shadow of a doubt that her mama loved her, but she didn't usually tell her right out.

Sarah continued to stare at her for several minutes. The silence built in the cabin until she seemed to make up her mind. "I got somethin' I want to tell you." Her voice was grave and quiet.

Rose sat silently, having no idea what her mama could have to say that would make her so serious. She had never seen her quite like this—with a mix of fear, determination and sorrow shining from her eyes.

"You wouldn't remember nothin' 'bout the old Master Cromwell," she began. "The one who be Miss Carrie's granddaddy."

Rose shook her head. Old Master Cromwell had died when she was still very young.

"He wasn't much like Carrie's daddy. He treated us slaves all right, but he didn't have no trouble usin' the whip if he thought it was needed. And he didn't always limit his time in bed to bein' with his wife." She paused a moment, seeming to remember. "Course, that still happens a lot now. When a man owns you, he figures he can do with you what e'er he wants. Old Master Cromwell, that be the way he figured."

Rose stared at her, wondering where in the world she was going with this.

"When I first done got to this plantation, I didn't look old like I do now. People done used to tell me I was right nice to look at," she said with a smile, before her expression turned sad. "Well, the old master must have thought the same thin'. Me and John, we'd just got married, but that didn't stop him from comin' down to my cabin one day. I was sick with a little fever and weren't workin' in the fields that day. John weren't nowhere around. I reckon the old master knowed that." She stopped and took a deep breath.

"Anyway, the old master had his way with me that day. I tried to stop him, but he just laughed at me. Told me he could do what he wanted with what was his. Told me the whip was waitin' for me if I thought I would like that better."

Rose fought to hold back her tears at the look of pain on her mama's face. Sarah's eyes were glazed with remembering.

"When John got home that night, I didn't tell him. I was afraid of what he would do, and I was afraid of the whip for him." She paused again, almost as if she couldn't go on. "Then, not too many weeks later, I came up pregnant. My John was so excited. He always wanted children. He was willin' to take the chance of being separated from them, even though it broke his heart to think they might be sold away from us. He wanted children—lots o' them," she said, her voice trailing off to a whisper.

All Rose could do was sit and listen.

Sarah tried to steady her nerves. "Miss Carrie's mama was the one who helped deliver you, Rose. You and your brother—"

Rose jerked forward in the chair. "My brother? What are you talking about, Mama? I never had a brother," she cried. "You mean to tell me I was a twin?"

Sarah nodded, asking her with her eyes to hear it all. "Yes, Rose, you was a twin. There were two of you. Two fine babies."

"What happened? Did he die right away? Why didn't you tell me?"

Sarah continued as if she hadn't heard her questions. "Miss Abigail was smiling when you done come out, Rose. You were the first baby. It was easy to tell right at the first that you were going to be a beautiful girl." She smiled, remembering. Then her smile faded. "I was surprised as anyone when I felt another baby comin'. I was excited, too. Ain't too many twins born 'round here. Then I saw Miss Abigail's face. She weren't smilin' anymore. First I thought my baby be sick or somethin' wrong with him. She didn't say nothin' at all. Just held my baby boy up so's I could see him. I think if she could have got him out of the room without my laying an eye on him, she would have."

"But why, Mama?" Rose felt as if her world was spinning. She knew the truth, but she couldn't bring herself to admit it.

"That baby boy was as white as Miss Carrie. He even had blue eyes peering up at me."

Reality hit Rose like a sledgehammer. "My daddy isn't really my daddy?" she whispered in shocked disbelief. "John isn't my daddy?"

Sarah shook her head, compassion flooding her face. "I'm sorry, Rose."

"You mean Carrie's granddaddy is my daddy?" She shook her head. "I'm half-white?" she asked. Her head was pounding, spinning with the shock of her discovery. Then another thought hit her. "You mean I'm blood-related to Carrie? Why haven't you ever told me?" she cried.

Sarah reached out and took her hand. "I need to tell you the rest of the story." She squeezed her hand and kept talking. "Miss Abigail didn't know what to do. What old Master Cromwell done may have been all right on other plantations, but she knew her husband didn't see eye to eye with his daddy. And the old master had taken real sick right before I had dem babies." She paused again, remembering. "Nobody had seen my babies yet 'cause ever'one was out in the fields. They done decided the best way to keep from having any talk and scandal was to take the white lookin' baby away." Sarah paused again, tears in her eyes. "I got to hold my baby boy once before they took him away. A carriage came rollin' up, and he was gone..."

"My brother is still alive?"

"I don't rightly know. I ain't never seen him again. Never was told where they took him. It was like he weren't never born. They told me I wasn't to tell nobody."

Rose tried to absorb all she was hearing.

Sarah squeezed her hand again and kept talking. "My John knew right away when he got home that somethin' was wrong. He thought somethin' was wrong with you. He held you so tender, so proud to know he had a daughter." She shook her head. "I couldn't hardly stand it. I couldn't keep the tears from pouring down my face. Well, John kept after me till I told him." Once again there were tears on her face. "I couldn't stand losing another baby, not after my babies got killed in Africa. I didn't rightly care who y'alls daddy was. I was yo' mama!"

Rose's heart wrenched. She reached out and took hold of her mama's other hand. She was shocked at how cold it was. "Mama..."

Sarah shook her head. "I ain't told you all the story yet. John was mad clear through. All he wanted to do was kill the old master. Carrie's daddy came down to the quarters when he was rantin' and ravin' in the cabin. Came right in without our even knowin' he was out there," she said. "Marse Cromwell be a good man, Rose, but he was in a right sticky place. He understood how my John felt, but he had to take care of his daddy, too. He told us he was mighty sorry for what his daddy had done. Said he wished he could go back and undo it." Sarah smiled wistfully. "Don't all of us have things we wish we could go back and undo?"

"Was that why Daddy was sold?" Rose asked. "He'll always be my daddy," she added fiercely, her mind full of the last precious days they had shared together before he died.

"You right, Rose. John was your daddy. He loved you as much as he could have loved any baby of his own," she declared with pride. "When Marse Cromwell told him he would have to go away because he couldn't risk any trouble, all John could think about was me and you. He told Marse Cromwell he would go away, and he promised he wouldn't never say nothing about there being another baby, but only if the Marse promised to keep me and you here. Only if he promised to take good care of us."

"Daddy said that to Marse Cromwell?" Rose whispered. She knew Thomas Cromwell was kind, but she also knew he felt like slaves were inferior people, certainly not in any place to make demands of him.

Sarah nodded. "Marse Cromwell promised that day. He said he would take good care of us and make sure you'd grow up workin' in the big house so's you didn't have to be a field hand. But I had to promise never to tell you. My John was sold the very next day."

Rose stared at her. "And you had no idea where he was for eighteen years? Didn't that tear your heart out?" She shuddered at the idea of being separated from Moses. It would be like part of her being ripped away.

Sarah nodded. "I didn't want John to go away. I told him we could go on the auction block together. I wanted us all to be a family. He wouldn't hear nothin' of it. Said he weren't going to take no chance of being split up and not knowing whether we were all right. He said he trusted Marse Cromwell to keep his word. And he did."

Rose's head was spinning from the revelations that had just been told her. Shaking her head in disbelief, she asked the only question she could think of. "Why are you telling me now, Mama? Why now after all these years?"

Sarah shrugged. "I done kept that secret for as long as it needed to be kept. I don't know how long I'm going to keep on living, and that secret didn't need to follow me to the grave. I reckoned a long time ago that you had the right to know the truth 'bout where you come from. Why, you could maybe have a baby that come out lookin' white. What would you have done if that happened? What would Moses have thought?" Abruptly she changed the subject. "Your Moses be a good man, Rose. He be like my John. He loves you with that burnin' kind of love. He'll take good care of you."

Rose nodded absently, still trying to absorb all she had learned. Finally she spoke. "Thank you, Mama. Thank you for telling me."

Sarah nodded and squeezed her hands again. "You need some time to think through everythin' I told you. I love you, Rose girl. You always remember that no matter how you got here, you had a mama and daddy who loved you with all their hearts—-who would do anything in the world for you."

Rose nodded, tears welling up in her eyes.

"You need to go spend some time thinkin'," Sarah said softly. "I'm tired. I think I'll lie down for a little while."

Rose leaned down to give her a kiss and walked slowly out the cabin door. All she could think was that she had to find Moses.

Carrie had been riding for over an hour, so deep in thought she hardly knew where she was. Granite, seeming to sense her mood, was content to walk along, his tail swishing constantly at the flies buzzing around his body. Every now and again his head would bob sharply in protest against an invading marauder biting his neck, and Carrie would reach out to brush it away.

A sudden shout caused both of them to lift their heads at the same time. In the distance, she saw Moses working with a group of the field hands. He was beckoning her over. She didn't really want to be disturbed, but she couldn't pretend she hadn't heard him. She turned and headed Granite toward him.

"Thought you might like to see this," Moses said with a wide grin, standing back and waving his arm toward the field.

"What?" Carrie asked in a bewildered voice as she looked out over the brown field. Then she leaned from her saddle to look closer. "Look at that!" she exclaimed, leaping easily from the saddle. In a moment, she was down on her knees, unmindful of the dirt. "Our first bean plants," she said joyfully. She stood and looked down the seemingly endless rows of tiny sprouts that had just pushed their heads up to welcome the sun. "Think of all the people these will feed."

Moses nodded. "I knew you'd want to see them. We can hope for a long summer and a mild fall. These beans went in mighty late, but they still have time to bear a lot of food."

Carrie's head shot up suddenly. "What did you say?"

Moses looked confused. "What do you mean?"

"The last thing you said about the beans. What was it?"

Moses looked at her as if he was afraid the hot sun had gotten to her. "I said these beans went in mighty late, but they still have time to bear a lot of food."

Carrie smiled and nodded. "Exactly!"

Moses waited a moment and then asked carefully, "Am I missing something here, Carrie?"

Carrie laughed and shook her head. "I'm sorry, Moses. I know I'm not making much sense. It was something I've been thinking about. I had lunch with Sarah today, and she said a lot of things that got me to thinking. I've been afraid that by the time I get off this plantation it will be too late to make much difference in the world."

"You're not but nineteen years old, Carrie."

"I know," she said. "But it seems like I'll be here forever, just running this plantation. I can do everything I can now to make my dream come true, but I had been wondering what I'll do if it's too late. You gave me the answer I needed."

"I did?"

"Yes. Don't you see? Even if I get started late, there will still be time for me to bear a lot of fruit, just like these plants can still feed a lot of people. Who cares whether they went in when most people plant crops. The people who eat this food will be glad they went in at all."

Moses nodded, appreciation lighting his face. "That goes for me, too, I reckon. There will still be things for me to do when I leave this plantation."

Silence fell between them as they stared down the long, even rows.

"Moses!"

Both Carrie and Moses heard Rose's voice long before she appeared on her mare around the curve in the road. Every muscle in Moses' body tensed. Carrie knew he was imagining trouble. She certainly was.

Rose rode up beside them, her eyes wide and her breathing irregular. "Carrie. I didn't know I would find you out here."

Carrie could hear in her voice that she was disappointed to see her. Why? She watched as her friend regained control and slid from the saddle to stand beside them.

"I thought I would come out here to say hello and to see how things are going," she said casually.

Carrie knew she was lying but had no idea why. Had she done something to upset her? She tried to hide her hurt feelings by climbing easily into her saddle and smiling down at the couple. "I need to be getting back to the house. I'll see you later." She turned and cantered off, her mind sifting through the possibilities of what could have made the shutters go down over Rose's eyes.

She was still searching for a reason when she rode past the road leading down to the quarters. She stopped and wheeled Granite around, eager to tell Sarah she had come to some conclusions about the talk they had. She wanted to thank her again for the challenge to think things through.

She rode slowly, taking deep breaths of the late afternoon air. The day was finally starting to cool off, especially in the shade of the tall oaks spreading their canopy over the dusty road. Late-blooming honeysuckle lent a sweet perfume to the heavy air.

The door to Sarah's cabin was open as usual when she rode into the quarters' clearing, but she was surprised when Sarah didn't step to the door to meet her. Maybe she was still resting. Carrie tied Granite's reins to the hitching post and walked over to the open door.

And stopped. She knew instantly.

"Carrie!"

She vaguely heard Rose's voice in the distance, but she didn't turn around. She was held rooted to the tiny step.

"Carrie, I'm sorry I was so silly back there. I'm sorry if I hurt your feelings. I'm glad you're here, though. I want us to talk with my mama." Rose was speaking as she tied up her mare, but suddenly she slowed, as if realizing her friend hadn't even acknowledged her presence. "Carrie?" Her voice grew sharp. "What is it? What's wrong?"

She was beside her then, peering into the tiny cabin. "Mama!" She ran inside and fell to her knees next to the still body. Sarah was sitting in the rocking chair by the window. "Mama..." Rose's voice fell off into soft sobbing as she laid her head on the white-clad lap. "*Mama...*"

Moses appeared on the steps next to Carrie.

She turned and looked up into his anxious face. "She's gone, Moses. Sarah has gone to be with John. She's gone home."

Chapter Sixteen

"My mama may have been a slave, but she was the freest person I ever knew," Rose murmured quietly.

Carrie nodded and slipped her arm around her friend's waist.

Sarah had been gone for over a week. Still, Rose liked to come out to the grave. She could remember her mama's words best when she was standing beside her grave. Every evening when the sun slipped below the horizon, she walked out to gaze down at the flower-draped wooden cross and remember.

"My mama left behind so much."

"I think maybe your mama lived life more than anyone I ever knew," Carrie responded. "She told me one time that it wasn't the material things in life that mattered. She wouldn't be able to take them with her anyway. She said the only thing that counted was how much love you left behind." She smiled. "Your mama left behind an awful lot of love."

"Your mama loved everyone," Moses said in his deep voice.

Rose edged closer to his towering body. The need for his physical presence had intensified since her mama had died so unexpectedly. It was only when she could feel him that she was sure he was there. She tried to stay busy during the days, but the grief over her mama was still too fresh.

Moses put his arm around her, and the three stood together quietly. They didn't speak again until the sun had flung its last golden ray and slipped behind a purple bank of clouds.

Moses was the one to break the silence. "I won't never forget the first time I saw her. I thought she was an angel. I'd just been sold on the block and split from my family. I wasn't nothing but a mess of anger and hurt. Your mama knew that. Her love that first night made those feelings a little easier to bear. Then she taught me how to let go of all that hate and hurt. I don't know what I would be without her."

Carrie nodded, remembering too. "Sarah has been like a mama to me all my life. She always knew what I was feeling. She was smart enough not to give me many answers. She just asked a lot of questions and let me figure things out. She trusted me to make the best decisions." Tears filled her eyes. "I'm going to miss her so much."

Once again, Rose felt the tears pouring down her cheeks. She didn't try to stop them. Her mama had taught her that trying to control grief was like trying to dam up a river. You could hold it back for a while, but sooner or later it was going to be stronger than your control. When it broke, the dam would do a lot more damage than if you let it flow natural like. She would cry for as long as she needed to, and somewhere in the future, time would work its magic and the hurting wouldn't be so bad. "I had the very best mama in the whole world," she whispered through her tears. "She'll be right in the front of my heart for as long as I live."

Finally, she forced a smile. "I'm ready to go back now. Thank y'all for coming with me."

When they reached the edge of the quarters, Rose and Moses turned toward their cabin.

"I'd like you to come to the house for a while if you would please," Carrie said.

Rose looked at her. "Got something on your mind?"

Carrie looked up from the sheet of paper she was holding in her hand. Moses finished lighting the lantern and sat back down on the loveseat beside his wife. Carrie settled in the wingback chair across from them. "I got a letter from my father today," she announced.

"Bad news?" Rose asked.

Carrie shrugged. "It could be. I really saw it more as a sign than anything else."

"A sign?" Moses asked.

Carrie nodded. "My father filled me in on what's going on. I told him I didn't ever want to feel so detached from current events again. It's all right being here on the plantation, but I don't like feeling so separate from the rest of the world. He's been writing me letters every few days to keep me abreast." She raised the paper, looked for her place, and began to read.

> *Our office received information today about one of the new bills to pass the House of the Northern Congress. We do all we can to stay in touch with Union politics. They are calling it the Crittenden Bill. Basically, it asserts that the war has been forced on the country by Southern malcontents. It also says the federal government's only aim in pressing on toward an assured final victory is to 'Preserve the Union with all the dignity, equality, and rights of the several states unimpaired.'*

Carrie looked up as she got to the end of the first page.

"What's all that really saying?" Moses asked.

Carrie frowned. "What it's saying is that the war the Union is fighting is being fought in such a way so as not to affect the institution of slavery in the slightest degree."

"Then what's the South fighting this war for?" Moses asked. "I thought they were convinced the North was going to abolish slavery. I thought that's what they were fighting about."

"The South doesn't believe them," Carrie responded. "Politicians in the North are trying to duck away from the issue in hopes of ending the rebellion soon, but no one down here is buying it. Here..." Quickly, she scanned the letter and picked up her place again.

> *Only two of their senators had enough guts to be honest about what they really believe. One was Congressman Riddle from Ohio. I, at least, admire his honesty. When someone tried to get him to change his vote, he let them have it. Told them*

slavery was doomed to die, and every sensible man knew it. He told them when it died it would not be simply voted out of existence—it would be abolished by convulsion, fire and blood. He believes the convulsion is the war we are in now. He wants the war recognized as the thing that will kill slavery.

Like I said, I can admire the man's honesty, but I pity his naiveté. The South will fight to the bitter end to protect our rights. Sooner or later, the rest of the Northern politicians will come out of the closet and admit their real intent. Not that it matters. We down in the South have seen the truth for a long time.

Carrie put the paper down.

Rose was the first to speak. "I thought the North wanted to see slavery end?"

"A lot of people do," Carrie said, "but I think right now their main focus is trying to restore the Union. I still don't think people up there realize how sacred the institution of slavery is down here and how afraid people are of what will happen if it ends... Or how determined the South is to fight what they perceive as forced control."

She shook her head then and leaned forward in her chair. "I didn't read that letter so that we could discuss politics."

"I didn't figure you did," Moses said with an easy smile, his massive frame settling back in his chair. "What's going on inside that head of yours?"

"It's time for y'all to escape," she said firmly.

Rose and Moses both bolted upright in shocked surprise, but Carrie didn't give them time to say anything. "I've thought it all through. I don't think this war is over by a long shot, but right now the South seems to be winning. They're already tightening up their control of the slaves, and they've brought on more militia to track down runaways. It's only going to get worse, especially if they win." She paused. "If the North wins, there is no assurance things will be any better. If they're truly not going to abolish slavery, things might get worse for blacks if the North tries to appease the South." She shook her head. "I think we need to move now to get you two to freedom."

Moses was the first to break the shocked silence. "How are you going to manage things around here if we leave?"

Carrie had thought about that, too. "That doesn't really matter. That is my problem." Rose opened her mouth to interrupt, but Carrie continued on. "My family has stolen your freedom for too long. What is important is that you be free. Right now, things are going our way here, but sooner or later, my father is going to find out the truth. I have no idea what will happen then. We can find a way to get you out of here now. I'm not so sure about later."

Rose finally broke in. "We can't leave you here alone, Carrie. We *won't* leave you here alone. Our time will come."

Carrie gazed at her friend, recognizing the determined tone in her voice. It meant she was settling in on a decision and wouldn't be moved. Carrie sighed, picked up the letter, and began to read again.

The governor is calling for more men to help build the defenses for the city. He is asking all slave owners to send slaves to help in the effort. He has given us until the middle of October to finish the harvest, and then he wants them sent. Pick five that you think would perform the work best, but make sure you send Moses. His strength and size would be a welcome addition to the work force here.

Silence filled the room when she finished. She looked up at her friends' shocked faces and smiled sadly. "You see, it really is the best time."

Rose sat quietly, tears pouring down her face.

Carrie leaned forward to take her hand. "I thought you would be excited," she said, confused. "You always told me you would never leave the plantation till your mama was gone. Sarah is safe with John now. There is nothing to keep you here. It's time for you to follow your dreams."

Rose brushed at her tears and tried to smile.

"I think it's time to tell her," Moses said, looking at Rose with a strange expression.

"Time to tell me what?"

"It's only fair, Rose. How would you feel if you were in her place?"

Carrie was suddenly alarmed. "What do I need to know?" she asked in a voice made sharp with anxiety.

Rose nodded at Moses and turned to Carrie. "My mama told me something before she died. I guess she knew her time was almost up. I was coming out to talk to Moses about it when I found y'all together in the field, but at that moment, I needed to talk to just him."

"That's why you weren't too happy to see me," Carrie said.

"I came back to apologize. I think I said something, but you didn't hear me. Then I saw my mama..."

Carrie nodded. "I understand."

"No, you don't. You need to know what she told me."

"I'm listening."

Rose took a deep breath and looked her straight in the eye. "My real daddy is your granddaddy."

Carrie slumped back against the cushion of the chair. It never even crossed her mind to wonder if Rose was lying. She knew better. "Maybe you should tell me the whole story," she said.

Piece by piece, broken by tears on both their parts, the story tumbled out. The room darkened, the lantern casting longer shadows on the walls, as they talked.

Finally, Carrie turned her head to gaze out the window. A moon was hanging, full and lush on the horizon. From where she sat, the golden orb seemed to perch right on top of the trees. She needed time to absorb all Rose had told her.

After several long minutes, she turned her head back to look at them. "The woman who has been my slave all these years is really my half-aunt?"

Rose stared at her. "I guess I never really thought of it like that," she murmured.

A faint smile formed on Carrie's lips. "I'd go back and undo all of it if I could," she said, "but I can't. Your mama always told me that if you can't change a situation, you might as well look for the good things in it and do the best you can with it." Her eyes filled with tears.

"What are you crying for?" Rose asked.

Carrie shook her head. "Your mama should have hated me." Tears spilled over and poured down her cheeks. "Sarah should have hated me," she repeated. "Every time she looked at me, she had to remember that it was my granddaddy who made her lose her little boy and her husband. How could she look at me? How could she love me?"

Rose leaned forward and took her hands. "You know my mama wasn't like that. She didn't judge people by things they couldn't help. She took them as they came and loved them for who they were."

Carrie nodded and wiped away the tears, forcing a tremulous smile. A new thought struck her. "We really are blood-related. All those years we thought we were like sisters... We really were related."

Rose nodded. "Yes. Now you see why we can't leave right now."

"No," Carrie said, standing up to make her point more firmly. "Now I see even more clearly that you *must* leave soon. Don't you see?" she said, waving her hands and speaking intensely. "The Cromwells have done nothing but rip your family's dreams away from them. It's time for that to stop. I can't bring back all the lost years with your daddy. I can't find your little brother for you. I *can* give you your freedom. I can make sure you and Moses are never separated by the auction block or an owner's whim." She stopped, looking at them beseechingly. "We don't know when it might be too late. I want to do this for you while I can."

Moses leaned over and took Rose's hand. "I think Carrie is right, Rose."

Rose shook her head. "She's the only family I have left," she said in a low voice full of tears. "The only blood family. How can I leave now? Now that I know?"

Suddenly, Carrie gasped and sat up straighter.

Rose looked at her. "What's that strange look on your face, Carrie Cromwell?"

Carrie jumped up from her chair and headed out of the room. "Come with me." She turned down the hall into her father's office. "I said I didn't have a way to bring your baby brother back, but I may have been wrong."

Rose and Moses looked at her blankly.

Carrie laughed. "Oh, I know I can't bring him back, but we might be able to find him. I was able to find your daddy after all those years."

Suddenly Rose understood. "The records! They might tell where my twin brother was sold and who bought him."

Carrie nodded, already opening drawers and hauling out the huge books her father had been keeping for as long as he had the plantation. There were more books that went back to the very first slave ever bought by her grandfather. As the three friends begin to pore over the books, Carrie's mind was spinning. Now she understood why there had never been much talk about her grandfather—how different her father was from him. That must be why Thomas had always been willing to understand her and accept her, even when her mother was ready to despair of her. He had at one time been where she was.

She blinked away tears as she flipped pages looking for the information they sought. How hard it must have been for her father to sell John and the little baby. She knew it went against everything he believed about taking good care of his slaves, but he had done it to protect a man he probably never understood. Her father suddenly became more human to her than he had ever been.

The chimes on the clock were striking midnight when Rose finally looked up from the book she was poring over. "I found it," she whispered in an awed voice.

Carrie and Moses leaned forward eagerly.

Rose's voice was low and hushed. "He was only one day old when he was sold. They got two hundred dollars for him." She paused, trying to control her voice. "A man by the name of Walker bought him. Came and got him and took him away."

"Where was Walker from?" Carrie asked. "Is there an address there? Any more information?"

Rose shook her head, looking disappointed. "A name's not very much to go on," she said.

Carrie sat quietly, not wanting to admit Rose was right. There must be a hundred Walkers in the Richmond area. How would they go about finding the one who had adopted an infant nineteen years ago?

Rose put down the book with a heavy sigh. "I didn't really think we would find him."

Carrie reached for the book and began to flip pages absently. She was surprised when a single envelope fell out. Her father kept his correspondence somewhere else. What was this doing in there? More for something to do while she tried to figure out how to make Rose feel better, she opened the envelope and pulled out the single sheet.

Suddenly she gasped. "Listen to this."

> *Dear Mr. Cromwell,*
>
> *I have no idea that you will wish to know what became of the tiny baby you sold three months ago, but I felt the need to write and tell you anyhow. Maybe someday someone will want to know. The little mulatto baby was sold by you to a man named Walker. He took it back to his plantation, planning on having a slave woman take it as her son, thus adding to his number. However, his wife would have nothing of it, saying she didn't want a white baby on her plantation. Said it would start bad stories. She also felt sorry for the wee thing.*
>
> *Mrs. Walker brought the baby to me. Actually, to the steps of my orphanage. Little Marsh has become a true joy to us here. He is being adopted tomorrow by a family who knows nothing of his black heritage. They are thrilled to be taking home their blond-haired, blue-eyed baby boy. I am confident they will give him a good home.*
>
> *Sincerely,*
> *Margaret Cramer*

Rose stared at Carrie, her eyes wide with disbelief. "My twin brother was raised in a white family?"

"Evidently. It will take some time, but we may be able to track down the family that adopted him."

"I ain't so sure that's a good idea," Moses said.

"Why not?" Rose asked.

"Think about it. Somewhere out there is a man who has been raised in the white world all his life. What's he going to think when a black woman comes and tells him she's his twin sister?"

"I see what you mean." Rose's face twisted with sadness and frustration.

Carrie felt the tears well in her eyes again. "I'm sorry. I should have thought of that. All I did was build your hopes up," she said remorsefully.

Rose shook her head. "Someday, when the world isn't so crazy, I'm going to find my brother. He may not want to have anything to do with me, but he's at least going to hear the truth about where he came from. I'm going to tell him he had a mama who loved him with all her heart. Whether he believes it or not is up to him." Her smile this time was genuine. "I'm glad I know what happened to him. May I have that letter, Carrie? Someday I'll use that information."

Moses spoke again. "We need to talk about the letter Carrie got from her daddy tonight. I don't intend to go work on defenses for Richmond."

"Of course not," Rose said calmly. "We'll have to escape before then."

Carrie gave a huge sigh of relief and sagged back against her chair. "Finally. What changed your mind?"

Rose shrugged. "I for sure won't be able to find my brother if I'm a slave. As a free person, I'll have more of a chance."

"You'll be nothing but a runaway around here," Moses reminded her.

"For a while," Rose agreed. "But that Mr. Riddle from Ohio was right. Slavery is doomed to die. Every sensible person knows it. God isn't going to continue to let it go on. When that time comes, I'll come back and find my brother. And I'll spend time with my niece," she said with a grin.

Laughter rang through the house for a long while, and then the three settled down to business.

It was very late when Carrie crawled into bed, but sleep wouldn't come. Finally, she got up and pulled her chair next to the window so she could catch the slight breeze wafting in. Her heart felt like it had been rolled on by several heavy wagons. The last week had been an endless assault on her emotions.

Losing Sarah... Finding out the truth about her grandfather... Realizing Rose truly was related to her... Making the decision it was time for Rose and Moses to leave...

She was content with her decision, but seldom had her heart felt so heavy. For a brief moment, she regretted her new position on slavery. It was taking from her everything she loved. First, she had turned down Robert's proposal of marriage, even though she was sure he would be the only man who would ever capture her heart. Now, she was about to lose her best friends.

So that they can have the freedom they so richly deserve, her heart reminded her. Carrie laid her head back on the chair with a sigh. She wouldn't undo any of her decisions, but she sure wished they didn't have to hurt so much.

She didn't know how long she sat there, quietly rocking, before peace began to steal into her heart. It was up to her to make the right decisions, and it was up to God to be responsible for the results. She saw anew that that was what trusting God was all about. You had to leave the results to him and trust he would do what was best.

A voice floated in on the breeze. *Do you believe I love you?*

Carrie stilled as the question poured into her soul. Wasn't that what it was all about? If she believed God loved her, couldn't she also believe God had only the best in mind for her, no matter how rocky and twisted the path to get there might be?

Carrie laid her head back against the chair and finally slept.

Chapter Seventeen

Thomas Cromwell spread open his paper and settled back into his favorite chair. He lay back against its firm softness for several moments before he lifted his head to begin reading. It had been a long day, and he was tired.

As always, when his body relaxed, his mind flew to Cromwell Plantation. How he missed the wide open spaces, the smell of the raw earth. Usually at this time the tobacco would be harvested, its pungent aroma filling the air. He could almost hear the chop of the huge knives as the field hands took down stalk after stalk. He loved the month of September. The starkness of winter was still far away, but the hot grip of summer was loosening, and the first leaves were twirling gracefully down to start their yearly carpet.

The memories continued to flood his mind, until he saw a picture of Abigail in her yellow dressing gown, running the brush through her blond hair. He frowned and sat up. He missed the plantation, but he wasn't ready to go back. His heart still ached when he thought of his beloved wife. Maybe someday he could think of her without a sharp pain running through every part of him. When that happened he would go back, but for now he was thankful for his job in the government. It kept his mind occupied and kept the long nights from being endless.

He picked up the paper again. It wasn't often that he got home this early. There was a stack of newspapers waiting for him to go through, and then he would write a letter to Carrie.

A sudden knock at the door several minutes later caused him to look up with a frown. He wasn't expecting any visitors. Was he to be called back to the Capitol? He laid down his paper, sighing impatiently. He could hear Micah's even footsteps moving toward the door, then, "Is Mr. Cromwell in?"

Thomas jumped up from his chair and hurried to the entryway. "Robert Borden! Come in. Come in."

Robert smiled and moved inside. "I hope I'm not bothering you, Thomas. I'm only here for the day, and when I found myself with some free time, I decided to take my chance and come."

Thomas smiled and led the way into the parlor. "Of course you're not a bother. We've been eager for news of you. It's wonderful to see you." He sat down and waved his hand toward an empty chair. "Make yourself at home." Then he spoke to Micah, who had appeared at the door. "We'd like cold lemonade and some of the cookies that were made earlier." Micah bowed slightly and left the room. Thomas turned back to his guest. "What brings you to Richmond?"

"General Johnston asked me to come down and confer with General Lee about some matters."

Thomas raised his eyebrows. "Sounds as though you're becoming rather important."

Robert shrugged. "I welcomed the opportunity to do something different. The Battle of Bull Run was six weeks ago, and yet, still we sit there—an army doing nothing. The most stimulating thing I've done in the last month was take part in a scouting party that went to check things out on the Potomac. The most exciting thing I saw was the unfinished dome of the Washington Capitol."

"I understand the generals are becoming quite impatient."

Robert nodded. "You understand right. That's why I'm here. General Johnston and General Beauregard plan on meeting with President Davis in a couple of weeks. I'm here to gather information and lay groundwork."

"It sounds as if this meeting will be rather crucial," Thomas observed.

"It will." Robert paused. "May I speak frankly?"

Thomas eyed him for a moment and then walked over to close the heavy doors to the parlor. "Not a word you say will leave this room."

"Thank you. I always find talking to you helpful." Robert settled back in his chair and began. "Everyone is getting impatient. General Beauregard proposed back in early August that we move forward and press an attack in hopes of forcing the Yankees into fighting a battle out in the open, outside the Washington lines. General Johnston decided we weren't strong enough to force such a confrontation and turned down the idea."

Thomas nodded. "I think that was wise."

"Maybe," Robert said. "We might have had the advantage then with their army so demoralized by the recent defeat." He shrugged. "It's too late to do it over, but now *both* men are eager to do something. They agree it is time to strike a blow rather than simply sit passively waiting to see what the Yankees might do."

"What do you think?" Thomas asked, leaning forward to gaze at Robert. The young man didn't have much military experience, but he was obviously well thought of if he had been granted this much information.

"I agree with the generals," Robert said. "Our intelligence tells us the Federal Army in front of Washington is growing much faster than our own. If there is going to be a Confederate offensive, I believe it must happen quickly. Decisive action before the winter is important to us."

Thomas listened thoughtfully. There had been much talk around the capital about making another move. "What will it take for it to be successful?"

Robert was ready with an answer. "The army must be strongly reinforced. They want Davis to double its size to sixty thousand men."

"And where do you propose they come from?"

"It can be done if we arm all of our new recruits, as well as pull in troops from every point in the South that is not actually under attack." Robert's voice grew excited. "With an army like that, we could cross the Potomac, bring on a battle northwest of Washington, and win a victory that would establish our independence."

Thomas looked at him, quietly mulling over Robert's words.

Robert spoke again. "It is my opinion, Thomas, that success here at this time saves everything. But I am afraid there will be disastrous results if we remain inactive throughout the winter."

Thomas shook his head. "I agree with you in principle, but I'm not sure it's possible in practicality."

"Why not?"

Thomas thought long and hard before he answered, all the while knowing he would have no final say in the decision. President Davis and his cabinet would make the final decision. "It's just my opinion of course, but I see several problems with your plan. I agree with you that there are plenty of recruits to be found. More men are signing up every day." He paused. "Our problem is weapons. There simply aren't enough to meet the need. They might come up with thirty thousand more men, but they won't find rifles to put in their hands."

"We need to speed things up," Robert said impatiently.

Thomas laughed. "Spoken like a true military man. But surely you haven't been away from politics so long as to have forgotten the roadblocks they are facing. Everything is new. The president is still trying to create order out of chaos. The demands have been made for the weapons, but Southern manufacturing facilities are too inadequate to meet the need. They're trying, but it's just too slow."

"What about overseas?"

Thomas shrugged. "The contracts have been placed, but the results have been negligible so far. I think Europe is still trying to figure out where they stand on all this, even though we have hopes they will recognize us as a nation soon. In the meantime, the blockade along the coast is starting to cause us some problems."

Robert shook his head in frustration.

Thomas picked up the paper he had been reading earlier. "You're not alone in your frustration. Let me read you something from the *Richmond Examiner*. '*The idea of waiting for blows instead of inflicting them is altogether unsuited to the genius of our people.*'"

Robert nodded. "They're right."

"It's also impossible to inflict those blows without weapons," Thomas observed. "There is another problem," he added. He didn't wait for Robert to ask what. "Your generals feel justified in demanding we concentrate our military strength at the point of greatest danger."

"Surely you agree with that, Thomas," Robert protested.

"Yes, I do," Thomas agreed readily. "It's not me you need to worry about. And it's not really the government. I think they agree with your generals, however, in many ways their hands are tied."

"How?"

Thomas smiled at his belligerent tone. "Our Confederacy is still as much an association of independent and equal states as it is a nation. We have governors who insist proper garrisons be maintained in places not under attack because the situation could change at any time. They are quite simply not willing to send their men. As frustrating as it is, their wishes must be heeded."

"I suppose President Davis has to exercise his authority within the limits of the system."

Thomas nodded. "A system where the wishes of the separate states are all but sacrosanct." He continued in a somber voice. "I don't see that Virginia could have made any decision other than the one she did, but I'm afraid the new Confederate government opted to wage war before they had counted the cost."

Silence fell on the two men as they contemplated the future. Thomas was deeply troubled, and his conversation with Robert had only intensified his concern. This could not just be a war to put down rebellion. Its elements were too violent. Men who had never learned to endure wrongs with patience had become convinced wrongs were being done to them. People eternally eager to dedicate themselves had grown to feel there were noble causes to be served. And there were enemies to be hurt in a land where the only rule about a blow struck in anger was that it must be struck with all the strength one had. This was a war in which anything could happen.

In spite of the glorious victories that had marked the first summer of the war, there was a dawning realization that all was not going well. The blockade was beginning to hurt. Impatient recruits were impotent without weapons. The Southern coast lay alarmingly exposed to the gathering Federal fleets. Thomas knew the North was settling down for a long pull. The offensives that lay ahead would mostly likely be conducted by the Union. The more he learned, the less confident he was that the North could be beaten back. To the average Southerner, the war had hardly begun, but he could see ominous signs in the still darkening sky. Time was passing. He sensed it was working for the wrong side.

Robert was the first to rouse himself from the contemplative silence that had cloaked the room. "How is Carrie?" he asked quietly. He had told himself on the way to Thomas' house that he wasn't going to ask. He had to learn to let her go. But once in the presence of her father, he could no more keep from asking than he could keep from breathing.

Thomas smiled. "I got a letter from her last week. She is doing fine." He shook his head and laughed. "I don't think she'll ever cease to astound me. Fifty acres of my tobacco have been plowed under and will soon be producing food for the city. She would have done more if there had been more time."

Robert listened in amazement as Thomas told him of Carrie's campaign to bring fresh food to the city— especially to the soldiers who were still convalescing and needed the nutrients.

"She cares very much about the wounded soldiers," Thomas said. "I think she got to see almost all of them when she was searching the city for you."

"When she did what?" Robert exclaimed.

Thomas nodded. "I wrote her and requested she come to Richmond during the battle. She humored her father, but then she refused to leave until she had satisfied herself you were not lying wounded in the city somewhere."

"My name wasn't on the wounded list," Robert said, thoroughly amazed at Carrie's concern, until he remembered her running forward to press a lock of her hair into his hand before he pulled out for the front.

Thomas nodded. "I know. That wasn't good enough for her. She insisted some of the soldiers could have fallen through the cracks. It wasn't until she found Hobbs that she was satisfied you were all right."

Robert shook his head again in amazement. "Carrie found Hobbs?"

"He was being nursed by a lady who had taken in two other soldiers. He left for the front again last week. He told her about how you saved his life. It was a brave thing to do," Thomas said warmly.

Robert shrugged his shoulders, embarrassed. "Anyone would have done it."

"I don't think so," Thomas observed.

Robert was glad to hear Hobbs was all right, but his thoughts were focused on the reality that Carrie cared so much. He could envision her going through the city, determined in her quest. Suddenly his frustration swept over him, and he almost groaned out loud. He wished this war would end. Maybe then he and Carrie could spend enough time together to work out their differences. But when he remembered the finality with which she had turned down his proposal, he knew they were worlds apart on an issue he couldn't imagine changing his mind about.

"There's something else you need to know, Robert," Thomas said, breaking into his thoughts.

Robert looked up, trying to control the frustration on his face. "About Carrie?"

"No. About Matthew."

"Matthew?" Robert asked, confused. "Matthew Justin?"

Thomas nodded. "He is here in the prison."

Robert took a deep breath and settled back against his chair. Was there to be no end to the surprises of this visit? "Matthew was captured at Bull Run?"

"Yes," Thomas said, "but not as a soldier. He was there as a correspondent for his newspaper."

"Can you get me in to see him, Thomas?"

"I thought you had to leave early tomorrow morning?"

"I am supposed to, but I will have to take the next train. I want to see him." Pain shot through him at the idea of his friend in prison. The faces of the Union men during the battle had all blurred into nothing but blue uniforms. It had not even seemed like he was firing at real men. They had simply become the enemy. Now one of the enemy had taken on an identity—the identity of one of his closest friends.

Thomas nodded. "I'll see what I can do. Meet me tomorrow morning at my office. There may not be time to get a letter, but I'll try."

Bright and early the next morning, before most of the city was even stirring, Robert stood outside the gates to the prison, staring up at its imposing walls. In his hand was the letter Thomas had managed to procure him. He knew Thomas had gone way beyond the call of duty to get it for him. He would find a way to pay him back.

The guard who opened the door snapped to attention and was immediately courteous when he saw Robert's uniform. "What can I do for you, Lieutenant?"

"I'm here to see one of the prisoners."

"I'm sorry, sir, the prisoners are not allowed to have visitors."

Silently, Robert handed him the letter. The guard looked at him more closely. "Come in, sir. I will get Lieutenant Todd for you."

Robert followed him into the building, looking around as they walked. He could hear the sounds of men moving around on the floor above him. Occasionally, he would hear a yell, or a bark of laughter.

"Wait here, sir."

Within moments, the guard was back with Lieutenant Todd. Robert had met him during the training days out at the old fairgrounds. "Lieutenant," he said with a smile. "It's good to see you again."

Todd nodded but didn't smile. "You are here to see Matthew Justin?"

"That's correct." Instantly, Robert was on his guard. "He is still here, isn't he?"

"Yes."

Robert held his gaze, waiting for him to continue.

"Who is this man? Why is he so important?"

"What do you mean?"

"None of the officers here have had visitors. This man, this journalist, has had three."

"Three?"

Todd nodded. "First there was that Carrie Cromwell. Then a black girl named Opal came with the same letter from General Winder. Now you. What's going on?" he asked suspiciously.

Robert shook his head. "I don't know. Matthew is a friend of mine."

Todd sneered. "I don't know if I would go around telling people you are friends with one of the enemy. It could be taken in the wrong way. People might wonder where your loyalties lie."

Robert flushed with anger. "No one who knows me will wonder where my loyalties lie, and the rest aren't important enough for me to worry about."

Lieutenant Todd's lips tightened, but he didn't say anything else. "Call Justin," he snapped to the guard, and strode from the hallway. Seconds later, a door slammed in the distance.

"Is he always so pleasant?" Robert asked with a grin.

The guard shrugged, but there was an apologetic look on his smooth face. "I guess the lieutenant don't want nobody questioning *his* loyalty."

"Why would anyone—" Robert stopped, remembering what someone had told him. "He's the president's brother-in-law."

"Yes. He may always feel like he's got something to prove. I can tell you, though, he's Southern through and through."

"I'm sure he is," Robert murmured. He was also quite sure he made an intimidating prison official.

The guard escorted him to a room and told him to wait. Twenty minutes passed before he heard approaching footsteps. He looked up as the door swung open. Matthew was leaner than when Robert had last seen him, but he looked to be in good health. And his blue eyes held the same sparkle.

"Robert Borden," Matthew said with a smile.

"Hello, my friend. Not much of a hotel you picked for your visit here."

"Oh, I don't know. I got me a place on the floor and three meals a day. That's probably more than a lot of people are getting around here."

Robert slapped his friend on the back. He hadn't lost his sense of humor. "It's good to see you, Matthew. Even though these aren't the circumstances I would have picked."

"Me either," Matthew remarked. "I've learned we don't always get to pick our circumstances, though. We just get to deal with them."

Robert nodded, eying him closely. "So how are you dealing with this one? Thomas said he has done all he can to try to obtain your freedom, but no prisoners are being released or exchanged yet."

Matthew shrugged. "Like I said, it's not that bad. I have become close to some of the officers. We find things to talk about. I'm even learning how to cook," he said with a grin. "I'm limited to bacon and biscuits, but even so, my mother would fall over in shock." Then he looked thoughtful. "I'm luckier than most, I guess. Carrie has one of her slaves who is working in Richmond bring me fresh vegetables every few days. I stretch them with the rest of the prisoners as far as I can."

"That sounds like Carrie," Robert murmured.

Matthew nodded. "And I've got lots of time to write. Carrie made sure that Opal brought me plenty of paper."

Matthew stopped talking and the silence stretched between them. Robert cast in his mind for something to say to break the awkwardness. Finally, he reached out his hand and laid it on top of his friend's. "I'm sorry. I'm sorry you're here. I wish I could do something."

"Thank you," Matthew said gruffly, blinking back a suspicious moisture.

Suddenly, the air between them was clear. As they looked at each other, the prison walls and the locked room faded away. Once more, they were college boys going on exploits together. They were young men who confided dreams and hopes to each other.

"This war is ripping friendships and families apart," Matthew said. "I had no idea you would come to see me."

"I would have found a way to get here sooner if I'd known. I just found out last night."

Matthew listened and then looked at him closely. "So you are now a lieutenant in the Confederate Army. How goes it?"

Robert shrugged, unsure of what he could say, even to his friend. How much would loyalty demand Matthew reveal? What if he had a way of imparting information? Robert hated thinking such thoughts, but he couldn't help it. There was too much at stake. He decided to change the subject instead. "I'd rather be at home on my plantation. I think of Oak Meadows daily. I got a letter from my mother a few weeks ago. She is doing the best she can, but things are hard."

Matthew understood what Robert was doing and searched for a safe topic. "I think this war is going to take on a face no one anticipated. Not even the men who authored it."

Robert sighed to himself with relief. The overall picture he was willing to talk about. It was the specifics he felt compelled to remain silent on. He nodded. "There were too many people, on both sides, who thought this war would never happen. Everyone waited for everyone else to back down."

Matthew nodded grimly. "I'm afraid my profession had its hand in bringing things to where they are now. The press was merciless about keeping the heat up. You could hardly read a Northern newspaper without hearing something about '*On to Richmond.*' In the end, I think it propelled both governments into a conflict neither was really ready for."

Robert wanted to protest that the South had overwhelmingly won at Manassas, but honesty kept him silent. He knew how disorganized the battle had been. He knew how many strokes of luck had put men in the right place at the right time. He also knew how hard the North was working now to build up their army to make sure the same thing didn't happen again. He chose ambivalence over a position. "Southern papers played their own part in what happened," he responded.

Robert grew impatient with the verbal game it was necessary for them to play. "Look," he said firmly. "Let's not talk about the war at all. We know it's out there. We know we're both involved. We know we stand on different sides. So be it. There is more to us than this war. Tell me about you. Tell me what you think about when you are locked up in prison."

Matthew smiled. "You're right. We may be a Northerner and a Southerner, but we are something more important than that. We are friends."

The two exchanged a long look of understanding.

"I dream about being free every day," Matthew continued. "I hate being watched all the time. I hate knowing my life has to be lived within these four walls. I miss the feeling of sunshine on my face. I miss the challenge of working. I miss the feeling I might be making a difference with what I do. I miss my friends," he added softly, the pain intense on his face and in his voice. "Every day I do what little I can to make a difference here, but the inactivity kills me."

"I dream, too," Robert replied. "I dream about being back on my plantation. I dream about having nothing more to do than increase the yield of my crops. I dream about smelling fresh earth as it is plowed for the spring crops. I dream about sitting on my porch with a drink in my hand, looking out over the rolling hills. I dream about Carrie being there with me." He knew his voice sounded hopeless when he uttered his last words.

Matthew remained silent.

Robert looked at him. "Carrie told you, didn't she?"

"That she turned down your proposal? Yes. That she still loves you? Yes, she told me that too."

Robert shook his head in frustration. "The whole thing is so ridiculous. We love each other. We should be together." He sighed. "Oh, I know the war would keep us apart right now anyway, but at least our hearts would be united."

Matthew gazed at him for a long moment. "The issue keeping you apart is not ridiculous. It is an issue strong enough to rip a nation apart. The Northern Congress is trying to edge away from it—take it out of the picture in hopes the picture will not be quite so volatile—but in the end, it will all come down to the issue of slavery." Matthew hesitated, as if he wasn't sure he should say more. "It is slavery that is fueling the passions of the South. It's funny, though. The South is fighting for the belief in individual freedom and the right to make your own decisions. At the same time, you are taking freedom from millions of people."

He hurried on before Robert could interrupt. "The North will have to develop the same passion. This is going to be a long war. In order to get men to fight a long war, they have to fight for something they can be passionate about. Men will quickly tire of fighting to hold the country together. They will begin to question why thousands of them are dying. But if you put a human face on it—if you give men a moral principle to fight for—they will fight to the bitter end."

Robert could feel the anger building in him. Matthew's next words caused it to die.

"Carrie has put a human face on the issue of slavery. When she thinks of slavery, she sees the faces of people she loves. She sees the faces of millions of people who have dreams like you and I do. She has faces to build her passion around. To her it is not ridiculous. It is who she is." He paused for a moment. "And she is not willing to sacrifice who she is, even for you."

Robert stared at him for a long moment. He knew his friend was right, and he didn't know what to do about it.

The guard knocked on the door and stuck his head in. "Your time is up, Lieutenant. You will have to leave now."

Robert nodded and stood. Reaching across the table, he clasped Matthew's hand and looked deeply into his eyes. Then he turned and left the room.

Opal watched Robert leave from across the road. Staying back in the shadows, she clutched the plate of biscuits she was holding. She almost hadn't recognized Robert in his Confederate uniform, but then she'd remembered the handsome young man who had visited Carrie several times and even spent Christmas at the plantation. What was he doing here?

Once he was out of sight, she walked quickly across the street. The guard was scowling when he opened the door. Instinctively, she shrank back a little.

He knew what she was there for. "Matthew Justin can't have no more visitors today," he said sharply.

Robert must have been there to see Matthew, she realized. She remembered Carrie saying they were friends and hoped he had just come to visit. Surely no one could have discovered what Matthew was doing.

She held out the plate of biscuits. "Could you please make sure he gets these?" she asked.

The guard scowled but reached for the plate, lifting the edge of the napkin to sniff appreciatively. "He'll get them," he said shortly.

"You're welcome to one of the biscuits, too," Opal ventured.

A smile lit the guard's rough face. "Thank you. They smell better than anything I get around here."

Opal breathed a sigh of relief and began to back away. "I'll be back later today for that plate."

"It'll be here," the guard said, and shut the door.

Opal was smiling as she walked away. She had expected to see Matthew today, but it was okay as long as he got the plate. Mrs. Hamilton had finally told her what she carried every time she went there. Once the men polished off their biscuits, they would open the false bottom of the warming dish and fill it with sheets of

Matthew's writing. The story of the prison and the fate of the men trapped there would be making its way north—along with other coded military information.

Once again, Opal had done her job.

Chapter Eighteen

As the guard escorted Matthew back into the large room crowded with his fellow prisoners, there was a pregnant silence. As soon as the guard's steps faded away, however, a cauldron of good-natured ribbing erupted around him.

"Your girl here to see you again, Matthew?"

"We've all decided to give you the most popular prisoner award, Justin!"

"If we'd known we were going to spend so much time in this hotel, we would have made contacts in the city, too."

Matthew laughed and rubbed his stomach. He was only thinking of one thing. "Is breakfast about ready?" he called. "I'm starving!"

"This visiting can really build up an appetite," another yelled, laughing.

"Am I going to have to fix my own breakfast?" Matthew yelled back. "Who's in charge of the mess around here this morning?"

Finally, Mike Blackman, a colonel from the Massachusetts regiment, stepped forward holding a platter behind his back. "It's ready, Justin. We were just waiting for you."

Matthew stepped forward with a smile on his face. Within seconds, all the men in his prison company were seated at the table, waiting expectantly. There was nothing but blank silence when Blackman proudly laid the platter on the table.

Matthew was the first to speak. "This your first time cooking, Blackman?" He tried to keep his tone casual, but the snickers of the men around him made it hard to keep the laughter out of his voice.

"Well, yes," Blackman responded, immediately defensive. "Something wrong with it?"

Matthew reached forward and picked up the limp, dangling strip of pork. "Did you like this pig so much you were afraid to cook it?"

"He may have liked that piece too much," another one hooted, "but he had something against this little guy." He held out the charred piece of meat to make his point.

Laughter rocked the room while Blackman turned red in the face. "If you're hungry, you'll eat it," he snapped.

Matthew shrugged. "I'll have to think about that. Do you suppose they give sick leave around this place?"

Blackman stared around at all of them and finally joined in their laughter. "So, okay, I'm not much of a cook. I've never cooked anything in my whole life. Sorry, men."

"Well, I guess we can fill up on biscuits." Matthew looked more closely at Blackman. "We've got biscuits, don't we?"

Blackman looked embarrassed. "If you want to call them that. I think maybe I put too much water in with the flour," he admitted. He reached down beside him for the other platter.

Matthew stared at the flat, pancake-like objects, which were rapidly taking on a rock-like appearance. He reached forward and picked one up.

"I'd watch it if I were you, Justin. That thing looks like it could break teeth," one of the men called out.

Matthew cautiously nibbled at one, then held it up and looked at it appraisingly. "Maybe we can mass produce these and use them in the next battle."

The laughter and ribbing continued. All the while, Matthew tried to ignore his growling stomach. All of them had quickly learned that the best way to handle their imprisonment was to laugh at whatever they could. Still, he had already taken in his belt two notches, and he couldn't deny he was hungry.

Suddenly, the door opened again. "Matthew Justin," the guard called out in a sharp voice.

"Yes, sir!" Matthew said, springing to his feet. What was it now? Surely he couldn't have another visitor.

"This was just delivered for you."

The room was silent as Matthew walked forward to take the proffered plate, controlling the wide smile that wanted to spread across his face. "Thank you."

The men around the table started cheering when the room was empty again. "Biscuits! Real, honest-to-God biscuits."

One man raised his hands toward the ceiling. "I don't know what we did to deserve getting you in our company, but I thank God," he said. "You may be what keeps us from starving around here."

Matthew grinned back and set the plate on the table. The fresh-baked aroma delighted his complaining stomach with its promise of gratification, but it also caused waves of homesickness. He could see his mama back in their mountain cabin, standing over the stove, kneading her dough. The tiny cabin would fill with the wonderful aroma, until she would reach into the stove and pull out the soft, fluffy treats. Dabbed with butter and laden with honey, there was not anything better in the world.

Matthew shook his head and reached for a biscuit. Thoughts like this would only make things harder. He had to stay focused on the present and not give up hope for the future. Sooner or later the country would figure out what to do with prisoners of war, and they would realize there was no sense in holding a civilian journalist.

An hour later, Matthew was lying on his spot on the floor, hands clasped behind his head, staring up at the ceiling. A strong odor caused him to turn his head toward one of the other prisoners, who was busy trimming his beard. Matthew had never before grown a beard but was now letting his grow out. All the officers, as was the custom, already sported beards when they arrived in the prison. They were determined to keep them neat.

Colonel Bagley had found a polished piece of tin he was using as his mirror. He had even fabricated a lantern out of a tin food can by cutting one side out and placing a candle inside. Matthew watched as he held a piece of wood over the candle until it was glowing. Once it was hot enough, he pulled it away and held it to the whiskers of his beard, singeing them. The smell was pungent, but he hardly noticed it. It merely mingled with all the other smells of the room—body odors, food, tobacco smoke, and the cologne Congressman Ely had persuaded the guard to purchase for him.

Matthew watched for a few moments and then turned back to finish his inspection of the ceiling. The spider he had been watching for days was almost done building the elaborate web spreading out over his head. Following the industrious little guy's progress had given him something to do.

He was jolted upright by the sound of the door crashing open and a voice shouting, "Fall in!"

"What the..."

Men sprang to attention all around him. Some were slower to move, so surprised were they by the sudden intrusion.

"I said, fall in!" Lieutenant Todd shouted from where he stood at the door.

Matthew hurried to his place in the line and turned to look at the three men accompanying Todd. All but one were holding pistols, as was Todd. The other one gripped a mean-looking bowie knife.

Todd, a fierce scowl on his face, strode along the hastily formed lines, looking the prisoners up and down. A deathly silence gripped the room. All eyes followed the officer as he returned to the front of the room.

"Gentlemen, information has been received that the officers have concealed weapons in this building. I have been ordered to conduct a search." Satisfaction was evident in his voice.

Colonel Bagley was the first to respond. "We have no hidden weapons here. You may search to your heart's content."

Lieutenant Todd sneered. "We have received information to the contrary."

Bagley shrugged. "Go ahead. You will find nothing."

Matthew watched as the four men spread out around the room. Protest and grumblings rose up as they pulled back and turned over bedding. Lieutenant Todd used his sword to pick at clothing as if he were afraid he would be contaminated by touching Yankee belongings. The other men poked through scant personal items lined up on the shelves, paying no heed when they fell to the floor.

One of the men, the rough-looking one with the bowie knife, picked up two papers lying on one of the beds and began to read them.

"That's a letter to my wife. Isn't it bad enough it has to go through the censors?"

The man holding the papers looked up with a sneer. "Bet she's right nice looking, Captain. Too bad she's probably in bed with one of your friends back home."

Matthew leapt forward just as the captain lunged for the man. "He's not worth it. Let it be," he urged, holding the angry man back. He gave a sigh of relief when the captain straightened and deliberately turned his back on his tormentor.

The other two men with Lieutenant Todd had remained silent up to this point. Finally, one, a Confederate captain, shook his head in disgust. "Gentlemen, I'm sorry. Our information was clearly wrong, and I apologize for this crude man's behavior." He turned to the man he was referring to. "You may leave, detective. We will complete the search without you."

Matthew peered at the offending man more closely. He must have been the one claiming to have the information about hidden weapons.

The detective flushed red. "Whatever you say, *Captain.* I don't cotton to coddling prisoners. Guess you and me feel different about that." He turned to leave the room, catching Lieutenant Todd's eye. He was laughing as he left.

The room fell silent as the search continued. At the end of a half hour, the only weapons found were several penknives.

Matthew almost smiled at the bitter disappointment on Todd's face. He had no use for the Confederate officer. He rarely saw him when he was not inebriated. The man's drunken condition seemed to only exacerbate the anger that seethed within him, as if his role in life was to subjugate his prisoners into constant indignity and hardship. Matthew was glad this search had given Todd no satisfaction.

Grumbling, the invading men finally left the room.

Matthew watched the door shut and then sagged against the wall with relief.

The voice beside him was quiet. "That was close."

Matthew nodded. "Fifteen minutes sooner and the game would have been up." He shook his head when he thought about what would have happened to him if his writings had been found. He knew one of the privates in the next building had been killed for sticking his head out of a window. He shuddered as he imagined what they would have done to him.

Slowly, he walked over to the table and picked up the plate Opal had delivered the biscuits on that morning. It had not attracted even a whit of attention. Matthew smiled as he balanced it on his hand. What the Confederates would have given to know the contents of the letters carefully hidden inside the false bottom. Not even all the prisoners knew that Matthew, aided by the light of a single candle, wrote long into the night about their life here, detailing all the officers, as well as the word-for-word comments spoken by the guards outside when they thought no one could hear them. It might not be worth anything, but then, other people might have a different perspective. They had received coded information in the plate requesting that the reports continue, so someone must think the letters had value.

Matthew replaced the plate on the table with a smile. He would call for the guard later that day when things had settled down. He knew Opal would be back for it tomorrow.

All was well.

Chapter Nineteen

Carrie's heart pounded as she climbed the steps to her father's house. Would he believe her story? Or would he see right through her subterfuge? She knew of no other way to accomplish what she needed to. She had to come to Richmond.

Micah answered her knock on the door. "Miss Cromwell!" he said. "I wasn't expecting you." He opened the door wide. "Your father should be home in a few minutes. May I get you something?"

Carrie shook her head. "No, thank you, Micah. And there is absolutely no reason you should have been expecting me. I came to surprise my father. Would you please make sure Sam has a place to sleep? He will be staying here until I'm ready to return home."

"Certainly, Miss Carrie."

Carrie had just finished changing out of her dusty traveling dress when she heard her father's carriage roll up. She took a deep breath, ran down the stairs, and opened the door before he could reach his hand out.

"Carrie!" Her father's voice echoed the surprise etched on his face. "What in the world are you doing here?" His face sharpened with concern. "Is something wrong? Something on the plantation?"

Carrie moved forward to give him a big hug and kiss his cheek. "Nothing is wrong, Father. Everything on the plantation is just fine."

"Then what are you doing here?" Thomas asked. He was obviously confused.

Carrie laughed. "I'm here because I missed you."

Thomas stared at her. "You're here because you missed me?"

Carrie felt a twinge of panic. It would not do for her father to become suspicious. She knew how it must look. She had never come to Richmond like this before. "Can't a girl miss her father? Aren't you glad to see me?" she asked with a slight pout falling on her lips. After her little game in the prison with Lieutenant Todd, she had wondered if she should go into acting. Now, as she watched her father's reaction, she was sure of it.

Thomas instantly became apologetic. "Of course I'm glad to see you. It's a wonderful surprise. I just wasn't expecting it."

Carrie breathed an inward sigh of relief. Another week and she could have come with the first load of produce, but she had been afraid to wait that long. The upcoming October deadline to send Moses and the other slaves to Richmond was scaring her. She had to take action.

Smiling cheerfully, she took her father's arm and walked deeper into the house. "Tell me all about what is going on."

"Of course," Thomas said. "But tell me first, how long are you here for?"

"Only three days."

There was nothing but pleasure in his voice when he responded. "You came all this way for three days?"

Carrie was relieved to see the suspicion gone. She smiled, feeling a pang of remorse as she had a glimpse of how lonely it must be for her father sometimes. She should have thought to come like this before. He had his work to keep him busy, but there were still long nights to endure alone.

"You must accompany me to the dance tomorrow night," Thomas said. "I had thought not to go, but now that I will have the loveliest date there, I wouldn't miss it for the world."

Carrie smiled in delight. "That sounds wonderful! I haven't been to a dance in ages."

"Not since Christmas," Thomas reminded her. "It's high time you had some fun again. Your life on the plantation is too much work. When you were here before, no one was thinking about dances. All eyes and hearts were centered on Manassas. I think you will find the city a much more joyful place. A dance will do you good."

Carrie, in truth, was delighted despite knowing it would be difficult being at a ball without Robert. Her thoughts must have conjured up her father's next words.

"Robert was here two nights ago."

Carrie stared up in surprise. "Here in Richmond?"

"Better than that," Thomas smiled. "He was here in the house. I have gotten more than my share of surprise visitors this week."

"How is he?" Carrie tried to control the eagerness in her voice. From the look on her father's face, she knew she had failed.

"He seems to be doing quite well. We had a good talk. He apparently has become very important to the military, because they sent him down here to confer with General Lee."

Carrie listened, envisioning his handsome face here in the room. She kept waiting for the ache of missing him to go away. Why then was it growing stronger? "I'm not surprised," she murmured.

"He went to visit Matthew as well."

"You got him a pass?"

"Just barely. I don't think General Winder will be willing to do me any more favors. I have stretched my position as far as I can, I'm afraid." He paused and frowned. "I have also heard talk that information is getting out of the prison somehow. There has been some information in Northern newspapers that could have only come from inside. They ordered a crackdown on security just yesterday."

Now it was Carrie's turn to frown. "Will I be able to see Matthew while I'm here? I was hoping to." She hoped his visit with Robert had gone well. She was sure they had been glad to see each other, but had they been able to bridge the gap of the war between them?

Thomas shrugged. "I don't know. All you can do is try."

Carrie was silent as dinner was served. Her thoughts were consumed with Robert. To have missed him by just two days! Slowly, her turbulent thoughts convinced her it was for the best. She would not have been able to concentrate on the job at hand if Robert had been in town. *It was for the best all around,* she told herself. The only way her heart could ever let go was to let more time pass. If she was constantly being reminded of what she had turned away, she was never going to get over him.

Having reached this conclusion, she was able to turn to her father with a natural smile when he asked her a question. The evening passed pleasantly as they talked long into the night.

Carrie watched her father disappear down the road in his carriage and then hurried to find Sam, who was hitching the horses up in back of the house. "I'm ready to go, Sam."

Sam looked at her with mild disapproval. "You shouldn't be comin' back here, Miss Carrie," he muttered. "How that gonna look? You need to wait inside for me to come get you."

Carrie frowned. She knew that was the proper way to do things, but she was in a hurry.

Sam read her expression. "I don't know what you be doin' here, Miss Carrie, but I do know one thing. You didn't just come to see your daddy. If you got some secret you be tryin' to keep, you better be keepin' it the right way."

Carrie nodded. She didn't want to do anything to draw attention to herself. "I'll be inside when you're ready, Sam. I'll meet you around at the front porch."

Sam turned back to his work, and Carrie retreated inside to wait.

It was almost ten o'clock when the carriage pulled up in front of the plain clapboard building just a few blocks from where Opal lived. To her left, Carrie could see the brick walls of the prison that held the captured Yankees. She could also see the maze of tents that had sprung up on Belle Isle to provide housing for the influx of prisoners that had outgrown the tobacco warehouses. She gazed at the tents for a moment and then turned her attention back to the building they had stopped in front of. "Are you sure this is it, Sam? It doesn't look much like a church," she said dubiously.

The only thing that distinguished the single-story building from the other buildings surrounding it, was that it was wearing an old, faded coat of white paint. No similar effort had been made on the others. That it was quite large could not be denied. Carrie was sure these must be old tobacco warehouses, no longer in use now that the brick ones had replaced them. She stepped from the carriage, gazing around her. Would she be able to find Marcus Anthony? What made her think he would be at the church at this hour?

Sam was looking at her with open curiosity on his face. "This be the address we got, Miss Carrie. You say this is supposed to be a church. What we be doin' here?"

"I need to talk with the pastor," Carrie said. She wished she could have come by herself so she wouldn't have to answer any questions, but she had been fairly certain it wouldn't be a good idea for a woman to come down into this part of town alone. As she looked around, she knew she had been right. Sloppily dressed men, both black and white, leaned against railings and porch supports up and down the street. The black men were busy inspecting the ground. It was the white men who were staring at her openly, making her very uncomfortable.

She took a deep breath and turned toward the church. "Wait here, please. I will be out soon." She could feel Sam's protective eyes on her as she walked up to the church and pulled the rope to the bell inside. She could hear its loud clanging, but there were no approaching footsteps to accompany it. Carrie leaned across the porch railing and peered in the window. Through the grime and dust, she could make out row after row of wooden plank benches. A homemade pulpit adorned the front of the building, its only ornament a crudely made cross.

Carrie straightened and pulled the bell rope again. At least she knew she was at the right place. It was most definitely a church.

"Don't look like nobody be there," Sam called helpfully.

Carrie could tell he didn't like bringing her to this part of town. *"Ain't no place for you,"* had been all he muttered when she had given him the address. Now she ignored him, not willing to give up her quest yet. She didn't know where else to look. Had her trip to Richmond been in vain? Impatiently, she pulled the rope again.

"Hello!"

Carrie looked up as she heard the call from down the road. Squinting, she saw a man hurrying toward her. She moved to the edge of the porch and waited. As the man grew closer, a smile lit her face.

"Hello. Are you here to visit the church? Is there something I can do for you?"

Carrie looked up into the kind face she remembered. The warm blue eyes still showed a deep capacity for caring. She was counting on that. "You are Pastor Marcus Anthony, are you not?"

He nodded, his eyes suddenly narrowing. "I know you from somewhere, don't I? You look very familiar."

Carrie nodded. "We met on the street one morning. You pulled me out of what became a rather nasty confrontation between two men."

Pastor Anthony smiled suddenly. "Now I remember. You were on your way to tell one of the soldiers goodbye."

Carrie gasped. "How did you know that?" She knew she hadn't told him her mission that morning.

Pastor Anthony laughed. "I'm used to seeing that look on young women's faces. I trust he made it through the battle all right?"

Carrie nodded. "Yes. Thank you."

"What can I do for you, Miss...?"

"Cromwell. My name is Carrie Cromwell," she said quickly. "May I have a few moments of your time, Pastor Anthony?" She looked around the street. There were too many places for listening ears. "May we go inside?"

"Certainly." He glanced toward the carriage.

"Sam is my driver. He will wait for me."

Pastor Anthony smiled in Sam's direction. "You are welcome to come in for something cold to drink, Sam."

"No, thank you, sir. I reckon I'll be stayin' right here with this here carriage and horses."

Pastor Anthony nodded and led the way into the dim interior of the church. The big, empty building echoed with their footsteps as he led her to a small office in the rear. He waved Carrie to a seat and then sat down behind his scarred desk.

Carrie spoke first. "I'm very glad I found you here today."

"It's very unusual," he responded with a smile. "I seldom come down here during the week. Hardly ever this time of day. I'd say God must think it pretty important I talk to you."

Carrie nodded eagerly. "I'm so glad to hear that." She stopped. Now that she was here, she wasn't quite sure how to proceed. The silence stretched between them as she searched for words.

Pastor Anthony watched her closely, but he didn't speak. He seemed to know she was struggling for what to say. After a moment, he leaned back in his chair, his blue eyes watching her, but his slim body relaxed. Carrie noticed how young he seemed, even though she was sure he was in his forties. The unruly brown hair made him seem like a boy.

She knew she had to say something. "I need to get in touch with the Underground Railroad," she finally blurted out.

Pastor Anthony's eyes widened a little bit, but his face remained calm. "And what makes you think I have access to the Underground Railroad?" he asked.

Carrie managed a laugh. "I'm sorry. That's not at all how I intended to start this conversation. I guess I'm a bit nervous." He waited for her to continue. She leaned forward to emphasize what she had to say. "I have two slaves I care about very deeply. Actually they belong to my father. I want to help them gain their freedom. I thought perhaps you could help."

"And why do you think I could help?" he asked carefully.

Carrie was frustrated, but she understood. Everyone had to be careful nowadays. "Because of your eyes, Pastor Anthony."

"My eyes?" he echoed.

Carrie nodded. "Your eyes say you care. Opal is another one of my father's slaves. She is now living here in the city with her cousins, Eddie and Fannie."

Pastor Anthony nodded, a smile on his face. "I know them well. They are fine people."

"And they think the world of you. Opal told me you have made God real to her for the first time in her life."

"I'm glad."

"That's why I'm here. There aren't too many white people in the South that see black people as human beings, but I know you see them that way. I figured if anyone would know how to get in touch with the Underground Railroad, you would."

Pastor Anthony leaned back in his chair. "Let me get this straight. You want to help two of your slaves go free. How does your father feel about that?"

"He doesn't know," Carrie admitted. She told him, as briefly as possible, of her struggle to know where she stood on slavery. "Several of our slaves have already run away," she said. "I told them they could go."

"Why don't these other two just take off, too?"

It was a fair question. "They are too special to me. Rose has been my best friend since I was a child. She is like a sister to me. I can't bear to think of her and Moses being chased by slave hunters and hound dogs. There has to be a way that is not so dangerous." She saw no reason to go into the recent revelation of Rose's actual relationship to her.

Pastor Anthony finally looked as if he were convinced of her intent. He stood and began to pace within the confines of his small office. "Any escape is dangerous, Miss Cromwell. Especially now. More and more slaves are escaping, thinking the North will welcome them eagerly. The war seems to have given them the motivation to pursue their freedom. Owners have responded by sending out more slave hunters." He stared out the window for a long moment and then swung back to face her, evidently having made up his mind. "I will help you."

Carrie leaned forward with a wide smile on her face. "Oh, thank you, Pastor Anthony. I knew you would be the right person to talk to."

"Does anyone know you are here?" he asked. "There must be total secrecy."

"No one but my driver. I would trust Sam with my life."

"Very well," Pastor Anthony said with a warm smile. "We have a lot of planning to do."

Carrie gasped as she entered the opulent ballroom on her father's arm. They had already greeted their host and hostess at the door. Their escort bowed slowly, flashed his white teeth, and backed away, leaving them standing at the door to the ballroom.

"Surprised?" Thomas asked with a smile.

"Of course I am," Carrie said, gazing around her. "You'd never know there was a war going on." At least not until you saw the preponderance of gray splashed among the sea of bright dresses. The contrast to the city she had left just six weeks ago was amazing. She had thought it silly when Rose suggested she bring a ball gown, but was glad she had acquiesced. She knew she was appropriately dressed in her brilliant green gown with the cream-colored trim. Her father had told her it matched her sparkling eyes to perfection.

Social functions had ceased leading up to Bull Run and afterward. All energy had been channeled into caring for the sick and wounded, but the crisis was over now. The South had been victorious, and it was time to celebrate. After all, Richmond was known for its high society, and now, with its influx of government officials and military personnel, it was time to live up to its reputation once again.

Carrie couldn't help the thrill of delight that coursed through her as she looked over the dance floor. There were many aspects of Southern society that didn't appeal to her, but she loved everything about the dances. The brightly colored dresses and impeccably attired men. The music that even now was causing her foot to tap. The long rows of food that tempted the eye and the stomach. And especially the dancing. Her body began to sway slightly in anticipation of what was to come.

Thomas smiled down at her. "May I have this dance, Miss Cromwell?"

Carrie smiled up at him radiantly. "It would be my pleasure, Mr. Cromwell."

The music flowed around them in a glorious waltz as Thomas swept her across the floor. It had been ages since she had danced with her father. He was the one who had first taught her, encouraging her to learn to love it when she said she would rather be out on Granite. He had insisted the time would come when she would love it as much as riding. She had laughed unbelievingly then, but now she knew he had been right.

The music swirled around them as they glided across the floor and around the room. Laughter and talk rang through the air. The touch of coolness in the air spoke of the reality of fall creeping up on them.

When the music stopped, a young man in gray approached. "May I have this dance, ma'am?"

Carrie smiled as her mind was transported back to the times of joyful revelry before there was a war. For this night, she would ignore the significance of the gray uniforms. She would simply see these young men as eager dancing partners. She nodded, then stepped into the young captain's arms and was lost to the music once again.

She had lost count of her partners before she finally begged for a drink and a brief rest. Her current partner, a dashing young lieutenant, immediately departed to fetch refreshments for her. Carrie sank into a chair and gazed around the room. All the best of Richmond society was here. There were several faces she didn't recognize, but the look of authority identified them as new Confederate government officials. The unfamiliar, beautifully attired women must be their wives.

"Having a good time?" a soft voice asked in her ear.

Carrie turned and smiled at the woman settling down in the chair next to her. "Mrs. Lewis! It's wonderful to see you again."

"I haven't seen you since the night at Spotswood when we were awaiting news from the battlefield. I hope your news was good."

"Yes, thank you. My friend is doing quite well. My heart still grieves, however, for the men who were killed or wounded."

"Mine as well. And please, call me Victoria."

Carrie nodded. "Only if you will call me Carrie."

Victoria nodded pleasantly. "That was quite a dashing man you started off the dance with," she observed.

"The most dashing man here," Carrie agreed. "That was my father, Thomas Cromwell. And you haven't seen me around town because I left a few days after we talked to return to our plantation."

"You don't live here in the city?" Victoria's voice was surprised. "Does your mother stay on the plantation with you? How hard it must be to not have your father at home."

"My mother is dead. I am in charge of the plantation while my father works here in town." Carrie caught sight of her father surrounded by a small group of men. He caught her eyes across the room and smiled.

"You run the plantation all by yourself?" Victoria asked, astonished.

"Well, I have a lot of help," Carrie said in amusement, as she turned her attention back to the conversation.

Victoria looked at her appraisingly. "You must be quite a resourceful young woman."

"I hope so. That's how my father raised me," Carrie responded with a smile. She knew other women were amazed by what she was doing, but there was nothing special about it to her. She was simply doing what she had to do. She suspected women all over the South were being forced to do the same thing, now that their husbands and fathers were fighting a war.

Just then the lieutenant walked up with two drinks in his hand. "Miss Cromwell," he said, handing her a tall glass of lemonade.

"Thank you, Lieutenant." Victoria made a move as if to leave, but Carrie put her hand on her arm. "Please don't leave." Then she turned to the Lieutenant. "If you don't mind, I'm going to sit here with my friend for a while."

The lieutenant responded with a bow. "I hope I may claim you for another dance later?"

"Of course," Carrie said graciously. She turned back to Victoria. Something about the woman with tired eyes drew Carrie. There was something real in her lack of care about the impression she made. Her clothes were well made and her hair was expertly done, but it lacked the flash of the other ladies. "You don't really like these affairs, do you?" Carrie asked.

Victoria shrugged. "They all tend to become the same after a while. Society is society. I have spent the last ten years in Washington, DC. When Louisiana seceded, we came here." She paused and smiled briefly. "All I really want to do is return to Louisiana and my flowers and gardens. I miss home terribly."

"I'm sorry," Carrie said.

"You must think me quite boorish."

Carrie shook her head. "Certainly not. I enjoy these events because I get to attend them so infrequently. I'm afraid if they were regular occurrences, I would become quite bored with them as well. There are too many other things I would rather be doing."

Victoria gazed at her for a moment. "Thank you," she said quietly. "I must say, in all fairness, that life here is more interesting than in Washington. Maybe I should say that I feel as if I serve more of a purpose. It's really quite interesting to see the changes taking place in ladies I have known all my life."

"What do you mean?"

"Well, instead of lounging around in rocking chairs, they are all terribly busy. Everyone seems to have a knitting or crochet needle in their hands nowadays. I have been to every store in this town in hunt of more skeins of wool, but there is none to be found. I am planning a trip to Petersburg next week in hopes of finding some there. I keep watching the paper, hoping there will be news of a supply that has gotten past the blockade or been smuggled in. I'm not sure how I feel about this war, but I most certainly want to see all our boys warm and cozy this winter." She took a breath and then continued. "Mrs. Henningsen brought home dozens and dozens of yards of cotton sheeting. That should keep us busy for quite a while."

"Cotton sheeting? What will you do with that?"

"Have you not heard about the new hospital to be built?" When Carrie shook her head, she continued. "Dr. William McCaw is behind the effort. He has recently received permission to convert some newly constructed barracks on Chimborazo Hill into a military hospital. I believe he plans on it being quite large."

"They are expecting more battles and many more wounded soldiers," Carrie said flatly.

Victoria nodded. "Most people are finally shedding themselves of the ridiculous notion this is going to be a short war. They have seen the number of wounded pour in from a battle we *won*. Reality says we must be ready if the tide turns the other way."

"Thank you for your candor," Carrie said. Her heart ached for the many soldiers she had seen in her hunt for Robert, and for the men who would return home without arms or legs to live the rest of their lives.

Victoria shrugged. "The South railroaded people into this war, as far as I'm concerned."

Carrie stared at her in amazement. This lady's husband was an aide to the president? When Victoria threw back her head and laughed, Carrie realized how attractive she was. New life leapt to her face, and her tired eyes took on a sparkle.

"Might as well be honest about it." Then her voice grew grim. "Now that we have so many of our boys fighting this war, I intend to do all I can to take care of them."

There was something about her eyes... "Do you have sons in the army?" Carrie asked.

Tears sprang to Victoria's eyes. "Three of them. Two are fighting for the South. One is a Union officer." She waved her hand. "I have a lot to be thankful for. My son in the North will probably never see action because of a vision problem. He works in the offices of one of the military departments. My other two boys are still down in Louisiana. They haven't yet had to fight."

Carrie gazed at her in sympathy, wondering what to say to this revelation.

Victoria read her face. "Don't feel you have to respond. There is really nothing to say. Almost everyone is in the same boat as I am. That's the one thing that makes these social gatherings bearable for me. I at least know I am with people who are united in interest and in heart. It helps me keep going."

Carrie gazed around the room with new eyes. How many more of the people here didn't really agree with the war that had been sprung upon them? As she looked, new understanding crept into her heart. It didn't matter to these people whether they agreed with this war in principle or not. The fact was they had loved ones who were fighting. They had loved ones who might never come home again, or might come home horribly wounded. They would pour forth all their efforts and energies for their loved ones. It was that simple. The big decisions had been taken from their hands. They would do the best they could.

Victoria seemed to read her thoughts. "It's sad, really," she commented, looking around the room as well. "Five months ago, practically every person in this room would have considered it unpatriotic not to push for the cause of Southern independence. Now, many of them still push for it, but not for the same reason. They're no longer making a stand. They are simply fighting for survival."

Carrie liked her new friend, but she was relieved when her father walked over to her. "Could I talk you into another dance?" he asked with a smile.

Carrie rose with an answering smile. After Thomas gracefully acknowledged the introduction of her new friend, he led her in a rousing Virginia reel. Carrie allowed herself to be once more lost in the music. She was here to have fun.

She and her father were both laughing and gasping for breath when the music came to an end. "You're still the best dancer in Virginia," Carrie exclaimed.

"Only because I have the best partner."

"Except for mother."

"Yes," Thomas agreed with a smile, "except for your mother."

Carrie gazed at her father with relief. This was the first time in the many months since her mother's death that the mention of his wife had not caused her father's face to be filled with pain. The look was one of fond remembrance. Carrie tucked her arm in his and squeezed it tightly.

A sudden movement at the door caught her attention. She looked over to see a tall, stern-looking man in his sixties, quite distinguished in his gray uniform, enter the room.

Thomas followed her gaze. "That is General Winder."

"The man who gave me permission to visit Matthew?"

"That's the one."

Carrie smiled. "I think I should go thank him."

"I don't think that is a very good idea right now."

Carrie looked up at her father with a frown. "Why not?"

Her father opened his mouth, but a shrill voice just beyond him drowned out any attempt to speak.

"There's the man in charge of those awful prisons. I do declare, it's shameful how he mollycoddles those prisoners."

Carrie stared in amazement. The lady speaking was one of the most influential people in Richmond society. Carrie thought back to her visit with Matthew. She had seen nothing that indicated mollycoddling.

Another woman, one Carrie had never seen, carried on the conversation. "It's bad enough that we have to have those heathens in our city. I don't know why our officials seem to think those men should eat our food and use our supplies."

"Not to mention the danger they represent every single day," the Richmonder snorted.

"What do they propose we do with them?" Carrie whispered to her father.

He didn't have to answer.

"They need to send all of them further south," the second speaker snorted. "I don't know why people think

Richmond has to do everything. The rest of this country needs to take on their fair share of responsibility."

Thomas took Carrie's arm and led her away. "Not exactly party talk, my dear. That is precisely why I suggested you not talk to General Winder. The poor man is being attacked on every side about these prisons. It's dreaming to think he could make it through a night without having to face it, but on the off chance..."

Carrie nodded. "Of course." Then she asked, "Have there been any conclusions about the prisoners?"

Thomas shook his head. "I understand a lot of them are soon to be moved to other locations. There is simply not room for them here. In spite of the abundance displayed here tonight, the blockade is having quite a negative effect on our city. Food and other supplies are growing harder to come by. Prices are shooting up dramatically. People are beginning to worry whether there will be enough to take care of the mass of people crowding into our city. I'm afraid they are not in a mood to be generous with the Yankees."

"What about you, Father?"

Thomas shrugged. "I think they need to be moved. Richmond simply cannot support all of them. There are more than two thousand of them in the city now. But as long as they're here, I think we need to take as good a care of them as possible. I keep trying to imagine Robert, or some of our other young men, in Northern prisons. I would hope they would be cared for."

Carrie frowned at the thought of Robert in prison. "I'm going to visit Matthew tomorrow," she said.

Thomas nodded. "I hope you're able to get in. I'm sure he will be glad to see you. There is no telling how much longer he will be here. Please give him my regards."

Just then the lieutenant she had put off earlier walked up. "May I claim my dance now?"

Carrie smiled and graciously assented, but the magic of the evening had been lost for her. Cruel realities had dragged her back to the present.

Chapter Twenty

Rose pushed open the door to her cabin. The cool bite in the air said that Moses would need to bring in an armload of wood for the first fire of the year. The vision of flames flickering in the stone fireplace again made Rose smile. She had always loved this time of year. She enjoyed watching summer lose its hold on the land as fall moved forward boldly, painting vivid streaks through the trees and making the days cooler and shorter.

She moved across the bare wooden floor, reached into a basket, and pulled out four ears of corn. Mindlessly, she began to shuck. She wouldn't take it out to the main cooking fire in the clearing. Tonight, she would wait and cook supper over their own fire. When the corn was ready, she cut two slabs of ham and mixed up some biscuits. It still amazed her they were eating so well. She had never seen the Cromwell slaves so healthy, or so happy. They worked hard all day, but the evening was theirs. Luxuriant gardens bordered each cabin, still producing fresh food for every table. They had built extra holding pens for hogs, and every family benefited.

Rose sighed. If only it would stay that way. She knew it couldn't, though. If the South won this war, Marse Cromwell would return, and with him a new overseer. There was no telling what would happen then. It was certain they would not operate with the newfound independence Carrie had granted them, although more work than ever was being done on the plantation. Rose knew their freedom would be viewed as a threat to white control and would be abruptly ended.

If the North won the war, the future was just as unknown. Would the abolitionists have their way, or would the North continue to appease the South by letting them have their slaves? If they were all set free, life would change immensely. Rose was smart enough to see that. People who had been told what to do every minute of their lives would suddenly be responsible for their own actions.

As Rose considered that, she could feel the old excitement growing within her. She didn't hear the door quietly open, or the footsteps crossing the floor. Suddenly, she was engulfed by a strong pair of arms.

"Where are you?" Moses whispered teasingly in her ear.

Rose smiled and turned around to kiss him. "Just lost in my thoughts, I guess." Then she changed the subject, noting the pile of wood on the porch. "I'll have dinner ready soon if you will build me a fire."

Moses finished eating and leaned back against his chair. "We brought in our first big load of beans and squash today. I think Carrie will have to start sending wagons in every other day for a while. With any luck, we'll have three or four weeks of crops before the first hard freeze."

"The potatoes and carrots are ready aren't they?"

Moses nodded. "Some of the women are working to put away all we'll need here, but it's not much. This spring's garden took care of that."

Rose looked at Moses' face. She could tell he was contented. He was doing what he had always wanted to do—be a farmer; watch the land produce food; take part in the miracle of growth. Was he really ready to give it all up?

"Let's talk about it," Moses said.

"About what?"

"Whatever you're thinking about. This has gone on ever since Carrie left for Richmond. You act like you're in another world."

Rose smiled sheepishly. "I guess I have been." She paused, gazing into the flames for a long moment. "I guess Carrie going to Richmond made it all real to me."

"About us leaving?" Moses guessed.

Rose nodded. "I know she went to make arrangements for us. She didn't say so, but I know it."

"I think you're right."

"Is this really what you want, Moses?"

Moses looked startled. "What do you mean? Are you asking if I really want to be free?"

Rose nodded.

"What kind of question is that?"

"You're so happy now. You're doing what you want to do. You can live your dream right here. It's *my* dream that is going to take us away. I worry you will resent it."

Moses threw back his head and laughed.

Rose frowned. She didn't find her thoughts funny.

Finally, Moses stopped laughing and looked at her. He sobered instantly. "Rose, I don't know what has gotten in your head, but you need to throw it right back out. You're not seeing things clearly. Sure, I can farm here, but that's not my *dream*. My dream is to be free. My dream is to have my own land that I can do whatever I want with. Land that will support my family. I'll never have that here. And I could lose what I have here any minute. You know what Carrie's father said. He wants me to come into Richmond next month. That means we'll have to be apart for who knows how long." He stopped and stared at her. "Your dream is as important to me as mine is. Even if I *could* live my dream here, I wouldn't. You got to make your dream come true, too. The only way for our dreams to happen is for us to be free. You know that." He gazed into her eyes for a long moment. "Where are all these thoughts coming from? Are you getting afraid of leaving?"

Rose was ashamed to admit it, but slowly she nodded. "I guess maybe I am," she said. "It's all I've ever dreamed of and all I ever wanted. I guess I just didn't really think it would happen. Now that it's close, it scares me." She paused for a long moment. "I guess I wonder if I can do it. If I can really be a teacher. If anyone will let me teach their children. If we'll really make it to freedom. What will happen if a slave hunter catches us?"

Moses smiled and reached across the table. "Your mama would say there isn't anything wrong with your fears." His voice grew firm. "As long as you don't let those fears stop you from following your dream."

"Mama..." Rose smiled in spite of herself. "I can see her saying that." Her eyes filled with tears. "I still miss her. It's been almost two months, and I still want to walk into her cabin and smell biscuits cooking."

"You gonna miss her for the rest of your life," Moses replied. "You and your mama were that close."

Rose nodded. "She'd like to know I was gonna be free."

"I think your mama already knew that. I think she knew it was all right for her to go on home to be with John."

Rose smiled. "I like to think of her with my daddy. I'm glad she doesn't have to be a slave anymore."

"She'd want you to be free, Rose. She wanted that for you all your life. She knew you wouldn't go free until she was gone."

A long silence filled the cabin while both of them tried to envision freedom. The logs crackled and sizzled as they welcomed the first cool night. Outside, they could hear the owls heralding a new season. It would soon be a new season in more ways than one.

"It will really be only the beginning, you know," Rose said thoughtfully.

"Our freedom?"

Rose nodded. "It's like everything we've done up to this point was to make us ready to be free. This isn't an ending—it's really the start."

Moses nodded. "All the things I've only thought about, now I can actually do." He paused for a long moment and looked up with a determined expression. "I'm not going to be satisfied until I find my family. Until I know they are free, too. I'll come back here you know."

"I know." Rose tried to push away the image of Moses coming back to the South once he was free. He wasn't the kind of man who could blend in. His size would always make him stand out, but she would never try to stop him. He was letting her follow her dreams. She had to let him follow his.

"Do you think we'll mess it up, Moses?"

"Mess it up?"

Rose nodded. "I don't want to be like other people. I see it in all kinds, black *and* white. They're free, but they don't appreciate it. They waste their lives afraid to do more than be like everyone around them. Sometimes I used to feel bad because learning came so easy to me. I thought I should hide it so other people wouldn't feel bad around me."

"Then your mama said something to you?" Moses guessed.

"Well, yes," Rose said with a smile. "She told me it wouldn't do no good to the world for me to hide what God done give me. She said other people might try to be differ'nt if they saw me doin' it." She said it just the way her mama had that day. It made her feel better.

For no reason she could identify, a surge of confidence went through her. She threw her head back in a loud laugh, spread her arms wide, and twirled around the room. "We're gonna be free, Moses. We're gonna be free!"

"You got that right, Rose."

Rose and Moses spun around toward the door as Carrie stepped into the cabin.

"I didn't even hear you, Carrie," Rose gasped. "You startled me." She ran to hug her. "When did you get home?"

"Just a few minutes ago. The storm today made the roads almost impassable. Two trees were down, and the carriage got stuck in the mud several times." Carrie shook her head. "I'm glad Sam was with me. To be so old, he sure has a lot of strength."

Carrie looked around the cabin and walked over to warm her hands by the fire. "Feels good," she said appreciatively. Then she turned to them. "We have to talk." She reached for the last remaining biscuit and took a big bite. "I'm starving," she announced. "I didn't take time to eat up at the house. I was too eager to come down here."

"I have some apple turnovers from last night."

Carrie grinned. "Like the ones your mama used to make?"

"Just like them," Moses said.

Carrie reached for them. "I won't be getting many more of these. I'd better eat all I can now." Her smile faded and was replaced by a look of sorrow.

"Carrie?" Rose asked.

Carrie shook her head and looked up, forcing a smile to her face. "Y'all leave next week."

Rose gasped and leaned against the table. Moses reached out and enfolded her hand in his huge one. Neither one knew what to say.

Carrie shrugged her shoulders. "I'm sorry, but I didn't know how else to tell you."

"Something like that you just got to spurt out," Moses agreed.

Rose found her chair and sank down in it. "Next week? We're going to be leaving here next week?"

Carrie nodded.

Rose felt a flash of excitement when the words penetrated her brain. There was so much she wanted to know. Now that the time was actually here, she had so many questions.

Carrie raised her hand. "Don't start in with your questions yet," she said with a laugh. "I can see them written all over your face. Let me tell you everything I can, and then you can ask me questions."

Moses took Rose's hand in his again. "We're listening," he said in his deep voice, his own eyes glowing with excitement.

Carrie began. "I went to Richmond to meet with a man named Pastor Marcus Anthony. Once he was convinced I was legitimate, he proved to be a wonderful source of information."

"Is the Underground Railroad still operating?" Rose couldn't help the question that slipped from her mouth.

"Yes," Carrie replied. "But they have to be even more careful. The old methods don't work as well. Several loads of slaves escaped around here last year by climbing into wagons. That won't work anymore. A few have gotten through, but the state has increased its militia and the number of slave hunters. They routinely check every wagon that goes by."

Rose felt a sharp twinge of uneasiness and turned to look at Moses. He was listening to Carrie intently, but there was no fear on his face.

He felt her eyes on him and turned to look at her, squeezing her hand. "Just keep listening, Rose girl. Ain't no use borrowin' trouble 'fore it find you."

Rose smiled as he repeated the words her mama had said to her so many times before. "You're right. I'm sorry, Carrie. Go on."

Carrie nodded. "We do have a plan, and I think it's a good one, but it's only fair you know all the risks beforehand."

Moses nodded. "We need to know what we're getting into."

Carrie continued. "Not all the slaves who have left here since last summer have made it to freedom. At least, not the freedom you want."

Rose gasped. "What do you mean? None of them were brought back here."

"You're right. They're in what the North is calling contraband camps. Seems some of them had heard there was protection to be offered by the Union Army, so instead of heading north, they headed east toward the coast. Some of the areas there are occupied by Union troops. They have offered them protection and a place to live, but little more."

Rose leaned forward, noticing the distaste on Carrie's face. "It's bad?"

Carrie shrugged. "I'm sure some of the slaves think they have reached paradise. I think Cromwell slaves might wish they were back here. Pastor Anthony told me the camps are dirty and crowded, and that food can be hard to come by. People are crammed into buildings. Seems the Union is trying to figure out what to do with them."

"Why don't they just send them farther north?" Moses asked.

"I asked the same question," Carrie responded. "They sent letters to Northern governors asking that very thing, but none of the fine men wants them in their state."

Rose sat back, dismay on her face. "Isn't there anywhere we can go?"

Carrie nodded quickly. "Not everyone feels like that, Rose. There are plenty of places where slaves will find support while they get started again. You just have to be careful."

Moses spoke up then. "We're not headed for any contraband camp, Rose. We're headed north, and we'll keep going until we find a place where we can make our home." There was both anger and determination in his voice. Rose turned to look at him. He held her with his eyes as he continued. "We knew this wasn't going to be easy, but people before us have done it, and so can we. Nothing in this life is guaranteed. You make the best choices you can and try your hardest." He paused. "I reckon we can trust God to take care of the rest."

Rose nodded again, once more filled with the peace and excitement she had felt before Carrie walked into the cabin. Her body and face relaxed. "You're right. Both of you are right." She laughed. "Tell me what we're going to do."

Carrie gave a sigh of relief. "The first leg of the journey we're going to be on our own..."

The fire had died down to nothing but glowing embers when all the plans had been laid.

"I think you'll see that everything will go smoothly," Carrie said with a smile.

Rose and Moses nodded.

The three friends stared at each other in realization of what their planning meant. Up until now they had shied away from the subject, but here it was again staring them in the face.

"I'm going to miss you, Carrie," Rose said softly.

Carrie said nothing, just bit her lip and blinked at the tears in her eyes. Mutely, she nodded her head.

Moses was the one to break the silence. "Let's go for a ride," he exclaimed, jumping up.

Rose and Carrie stared at him.

"It's after midnight," Rose finally managed to say.

"Exactly." Moses said with a grin. "Haven't you always wanted to ride under a full moon? You may never get another chance."

Carrie added her grin to his own. "He's right, Rose. We have to make the most of this next week. Let's go do something crazy."

Rose laughed, caught up in the new spirit infusing the cozy cabin. "Let's do it!"

Carrie led the way into the barn. "Be quiet," she whispered. "We have every right to do this, but there's no reason to make everyone else think we are absolute nuts."

Moses snorted. "Most everyone is sound asleep, but I can guarantee you Sam is watching us right now. He never misses a thing around here."

Carrie laughed. "You're right."

"We can wave at him on our way out," Rose said lightly.

All three horses were saddled quickly and led out into the beautiful night. By unspoken agreement, once they were on their horses and headed out, not another word was said. The glory of the night spoke for itself.

Carrie gazed around her and felt her throat thicken. It had been years since she had ridden at night. Even her father didn't think she should go out alone at night, and he had been too preoccupied with other things to join her. Now she realized what she had missed.

A soft, cool breeze was blowing, caressing her skin in a way that made her thankful for the wraps they had put on before coming out. The moon was past full but still cast a luminous glow over the earth. The silvery landscape with its lightly tossing branches seemed to send laughter back up to the moon. Trees and brush seemed larger than life as they cast dancing shadows onto the ground. Crickets, frogs, katydids and owls all joined in to perform a final concert for the departing summer. An occasional firefly blazed in accompaniment.

Carrie led the way down the road at an easy trot. She was in no hurry. After about thirty minutes, the trio emerged on the shore of the James River. Carrie pulled her breath in with delight. The gently riffling waters acted as a living mirror, reflecting back the silvery light of the moon.

"It looks like diamonds out there," Rose said with quiet awe.

Carrie nodded. The river was prettier than any picture she had ever seen. The dark shapes of the trees formed a perfect border for the exuberance reflected before her. As she watched, a low flying heron, long and graceful, broke through the edge of the picture and glided across the water in front of them. A fish split the surface and was quickly followed by more.

"They look like they're playing," Moses observed with laughter in his voice.

The deep, sudden bass of a nearby frog startled them all out of their thoughtful reverie. Carrie had enough of contemplative thought. She knew it would soon carry her back into depressing waters. She wheeled Granite around, urged him into a canter, and then yelled back over her shoulder. "The first one back to the house gets the rest of the chocolate cake!"

She could hear answering whoops behind her, and then she lost herself in the feel of her horse beneath her. The moon was bright enough for the road to be easily seen. Leaning forward, she buried her face in Granite's mane and let him run. Only she knew she was hoping the wind would blow all the sorrow and tears from her heart. The idea of Rose and Moses being gone was almost more than she could bear, yet she knew she was doing the right thing. She just wished she could feel better about it.

Two days later, Rose finally caught Sam alone. "Sam, can I talk to you?"

Sam eyed her closely and sat down next to the woodpile, laying down his heavy burden first. "You gonna tell me the secret you been carryin' round?"

Rose smiled. She wouldn't even ask how he knew. Sam had always been able to see inside her heart. "Yes," she said simply.

Sam leaned back against the tree. "I'll save you the trouble. You're leavin' here aren't you, Rose girl?"

"How did you know? Does anyone else know? It's supposed to be a secret," she cried, looking around to make sure no one was listening to her outburst.

Sam laughed. "Oh, it's a secret. You don't got to worry 'bout nobody else knowin'. It's only me that can see inside your heart."

"I know," Rose agreed, tears springing to her eyes. "You've always been like a father to me. That's why I couldn't leave without telling you—without saying goodbye."

"When you and Moses be leavin'?"

"In five days." Rose paused. "I can't tell you anything. I promised. But I'll find some way of letting you know I'm all right."

Sam nodded. "It's best that way. A body can't tell what he don't know." He smiled. "I guess I'll be headin' on soon myself."

"You're going to leave here?" Rose couldn't imagine Sam anywhere but on Cromwell Plantation.

"With you gone, my job will be done."

Now Rose was confused. "Your job? What are you talking about?"

Sam smiled at her. "Let me tell you a little story, Rose girl."

Rose leaned back against the tree and waited. She had never seen such a tender and serious look on Sam's face.

"I know 'bout that twin brother of yours."

Rose gasped. "How, Sam? I thought mama never told anyone. How did you know she told me?"

Sam shrugged. "I know your mama. I knew she wouldn't go home to be with John until her baby girl knew the truth. All those years, your mama didn't know I knew 'bout her baby boy."

"Why not?"

"'Cause I promised your daddy. When he found out they was gonna sell him so that nobody would ever learn the secret 'bout Miss Carrie's granddaddy, he came to me late at night. He was scared to leave you here alone. Said it weren't right that you wasn't gonna have a daddy. He made me promise that night to take care of you for him. I reckon I did all I could."

Rose smiled, remembering all the times he had waited up for her when she had been teaching her little secret school in the woods. She remembered him teaching her how to act right in the big house when she was just a little girl so she wouldn't get in trouble. How he used to save her an extra biscuit when she had been working hard. "I reckon you did a wonderful job," she said softly. She had to speak around the lump in her throat and blink back the tears brimming in her eyes.

Sam reached out his big, weathered hand. "I'm gonna miss you, Rose girl, but I'm glad you're gonna get your chance to be free. You done got a lot to give, girl. Don't you let nobody keep you from givin'. You run into hard things, you find a way to go over them. If you can't go over them, then go around them. Remember there always be a way to get where you're supposed to be. You just got to find it." His voice was thick with emotion.

Rose listened closely. "I'm gonna miss you, Sam. Thank you for all you've done." She reached out and clasped his big, rough hand.

Sam nodded. "I reckon we'll be seein' each other again. This here be a mighty big world, but God has a way of connecting folks' hearts. We're connected in our hearts sho 'nuff. I reckon God will find a way to let us see each other again." He looked off as if he could see something she couldn't. "Yes, I reckon we'll be seein' each other again."

"When do you figure you'll be heading on?"

"Why you askin'?"

Rose hesitated. She wanted to say she was only curious. He wouldn't believe her, but she didn't want him to feel obligated either. If it was time for him to be free, she didn't want to do anything to stop it.

Sam answered her dilemma. "The truth usually be the easiest to say, Rose girl."

Rose nodded. "You're right as usual." Her voice grew intense. "I'm worried about Carrie."

Sam looked at her closely. "She know who you really are?"

Rose nodded. "She knows..." Her voice broke at the thought of leaving her best friend.

Sam was quiet for a moment and then squeezed her hand tightly. "I reckon I still got me a job to do. I'll look out for Carrie for you, Rose girl. I'll do my best to make sure no harm comes to her."

Rose frowned. "But what about you going free?"

Sam shrugged. "As long as I got a job to do here, I aim on doin' it. I wasn't so sure I was supposed to be movin' on right now, no hows. This lets me know for sure."

Rose jumped up and slung her arms around his neck, tears pouring down her face. "I love you, Sam," she whispered fiercely in his ear, clinging to him for several long minutes.

"I love you, too, Rose girl," he managed between his own quiet sobs.

Chapter Twenty-One

Swing low, sweet chariot
  Coming for to carry me home
Swing low, sweet chariot
  Coming for to carry me home.
I looked over Jordan and what did I see
  Coming for to carry me home
A band of angels coming after me
  Coming for to carry me home.

Moses' voice drifted into the still evening air, carrying with it the prayers of millions of slaves still in bondage. With those prayers went the hope that was the light enabling them to endure the darkness.

Rose looked up from where she was kneeling by her mama's grave. "Is it true, Moses? Are we really leaving tomorrow?" She was still trying to make herself believe it was actually going to happen.

Moses walked over and knelt beside her. "It's true," he said softly. He was silent for a long time. "I've dreamed so long about being free," he finally said. Then his face hardened. "We got a lot to go through before we're free, though."

"Do you really think we can make it?" Rose shook her head at her thoughts and chuckled. "I'm laughing at myself, so don't you bother." She looked at the grave and added, "And don't *you* laugh, Mama. We're going to make it through everything just fine. We're going to go through every hard time and over every obstacle." Saying the words out loud helped.

Rose had come to say goodbye. She knew her mama was in heaven with her daddy, but this was the only earthly contact she still had. Her eyes filled with tears. "I know she's not here, but when I need to talk to her so badly my heart hurts, I can come out here and pretend. Soon I won't even have that."

"You've got something much better than this grave," Moses said. "You've got your mama locked in your heart. No one can ever take that away from you."

Rose looked at him with sudden understanding. "That's how you can stand being away from your mama, isn't it?"

Moses nodded, his face softening. "Someday I'm going to find out where she is, and my sisters, too. They split us up on the auction block, but they're not going to keep us apart forever. I've got all of them locked in my heart. When I come back, I'm going to find my family, and I'm going to give them their freedom as well."

Rose stood and walked into her husband's arms. She had so much to be thankful for. Her mama might be gone, but at least they had known each other and been close. At least they had never been separated by the cruel realities of the slave system. "I aim to find my brother someday, too," she said, speaking more to herself than to Moses.

Moses' arms tightened around her. "I know you are. And I'll help you."

Rose smiled as his strong voice sounded over her head. She could face whatever was coming as long as they were together. She thought she had been fine all alone before Moses had come into her life. She had been content with her teaching and her dreams. Now she only felt complete when Moses was near. "I heard Mama say one time that she only felt complete when my daddy was with her. I don't know how she survived all those years without him."

"She survived because she had God."

"Yes," said Rose thoughtfully, "but it still had to have been hard. It's different when you have someone with flesh on right beside you."

Moses threw back his head and laughed, the deep sound rolling across the trees and reaching into the night. "I reckon you're right, Rose girl." Then he drew her into his arms and kissed her deeply.

Somewhere in the depths of his tender kiss, Rose lost all her fears. Love pulsed through her being as she returned the kiss with all her heart. They clung to each other for several long minutes before they pulled away and stared into each other's faces, giving each other the strength and love they would need to overcome what was ahead.

Finally, Rose was ready. She turned, knelt down once more and reached out to touch the cross above her mama's grave. "Goodbye, Mama. Thank you for everything." Tears flooded her eyes, but her voice was strong.

The night sky was twinkling with a sea of stars when they finally turned and walked away.

Carrie was waiting for Rose and Moses when they reached the barn in the early morning hours. The sun was just beginning to transform the inky sky into a glowing cobalt. If they were going to make their first connection, it was imperative they get an early start. Unable to sleep, she had been at the barn for over an hour already. Granite and the two other horses they were going to ride were already fed, tacked and ready to go. She was just leading them out when she saw her friends emerge from the darkness of the surrounding trees.

"You couldn't sleep either?" Rose whispered.

Carrie shook her head and held her finger to her lips. She didn't want anyone to know what they were doing. If they left no trail, there wouldn't be one to follow later. Pastor Anthony had been very stern about the procedures they needed to follow if their hastily contrived plan was to work.

Rose nodded and held up the meager roll holding the few belongings she was taking along. Carrie winced but nodded in approval. Rose could get more material things when she reached freedom. What was important now was not to attract any attention. A black couple with a large pack on their horses or in their hands would surely attract attention. Carrie reached for it and quickly tied it on behind Rose's saddle. Then she did the same with Moses'.

Just before they climbed into the saddles, she held up a hand to detain them. "Come inside the barn," she whispered.

Rose and Moses looked at each other in surprise, then followed. Once inside, Carrie reached for the coats she had laid on top of one of the feeders. "You're going to need these," she whispered. Already the mornings were getting colder. The first hard frost was not far away. Both of them were wearing coats, but not ones that would stand up to the cold farther north. "One belonged to my mother. The other is an old one of my father's. He will never miss it."

Moses smiled and put on the coat she handed him. It was tight across his broad shoulders, but it fit in most other ways. Rose's fit perfectly.

Carrie nodded and led them from the barn. In minutes, they were out of sight of the plantation house. She kept Granite at a steady, ground-eating walk. She didn't want hoofbeats to alert anyone to their actions. Only when they were out of sight and out of earshot did she talk normally. "Are you sure no one saw you leaving?"

Rose nodded. "We're sure. We left a note for Sam, just like you said. Told him it was our time to go, and we were leaving. He'll tell everyone." Her face was a mixture of sadness and excitement.

"You two are going to be missed very much." Carrie thought of how the other slaves had flocked to Rose after Sarah was gone. How everyone counted on Moses to take care of things for them. "It's not going to be the same around here." She didn't say anything about how her own heart ached over their leaving. They already knew.

Silence engulfed them as, occupied with their own thoughts, they rode on. The rising sun transformed the deep cobalt into a rich violet and then suddenly diffused it with streaks of orange and pink as it crept over the horizon. The morning air was chill and fresh, seeming to hold everything in suspension. All the horses moved easily, invigorated by the fall air.

Suddenly the sun exploded onto the scene, throwing its brilliant rays like lightning rods into the glorious sky.

The brilliant blue sky seemed pregnant with fluffy orange and pink puffs of clouds.

"I reckon we can trust a God who can paint a picture like that," Moses said in a reverent voice.

Carrie took courage from the display dancing above her head. Moses was right. She knew there were times ahead when she was going to have to hang on to that knowledge.

They came to the first fork in the road. Carrie deliberately took the one that would lead them east of Richmond. They needed to stay as far away from the city as possible. Too many people knew her. If she was seen, someone was sure to ask questions, and sooner or later the information would reach her father.

Carrie's heart ached as she thought of her father. He was such a loving and kind man in so many ways. That they were so far apart on this issue caused her great pain. She knew he would be hurt and angry if he learned what she was doing right now. She shook her head to force the pictures out of her mind. She was doing the right thing. Maybe someday she and her father would see eye to eye.

"How we doing on time, Carrie?" Rose asked when the sun was high in the sky and the colors had faded to reveal a startlingly clear blue sky.

"We'll make it. If we keep up this pace, we should be there ahead of schedule. That will give you a little time to rest before you have to go on."

"What if the conductor isn't there?" Moses asked.

Carrie tried to smile reassuringly at Moses even though she had entertained the same doubts herself. "He'll be there," she said. "If he's not," she added after a moment, "we'll think of something." She had no idea what, but she saw no need to say that. It was too late to turn back now. "We'll cross all those bridges when we get to them. You'll have to do the same."

Rose laughed then, a welcome break in the tension. "Seems like we're crossing bridges in a lot of ways."

Carrie laughed, too. It felt good and released some of the heaviness in her heart. They were meeting their first conductor under the bridge that ran across the

Pamunkey River. Just a few minutes before, they had made the turn that dumped them onto the Mechanicsville Turnpike. Pastor Anthony had at first been concerned about using this route because it was a favorite, heavily used route for runaways, but finally he had surmised it was the best way. Carrie's presence would throw off most suspicions. Once she had to turn back, they would face more danger, but every precaution would be taken.

"Still seems strange to be running away in broad daylight."

Carrie nodded. "I know, but Pastor Anthony said it would be the best way to throw off suspicion. They patrol these roads with the militia pretty heavily at night, but during the day they largely ignore it."

After a few more minutes she stopped and pulled her coat off. "I don't think I need this anymore." The sun, rising steadily in the sky, had taken the early morning chill out of the air. Moses and Rose followed her lead, quickly tying their coats on top of their packs. "It will work well to keep anyone from asking questions about your packs, too," Carrie said.

She reached down into her saddle bags and pulled out a carefully wrapped package of biscuits and bacon. "We have a few minutes. Let's stretch our legs and have a bite to eat." Once they had tied the horses, they found a large rock under a tree and settled down to eat.

The sound of hoofbeats caused Carrie to lift her head. Headed straight toward them were several Confederate soldiers. "Remember what I told you," Carrie said quietly. It was all she had time to say.

"Good morning, ma'am," the one in charge said courteously.

"Good morning, Captain," Carrie responded, hoping her tone didn't reveal her nervousness. "Beautiful day isn't it?"

"That it is, ma'am." He looked carefully at the three horses.

Carrie watched him closely. She saw the spark of suspicion in his eyes. She knew it looked strange. Surely he was wondering why they weren't in a carriage, and why Moses and Rose were riding horses of their own. Too late, she realized the very quality of their coats would be suspicious. What were slaves doing with coats like that?

"Where you headed, ma'am?" The Captain turned to look at her with sharp eyes.

Carrie smiled brightly. "Why, Captain, I'm headed to visit some of my family just the other side of Mechanicsville. Surely you know the McCormicks!" she gushed enthusiastically. "They are just the most wonderful people. First cousins you know. It's been simply ages since I was able to see them. My father, bless his heart, insisted I take the family carriage, but my dear mother is so ill." She stopped speaking to dab at her eyes. "I simply couldn't see taking the family carriage. What if she were to take ill and need to be transported somewhere?" She almost laughed at the confusion on the captain's face as she rattled off her prepared speech so quickly she could almost not keep up with it herself.

The captain frowned slightly. "I see what you mean, ma'am." Then he opened his mouth as if to ask another question.

Carrie was afraid he was going to ask her where the McCormicks lived. Since it was an entirely made up name, she had no idea. If he knew some McCormicks and was aware of where they lived, a wrong answer could be their undoing. "Oh, Captain, I was sure you would understand. Our boys in gray are so wonderful. What y'all do for us is simply amazing. I'm grateful from the bottom of my heart."

"Thank you, ma'am."

The captain seemed to be looking at her a little closer. The look said he wasn't necessarily thinking of his job anymore. Still, she couldn't be sure. "This really is the first little fun thing I've gotten to do since this war began. I just couldn't see going about having a good time while y'all suffer and fight for our protection. Why, I've spent almost every day working on mittens and scarves for our troops this winter." She paused for a moment. "And my daddy says y'all do such a wonderful job protecting us. Why, do you know what he told me?" She pretended to shudder. "He told me there are runaway slaves trying to use this very road to leave their beloved masters..." She caught her breath in a gasp.

The captain nodded his head gravely. "Your daddy was right, ma'am. That's why we're checking with you now." His voice became a little sterner. "Are these your slaves, ma'am?"

"Oh, yes, sir," Carrie said with a breathless laugh. "I would be so terrified to be with any but our own dear slaves. You really have no idea of what to expect from some of these people, you know." She let her eyes open wide.

"Yes, ma'am. I do know."

Carrie decided to take a risk. She reached into her deep pocket and pulled out a sheaf of papers. "These are their papers, sir. I would be so happy to let you go through them. You will see they are mine. My daddy insisted both of them come along when he knew I was determined to go." She paused, giving a pretty little laugh. Her tone became confidential. "You see, we're taking a little break now because my slaves here have never been on a horse much. I'm afraid it's rather taxing on them. We were just getting ready to leave. Our cousin is expecting us, and I'm afraid we're running a little late." She glanced at her watch and then held her hand to her mouth. "My goodness, I had no idea it was getting to be so late. Here are their papers," she said handing them up to him. "You are certainly welcome to look through them. I'll simply do anything to help our boys."

The captain looked suddenly embarrassed. He smiled, took the papers, but handed them right back. "That's all right, ma'am. I don't want to take up any more of your time. I'm sorry to have delayed you."

Carrie smiled up at him brilliantly, all the time gathering up the breakfast items and stuffing them in her bags. "Why, that's not a problem at all, Captain. I did so enjoy talking to you."

"The same, ma'am." The captain tipped his hat courteously and rode off with his men.

Carrie watched him leave and then sagged against Granite. The three of them mounted quickly and began to trot down the rather rutted road. Carrie's heart was beating rapidly as she replayed the incident in her mind. A movement to her right caused her to glance over. Moses' shoulders were shaking convulsively.

Carrie's laugh rang out in the morning air. Soon the three of them were laughing so hard they were gasping for breath. Thankfully, the road was now empty of anyone who would wonder if they had taken leave of their senses.

They had just begun to regain control when Rose sang out in a high Southern drawl, "*Why, Captain...,*" and batted her lashes furiously.

Once again they went into convulsions of laughter. It was several minutes before the sight of two carriages headed toward them caused them to regain control. Carrie was able to smile naturally at the two men in the carriages as they rolled by. "Good day, gentlemen."

Rose was the first to sober. "I'm going to miss you so much, Carrie."

The reminder was enough to sober them all. The sun continued to rise as they rode. When it was almost directly above them, Carrie caught sight of the bridge they were looking for. Her heart leapt with gladness that they had made it, but at the same time it dropped with the knowledge that the time to say goodbye had finally come. The silence between them was deep as they rode the last few hundred yards.

Carrie watched closely as they drew nearer. Would their conductor be there? The plank bridge over the river was devoid of life. The clear waters of the Pamunkey glistened as the river wound its shallow way through bulrushes and tall clumps of razor-sharp grass. The clip-clop of the horses' hooves sounded deafening as they rode slowly over the bridge, trying not to be obvious they were looking for someone.

Carrie glanced at her watch. The interlude with the captain had delayed them, but they were still right on time. She knew it was too soon to be worried. Trying to make all the arrangements for the Underground Railroad was a daunting task—anything could have held their conductor up. She glanced over at her friends' anxious expressions and smiled. "It will be all right," she said soothingly.

They reached the end of the bridge, moved a little to the other side, and then pulled their horses to a halt.

"You really think this is going to work?" Moses asked suddenly. "You really think we can just ride right through to where we're going?"

"What if that captain had asked to see our papers?" Rose added. "He would have known who you were and maybe would have remembered seeing us if your father puts out a reward flyer for us."

"The captain *didn't* ask to see the papers," Carrie reminded them, "and, yes, I do believe it's going to work." She took a deep breath. "You've got to take one minute at a time," she said. "To answer your last question—yes, I think you're going to be able to ride through, but if you can't, the conductor who is leading you will find another way." She turned to Rose. "As for you, my darling aunt, what-ifs will control you for the rest of your life if you let them." She took on Sarah's scolding tone. "Why, you could sit still the rest of yo' life and never have nothin' happen if you start thinkin' about all the what-ifs."

Their laughter once again cleared the tension in the air.

"I couldn't have put that any better myself," a deep voice said from behind them.

Carrie gasped and spun around on Granite. Standing just behind her was a tiny man, barely five feet tall, with dancing eyes as green as her own. "Where did you come from?" was all she could think to ask.

"From right there," he said cheerfully, waving at the bridge. "I figured I would take a wee nap while I was waiting for you. Your horses' hooves woke me up, like I figured they would." He laughed and then bowed quickly. "The name is Mike O'Leary. I'm your conductor."

Carrie looked at him with delight, liking him immediately. The wrinkles said he was older than her father, his twinkling eyes and ready laugh spoke of someone much younger. And in the midst of his cheer was the look of steady courage and determination in his eyes. She began to feel better. She knew instinctively she could trust Rose and Moses with this man.

"It's a pleasure to meet you, Mike O'Leary. My name is Carrie Cromwell. This is Rose and Moses." She smiled and handed over the forged papers that would identify them as his slaves if they were stopped and questioned.

O'Leary acknowledged the introduction with a broad smile, looked carefully at the papers, and then checked his watch. "You're right on time. That's good. But we got a long ways to be going. I reckon we'd better be on our way." He turned and strode quickly into the woods, emerging moments later on a towering bay gelding that made him look even smaller.

Carrie turned to Rose and Moses, the lump in her throat making it impossible to smile. She dismounted from Granite slowly, thankful there was no one to witness their farewell. Rose and Moses swung from their horses as well.

Carrie and Rose stared at each other for a long moment before they fell into each other's arms. Their emotion was too deep for tears. They simply clung to each other, trying to gain strength.

Carrie finally pulled away, allowing all the love in her heart to shine through her eyes. "Please be careful," she whispered.

Rose nodded, staring back into her eyes. "Thank you, Carrie." Her voice broke as she reached out again to hold her friend. "I love you," she whispered.

It took Moses to pull her away. He wrapped Carrie in a warm embrace. "You are a very special woman, Miss Carrie Cromwell." He held her back and looked into her eyes. "Thank you for everything."

Carrie nodded, unable to trust her voice to say anything. Finally, she whispered, "Take good care of yourselves. I love you both."

O'Leary was the one to lighten things up. "Shucks, you'd think you weren't never going to see each other again. Why, I reckon before all this is over you folks are going to be free. Then you can be seeing each other any time you want."

Carrie managed a smile. "I hope you're right, Mr. O'Leary."

"Now, you can't be calling me by such a big handle. The name is Mike. The same to you two," he told Rose and Moses cheerfully. "We're going to be seeing a lot of each other the next few days. Might as well be on a first name basis." Then his voice dropped and became more serious. "We'd best be going, though. We have quite a ways to go before we reach our place for tonight."

Carrie nodded and stepped back while Rose and Moses mounted their horses again. With an ache in her heart, she watched until they were out of sight.

Chapter Twenty-Two

Rose could hardly move the next morning when she woke up. She had never been so sore in her life. She rolled over to see if Moses was awake.

"Don't remember feeling pain in quite these same places before," Moses said with a smile. He was lying on his side, watching her.

Rose allowed herself a small groan. "Are we really going to spend all day in a saddle again?" she asked. "I think every single part of me hurts." This was the first time they had talked since they arrived at their station the night before. When Mike pointed them toward the barn where they would spend the night, they fell into their hay beds, exhausted. Within seconds, they were asleep.

Moses looked at her lovingly. "It's amazing."

"What is?"

"How you can still look beautiful after all day in a saddle and all night in a hay loft."

Rose smiled and leaned over to give him a kiss. Then she fell back as every muscle screamed in protest of movement. "That's what I love about you, Moses. You're such a good liar."

Moses opened his mouth to protest, but they heard the barn door creak open.

"Anybody alive in there?" the now familiar Irish voice sang out.

"We're alive," Moses called back.

"That's good. I have some breakfast here for you. Then we've got to hit the road. We've—"

"Got connections to make," Rose completed for him. Then she brightened. Each connection with the Underground Railroad was taking them that much closer to freedom. She stretched long and hard, forcing her stiff muscles to respond.

"You gonna make it, Rose girl?" Moses asked playfully.

Rose stuck out her tongue and jumped to her feet, ignoring the pain that shot through her body. "I'll be ready before you are," she shot back. In a flash, she climbed nimbly down the ladder leading to the loft and headed in the direction of the well.

"Hey, you!" Moses cried. Seconds later he ran up behind her and grabbed her in a hug.

Laughing, the two of them quickly got ready.

It was almost dark when they rode up to the banks of the Rappahannock River. In spite of her exhaustion, Rose was thrilled at the sight of the vast river spread out before her. It was like being back on the James. The sight of it made her heart long for Carrie. "You think she made it back home, don't you?" she asked for what was probably the hundredth time.

Moses answered patiently. He knew how worried she was. "Carrie Cromwell is an incredible woman. I *know* she made it back home."

Rose nodded again, but still her heart wondered. Carrie had to ride back that long distance by herself. Had anyone stopped to question her? Had she encountered any trouble? Were things going to run smoothly on the plantation?"

"Honey, you're going to have to let it go."

Rose looked at Moses. "I know. Mama always told me it was a waste of precious energy to worry about things you couldn't do anything about. I'm trying to let it all go. Honest."

Mike broke through the brush surrounding them and smiled brightly, though fatigue showed on his face. Minutes later, they were seated in a large boat, moving quickly through the water.

Rose watched as the land slipped further away. Mike had assured them the horses they had left tied would be picked up by someone that night. They would be well taken care of and used for more escape attempts. Still, it had been hard to leave them. They had been her last tangible connection with Carrie. She watched until the encroaching darkness made it impossible to see anything but the water surrounding her. Then she turned her head to see where they were going.

Moses and Mike were leaning hard into the oars as the man who had met them skillfully navigated the dark waters. Rose watched for a few minutes and then laid her head back to stare up into the sky. The first stars had begun to shimmer, and a mere sliver of the moon seemed to hang from a thread. She was grateful the sky was clear. She couldn't imagine being in this boat during a storm.

The only sound was the men's heavy breathing as they hauled hard on the oars. Rose smiled as she caught her first glimpse of the approaching shore. Mike had said they were making good time.

The last two days had been full of heart-stopping moments for her. Every strange face had the potential to be the one that would result in her being sent back into slavery. It had been hard to leave Carrie, but as they moved steadily north, the desire for freedom had become a steady flame in her heart. She could feel the desire pulse with every hoofbeat, and now with every stroke of the oar.

Freedom... Freedom... Freedom...

So far they had run into no obstacles. The closest they had come to trouble was meeting the captain on the road. True, they had a long way to go to reach Philadelphia, but they were soon going to be out of Virginia. She could feel the excitement growing in her heart.

Two days later they reached the banks of the Potomac River. The twenty miles they had covered after leaving the Rappahannock had been grueling. Being on foot now meant they must travel by night. The narrow, rutted roads they had walked down would have been difficult in the day, but by night they were relentless. Rose had fallen more than once, quietly getting back up every time to continue on. The nights were getting colder, and she was increasingly grateful for the warmth of the coat Carrie had given her.

Mike returned from scouting the shore with a worried look on his face. "The boat should have been waiting for us. We will stay here. They're probably running late."

Rose said nothing, just stared across the huge expanse of water. The sky was beginning to grow light. If they didn't cross soon, they would have to spend another whole day by the river, risking discovery, even though their location must truly be remote.

The sky was glowing orange when Mike turned to them with a smile. "Looks like we get one more day in Virginia."

Rose could tell he was trying not to worry them.

"Will there be a boat, Mike?" Moses asked quietly. "You can be honest with us."

Mike shrugged his shoulders. "I can't be knowing that. There was supposed to be a boat. That's all I was told. Any number of things can be happening to mess up the plans, though."

"And if there's not a boat?" Moses asked.

"Then we'll be looking for another way across that water," Mike said. He stretched mightily. "As long as we don't have somewhere to be getting to, I think it would be a fine time for a wee bit of sleep." He lay down on the ground and was soon snoring.

Rose and Moses looked at each other. Moses smiled. "He's right. We might as well get some rest."

Sometime later, an angry shout startled them awake. It came from the direction of the water.

Rose started upward, only to be stopped by Moses' big hand on her arm. He had a finger laid across his lips. Mike was already up, crouched at the brush, trying to see where the noise was coming from. When he saw Rose and Moses watching him, he motioned them to move farther back into the woods. Moses stood easily, took Rose's arm, and crept away. Only when they were another hundred feet back, settled behind a large tree surrounded by low growing brush, did he stop.

All they could do was listen. For a long time, they heard nothing. Then voices erupted again.

"I thought you told me you saw movement up there," a deep voice called.

Moses leaned close to Rose's ear and whispered. "Whoever it is must be down on the little trail that runs along the bank. I saw it earlier."

"I *did* see something move," a voice slurred back. "It was a deer I tell you!"

Rose frowned. The sound of their voices told her they had been hitting the bottle too hard that morning. She pushed down her sudden panic. She couldn't let memories have the best of her now. Letting her imagination run wild now would do no one any good.

The unseen voices continued. "Daddy said we better not come back without some deer meat. It's your fault we're getting such a late start."

"Ain't my fault! You're the one who brought along that bottle."

Just then a shot rang out.

"I got one!" a voice yelled in triumph. "Did you see it move up there on the bank? We'll be taking our deer home tonight."

Rose could hear brush cracking and limbs breaking as the two men made their way up the bank. Was Mike in a place they couldn't see him? She thought of his nimble body and smiled. He was probably up a tree, staring down at the men, trying to figure out how to get rid of them.

Suddenly, the air was rent with heavy cursing. Then the older voice spoke. "That ain't no deer, you fool. That's a man. You done killed a man!"

Rose gasped, staring at Moses in horror. His eyes were wide as he grabbed her arm, warning her to be quiet.

"Well, how'd I know it was a man up here?" The voice grew suddenly suspicious. "What was he doing up here in the woods, anyhow?" The reality of what he had done seemed to have sobered him up somewhat. "He must not have been doing something right if he was up here hiding in the woods."

"Well, what are we going to do with him?"

"I say we leave him right here. Ain't nobody gonna find him."

"We can't just leave him here to rot," the other voice said with disgust. There was a brief silence before he continued. "I reckon we can put him in the river. That way no one will connect him with us."

The killer had obvious relief in his voice. "That's a great idea."

There was another brief silence and then the other man spoke again. "What's this here in his pockets? Some kind of papers..." Silence and then, "These here be slave certificates. Says his name is John Salem. These here papers be for a couple of slaves named Rose and Moses."

The killer laughed again. "Well, dead men can't tell no tales. I say his papers go down the river with him."

The other voice spoke up. "These here papers are for slaves. You think they're around here somewhere? If they are, they know we killed him." There was a short silence. "Maybe we ought to look through them woods."

The killer protested immediately. "You crazy? They're ain't no slaves around here. If there were, they've probably already run far away. We wouldn't never find them." His voice rose to a whine. "I say we get rid of the body. Let imaginary slaves take care of themselves."

"I reckon you're right. We've got to get a deer, not hunt slaves."

There was another silence and then a loud splash.

"Goodbye, Mr. John Salem," a voice called. "Too bad we can't take you home to put in our smoke shed."

Both men laughed, and moments later, their voices faded from hearing.

Rose allowed the tears to come then. She turned to Moses for comfort, but he was already up and running. She wanted to call to stop him but was afraid the two men were still close enough to hear her voice. She leapt to her feet and followed.

She found him standing on the river bank, scanning the water. She looked fearfully down the bank, praying the two men would not retrace their steps. "Moses! What are you doing?" she whispered.

"Mike O' Leary was a good man. The least we can do is give him a proper burial."

Rose nodded, but their scanning of the water revealed nothing. The two men must have thrown Mike's light body into the current. He hadn't been dead long enough for his body to float, and neither one of them knew how to swim. Finally, they had to admit defeat. Heavyhearted, they climbed back up the bank and took their hiding place again.

The sun was now high, but a thin layer of clouds covered the clear blue sky. The already cool day was getting colder. Rose shivered, partly from the shock of what had happened and partly from the cold. Without saying anything, Moses turned and wrapped his arms around her. They sat that way for a long time, each dealing with the new reality of their situation. They were in the middle of nowhere, with no guide, no boat to take them across the river, and very little food.

Moses was the first to speak. "Looks like we have an obstacle to overcome."

His strong voice released the dam holding back Rose's emotions. Sobs racked her body as Moses continued to hold her close, stroking her head gently. She cried for Mike O'Leary, and for the family he had told them about who would never see him again. She cried to release the fear that had gripped her as they had listened to the shot that killed him. After a long while, she grew quiet again. "What are we going to do, Moses?" She wiped at her tears and stared up into his face.

He looked thoughtful for a long moment. "We're going to find us a boat," he said finally.

Rose stared at him. "How are we going to do that?"

Moses shrugged. "We're going to walk until we find us a boat. I don't know what else to do," he admitted. "We can't swim across that river. As wide as it is here, there's no telling how far we'll have to go before we find a place narrow enough to cross. And we're not going back," he said with firm resolve. "That leaves us only one thing. We've got to find a boat."

Rose nodded. She had never seen such a vulnerable look in his eyes, and she knew he needed her support. "We should wait till it's dark," she said.

Moses gazed at her tenderly. "I love you, Rose girl." Once more he wrapped her in a warm embrace.

They fell asleep that way. When they awakened, the sun was dipping low on the horizon. They quickly ate the last bit of food they had, then put on their coats and began to move through the woods. This way they could keep the river in sight and stay invisible to seeing eyes. When it was too dark to see their way through the woods anymore, they moved down onto the narrow trail.

"What if those two men come back this way?" Rose asked nervously.

"They won't," Moses said. "They went back home by some road. They won't be in any hurry to come down on this part of the trail any time soon."

Rose took comfort from his words and continued to press on, trying to ignore the pangs of hunger. She lost track of the number of times she stumbled over some unseen root or rock in the trail. The moon, which had been visible at first, was now hidden behind a thickening layer of clouds. A stiff wind had sprung up, causing the cold air to infiltrate even their heavy coats. Her feet were wet from plodding along the shoreline and now were beginning to feel numb. Rose gathered her coat even closer around her, bit her lip, and continued on.

"You all right, Rose?" Moses' voice was deep with concern.

"I'm fine, Moses. I'm sure we will find a boat soon." What difference did it make that he knew she was lying? He needed all the support he could get. She was determined not to become a burden.

They plodded along all night, not finding anything. Rose was becoming weak from hunger and exhaustion when Moses gave a low, triumphant cry.

"A boat!" Immediately, Moses pulled Rose back into the bushes.

"What are you doing?" she whispered, pushing back the branches grabbing at her face.

"If there's a boat, that means there are people somewhere around." Moses continued to peer through the bushes. "It's not very big, but I think it will do the job. Now we only have to hope it's here tonight when we need it."

Rose stared at him in the darkness. "Tonight? What do you mean tonight?"

Moses' voice was patient. "We're going to have to cross at night. Just like we were supposed to do. People will see us if we cross during the day."

"What are we going to do all day?" Rose hated the frightened sound in her voice but she was close to the limits of her endurance.

"We're going to hide," came his firm, quick reply. "The sun is going to be coming up soon."

Rose glanced at the horizon and was stunned to see it beginning to turn light. They had walked all night long. Her body and her gnawing hunger verified the fact.

They moved a hundred feet back into the woods until they found a sunken area surrounded by brush that would provide them protection from the wind and from prying eyes. Rose sank down gratefully.

Moses touched her shoulder. "I'll be back soon. I'm going to get some food."

Rose looked at the determined set of his jaw and knew there was no stopping him. She swallowed her fears. "Be careful," she whispered.

Moses nodded, kissed her briefly, and began to move away. "Stay right here. I'll be back as soon as I can."

Rose watched from her hiding place as the sun brightened the still cloud-laden sky. She tried to ignore the cold that had seeped into every pore of her body. She had known escaping could be difficult.

Freedom!

Just thinking about it gave new strength to her heart. All of this was worth it. It would all be over someday, and when it was, she would be living a new life of freedom.

It seemed like eternity before she heard footsteps. Shrinking back into the brush, she made not a single sound until she saw Moses searching for where he had left her.

"I'm right here," she whispered, stepping out into the open.

Moses smiled brightly, acting as if the labors of the night before had not even affected him. He took her hand and pulled her back into their hiding place. "Have a seat, wife. Breakfast is served."

Rose sat and stared at him with love and gratitude. He returned her look and reached into his deep pockets. Rose gaped as he laid the food on the rock in front of her. There was a small loaf of bread, a thick slab of cheese, and two apples. In addition, he pulled out several carrots and two small tomatoes. "Where in the world..."

"You don't want to know," Moses said with a smile.

The mere idea of the danger he must have put himself in to get this food made her shudder. "You're right," she murmured. Then she reached for the food.

It had been dark for quite a while before Moses ventured back out into the open. Rose waited for him impatiently. She was ready to resume their journey. The food and a good day's sleep had renewed her strength and revived her spirits. When Moses reappeared with a smile on his face, she rose and followed him. The boat was right where they had seen it last night. No one had been near it. The sky had still been a threatening gray when the sun went down, but at least there was no stiff wind blowing. Moses led the way onto the shore, looking carefully in every direction. When he was satisfied no one was around, he signaled for Rose to join him.

Rose moved quickly and settled herself in the front of the boat, trying to control the fear rolling in her stomach as she looked into the black emptiness of the water that stretched before her.

Moses stepped in behind her and then settled himself at the oars. "I haven't done a lot of this, but I think it won't be too hard to handle."

Rose merely nodded. "I trust you," she said lovingly. She was determined to be brave. At his signal, she reached forward and undid the thick rope holding the boat.

Rose looked back as the shoreline disappeared. Soon all she could see anywhere was water. She sat as still as she could as Moses pulled the oars steadily.

"How in the world can you see where you're going?" she finally asked.

"Can't. But I know it's taking us farther away from the South. That's good enough for me."

Suddenly, the wind that had died down picked back up. Moses worked harder, grunting with each stroke as the water kicked up whitecaps around them. The boat bobbed like a cork. Rose took deep breaths to calm herself. Then, to make matters worse, the clouds that had threatened all day, delivered on their promise. The drops started out slowly but were soon a steady downpour. Soaked through to the bone, Rose was shivering uncontrollably.

"You all right?" Moses called in between gasps of air.

"I'm fine," Rose called back. To combat her fear, she began to sing the song that had become their beacon of hope.

> *Swing low, sweet chariot*
> *Coming for to carry me home*
> *Swing low, sweet chariot*
> *Coming for to carry me home.*
> *I looked over Jordan and what did I see*
> *Coming for to carry me home*
> *A band of angels coming after me*
> *Coming for to carry me home.*

Her voice had started low, but as she sang on to the end, it raised in determined triumph against the elements that were battering them. The rain continued, and the waves battered the sides of their small boat, but her heart was strong and her courage intact.

Once she had finished that song, she launched into another. She knew without asking that her songs gave

Moses strength. From one song to the next, she sang without stopping.

> *You call yourself church-member,*
> *You hold your head so high,*
> *You praise God with your glitt'ring tongue,*
> *But you leave all your heart behind.*
> *O my Lord delivered Daniel,*
> *O Daniel, O Daniel,*
> *O my Lord delivered Daniel,*
> *O why not deliver me too.*

Rose lost all track of time as they forged through the water with her singing, and Moses rowing. Suddenly, she gave a sharp cry.

Moses, with his back to her, stopped rowing. "What is it? Is somethin' wrong?"

Roses shook her head happily but realized he couldn't see her. "Land! I see land, Moses!"

Moses whipped his head around for a brief look and then bent himself to his task once more. Her announcement seemed to give him added strength, for it was only moments until the small boat scraped against the shore.

Rose stepped out, her trembling limbs barely able to support her. A moment later Moses was standing beside her. They embraced wordlessly. The night was still dark and the rain continued to pelt them, but they had completed the next leg of their journey. Somewhere in the middle of the vast river, Rose had grown up a little bit more. She would no longer ask what they were going to do next, or whether they would make it or not. God had brought them this far. They would continue. One day at a time. One step at a time. What did it matter that they were lost in the middle of nowhere? They were together. Together, they would make it.

Rose looked up as Moses moved through the woods toward her. "Any luck?" she asked calmly.

Moses nodded, his voice strong in spite of his obvious fatigue. "I found a house."

Rose watched him, waiting for him to continue. The day was chilly, but the sun had finally dried out her clothes. She had just finished re-braiding and coiling her hair. Her coat, laid out on some rocks, would be dry soon. Moses had shucked his coat before going on his exploration trip. It would soon be dry as well.

Moses plopped down on the ground beside her. "I watched the people for a while. I think we should ask them for help."

Rose felt a twinge of fear before she remembered her resolve from the night before. "When?" was all she asked.

Moses looked at her carefully. "You doing some changing, Rose girl?"

"I hope so," Rose replied. "My mama always told me hard times make you grow up. I reckon she was right again. I know I have a lot of growing up I need to do."

Moses nodded. "I reckon we all do." He settled down beside her. "The family in the house is black folks."

Rose looked up with excitement. "That sure is better than charging in on white folks."

"That's the way I figured it," Moses said with a sudden grin. "I'm hungry. I don't see any need to wait."

Rose watched as Moses walked steadily up to the door of the little cabin. He had insisted she stay hidden until he knew it was okay, but she stood and walked quickly to join him. He didn't notice her until he was almost to the door. When he did, he spun around with a protest on his face.

"We're escaping together. We're going to do this together, too," she whispered.

Moses looked at her hard for a moment, then nodded. With a deep breath, he raised his hand and knocked on the graying wooden door.

"Who be there?" came the sharp reply.

Rose held her breath. Would the code of the Underground Railroad work? Or would it be their undoing?

"We are friends," Moses replied.

The door swung open slowly. A large black man, wrinkled and gray, stepped out into the yard. Carefully he looked around. Then he looked them over, peering into their eyes. What he saw must have satisfied him.

"Welcome. I am a friend of a friend. You two look mighty done in. Come on in for a bite to eat."

Chapter Twenty-Three

Rose smoothed down her dress one more time and patted her hair. She knew her dress looked worn and old, but at least it was clean. Moses was wearing a nice shirt one of their new friends had found them, but his pants looked like what they were—refugee pants. Fighting to control the butterflies in her stomach, she looked up at the three-story row house in front of her. Moses, standing beside her, seemed just as nervous as she was. Somehow, the thought comforted her.

"We can't stand out here all day, you know," she said. She took Moses' hand, and together they walked up the stairs surrounded by a wrought iron railing.

Moses took a deep breath and raised his hand to the knocker. He rapped it sharply three times and then stood back.

Rose held her breath as she heard footsteps approaching the door. "She's home," she whispered. She had thought they might have to come several times before they caught her at home. Their evening arrival seemed to be timed perfectly, unless of course it was one of her servants. Then she remembered Carrie saying she had none. Her thoughts were cut short when the door swung open.

Rose stared at the attractive woman before them. She was just the way Carrie had described her—tall, with a regal bearing softened by light brown hair pulled back into a bun, and laughing gray eyes. Rose liked her immediately.

"May I help you?" the woman said graciously, not seeming to take notice of their worn condition. She was both courteous and pleasant.

"Are you Abigail Livingston?" Moses asked.

"I am," she responded. "And who might I have the pleasure of talking with?"

Rose stepped forward. "My name is Rose. This is Moses." She stopped, not knowing what else to say.

Finally, she reached into her pocket and pulled out the letter she had kept protected for so long. She held it out wordlessly.

Aunt Abby looked at her curiously but reached for the letter and opened it. Quickly, she scanned the contents and then gave a cry of delight. "You are friends of Carrie Cromwell! She has told me so much about both of you." She stepped outside and embraced both of them. "Please come in at once."

"Thank you," Rose and Moses murmured as they followed the glowing woman into her immaculate home. Carrie had promised them she would give them a warm welcome. Their fears had been futile.

In moments, they were seated in her parlor. "First things first," their hostess announced. "I find Mrs. Livingston much too big a handle for anything but a business environment. Will you please call me Aunt Abby? Anyone who is a friend of Carrie's is a friend of mine, and I practically feel like I know you both."

Rose smiled. "We'd like that." She paused and then added softly, "Aunt Abby." She could feel tears building in her throat. Aunt Abby was so much like her mama. Oh, the differences were obvious, but it was easy to recognize the same caring heart and the same willingness to give love.

Aunt Abby turned her attention back to the letter she had read so quickly. Then she looked up with a frown. "Carrie wrote this letter on October first. Today is October the twenty-ninth. It has taken you quite a while to make your way here. I take it there were difficulties?"

Moses nodded. "I guess we ran into our share of them." He filled her in on the details leading up to where they had crossed the river after losing their guide. They laughed together over Carrie's acting with the Confederate captain, and shed tears together over Mike O'Leary's death.

"And when you crossed the river? What did you do then without a conductor?"

Rose spoke up. "We were blessed enough to find another conductor for the Railroad. A former slave by the name of Isaac Waters. He convinced us it would be too hard to go over land with winter approaching. I'm still not sure how he arranged it, but we've only had to walk from the dock down on the end of Washington Street to here. The rest of our trip has all been on water."

"They were able to secure you passage on a big boat?"

"I wouldn't exactly call them big," Moses said with a smile. "Most of them were rowboats."

Aunt Abby gasped. "You came all the way up the Chesapeake Bay and the Delaware River in rowboats?"

"Yes," Rose said. "And we made many wonderful friends along the way. One man would take us a day or so north, then another would pick us up. We had quite a few days when we had to be put up while we waited for our next conductor, but we were always well-fed and cared for." She smiled. "Not that I wasn't glad to finally reach Philadelphia. I have had quite enough of boats for as long as I live." She saw no reason to tell Aunt Abby of the long, bitterly cold days on the water. Or the days when waves threatened to overturn their tiny crafts. They were here. That was all that mattered.

Freedom had beckoned. They had answered its call, doing just what her mama would have told them to do, by going around every obstacle and embracing every hard time as if it were a friend carrying them to their final goal. They had persevered, and they were stronger for it. Rose knew she was not the same young woman who had left Cromwell Plantation a month earlier. She was ready to face whatever life had to offer here in this new city.

"And Carrie?" Aunt Abby asked. "How is she? I miss her so much. Even our correspondence has become impossible."

"Carrie was doing well when we left her," Rose answered. "She received your last letter."

"She did?" Aunt Abby exclaimed with a smile. "My conductor friend made no promises, but he said he would do what he could to get my letter to her." She paused, her eyes glistening with tears. "Please do tell me all about her. She's like a daughter to me, you know."

Rose nodded. "She has talked of you so much. She wanted me to tell you she has written you at least two letters a week. She's saving them for the time when they can reach you again." She thought for a moment. "I'm sure she told me she tried to send a letter to you through the network. It must not have made it."

Aunt Abby smiled, her eyes shining with delight. "It's just wonderful to know she is all right."

Rose filled her in on all the details of what Carrie was doing on the plantation. "She had delivered twenty wagons of food to the city when we left. There is no telling how many were sent before the first hard frost."

"I should have known she would find a way to make a difference," Aunt Abby said with admiration. "I can only imagine how much she must miss you two." She leaned back in her chair. "Does Carrie feel safe on the plantation now?"

Moses shrugged. "She believes she is where she is supposed to be. Her father called her to Richmond for the Battle of Bull Run. She went to make him feel better then, but I don't believe she'll leave so easily again. She feels like she has a mission to accomplish there now."

"That sounds like Carrie," Aunt Abby asked. She turned to Rose and looked at her sharply. "There are things you're not telling me. Is there something Carrie has asked you not to talk about?"

Rose shook her head. She should have known Aunt Abby would have the same perceptiveness of her mama. "It's not anything I can really put into words. I just worry about her sometimes. The plantation has become her whole world, but it's out of necessity, not because her heart is really there. I want her to have her chance, Aunt Abby. She made it possible for Moses and me to be free...to follow our dreams." Her voice broke as she spoke, Carrie's smiling face rising up in her mind.

"You love her," Aunt Abby said softly, watching her closely.

"I love her," Rose agreed in a whisper. "It was like leaving part of myself to have to leave her." Suddenly, she felt a desire for Aunt Abby to know the truth. She looked to Moses, and he nodded his head. Once again, he was reading her thoughts.

Rose took a deep breath and gazed at Aunt Abby. The warm eyes encouraged her to continue. "Carrie is more to me than a friend." She told Abby the story her mama had shared with her before she died.

Aunt Abby listened carefully, asking quiet questions as Rose went along. "So what do you two do with your lives now? Your old life has ended for at least as long as God sees fit to reunite you with Carrie somewhere in the future. You have a new life ahead of you. What do you want to do with it?"

Rose smiled. How much Abby was like her mama. Aunt Abby had listened with her heart to all she said, but there was nothing she could do to change the past. All she could do was try to be involved in the present and the future. Rose sensed this caring woman would do all she could for them.

"I want to teach," Rose said firmly. "I want to help black children follow their dreams. But I want to go to school first. There is so much I want to learn. So much I still want to know."

Aunt Abby listened and then turned to Moses. "And what about you?"

"I want to find my family. That is the dream that burns in me above all others. My daddy made me responsible for them when he died. I'll do whatever it takes to see us all together in freedom." He paused for a long moment. "And I want to fight for the Union, or be involved somehow. This isn't just their war. It's the black man's war, too. I believe our freedom hinges on it." He stopped when he saw Aunt Abby's frown. "What?"

Aunt Abby shook her head. "Both your dreams are going to be hard to accomplish. There are many blacks here in Philadelphia eager to fight. They have all been turned away."

"Why?" Moses asked.

Aunt Abby shrugged. "The North, for all its talk about equality, is not really willing to embrace it themselves. They wanted the South to let the slaves go, but they didn't count on having to pay a price themselves for it to happen. Quite simply, I don't think they believe blacks are capable of being soldiers."

Moses frowned. "I thought I was leaving that kind of thinking behind in the South. I thought things were different here. Especially in Philadelphia."

"I wish I could tell you that was true. Oh, things are different, but I'm afraid you won't find it to be the way you envision. Let me tell you something about the city you have chosen to call home." The chiming of the hall clock drew her attention. "Have you eaten yet? I was just getting ready to have a bite."

Soon they were seated around the table in the kitchen, munching on bread, cold ham, cheese and pickles.

Abby returned to what she had been saying. "Now, about Philadelphia. You will find quite a large number of blacks in our fair city. In fact, we have more blacks here than any other city besides Baltimore. And you will find most of them congregated not very far from where we are right now. Most of the women serve in the capacity of domestics, and they find it easier to be close to their work."

Rose nodded. Carrie had said Aunt Abby lived in one of the wealthiest areas of the city.

Aunt Abby continued. "Philadelphia has the privilege of two very different distinctions. You are probably aware that the Pennsylvania Anti-Slavery Society is based here."

Moses nodded. "Carrie has told us about how much you do for the effort."

"I wish I could do more," Aunt Abby said. "The other distinction we have is one Frederick Douglass himself gave us. I'm afraid it's not one I am proud of. After one of his trips here he said, '*Colorphobia is more rampant in Philadelphia than in the pro-slavery, negro-hating city of New York.*' I'm afraid there is a great deal of truth to that."

Rose felt the sick feeling of disappointment rise up in her. "I'm sorry to hear that." She didn't know what else to say.

"I feel it's only fair to give you a clear picture. Don't misunderstand me. There are opportunities here for you, but you will have to fight hard. You will have to want it with all your heart."

Moses smiled. "I know we fit that bill, Aunt Abby. We've been through a lot of hard things already. We'll just keep on until we get where we want to be."

Aunt Abby nodded, looking at them both closely. "I believe you," she said. "I see the same spirit in you two that I saw in Carrie." She paused for a moment. "Let me tell you what else you can expect. Prejudice against color is quite rampant here. We have white schools and colored schools. White churches and colored churches. Why, I think we even have what I call white Christianity and colored Christianity. The lines are tightly drawn everywhere. No colored people, no matter how well dressed or well-behaved, are allowed to ride on public transportation."

Rose frowned. "What are they so afraid of?" she asked.

Aunt Abby regarded her somberly for several long moments. "People are afraid of what is different. Instead of embracing the differences as something that can enrich them, they try to bottle them up and put them somewhere they can't touch their lives. The very reality of how blacks came to America works against you. Rightly or wrongly, people's mentality is of people who are slaves. People have to have someone to look down upon. I guess it makes them feel better about themselves if they think other people are even lower than they are."

"It was hardly our choice to come to America at all," Moses protested in an angry voice.

"Of course it wasn't, Moses. My experience has taught me that darkness follows darkness. It was the darkness of men's hearts that brought your people from Africa. The darkness is continuing in people's attitudes and actions now. Many people talk about wanting the slaves to be free, but they haven't looked in their own hearts. They don't realize if they were talking about the word *free* in relation to themselves, they would also be talking about equality. Too many people aren't willing to look at their hearts and attitudes with honesty."

"What makes you that way?" Rose asked. "Why are you different?"

Aunt Abby smiled. "I'm lucky I think. Oh, I grew up with a tremendous amount of prejudice all around me. My family are Virginians you know. We never owned slaves, but my father always wanted them. Then I came to Philadelphia on a visit and met my husband. That was during the forties when riots were erupting in protest of the blacks in the city. My husband had grown up farther north where the abolition movement was already active. He had many black friends when he was a child. I learned to see blacks through his eyes. I had to fight to overcome my prejudices, because they were deeply ingrained. I was involved with the fight for freedom before I realized my own heart was struggling with the equality issue."

When she paused and looked thoughtful, Rose gazed at her in admiration. She understood why Carrie was so drawn to this honest woman. She knew she had found a friend.

Abby continued. "I'm afraid it's a condition of the human heart, this desire to believe we are better than other people around us. It took God quite a while to teach me I was absolutely no different from my black brothers and sisters. God sees us all the same. Given the same chances, some of us will succeed, and others won't. Given the same chances, some will give their all to follow their dreams, while others will fall by the wayside. I pray every day that God will cleanse the darkness from my heart."

"You are a remarkable woman, Aunt Abby," Moses said with a catch in his voice.

"Nonsense," Aunt Abby responded. "I am merely human like you are. We all have to come together if we are going to make any sense out of this world we live in. Especially at this time."

"Has anything new happened with the war?" Moses asked. "Obviously we haven't gotten any news lately."

"Not much, actually. The Battle of Bull Run had a very sobering effect on the North. General McDowell was replaced by General McClellan. They seem to be looking more long-range than they were before. The last I heard is that a tremendous effort is being made to build a strong, well-equipped army. Congress has authorized the building of an army of one million men for three years, or the duration of the war."

"A million men," Moses whistled.

Aunt Abby nodded. "There has been quite a lot of enthusiasm among men eager to defend the Union. At least for now."

"You think it will change?" Rose asked.

"I think the realities of war are going to change attitudes and dampen enthusiasm everywhere. The Battle of Bull Run seems to have galvanized men eager to defend their honor and the honor of their country, and right now the war is good for our economy. But I think that will change."

"Why?" Moses asked.

Aunt Abby shrugged. "I believe we are in for a long, hard war. As the casualties and suffering mount, the enthusiasm will fade, especially here in Philadelphia. In spite of the strength of the abolition movement here, Philadelphia has long had a traditional sympathy for the South and an antipathy toward blacks. I fear those realities will cloud its dedication to the Union."

"Are we safe here in the city?" Rose asked. She was not feeling afraid, but she wanted to be aware of any precautions they needed to take.

"I think so," Aunt Abby responded. "You should spend the next week or so getting to know Philadelphia. I will show you the areas where you need to be most careful, and also some places you will feel comfortable."

"We don't want to impose on you," Moses protested.

"Nonsense," Aunt Abby said crisply. "I know I haven't really said anything, but I hope you know I want you two to stay here with me. I have plenty of room."

"I was hoping you would want us to," Rose admitted with a smile. "I feel like I'm at home. My mama was so much like you."

"Your mama was Sarah, wasn't she?"

Rose nodded.

"Carrie told me so much about her. She sounds like she was a wonderful woman. I'm so sorry you have lost her."

Rose managed to smile. "She knew I had Moses. She wanted to go and be with my daddy. I know she's happy."

A brief silence followed before Moses asked, "Will I be able to find a job here? We have no intention of letting you take care of us."

"I didn't think you did," Aunt Abby said, "but finding a job will be difficult, I'm afraid. Employment in the new factories is pretty much closed to blacks. Even semi-skilled and unskilled occupations are harder to come by because of the Irish who have flooded our city."

Rose could tell she was trying to be honest, yet not discouraging at the same time.

Moses nodded. "I'll find something," he said.

"What do you want to do in the long run, Moses? When you've found your family and they're free?"

"I want to be a farmer, ma'am." His eyes shone as he talked. "I love working the land and watching a tiny seed grow into a plant that can feed a lot of people. There's magic in that, you know. Growing tobacco and corn was all right, but growing the food crops the last two months for Carrie lit a new fire in my heart. I watched those plants every day. I imagined how many people they were going to feed. I want to feed people, Aunt Abby. Someday, on land of my own, I want to grow crops that will feed people." His eyes glazed over as he looked far into the future.

Aunt Abby nodded. "Hang on to your dream, Moses."

"I aim to, Aunt Abby. I aim to."

Aunt Abby turned to Rose. "You want to teach."

"More than anything in the world," Rose said eagerly.

"Why?"

Rose thought through her answer. She could feel Aunt Abby's eyes on her, and she sensed it was more than just a casual question. "I've wanted to be a teacher ever since I learned how to read and write. I would have been in a lot of trouble if anyone found out that I was learning, but it meant too much to me. I discovered a whole world beyond the narrow one I lived in. I want other people to know that." She paused.

Aunt Abby continued to watch her, listening. She seemed to know Rose had more to say.

Rose continued. "I read somewhere that Thomas Jefferson said the relationship between a free society and education were inseparable. He believed Virginia's peace, prosperity and civilization depended on the education of its people. I know it is also believed that the same things are just as dependent on the containment and repression of education among the black population. It is obvious to me that the white population understands the power of education. I want my people to understand it as well."

Aunt Abby stared at her for a long moment. "It's amazing that one from the slave system could be so intelligent. Not just intelligent," she hastened to explain. "I know all people have that capacity. I am very impressed at your understanding and how much you know. Did Carrie teach you all that?"

Rose shrugged and decided to tell the truth. There was no one to punish her anymore. "I went beyond what Carrie was teaching me," she admitted with a smile. "I used to sneak into her daddy's library when no one was around. I always came out with a book or two. It didn't matter what they were. I would read them by candlelight late at night, and then I would sneak them back in."

Aunt Abby laughed in delight. "You are truly an extraordinary woman."

Rose shrugged. "I did what I had to do."

"Exactly," Aunt Abby responded. She lost herself in thought for a moment. "I'll have to do some digging to see what opportunities there are here for you. In the meantime, I've been thinking about hiring someone to help me around the house. I find my business is keeping me away from home more and more. Trying to keep the house is becoming quite a burden. Would you be willing to help me?"

"Of course," Rose said. It would make her feel so much better about taking advantage of Aunt Abby's hospitality. Later, she could try to find a job that would allow her to make a little money while she went to school.

"I will pay you of course," Aunt Abby continued.

"We couldn't think of taking money from you," Moses protested, before Rose had an opportunity to do so. "You are already doing so much for us. You can consider it payment for room and board."

"I will do no such thing," Abby said firmly. "You are staying here as my guests. It just so happens I need help as well. We are meeting each other's needs."

Rose stood and gave Aunt Abby a hug. "Thank you so much. I have dreamed so many times of finishing our journey and reaching your home. Carrie loves you so much that I was sure you must be very special. Now I know for myself you are."

Aunt Abby returned her hug, blinking away the sudden tears. "Thank you, Rose." Suddenly, her shoulders were shaking with quiet sobs.

Rose continued to hold her, patting her shoulder until slowly the sobs subsided.

"Well!" Aunt Abby said shakily. "I don't know the last time I did something like that."

Rose waited quietly. She was sure there was a reason for the display of emotion.

Aunt Abby brushed at her tears. "I guess my emotions have been building up. I seem to have been losing a lot of people I love lately. My husband went first. It took me a while to get used to living alone, but I adjusted. Then Carrie came into my life, and she became the daughter I never knew. The war has taken her away from me. Then Matthew Justin..."

"The journalist," Rose said.

"Yes. He and I became very close. Now he is in prison in Richmond. I worry about him daily. I have been feeling like a very lonely old lady. You two are like a gift to me. I'm so glad you're here."

Rose smiled and hugged her again.

Moses spoke for all of them. "Looks like God knew how to fit together the pieces of the puzzle."

Chapter Twenty-Four

"The house looks real nice, Miss Carrie."

Carrie smiled as she looked up into Sam's strong face. "Yes, I suppose it does," she responded, even though she didn't really think so. She knew the house servants had done the best they could in preparation for the big times of Christmas, but it lacked the sparkle of former years. "Not that it matters so much," she sighed.

"Feelin' sorry for yourself?" Sam asked quietly.

Carrie stared at him in astonishment, with just a touch of anger. Then she shrugged her shoulders and admitted, "Yes, I suppose I am."

"You done got a lot to be proud of, Miss Carrie. I don't reckon I know any other woman who could do the things you done. Why, you be runnin' this here plantation all on your own."

Carrie shook her head. "No, I'm not. And you know it. I couldn't begin to run it without all of you helping me. I don't know what I would do if the rest of the Cromwell people were to leave."

"I don't think you got to worry 'bout any more folks leavin'. They figure on stayin' right here."

"Why?" Carrie asked. "Why don't they go free while they have the chance? Why do they choose to stay in slavery?" She trusted Sam to be honest with her.

Sam looked at her for a moment. "Some people got too many fears inside to try to do somethin' new. They talk 'bout what they want, but they don't put no action behind it." He paused. "I figure they's some of them hopin' things will be different 'round here after the war."

"Why? Who do they want to win?"

Sam shrugged again. "Depends on who you be talkin' to. Somes wants the North to win. They figure they goin' to come down here and set them all free. Then they won't have to face a scary escape. It will be done for them."

"And some want the South to win?"

Sam nodded. "They's not sure 'bout them people up North. They don't know what it will be like. They figure if they work hard here and the South done wins this war, that they will be treated better and given more rights as a kind of reward."

Carrie couldn't miss the contempt in his voice, even though she knew he was trying to hide it. "What about you, Sam? Why do you stay?" It was a question she had been wondering about for a while. She had thought he would leave when Rose and Moses were gone.

Sam was silent for a long while. "I got me a job to do here, Miss Carrie. I won't be goin' nowhere till that job be done."

"What kind of job is that?" Carrie was surprised at her own directness. She usually allowed the slaves their privacy, but she and Sam had grown close. With Rose and Moses gone, she depended more on his solid, kind strength.

Again Sam hesitated, opening his mouth as if he wanted to speak, and then shutting it again.

"I'm sorry, Sam. I don't mean to pry."

Sam shook his head. "It be okay, Miss Carrie." He looked at her with warmth in his eyes. "My job be to take care of you."

Carrie stared at him. "What?"

Sam nodded. "I know all about Rose and your granddaddy. Been knowin' bout it ever since Rose girl was born." Carrie listened while he told his story. "Rose told me she was leavin'. She knew my old heart would break if she just disappeared without telling' me. But she was worried about you, Miss Carrie. I told her I would watch out for you."

"You're staying here just for me?" she whispered, her eyes flooded with tears as she battled her emotions. She was grateful Rose had asked Sam to look out for her. She didn't know how she would have made it through the last two months without Sam. There was also sorrow that her faithful friend could be free if he didn't feel responsible for her.

Sam smiled. "I wouldn't been takin' that job if I hadn't wanted it, Carrie girl."

Carrie smiled in return as he slipped away from the more formal "Miss Carrie." She shook her head. "I know I should tell you to go on and find your freedom, but somehow I can't bring myself to say it. I depend on you so much. You have become so special to me, and I don't want you to leave." She frowned. "I'm afraid I'm being terribly selfish."

Sam shook his head. "I don't reckon you're being selfish, Carrie girl. Ever'body need someone to draw strength from. Wouldn't do you no good to tell me to leave anyways. I don't reckon I'll be movin' on 'less I know you're all right." His tone left no room for argument.

Carrie gazed at him, tears once more swimming in her eyes. "Thank you," she said. She should say more, but the words wouldn't come.

Sam nodded and then changed the subject. "When you gonna want the big tree cut?"

Sam's question brought Carrie back to the present. "I'm not going to have a tree this year, Sam." She reached in her pocket and pulled out a letter. "This came from Father yesterday. He would like me to come to Richmond. I'm going to go."

"When you leavin'?"

"Today is the fifteenth. I'm going to leave in three days. I would appreciate it if you would drive me."

"Yessum," Sam replied. Then he turned and disappeared into the house.

Carrie lingered on the porch and stared out over the brown pastures. The lush green of summer had been swallowed by the harshness of winter. The barren trees formed a stark border to the picture, and yet, still she loved it. No matter how much she wanted to leave someday to fulfill her dream, her heart would always be here at Cromwell Plantation. It grew more special to her every day.

She was glad her father had written for her to come to Richmond. There were too many memories from Christmases past to taunt her. Christmas had always been such a wonderful time for her. She was like a child when it came to decorating, entertaining and giving gifts.

Too much had changed, though. Last Christmas, her father, Robert and Matthew had all been here to share in the joy. Now her father was too busy in Richmond, Robert was on the front somewhere, and Matthew was still in prison.

Her mind turned, as it did every day, to Rose and Moses. Had they made it to Philadelphia? Would she ever hear from them? Would she ever see them again? Carrie tried to shove down the ache in her heart, but it was harder today than other days. The one year anniversary of her friends' wedding had come and gone. Every time she made a trip to the quarters, she had to look at the cabins that were once home to Sarah, and Rose and Moses. Their emptiness echoed the emptiness in her own heart.

Carrie faced what was eating at her. She was lonely. Being alone on the plantation had not bothered her before when she had Rose and Moses to talk with, laugh with, learn with. Now, it seemed as if every day stretched out before her endlessly. She found ways to keep busy, but the relative inactivity of the winter months weighed heavily. Every day had become a chore. Carrie frowned, not liking where her life was taking her.

"Miss Carrie, the children are ready to go on the hunt."

Carrie turned quickly. "Thank you, Sam. I'm afraid I almost forgot."

Sam frowned. "Your heart be too heavy for Christmastime. It prob'ly do you good to get out in the woods with the children."

Carrie sighed. "I'm sure you're right. It will be good to be with them."

She had been with them only a few minutes before she could feel her spirits rising. Their excitement and enthusiasm was contagious. At first she had regretted saying she would take over Sarah's job of leading the hunt, but now, with the quarters' children swarming around her, she was glad. She smiled down at them and cried out, "It's time!" She turned and led the giggling bunch down the path.

Carrie kept a sharp eye on the woods as they walked. She pointed up at a bunch of glistening yellow persimmons. It was too late in the year to find many of them, but the few they took back would be like golden treasures. As the children gathered around her, she knelt down on one knee and repeated the words she had heard Sarah say for so many years.

"Chilun, we be finding gifts for Jesus like the wise men did. They brung the baby Jesus three gifts—gold, sweet smelling spices, and bitter herbs. Some of the very herbs and fruits we be findin' now."

The children giggled as she imitated Old Sarah. Carrie picked Jubal to climb for the golden treasure. His eyes shone bright with excitement and pleasure when she pointed at him. Quick as a wink, he shimmied up the tree and stretched out on the limb holding the fruit. All the children held their breath as they watched wide-eyed. The limb bent under his weight as he reached for the late fruit. Instinctively, Carrie moved to stand under the limb. At least she could break his fall if the limb broke. With one final reach, Jubal nabbed the fruit and retreated back toward the tree trunk, a wide grin on his face.

"He got it, Miss Carrie. My brother done got the 'simmons!"

Carrie leaned down to give the excited little girl a hug. "You're right, Hannah. Jubal got it. He's a very brave tree climber, isn't he?"

Hannah returned her hug with an even tighter one of her own and then danced away to meet her brother as he slid back down the tree.

Carrie felt her loneliness lift from her like a cloud on a rainy day when the sun finally breaks through. Out here in Sarah's world, where her old friend had taught her so much, she could hear her voice clearly. *"The only cure for loneliness be givin'. When you be givin' you ain't got time to think 'bout what you don't got. But you got to give with your heart. You got to give from your heart. That's the only sure way to beat back that old demon o' loneliness."*

"Thank you, Sarah," Carrie murmured as the children sprinted ahead of her. She walked along slowly, watching for the treasures they had come to seek, but letting the woods work their magic on her. The peace she had been missing for so long began to creep back into her heart. Yes, her life was changing, but life was always like that.

"Girl, the only thing you can depend on is change. Things always gonna be changin'. But changing ain't neither good nor bad. It's what you do with it. You can fight it and let it get the best of you. You can feel sorry for yourself 'cause thin's ain't stayin' just like they was. Or you can look for the good in what's new. You can search for ways to make thin's better. It's all how you look at it, and what you figur' to do with it."

Once again, Sarah's words rang in her head. Solemnly, Carrie made a vow to spend more time in the woods. It was so easy to lose perspective when she was engulfed by the daily operations of the plantation. It was so easy to become overwhelmed. She knew she needed time alone to make sense of all that was happening in her life.

"Miss Carrie! Miss Carrie! We done found some of them berries Old Sarah said were magic."

Carrie smiled down at Hannah's glowing face as the little girl skipped up to her. She took her hand and began to run down the trail to where she could hear the other children. Her voice rang out in the clear air. "Let's go get them, Hannah."

Carrie gazed around her as Sam drove the carriage along Broad Street. She could already sense the difference in the city. Gone was the dour gloom that had prevailed after the Battle of Bull Run. Gone was the stunned reality of the consequences of war. The dead had been mourned. The wounded had been nursed and sent back to the front. The reality of victory had replaced the reality of death. And it was Christmas!

People thronged Broad Street. The population had exploded even more since she was last there. Men in gray were everywhere. The buildup of the army continued.

With no battle front, they joined the crowds already causing Richmond to bulge at the seams. Faces were happy and laughing.

Carrie watched as one handsome young man in uniform approached a tightly knit group of ladies on the corner. They watched him come, glancing coquettishly over their fans. Their brightly colored dresses, peeking from beneath their heavy coats, were a vivid splash against the dullness of the road.

"Good afternoon, ladies," the young soldier said, his deep voice carrying to where Carrie sat in the carriage.

"Well hello, soldier boy." Carrie frowned at the sound of the woman's voice. Its tone went beyond politeness. As she watched, the young lady standing closest to her took the soldier's arm and smiled up at him. "Going my way, honey?" Then they began to walk down the street together, talking quietly.

Carrie shook her head. Things certainly were changing.

Sam watched her with a grin on his face. "I take it you've never seen one of the new Richmond *ladies* before."

Carrie was confused. "I'm not sure what you're talking about, but she was a little brazen, I think."

Sam nodded. "That's how they make their money."

Carrie stared at him. "How they make their money?" Suddenly, she understood. "That young lady was a prostitute?" she gasped.

Sam nodded, turning his attention back to the road.

"But what are they doing on Broad Street? Oh, I'm not so naive to not know they exist, but they've always stayed away from the nicer parts of town. Men who wanted that kind of entertainment had to go to it."

"Looks like it be comin' to them, now," Sam said with a grin. "You put this many people in one place, and things ain't gonna be the same no more."

Carrie gazed around her. "I guess you're right," she murmured.

Carrie kissed her father on the cheek and ran out to the carriage waiting for her. "Good morning, Spencer. It's good to see you again."

"Thank you, Miss Cromwell. It be good to see you too." Spencer picked up the reins and clucked lightly to the team of horses. "You be back in Richmond for a while?"

"Just until after Christmas, then I will return to the plantation. My father wanted me here for the holidays."

"Christmas is made for families," Spencer agreed. "Mr. Cromwell told me you wanted to go to one of the prisons?"

"That's right. The officers' prison in the old Harwood Factory."

Spencer merely nodded his head.

Carrie looked around her as the carriage rolled along. Not too far from her father's house, people were hard at work transforming military barracks into the Chimborazo Hospital. From all Carrie had heard, it was going to be quite an impressive operation.

Maybe...

She pushed down the longing in her heart. Her place was still on the plantation.

The day was bitterly cold, with gray, overcast skies and a stiff northern breeze. Her father had told her this morning he wouldn't be surprised if they got snow. Carrie stared hopefully at the sky. Now that she was back in Richmond, the Christmas season had regained some of its excitement for her. She had worked hard the last four days to transform her father's house into a festive home. He had been thrilled to see the tree she had decided at the last minute to have Sam cut and bring along with them. They were going to decorate it together tonight. It was nowhere as big and impressive as the ones they usually had, but it would bring the spirit of Christmas into his home.

Now she was on her way to visit Matthew. His present was carefully wrapped and sitting beside her.

"We be here, Miss Cromwell."

Carrie started and looked up. She had been so immersed in her thoughts, she hadn't even been aware of where they were. The prison district looked even more depressing on a day like today. As the cold wind whipped around the buildings, she glanced up at the open windows and shuddered. Those men must be freezing.

She looked at Spencer as she stepped from the carriage. "I expect I will be at least forty-five minutes. It is much too cold for you to wait here for me." She paused and almost smiled at Spencer's look of surprise. "You may go find somewhere warm if you would like. I will meet you back here at eleven-thirty."

"Thank you, Miss Cromwell," Spencer said, his eyes speaking his gratitude.

The guard who answered the door in response to Carrie's knock was a new one. She wondered if she would have the same trouble as the first time but need not have worried. He carefully read the letter she handed him and stepped aside to let her enter. "I will notify Lieutenant Todd."

Carrie waited in the hallway, shivering from the damp chill of the building. She gripped her gift to Matthew tighter.

"Hello again, Miss Cromwell."

"Good morning, Lieutenant Todd," Carrie replied pleasantly. The man standing before her looked as if his months in charge of the prisoners had done nothing to improve his state of mind. While he had kept his voice light, his eyes spoke his disdain. He didn't attempt to hide it with his next statement.

"I understand you are here to mollycoddle one of our prisoners again."

"Those are not the words I would choose to use, Lieutenant," Carrie replied evenly.

Todd smirked, but nodded as if he had no stomach for a parley today. "I will have Justin called for you. Good day," he said abruptly, turning to reenter his office.

The guard led Carrie to the same room she had visited Matthew in before. She had no idea of what to expect. When the door opened again, she quickly rose to her feet. She almost cried aloud when she saw Matthew, but she managed to force a smile to her lips instead.

He saw right through her. Moving forward to take both of her hands, he smiled down at her. "I know I look bad. You don't have to pretend."

Carrie shook her head and squeezed his hands warmly. "You still have a sparkle in your eyes. I'm glad to see that at least."

Matthew had lost a lot of weight since she had last seen him. He had had none to spare then. His skin was pale and dull from his long months of confinement. His hair had grown long and scraggly but was pulled back from his face, accentuating the sharp contrast of the sunken cheeks that now sported a thick red beard. The clothes he was wearing were inadequate to protect him from the harsh weather. Yet, still his bearing was erect, and his eyes and voice were strong. Prison life may have been hard on his body, but his spirit had not been conquered.

"Merry Christmas," she said with a smile. "I brought you a present."

Matthew reached for it, his eyes clouding for a moment. "It seems like a different life than the one last year. I can hardly believe it was just one year ago that I was sharing Christmas with you, your father and Robert on your plantation." He paused and looked at the package. "Thank you."

"Open it," Carrie urged. She wanted him to have what was inside.

Matthew tore into it. Seconds later he gave a whoop of delight. "A coat!"

"Put it on, Matthew." She was glad he liked her gift. She had thought long and hard before selecting it. Finally, she had remembered the open-air windows and hunted down the warmest coat she could find.

Matthew put it on quickly. Then he stared at Carrie.

She returned his stare and dissolved into laughter at the same time he did. The coat looked like it had swallowed him.

"I bought it for you the way I remembered you," Carrie choked out between laughs. Thank God they were able to laugh about it. It would be so easy to cry.

"It's wonderful, Carrie," Matthew said, controlling his laughter and speaking warmly. "You don't know the number of times I have longed for something to keep me warm. Thank you."

"Tell me how you are doing," Carrie asked, eager to turn the attention away from herself.

Matthew shrugged. "The days are long. The nights tend to be longer. It has become harder in the cold to keep my spirits up. The officers I reside with are wonderful, though. We keep each other from feeling sorry for ourselves. We spend long hours dreaming of what our release will be like. We regale each other with stories of home. I could probably tell you every man's life story up there."

"Ever the journalist," Carrie observed.

"No," Matthew said thoughtfully. "It's more a preservation of sanity. We have to remind each other that there really is another world out there."

Carrie nodded but realized she had no way of truly understanding what he was going through.

Matthew shook his head. "I really have very little to complain about. I live in paradise compared to the enlisted men. However bad the food may be, they at least give us provisions for three meals a day. The enlisted men only get two. I have a straw mattress to lay on, while the enlisted men sleep on the floor. And we do find ways to pass the time. I find I am becoming quite good at chess," he said cheerfully.

"You have a chess set?" Carrie asked.

"Of a sort. It is quite a popular game here at Harwood's. The playing pieces are a bit crude. They are carved from meat bones, but they serve their purpose." He laughed. "One of the officers has become quite fanatical about the game. Last week when he was playing, he became so excited about checkmating his opponent that he fainted dead away. We told him he needed to play a little less and eat a little more."

"Have you heard anything about the possibility of your being released?"

"I'm afraid not, but I have not given up hope."

"Hope becomes our light during our darkest times," Carrie murmured.

"What?"

Carrie repeated what she had said. "Old Sarah used to tell me that. I find it to be very true."

"Sarah was right. My hope is what gets me up every morning." He smiled. "There are things happening to give hope. Our famous Congressman Ely was released yesterday. Seems he was exchanged for Charles James Faulkner."

"The Virginian politician who was arrested in the North for disloyal conduct?"

"That's the one. Anyway, the Federal government released him. The Confederates reciprocated and released Ely since he was also an important politician."

"How happy he must be!"

"Yes, and we were happy for him. Not only is he free, we know he will spread the news in the North about what is happening in the prisons. We all pray he will have influence to force some exchange of prisoners."

Carrie nodded. "I hope so," she said.

"So, Carrie Cromwell, how are you doing? Still running the plantation by yourself?"

"I'm afraid so. Even more by myself than I was before." Briefly, she told him of Rose and Moses' escape. "I have great hopes they are with Aunt Abby even as we speak."

Both of their eyes misted over as they thought about the lady they loved so much.

Finally Carrie cleared her throat. "I am only here for the Christmas holidays, then I will go back to the plantation and begin to prepare for spring planting. There is much work that needs to be done."

Matthew gazed at her with obvious admiration and asked quietly. "Are you planning on seeing Robert while you are here?"

Carrie's mouth fell open. "Robert is in Richmond?"

"I thought you knew," Matthew said. "He was here to visit me yesterday."

"Did he speak of visiting me?" Carrie hated to ask the question, but she simply had to know.

"Well...no, but then, I don't think he has any idea you are here. He arrived in town night before last. He spoke of visiting your father today."

"I'm sure Father will be glad to see him," Carrie managed, even though her heart was spinning.

Matthew leaned forward and took her hands. "I'm hoping things can work out between you and Robert."

Carrie took a deep breath and regained control of her emotions. Why could she not control her heart and mind when it came to Robert? It would be better if he didn't discover she was in town. Only time was going to heal her heart, while continuing to see him would do nothing but keep the wound raw.

"Thank you, Matthew, but I don't see that happening. I'm glad he was here to see you yesterday, though."

Matthew nodded and watched her quietly.

Carrie sought for a way to change the subject. Her mind drew a blank. All she could do was sit, fighting to control her emotions.

Matthew came to her rescue, relaying stories of prison life. It gave her time to pull her thoughts back together.

"Time's up!" the guard called into the room.

Carrie flushed. "Matthew, I'm so sorry."

"Nonsense," Matthew responded with a warm smile. "It has been wonderful to have you here. You have given me a gift I have longed for, and..." He paused. "I understand unrequited love," he finished softly.

Carrie stared at him. She hadn't known about a lost love in his life.

"Time's up!" the guard called again, appearing at the door.

"Merry Christmas, Carrie. Thank you for coming."

"Merry Christmas, Matthew." Carrie said with a catch in her throat. "I will be thinking of you."

Two nights before Christmas found Carrie on her father's arm as they swept up the stairs leading to a gloriously lighted home. Carrie gazed at the elegant mansion as they approached. Candles were burning in every window. Festive greenery adorned every door, window and sash. A large tree, resplendent in its Christmas finery, was the center of attention in the grand foyer.

A doorman was waiting to take their wraps. Music played in the background as the guests entered. Carrie looked around her. Would Robert be here tonight? She tried to pull her attention back to her father and the hosts they were waiting to greet. She was being silly. She knew she must stop looking for Robert everywhere she went; after all, what good had her decision been if she was going to pine over him for the rest of her life? It was high time she focus on other young men. Maybe that would keep her mind off Robert.

When Carrie stepped into the ballroom, her plan was perfectly formulated in her mind. She would have so much fun and meet so many new men tonight, she would have no time to think of Robert.

"The first dance belongs to you, Father."

Thomas turned to her with a bright smile. "I was never in doubt of that, dear. I was simply going to turn the young men away until I had had my fill. By the way, have I told you how ravishing you look in your Christmas gown?"

Carrie laughed. "Yes, you have. I still think you are trying to make me feel better about wearing last year's gown." She laughed again. "Not that I care. I've always thought it was silly to wear a gown once and then retire it to search for another. I loved this dress when I bought it, and I still love it," she said. She knew she looked her best in the sweeping, red satin gown with green velvet trim. Robert had loved her in it...

Too late she remembered her vow. When the music started, she moved into her father's arms. The dancing would claim her attention. She would make sure of it.

Laughter and chatter filled the ballroom as the music swept its way through the room. Carrie put all thoughts out of her mind and fell into the spirit of the evening. Hard things were to be ignored and banished from significance. This was a night for enjoyment. One willing partner after another swept her through dance after dance. The music swirled around and through her.

"May I have this dance, Miss Cromwell?"

Carrie felt a tap on her shoulder and turned to meet her new partner with a smile. "Why, of course—" The words died on her lips. She struggled for control until managed to say quite naturally, "Hello, Robert."

He continued to look at her, almost seeming to drink her in with his eyes. She blushed but didn't look away. He held out his arms and Carrie moved into them. The magic that had engulfed them the first night they had danced together at the Blackwell Ball swallowed them once again. Carrie lost touch with everything around her. All she could see was Robert. All she could feel was the beating of her heart and his arms around her. The music faded into the background as they swirled through the room.

When the music stopped, he said nothing, just watched her quietly. When it started up again almost immediately, he swept her once more onto the floor. They were one as they glided from one dance to the other. Carrie had no need to talk. She didn't want to break the magic. She didn't want reality to dash her hopes one more time. She was giving herself a Christmas present.

Finally, the music died away. They had completely ignored the call to the supper table. All around them they could hear guests calling for their wraps and carriages.

Carrie, breathing hard, stepped back.

Robert stepped back as well but didn't release his hold on her shoulders. Finally he spoke, his voice registering an intensity she had never heard. "I would like to talk to you. May I come by tomorrow morning?"

Carrie nodded. The magic of the evening still had her in its grip. Perhaps it would continue.

Robert's mouth tightened with frustration. He took her hand and led her through the throng of people.

Carrie followed willingly.

Robert pushed open the door to the study and pulled her into the dimly lit room, cozy from the heat of the flickering fire. Still not speaking, he led her to the large window overlooking the city. They stood silently for a few moments as they watched sparse snowflakes dance in the lights along the street.

Robert turned her to face him and gazed down at her. "I've missed you, Carrie."

Carrie met his eyes. "And I've missed you, Robert." She knew her face was saying much more. She didn't care.

Robert continued to stare at her, obviously unsure of his words. Carrie sympathized with him. What was there to say? She had turned down his proposal of marriage. It would be insane to deny the magic that still pulsed between them, but it hadn't been enough before. Why should it be now?

A sudden spark from the fire exploded and shot up the chimney. Robert glanced at the fire and seemed to make up his mind. He watched her closely as he drew her toward him.

Carrie did not resist. The magic of the evening held her captive. She closed her eyes and leaned forward slightly as Robert's lips claimed hers. Her whole body trembled as his hold on her tightened, and his lips sent trails of fire down her spine. She could no more control her response to him than she could control what was happening in her country. She shuddered slightly as her arms reached up to encircle his neck, and her lips sent their own message.

A sudden noise in the hallway startled them. They drew apart simultaneously and looked at each other, breathless. Carrie fought to control her trembling. She knew she needed to regain control before someone walked in on them. The sound of footsteps heading toward the study said that would be soon.

Robert bowed and moved away, still holding her with his eyes. "I'll see you in the morning," he said gravely.

Then he turned and walked away.

Carrie turned away from the window in disappointment.

Thomas watched her from his window chair. "He'll be here," he said comfortingly. "Something must be holding him up."

Carrie shook her head. "It's almost noon. He must have changed his mind." She tried to hide the bitter disappointment in her voice. She turned and took a seat far from the window. She had been silly to hope again. Silly to lie awake most of the night, dreaming that things could have changed. Silly to dance each dance over and over in her mind. Silly to relive their magical kiss.

"I've had a wonderful Christmas with you, Father," she forced out. "Thank you so much." The clock struck noon, and she rose to head for the stairs. "We will have to leave soon if we want to get all our visiting done. I will get my wraps."

Thomas played along. "The Clays are expecting us for dinner around five o'clock. We should have plenty of time to make all our stops."

Carrie nodded and moved toward the stairs.

Just then there was a sharp rap on the door. Carrie started and held her breath as Micah came from the back to answer it. She had not heard a carriage. Hope began to flutter once more.

"I have a message for Miss Carrie Cromwell," a strange voice said.

Carrie moved to the door. "Thank you, Micah." She turned to the young boy in uniform standing before her, his face intense with his mission. "I am Carrie Cromwell. What can I do for you?"

The boy looked at her admiringly and held out a thin envelope. "Lieutenant Borden asked me to deliver this," he said. He hesitated a moment and blurted out, "He said the prettiest girl in Richmond would be the one to claim it. He was right." The soldier flushed crimson.

Carrie smiled gently and reached out to take the envelope. Already, her hopes were withering. "Thank you," she said graciously. "And Merry Christmas." Then she closed the door and stood in the entryway, staring at the letter.

"What is it?" Thomas called.

Carrie walked woodenly into the parlor. "A note from Robert."

Her father said nothing, but she knew he was waiting. She peeled open the envelope and pulled out the single sheet.

> *My dear Carrie,*
> *It is with great disappointment and sorrow that I write this letter. I have been called away to join Jackson on the front. I am leaving early in the morning. My heart longs to talk with you, but I'm afraid that is impossible. Thank you for a wonderful evening of magic. I will carry you in my heart. Merry Christmas.*
> *Love,*
> *Robert*

Carrie read the first three sentences out loud to her father and then carefully folded the letter and put it in her pocket. "I believe I hear the carriage being called. We'd best be on our way."

It wasn't until late that night that Carrie let the tears come that had been choking her throat. Somehow she had managed to hold them back all day, smiling brightly as they visited from house to house. The effort had left her exhausted. After kissing her father goodnight, she had escaped to her room. Too exhausted to prepare for sleep, she had fallen across her bed. It had taken only moments for the hot tears to push past the barriers she had erected. Finally, too drained to cry any more, she lay quietly on her bed, her heart squeezed with pain.

She heard the clock chiming midnight before she moved again. She walked over to the desk in her room and found a piece of paper and a pen. She began to write.

Dear Robert,

I have a confession to make. I love you with all my heart. In spite of the fact that you have hatred and anger toward the black people I love so much, I love you. I have tried not to. I have told myself that I didn't. But the truth is inescapable. You are the only man who has ever captured my heart, and I will love you forever.

I am convinced, however, that marriage between us would never work. The tensions and misunderstandings would someday destroy the love that burns so brightly between us. I would rather endure the pain I am suffering now than watch that happen. My heart could not stand it.

I have searched my heart deeply tonight, and I have come to accept the truth. I merely thought I had let you go, but I didn't really. I was sure you would change your mind—that your heart would change, and we could be together. I have been living my life, but not as fully as I should because I have been waiting for you. I cannot continue to live that way.

I have reached a decision tonight. Once again, I have completely given you up. It is the only way I can live. Given enough time, I am sure my heart will move past its love for you. I love you too much to continue seeing you. Please do not make any attempts to communicate with me. If you love me, you will heed my wishes.

I hope for you a wonderful life.

Love,

Carrie

Carrie wiped the tears away from her eyes as she finished the letter and carefully sealed and addressed the envelope.

Unbidden, a picture of Robert on the front, suffering cold and fatigue, sprang to her mind. For several long minutes, she held the letter in her hand and stared at it.

She stood and moved toward the crackling fire that still flickered in her fireplace. Kneeling, she held the letter to the flames and watched as the words that poured from her heart crumbled into ashes.

Chapter Twenty-Five

January 1, 1862 dawned clear and unseasonably mild in Winchester, Virginia. Robert stretched as he came out of his tent, taking deep breaths of the fresh morning air. All around him there was movement as the eighty-five hundred men Jackson had mustered for his winter campaign prepared for the march to come. Spirits were high and confidence was strong that their campaign to take control of the western portion of Virginia would be successful.

Robert dashed water onto his face to wake himself up and then moved over to the cooking fires. It took him only a few minutes to cook a piece of beef on the tip of his sword. Hardtack and a cup of coffee finished his breakfast. As he ate, he pondered what was to come.

"Good morning, Lieutenant," a voice said cheerfully.

"Good morning, Hobbs." Robert had been pleased to discover Private Hobbs had been assigned to his regiment. His wounds were completely healed and he was still as dedicated to the cause as ever. He had proudly informed Robert that he had signed up for the duration of the war.

"Hey, look, Lieutenant. I won the contest this morning. I got me three." Hobbs lifted his coffee for inspection.

Robert grimaced as he walked over and gazed down into the murky liquid. He knew the men had competitions each morning to see who came up with the most weevil larvae from the hardtack. Hobbs had three floating at the top of his coffee.

"This hardtack really been around since the Mexican-American War?" one of his other men asked. "We're eating grub that was made in 1846?"

"Sheesh!" Hobbs exclaimed. "That's sixteen years." He held up his hardtack and looked at it with astonishment. "Somebody made this stuff the year I was born." He reached down with his knife and skimmed the larvae off the top of his steaming liquid. "I reckon it's all right now," he said.

Robert smiled as most of the soldiers followed suit. They were good men, doing their best to find humor in their hardships. He knew they dipped the rock-hard biscuits in their coffee to soften them, but also to dislodge any insect infestation caused by improper storage. The army was making the most of every provision they had—including hardtack baked for earlier military use.

"This campaign should be a cinch after the first one we fought together," Hobbs remarked.

"I certainly hope so," Robert replied. "A lot hinges on this."

Hobbs nodded and took a sip of his coffee. "I reckon it won't be too hard to regain control of western Virginia. I hear tell the Yankees are going to be powerfully outnumbered by us. They'll probably run when they see us coming."

"If they know what's good for them they will," Robert agreed. His face hardened. He knew more hinged on this than his men were aware. President Davis had told him Jackson's full intent during a strategy session.

Jackson's plan was to concentrate his entire force on Romney in order to drive the enemy, about six thousand strong, from the South Branch Valley. He hoped his thrust would lure the North's General McClellan out of his fortifications around Alexandria where he was opposed by General Johnston. Then Jackson would move with his troops to reinforce Johnston and secure a victory. Jackson deemed it of great importance that northwestern Virginia be occupied and controlled by Confederate troops this winter. President Davis had rejected a proposal by General Beauregard to invade Maryland. Jackson's plan, he approved.

The day for action had arrived. Fortune appeared to be on their side, as the warm weather lifted everyone's spirits and made the idea of a mere forty-mile march seem like a picnic.

Robert was ready with his men when the call came to move out. "Let's go get them, men!" he called loudly. He urged his horse forward as his men stepped out behind him.

Excited talk and laughter filled the air for the first part of the march, but then the wind shifted and began to blow from the north. The week of mild weather ended abruptly as a strong front blasted its way toward them. Robert looked up at the sky in concern. He had been aware of the dangers inherent in a winter campaign, but he had hoped somehow they would not have to deal with them. He had also received information earlier that concerned him greatly. Even though Romney was Jackson's ultimate goal, the general had decided on a circuitous route that would more than triple their distance to Romney. Robert was afraid the men would not be able to hold out that long on foot in bad weather, but it was not his decision. All he could do was follow orders.

He had grave misgivings about the men's capability to do what they were being asked to do, but he understood why they were being asked. Had General Jackson gone straight toward Romney, he would have left a larger force hanging on his right flank than he cared to worry about. At the same time, he would have left Union forces free to communicate on their Romney relief efforts. Instead, he had decided to march straight for Bath, scattering the force on his right before striking west toward his real goal. He would cut telegraph lines and burn bridges along the way. It would at least delay the organization of any new force to harass him.

By nightfall, the threatening sky had erupted into a snow and ice storm. Jackson's troops were in an uncomfortable bivouac, attempting to stay warm.

Hobbs smiled at Robert when he walked over to check on his men. "Fine night, isn't it, Lieutenant?"

"I suppose it is if you're a bear, Hobbs. How are you?"

Hobbs shrugged. "I could be a little warmer, but I reckon I'll make it. I used to go on hunting trips in the winter in these mountains. They can be pretty brutal." His face said much more than his words did.

Robert nodded in agreement as he gazed around at the hundreds of campfires battling the cold sweeping down on them. Men surrounded them, their faces pinched with cold as they wrapped themselves in thin, inadequate blankets. Supply wagons had not been able to keep up with the troops. The men were without food or shelter. Wind raced over the hills, whistling through the trees, and whirling sparks and smoke into their eyes.

One young soldier caught his attention with his hacking cough. Robert frowned and walked over to where he was curled up on the ground with his back to the fire. "That cough doesn't sound so good, Clark." The slightly built North Carolinian gazed up at him, but when he opened his mouth to speak another spasm of coughing erupted. "Get this man something hot to drink," Robert snapped. If anyone heard him above the increased whistling of the wind, they didn't acknowledge it. Their faces seemed frozen as they stared into the fire.

Robert growled, cursing under his breath the necessity of bringing these men out into weather like this. He stalked over to one of the cook fires and poured some water into a pot to boil. It was twenty minutes before the water was hot enough to make coffee—just long enough to numb his hands and feet. He rubbed his hands together furiously, then made a large cup and carried it over to Clark. The man was still coughing violently, his body shaking with the cold.

"Drink this," he commanded. He knelt down and put his arm behind Clark's shoulders to support him while he drank the hot brew.

Clark sipped at the drink slowly in between coughs. The shaking and coughing subsided somewhat, and he smiled up in gratitude. "Thank you, Lieutenant."

Robert nodded and stood up, clapping his hands to get the attention of his men. "We're in this together. All of us. Nothing we do is going to change this night, so that means we have to make the best of it. And we have to help each other."

His men looked at him dully. Robert turned, strode back to his tent, and grabbed up his blankets. When he returned, he put one around Clark, wrapped the other one around himself, and then sat down next to the fire.

Hobbs stared at him in astonishment. "You staying out here with us tonight, Lieutenant?"

"I said we were in this together, didn't I?" Surprised faces took on new life. "We've got to fight this cold," Robert continued. "That means we have to take turns keeping the fires burning hot."

"I'll stand the first watch," one man volunteered.

"I'll watch next," another spoke up.

"It also means we have to keep hot liquids in us," Robert snapped.

Without speaking, two men stood and headed toward the cook fire. One piled on more wood while the other filled pots with water.

"And we have to share our body warmth," Robert finished. Soon there were groups of four or five soldiers huddled together, offering each other protection from the wind, sleet and cold.

Robert looked longingly at the tent that would offer him at least some protection against the storm, but he turned away. He would stay with his men. If he expected them to stand together, he had to stand with them. He laid down as close to the fire as possible, pulled his blanket tightly to him, and tried to think of other things. Carrie appeared, full-blown in his mind. He felt as if he could reach out and touch her glowing skin and sparkling eyes. Suddenly, the laughter in her eyes faded and was replaced by something else. Robert craned forward in his mind to determine what it was. And then he knew. There was a look of warm approval—even pride—on her face. Strangely encouraged, Robert slept.

Five days later, Robert found himself wondering if he would ever be warm again. So far the campaign had been successful. The town of Bath had been easily occupied after a brief skirmish in which no one was injured. When Jackson followed the retreating troops to the town of Hancock, the Yankees had returned their fire with heavy fire of their own and refused to surrender. General

Jackson had considered using his superior force to overwhelm the city but decided he would wait for his widely scattered troops to come back together. He had contented himself by ordering several shells lobbed into the town after giving Hancock time to remove their women and children.

"Lieutenant Borden."

Robert spun around at the sound of the voice behind him. "Yes, sir, General Jackson!" he returned.

"Take a unit of your men to guard against any curiosity the Yankee cavalry might have to investigate us tonight." The general issued the orders in his usual quiet voice then turned his mare, Little Sorrel, back toward his tent.

Robert watched him go, amazed once again at how unlike a general he appeared. His other Confederate counterparts were all pomp and circumstance. From the beginning, Jackson and his cadet aides were content to go about their duties clad in the plain blue uniforms of the Military Institute. His seat in the saddle was rather ungraceful. His threadbare cadet hat, worn even in this cold, was always tilted over his eyes. He spoke only when necessary, and he seldom smiled. Yet, the loyalty of his troops was wholehearted. To a man, they would stand with him.

Robert had watched as the misery of the troops intensified. Today was the first day of a break in the weather. There was plenty of grumbling and complaining, but he had heard no one suggest they turn back. The men would continue to press forward to Romney. That is, if any were healthy enough to stand. Robert frowned at the wave of hacking coughs that rolled toward him. Many of his men were sick, wracked with fevers and coughing. Once again, Carrie's face rose to his mind. What he would give to have her here to care for his men. Then he shook his head. He could not imagine Carrie being in a place like this.

"Hobbs!" he called as he turned toward his men. Immediately, the freckle-faced mountain boy was at his side.

"Yes, Lieutenant?"

Robert smiled at the lad. Hobbs and his constant good cheer had become indispensable to him. "Select fifty of our men and tell them to prepare for a little scouting trip." He paused. "I want fifty *healthy* men."

Hobbs hesitated for a moment. "I will do my best, sir."

"It's that bad?" Robert asked with a scowl.

Hobbs shrugged. "It's not just our men, sir. The troops are sick everywhere. I'll find the fifty healthiest men I can."

Robert nodded and turned away to gather his own gear. This blamed winter would have to end sometime. The thought of the long weeks stretched out before them were daunting, but there was nothing to do but endure.

Robert talked briefly with the cavalry detachment that rode out to meet him. "I have orders to stand watch against the Yankee cavalry," he said to the captain who rode up to confer with him.

The middle-aged man regarding him answered with amusement. "You ain't got nothing to worry about, Lieutenant. Them Yankees ain't coming out to look for no trouble tonight, and my boys are keeping a sharp eye on them."

"I have my orders," Robert said.

The captain shrugged. "Suit yourself, Lieutenant. We can all watch nothing happen together." He paused. "Or you can let your men get some sleep. Looks to me like they need it."

Robert knew he was right. Hobbs had tried to pick fifty healthy men, but that was simply asking too much of a unit decimated with sickness. "Let me know if you have need of our services," he said, relaxing. Then he turned and waved his men back.

Robert searched until he found an area he was convinced would be safe—an open field that commanded an advance on either end. They would have time to take action if the enemy tried to surprise them during the night. After telling his men to get some sleep, he wrapped up in his blanket and laid down on the cold ground. He looked up into the sky for a few moments. It was cloudy, but not nearly as cold as it had been. Within minutes he had fallen into an exhausted slumber.

"Great Jehoshaphat!"

A loud, startled voice snapped Robert from his sleep. Just as quickly, he was aware of an oppressive heat. He threw off the blanket with which he had completely covered his head during the night and was amazed to see snow flying in every direction.

"Look at that, Lieutenant!"

Robert gazed in the direction Hobbs was waving his arm. The scene stretched out before him was a strange one. The field, blanketed under five inches of snow, looked to be the home of great fallen logs. As he watched, one by one, the "logs" came to life and sent snow flying in every direction.

"First good night's sleep I've had since we started this crazy march," one voice called. "I was warm as a pup all night long!"

Choruses of assent rose around him. Robert smiled, realizing now why farmers in the mountains and in the North prayed for a deep layer of snow to protect their wheat from intense cold. He jumped up, gave orders to the men to prepare breakfast, and then rode up to check with the cavalry unit.

"Still as a church mouse around here," the captain reported. "You can tell Jackson these boys ain't gonna cause no one any trouble."

A horse galloped up and skidded to a halt where they were standing. "What is it, Smith?" the captain asked sharply.

"Reinforcements, sir. There are a large number of reinforcements marching into Hancock. I don't reckon they intend to give it up."

Robert listened as the young scout revealed all the information he had and then turned to race back in the direction he had come from. "I will take this information back to General Jackson," he snapped.

Later that afternoon, General Jackson withdrew his troops and once more continued on his way to Romney. He had abandoned his idea of crossing the Potomac and raiding north. His efforts in taking Bath had not been in vain, however. He had accomplished his primary objective. Earlier that morning, he had sent a command of men to destroy the Big Cacapon Bridge over the Potomac River. They had driven off its defenders and decimated it with their artillery, before proceeding to rip down telegraph lines as far as they could go.

Carrie stopped her work long enough to straighten her shoulders and stretch in an effort to bring relief to her aching muscles. Not even she knew why she was working so hard at the task she had set for herself. She stepped back from the table she had erected in the basement of the house and reviewed her work. Bottle after bottle lined the table in front of her, as well as the shelves surrounding her. Their carefully prepared labels proclaimed their contents. *Yarrow, mistletoe, onion, mint, poppy, broom, thistle, dandelion...*

Carrie gave a sigh of contentment as she looked at how the supply had grown. There were still bags of herbs and plants to take care of, but she was making progress. The idea had come to her late one night when she was poring over the medical books Aunt Abby had sent. The long winter nights had given her an abundance of time to study them. The more she learned, the hungrier she became to know more.

One particular night, as she read through the volume about medicine and its uses, she had a sudden vision of the crowd of Union gunboats choking the Virginia shoreline. The citizens of Richmond were already feeling the results of the blockade. What would happen if medicines started to run short when the need was the greatest? That vision had started her on her current mission. She was sure she would be laughed at if the medical community was ever to see her growing store of herbs, but she didn't care. Even if she only had opportunity to use it for her people here on the plantation, it would be well worth her efforts.

The door above her cracked open, and Sam called down to her. "You plannin' on eatin' sometime today, Miss Carrie?"

"Is it late, Sam?" she called back.

Sam chuckled before he answered. "It be almost four o'clock, Carrie girl."

"Four o'clock," Carrie gasped. No wonder she was beginning to feel faint. She had been down here since ten o'clock that morning. She brushed her hands off on her dress, reached forward to cork the last bottle, and quickly climbed the stairs. "I'm starving," she announced when she reached the top.

Sam chuckled again and pulled out the plate he had been holding behind his back.

Carrie smiled when she saw the steaming bowl of soup surrounded by thick slices of fresh bread and butter. "You're an angel," she exclaimed. Her stomach chimed its agreement. She took the plate and walked past the dining room straight into the parlor, sinking down into the chair pulled closest to the fire. A sharp, cold wind blew outside, making the heat from the fire even more welcome. Branches smacked against the windows of the house, reminding Carrie she needed to have some of the men cut them back for her.

"You need anything else?" Sam asked from the doorway.

Carrie shook her head as she dipped her spoon into the fragrant brew. "This is wonderful. Thank you." She sighed as the first spoonful of soup warmed her all the way down to her stomach. When she finally put her spoon aside, she could feel the strength returning to her body.

Sam reappeared at the door to the parlor, a wide smile spread across his face.

"Yes, Sam?" Carrie asked, returning his smile. "What is it?"

Sam walked forward, holding something in his hand. "We had company," he announced, his eyes sparkling with joy.

"I didn't hear anything." Carrie frowned. "What in the world is someone doing out on a day like this? It's almost dark."

"They didn't come to the front door," Sam announced, still wearing his smile. "They done come to the back door."

Carrie, confused, sat back in her chair. "Will you please tell me what you are talking about? Who came and why were they at the back door?"

Suddenly, her eyes opened wide. She could think of only one reason someone would be out on a night like this and appear at the back door. Someone connected with the Underground Railroad had made a delivery. "Sam...?"

Sam nodded and held out the envelope to her. He held up another one, already opened. "I got me a letter, too," he said proudly. Only then did his eyes mist over. "I'll leave you to read."

Carrie, her heart pounding and her hands trembling, quickly opened the envelope and pulled the thin letter out.

> *Dearest Carrie,*
>
> *I am limited in what I write in case this letter falls into the wrong hands, but I wanted you to know we have safely reached our planned destination. Our hostess sends her deepest heartfelt love to you. Our journey took us longer than expected, but we reached our destination at the end of October. We are both doing well. Our hostess is taking good care of us and opportunities are opening up.*
>
> *Our hearts are with you, and we think of you often. We miss you greatly and long for the day we can all be reunited. Thank you for making all this possible. We will never be able to fully express our gratitude. Please take good care of yourself.*
>
> *Love,*
> *R & M*

Quiet sobs shook Carrie's body. Rose and Moses had made it. They were safe in Pennsylvania with Aunt Abby. Relief flooded her as visions of them struggling through months of winter cold vanished from her mind. It had taken the Underground Railroad over two months to deliver the letter, but there was no telling what route it had been forced to take.

Contentment filled Carrie as she stared into the flames of the fire. Rose and Moses were safe. They had accomplished the first step toward fulfilling their dreams. Unbidden, her thoughts turned to Robert, but it wasn't the longing for him that shook her to the core. It was the sudden intense feeling that he was in danger. Gasping, she gripped the letter tighter and stared out the window, shaken with the knowledge that something horrible was happening to Robert.

She slipped to her knees and buried her head in her hands. Quietly, she began to pray.

Robert had never been as miserable in his life as he was now. After the successful moves to cut the North's communication lines, General Jackson had ordered the troops to move on to Romney. They had marched headlong into the worst weather they had encountered to this point. The temperature plunged dramatically, while snow and sleet pelted them and coated their bodies. Underneath their feet, the sleet transformed itself into a solid sheet of ice.

The first steep incline had forced them off the roads and into the ditches and open fields. It was the only way they could make any progress.

"Look at that, Lieutenant," Hobbs yelled, pointing back toward the road as Robert's troops scrambled to gain footing on the steep hill.

Robert glanced back. "Good Lord," he muttered. "They'll never make it." He stopped and watched as the first of the supply wagons reached the hill. The smooth-shod horses were doing their best to haul the wagons, but the slippery road was too much for them. Robert groaned as he watched their struggle. One slipped, fell, and fought frantically to regain its footing as the other horses slithered around it. The shouts of men filled the air as they encouraged the horses and tried to force them to move forward.

Robert watched for several long minutes. "Come on, men. We have to help." Silently, his men turned and followed him.

Robert sized up the situation and stationed his men behind the wagons. "We have to help the horses. They can't possibly pull this up, but if we put our weight into it and push, the combination of our efforts may make it possible," he yelled over the commotion. He was the first to put his shoulder into the back of one of the wagons. The men around him sprang into action, grunting as the heavy weight of the wagon pressed back against them. Encouraged, the watching wagoners cheered as the wagon began to move forward slowly.

Robert was gasping for breath when they reached the top of the hill, but at least he wasn't cold anymore. Sweat poured from his body, even as ice caked his beard. He peered down the hill in front of him. The driver lifted his reins to send the horses on, but Robert reached out to stop him. "You'll never make it," he snapped. "The wagon will slide right over the horses. They won't be able to stop."

The driver glared at him, obviously short-tempered. "What am I supposed to do?" he growled. "Perch here on the hill? I got other wagons coming up behind me."

Robert thought quickly. An idea came to mind. "Do you have rope in here?" he asked.

The driver nodded and rummaged behind him, pulling out several long coils.

Robert grabbed them and tied four lengths to the top of the wagon. He handed the ends to the four men standing with him. "Spread out to the sides of the road where you have some traction. Use trees for leverage wherever you can. Just keep the wagon moving slowly," he shouted. The four men sprang into action, and with a look of surprised admiration, the driver once again lifted his reins.

Robert stepped back to watch. Would his idea work, or would the four men plunge down the hill after the horses? The wagon began to move. Cursing and shouting filled the air as the men struggled to hold its weight back. There were moments when it seemed the wagon would slide right off the road, taking the horses with it, but finally it reached the bottom of the hill. Not too far ahead, another hill loomed.

"It's going to take us until spring to reach Romney."

Robert turned and smiled weakly at Hobbs. "I'm afraid you might be right." He shrugged. He was aware of the discontent brewing among the troops. "We have one order—to move forward. Somehow we have to figure out how to do that."

Hobbs moved to the back of the next wagon and attached the ropes Robert handed to him. "We're ready, sir," he finally called.

"Move on," Robert called to the driver.

One by one, the ammunition and supply wagons, as well as the ambulances, slithered their way to the top of the hill. The last one was on its way up when one of the men fell and refused to move. His eyes were glazed with pain, fatigue and cold as he stared up at Robert.

"I done brought five wagons up this hill, Lieutenant," he said faintly. "I ain't got nothing left."

Robert helped him to his feet and led him to the side of the road. "You did great work, Clark. Rest here. I'll take your place." Robert leapt over to the wagon and threw his weight into it.

They were almost to the top when it began to slide sideways. The driver cursed and snapped his whip, calling encouragement to his struggling horses, but the ice had continued to thicken, and there seemed no way to stop it.

"Hold it men!" Robert cried, stepping more to the side and throwing his weight into the wagon to stop its slide. A quick glance across his shoulder revealed a gaping ravine yawning just feet from where he stood.

"We're not going to stop it, Lieutenant!" one of the men cried. "It's going!"

Robert shook his head. "No!" he yelled. "This wagon is full of food. Keep pushing!" Every muscle in his body screamed in agony as he fought to stop the inevitable.

Suddenly, the ground gave way beneath him. He reached for the wagon but missed. Robert slid down the ditch, grabbing for something to stop his fall as he stared up at the wagon teetering on the edge above him. He crumpled into a heap at the bottom of the ravine.

"Lieutenant!" he heard a voice scream.

Robert stared upward, his energy and strength spent. So this was how it was going to end. There was no glory in being crushed by a wagon. A picture of Carrie flashed in his mind, and searing regret shot through him that he would never see her again.

Move!

The word exploded in his head as if he had received a verbal command.

Move!

From somewhere, Robert found the strength to stand and lunge for the top of the ravine. His wildly groping hand found a root. Groaning with the effort, he pulled himself up. His shoulders had barely cleared the top when he heard a yell behind him. There was a scream as the horses lost their fight and the wagon plunged down the slope, carrying the horses with it. Robert felt the wagon brush his leg as it crashed into the bottom of the ravine, but his grip on the root held.

Robert's men rushed over to grab his hands and haul him up the rest of the way. He collapsed at the top, gasping for breath.

Finally, he looked down. Three of the horses were still thrashing, one was ominously still. Robert felt sorry for the three—at least the dead one was free from struggle. Then his breath caught. What had happened to the driver? A quick glance reassured him. The driver must have jumped just as the wagon plunged over the edge.

Jackson was there, staring down at the wagon. His voice was sorrowful. "The wagon is done for, men, but we have to get that food." His voice hardened as if he were trying to fight his own feelings. "Cut the horses free. There is a place about a hundred feet up where you can lead them out. If any of them have broken a leg..." He didn't finish his command. He didn't have to. The men knew what they would have to do.

Jackson looked over at Robert. "You all right, Lieutenant? The men told me you are responsible for moving the wagons. Thank you."

Robert nodded and raised his hand. "I'm fine, sir." But he didn't move. His close brush with death had left him dazed.

Clark led a group of men down into the ditch. Several minutes later, the men led a pair of horses away and out of sight. Robert closed his eyes as two shots rang out.

It was almost dark when the wagon was completely unloaded and the food transferred to another. The men spread out into the surrounding field and settled in for another long, miserable night.

Robert crawled into his tent and listened to the wind and sleet assaulting their position. He knew how close he had come to dying. He had been sure when he saw the wagon teetering above him that it was all over. Then the voice had surged through his being, giving his body a strength he didn't know he possessed.

He had tried to fight the knowledge ever since, but here alone in his tent he faced the truth. It had been God who saved him. God who shouted the command. God who had infused his body with strength.

God had always been a thing to know about. A thing that preachers talked about. A thing that he thought about when he went to church, which had only been on rare occasions. He had always believed in God, he supposed. It had just never touched him.

Now he knew God was real, and for some reason God must want him alive. For the first time in his life, Robert felt the warmth of love in his heart. Not the kind of love one sent, but the kind of love one received. The thought both scared and exhilarated him. What was he supposed to do with this new knowledge? The question was still spinning in his brain when he fell into an exhausted sleep.

Chapter Twenty-Six

Rose walked quickly down the crowded sidewalk, her head bent forward against the breathtaking cold. Already, she longed for Virginia. She was sure she would never get used to the brutal winters of the North. Snow was mounded in great heaps along the sides of the road and the sidewalks. She had always loved the occasional white wonderland that descended on the plantation; however, this was different. There were no wide open spaces nearby to turn into a crystalline fairyland. What lay on the streets and walkways was now covered with the gray grime of a coal-driven, industrial society.

As the wind howled down the street, she pulled her jacket and scarf closer and continued to press on. A now familiar noise had her looking up with longing. A horse-drawn car, moving easily on the railroad tracks the city had laid for it, was pulling up beside her. People stared down on her as they eased by. They were traveling to other parts of the city, or maybe they were making their connection to the railroad station across town. Rose swallowed her longing and flash of bitterness. The horsecars were off limits to blacks.

She was gradually learning the rules of this new city she called home. Her dreams of equality had been shattered by the reality of distinct race divisions in the city, but if it had disillusioned her, it had also challenged her. Someday things would be different. She shook her head and pressed on harder. She had housework to do, as well as a heavy load of schoolwork. The very idea caused her heart to lift and her legs to move faster. She was in school!

"Rose!"

Startled, Rose looked up as she heard her name called. Only then did she notice the carriage that had pulled up beside her. "Aunt Abby," she said with a smile.

"Get in quickly," Aunt Abby urged. "Your feet must be nearly frozen." She gazed with horror at Rose's soaked shoes. "You poor dear."

Rose stepped into the carriage. The sidewalks had not been as clear as usual after the heavy snow a few days earlier. She had tried to avoid the drifts, but large groups of whites moving down the sidewalk often meant she was forced to go through them. She had gotten used to it. "They'll warm up when I get home."

Aunt Abby shook her head. "I wish I had another carriage to provide you with transportation," she said regretfully.

Rose laughed aloud at the idea, yet appreciated the warmth that spread through her at yet another indication of Aunt Abby's genuine affection. Impulsively, she reached forward and squeezed the woman's hand, ignoring the pointed look of Aunt Abby's white driver. "You are wonderful," she said with a smile, "but the idea is really rather ridiculous. Could you imagine what people would think if a carriage were to deliver me to the Quaker school?"

Aunt Abby joined in her laughter but quickly sobered. "I'll be glad when this horrendous winter is over. I hate the idea of you walking to school. And knowing that Moses is outside working..." She shuddered.

"I am thrilled to be in school, no matter how hard it is to get there. Besides, it's much better than being consumed by mosquitoes and battling fire smoke in the little clearing in the woods on the plantation. You have no idea what a thrill it is to be able to carry books openly, and to have sufficient paper to write on. I'm learning the things I've always yearned to know." She paused. "And Moses. Yes, he is working hard and is mighty glad to come home at night, but at least he is now master of his own destiny."

Aunt Abby looked at her fondly. "When you put it that way..." She paused and looked thoughtful. "I guess all of us who have a dream have to go through hard times to reach it."

Rose nodded. Aunt Abby had told her of the hardships she had faced when she had taken over her husband's business. "My mama always told me you have to work hard for what you want. Work hard and dream big," she said.

The carriage rolled up to Aunt Abby's house, and they quickly stepped out and dashed up the stairs. The warmth that enveloped Rose as she entered the house was wonderful. She was still in awe of the coal furnace that kept it heated at all hours of the day. Cooking on the gas stove was a luxury she had never even imagined on the plantation, where even in the big house cooking was done on a wood stove. And the running water was truly a miracle after spending her whole life hauling heavy buckets of water from the well. She realized that not all Philadelphians lived the way Aunt Abby did. Wealth was necessary to have these conveniences, but they were becoming more common.

"You have such a serious look on your face, Rose. What are you thinking about?" Aunt Abby asked.

Rose looked at her with a smile. "I'm thinking that someday Moses and I will own a house with all these wonderful things." Even though she was smiling, her voice was firm.

Aunt Abby nodded. "I believe you will, my dear. I believe you will."

The clock struck four, and Rose knew Moses would be home soon, starved from his long day of working in the cold. She unbuttoned her coat and hung it on the coat rack. "I'm going up to put on my other pair of shoes. Then I'll get started on dinner." She turned and walked up the stairs to the room she and Moses shared.

Today, as she had every day since she had arrived, she stopped when she entered the room and gazed around. It was still a marvel to her. A large, four-poster feather bed with a canopy occupied the center of the room. Two Chippendale chairs flanked the fireplace, with a Currier and Ives print above it that demanded attention as soon as one entered the room. A light blue carpet picked up the same color in the drapes, which hung gracefully at the tall set of windows looking out over the busy street. It had taken them a while to get used to the rumble of traffic outside their window, but now it merged with the other background noises and they hardly noticed it. Under the window sat her desk, where she did homework by her own gas lamp. A door to the side of the room led into their own washroom, complete with a bathtub.

Rose shook her head as she took in the scene. She still felt like she should pinch herself when she walked into this room. She had never imagined she would share in such splendor. The other slaves in the quarters had been so jealous of her tiny room in the big house. What would they think if they could see her now? Rose chuckled. Her friends on the plantation would not even be able to imagine such splendor. You had to see it to believe it.

Rose changed her shoes and dashed back downstairs to the kitchen. Aunt Abby was already there, reaching into the icebox to pull out a container of clams. "What are you doing, Aunt Abby?" Rose cried. "I told you I would fix dinner. I'm sorry I took so long upstairs."

Aunt Abby turned and placed the container on the table. "Nonsense. You did nothing of the kind. Believe it or not, I find I miss cooking occasionally. You have so completely taken over the household work, I find myself feeling guilty at times, but I am in here tonight out of nothing but desire. I will be more than happy to leave the cooking to you—you are much better than me, and I am being treated to foods I never dreamed about—but tonight I would like to help."

Rose smiled and moved forward. "What are we cooking?"

"Clam chowder seems to hit the spot for me tonight."

Rose nodded. "That sounds wonderful." She and Moses had grown to love the seafood chowders so common in the North. "I'll cut the potatoes while you make the base."

Silence prevailed in the kitchen as the two women worked side by side. Wonderful aromas soon permeated the air. When Rose had dumped all of the potatoes into the waiting cream base, she cut several thick slabs of bread and pulled the butter out of the icebox. When she turned back, she saw Aunt Abby watching her closely.

"Are you happy here?" Aunt Abby asked.

Rose stared at her. "How can you not think I'm happy? I have everything I dreamed of. I'm in school. I'm free. What more could I want?"

"You could want to go back home and make a difference for your people," she suggested.

Rose flushed. "You're right, Aunt Abby. I truly have everything I want here, but every day I think of the millions of blacks in the South who could never even dream of these things. My mama always told me that God gave me gifts so that I could use them to help his people. I think black people need my gifts more than any other. I miss seeing children's eyes light up when they finally understand what I'm teaching them. It is a thrill like no other."

"What if the South wins the war and your people don't go free?"

Rose shrugged. She had thought about it. "I'll find some way to help," she stated. "I have a dream of all Southern black children attending school like white children do here in the North." She shook her head. "Not even most white children go to school there now."

"Why not? Surely people see the benefits of children being educated."

"I'm afraid they don't," Rose responded. "I used to hear Marse Cromwell talking about it with visitors at the dinner table. The high society of Virginia tolerates the idea of some education for poor white children, but state-enforced public education is a whole different matter. The planters believe that government has no right to intervene in the education of children. They see it as also trying to interfere in the larger social arrangement. They talk about how much money is being spent on the public school effort, but it seems to be only a drop in the bucket of what is needed."

Aunt Abby looked up from stirring the chowder. "Whatever makes them feel that way?"

"They believe public education will violate the natural evolution of society," she said, remembering the many discussions around the table late at night. "They think it will threaten the family's authority over their children.

They are afraid it will damage the relations between business owners and laborers if workers are all educated. They also believe it will usurp the function of the church."

Aunt Abby turned and stared at her. "How in the world could learning usurp the function of the church?"

Rose shook her head. "I think it's crazy too. I can't really say I understand it. Just seems to me like people call on the power of the church to stop things they don't want to happen."

"It's fear," Aunt Abby said. "Everything you have told me is nothing but fear that the life they have built for themselves and always known will disappear if other people are given the same opportunities as themselves."

"I guess all of us are motivated by fear in some way," Rose acknowledged. "I don't think most of the Southern planters have any idea that what they are doing is wrong. It's simply the only way they have ever known."

"You are defending them?" Aunt Abby asked in astonishment.

Rose shook her head. "Not defending them. Just trying to understand a little bit. It helps me not to feel so bitter about all the wasted years when I can grasp some kind of understanding." She paused and continued. "The South may win this war, but I don't believe, even if they do, that they will be able to return to the life they once knew. Too many soldiers will have risked their lives while standing in equality beside rich planters and their sons. They will not so easily go back to their place in society. And if what I am hearing is correct, thousands of slaves are fleeing from their owners already."

"Yes, I understand the number in the contraband camps is growing."

Rose nodded. "And they're going to school. Missionaries from the North are going down and setting up schools in the camps. I learned today about a free black woman by the name of Mary Peake who organized one of the first public schools for blacks. It's down in Fort Monroe in Hampton." Her eyes glistened with excitement. "That's not all that far from where I came from, you know."

"How many students does she have?" Aunt Abby asked with interest, raising the spoon to her lips to taste the chowder. "Needs to cook a while longer," she interjected. She waved Rose over to sit down at the table.

Rose followed, then answered her question. "Within two weeks she had forty-five students. There is no telling how many she has now. She opened the school in September. Her students are learning spelling, reading, writing and arithmetic. Why, they're even singing in school."

Aunt Abby regarded her closely. "And you want to go down to help."

Rose answered honestly. "Slavery has robbed my people of the right to education for too long. Yes, I want to help, but not yet. I still have so much I want to learn myself before I can be the teacher I want to be. I keep telling myself to be patient. To make the most of where I am now." She leaned forward and took Aunt Abby's hand. "And I can't even imagine leaving you right now. This may sound presumptuous coming from a black woman, but I love you very much. Being here with you has taken away some of the pain of not having my mama."

Aunt Abby smiled and squeezed her hand. "And having you here has taken away my awful loneliness. I love you and Moses, too," she said sincerely. "My house needs to have young people in it. I need someone to care for other than myself. Thank you for letting me do that."

They heard the front door open and a small blast of cold air circulated its way back to the kitchen.

"Moses!" Rose jumped up and hurried to meet him. She stopped when she saw him. "It's snowing again?"

Moses grinned and began to peel off his coat. "I tried to get most of it off on the doorstep, but it's coming down mighty hard."

Rose laughed. "You look like a snowman." Just then the chimes on the clock burst forth with their pronouncement of the time. Startled, Rose looked at it and then peered out the window. "It's dark. I must have lost track of the time when I was talking to Aunt Abby. Why are you so late?" Moses was usually home before it was dark. The wagons that hauled the trash from the city didn't operate that late.

Moses smiled as he turned to hang his coat up on the rack.

"You look like the cat that got the canary," came Aunt Abby's voice from behind them.

Rose nodded. "She's right. What are you looking so pleased about?" The quiet look of satisfaction on Moses' face, along with the excited glow in his eyes, intrigued and somehow discomfited her at the same time.

Moses merely moved in the direction of the kitchen. "Can't a guy eat around here?"

Rose stamped her foot in frustration and glared at him.

Moses laughed then. "You know good and well I'm going to tell you what's going on, but how do you expect a man to tell important news when he's starving?"

"All right," Rose muttered, "but you'd better eat fast."

Moses finally looked up from his third bowl of chowder and fourth slice of bread. "Thank you. That was delicious." He patted his stomach and pushed back in his chair. "I went to see Mr. Walker today, Aunt Abby."

Aunt Abby looked at him in surprise. "My friend Albert Walker?"

"Remember telling me about how he had connections with the government?"

"Why, of course. He's quite an important man." Aunt Abby looked at him more closely. "What prompted the visit today?"

Rose watched Moses carefully. She knew the determined light in his eyes. It meant he was preparing to do something important.

Moses shrugged. "I've been hearing things. We got done with the trash route early today, so the boss let us go. I was walking home when I looked up and saw his name on a placard."

"Yes," Aunt Abby said. "He has had his law office on Fifth Street for years. His efforts on behalf of the Anti-Slavery Society have been invaluable."

"He's a fine man," Moses agreed.

Rose couldn't stand it any longer. "What kind of things have you been hearing? What happened when you saw Mr. Walker?"

Moses turned and looked at her, a tender light in his eyes. For some reason, that light made her more nervous. She struggled to push down the uneasiness rising in her. She had no basis for it.

Moses must have sensed her struggle, because he launched right into his story. "I've been hearing rumors about the Union Army."

Aunt Abby regarded him quizzically. "Excuse me for how this might sound, but how in the world do you hear rumors about the Union Army in your work as a trash man?"

Rose laughed. She had wondered the same thing herself.

Moses laughed along with them. "You would be amazed the things men will say when they're standing around on the street corner. Since my trash route runs through the heart of the business district, I hear a great many important men talking. I believe they must think all blacks are either deaf or stupid, 'cause they continue with their talking just as if we weren't there. I have found myself moving very slowly at times while I listened to their conversations," he finished with a grin.

Rose nodded. Aunt Abby looked chagrined.

"Anyway," Moses continued. "Like I said, I've heard rumors. General McClellan is building up a huge army outside of Washington."

Aunt Abby nodded. "He took over as commander of the Army of the Potomac in July. They made him commander-in-chief of all the Union forces in November."

Moses nodded. "He hasn't done much with his troops in all this time, other than continue to build his army bigger and stronger. There is a lot of pressure on him to do something."

Aunt Abby nodded again. "There have been some rather nasty rumors about the man himself. Evidently, McClellan was the protégé of Jefferson Davis when he was in the peacetime army. That would be enough to make people look at him suspiciously. Then I heard that he had ties to the filibusters."

"The filibusters?" Rose echoed. "What is that?"

"The filibusters were private armies in the fifties that menaced Central and South America and sought the expansion of slavery." Aunt Abby paused. "Many of my friends in the Anti-Slavery Society are concerned as well. When McClellan took charge of the Army of the Potomac, he told them he would not fight either for the Republican Party or for the abolition of slavery, but only for the restoration of the Union. It has deeply concerned many of my friends."

"I think, from what I hear, that all the rumors are putting pressure on McClellan to do something," Moses commented. "We're closing in on the last week of January. He will have to take some kind of action soon."

Aunt Abby frowned. "I thought he had taken ill with typhoid fever at the beginning of the year."

Moses nodded. "I heard today that he was almost fully recovered."

Rose listened impatiently to all the talk surrounding her. Finally, she spoke up. "What do rumors about McClellan have to do with that look in your eyes?" She made no effort to hide her impatience.

Moses turned to her immediately. "I'm sorry, Rose. I am going somewhere with all this."

"I certainly hope so." Rose tried to battle the mounting fear inside of her.

"I heard some men talking today about McClellan's supposed plans. What they know of them, anyway. The general is pretty closed-mouth about his campaigns. From what I heard, though, he is going to try to approach Richmond from the mouth of the Rappahannock River at Urbanna."

Rose looked at him in surprise. "That's less than twenty miles from the plantation."

Moses nodded. "I know. Landing his forces there would put Union forces less than fifty miles from Richmond." His eyes flashed brightly. "When I heard that, I decided it was time to pay a visit to Mr. Walker."

"Because you want to be a part of it," Rose said.

Moses nodded and turned to her, his eyes pleading. "You've known all along that I want to help the Union win this war."

"What did you discover today?" she asked quietly.

"Mr. Walker greeted me most graciously when I arrived at his office, especially when I told him who I was living with." He turned to smile at Aunt Abby. "He thinks very highly of you."

Aunt Abby smiled and inclined her head. "He's a very gracious man."

Moses continued on. "He became more interested when I told him I had lived in that general area of Virginia for the last two years, and that I was quite adept at making my way around there."

"I thought the Union was still adamant about not using blacks in the military?" Aunt Abby interrupted.

Moses shrugged. "They are, but I convinced Mr. Walker, at least, that they need someone with them who knows the area well. Just in the few minutes we talked, I cleared up one misconception for him. I'm not sure of his connection with all this, but somewhere he had gotten the idea that the roads through there were sandy and well-drained."

Rose chuckled.

"Exactly." Moses grinned. "I assured him his information was wrong and used it as yet another point of how I could make myself useful."

Rose stared at him. "You volunteered your services as a spy?"

Moses nodded. "I don't know yet if they will be accepted, but Mr. Walker is going to put in a good word for me. He seems to carry some influence."

Aunt Abby nodded. "Albert Walker is a very powerful man in this city. He is well known in Washington as well. He was influential in getting Lincoln elected. He most definitely carries influence."

Moses listened carefully, his eyes glowing brighter. "He told me he would stay in touch."

"Do you really think the army will let a black man act as a spy?" Rose asked.

Moses shrugged. "I don't know. I do know, however, that before this war is over, thousands of black men will play a part in winning the victory."

Aunt Abby looked at him closely. "You really believe that, don't you?"

Moses nodded. "Not only are there free black men willing to lay their lives on the line, there are thousands of former slaves willing to do anything to see slavery abolished. Rightly or wrongly, we believe this war—if we win it—will be the end to slavery."

"Lincoln has made no statement to that effect," Aunt Abby said in a troubled voice.

Moses shrugged again. "Let's say it's something all of us feel in our bones. That's good enough for us."

Rose watched him. "How long would you be gone," she asked.

Moses shook his head and laughed. "I have no idea. I don't even know if I'm going anywhere. Mr. Walker told me to keep on collecting trash and learning from you. Any notification I get could come at the last moment." He paused. "Only time will tell."

Rose nodded, trying to calm her insides. She had known all along that Moses wanted to help the Union, but knowing something and dealing with it were two different things. She and Moses had not been apart even one day since he had arrived on the plantation. She couldn't help the tears that sprang to her eyes.

Aunt Abby reached forward to grip her hand. "Great causes require great sacrifices, Rose. They always have, and they always will." Her own eyes filled with tears.

Rose knew she was thinking of Matthew Justin.

"Moses is still with us for now," she continued. "If duty takes him away, we will continue to take one day at a time. At least we will have each other for comfort and encouragement."

Rose nodded. She shouldn't let her fear overwhelm her. Suddenly, in her mind, she was back on the boat in the middle of the Potomac River as Moses battled the wind and rain. The lesson she had learned came back to her. *She would no longer ask what they were going to do next, or whether they would make it or not. God had brought them this far.* She smiled and leaned forward to take Moses' hand. "I believe in you, Moses. If there is something you can do to help make a difference, I'll support you all the way."

Moses lifted her hand to his lips and kissed it gently, his eyes expressing his love and gratitude. "Thank you," he murmured.

Chapter Twenty-Seven

Robert emerged from his tent and walked over to the fire. Jackson's troops had arrived at Unger's Store the night before, after two days of brutal traveling. His men's voices floated out to him.

"I think Jackson is crazy!"

"Those crazy stories we heard about him at the Virginia Military Institute must have been true," another announced bitterly.

"Who but a crazy man would have troops out in weather like this?" another interrupted.

"I think he must really be a Yankee. That's why he's trying to kill all of us," a fresh-faced boy added.

"I don't ever want to hear anyone call General Jackson a Yankee again," Robert snapped as he emerged from the shadows and stepped up to the fire. He glared around at the men. All of them stared fixedly at the ground. Robert could feel the tension in the air. He understood how much the men had suffered. He himself had never been so miserable before. But this kind of talk was mutinous. None of them would make it out of this campaign alive if they didn't stand together.

"Come on, Lieutenant," one of the men finally said, looking up defiantly. "Don't you think it's crazy to have us out in the dead of winter?"

Robert kept his voice cold. Now was not the time to show sympathy. "I think if anyone of you wants to be a general, you should think about paying the price it takes to become one." He stared fixedly at the men again. "Did General Jackson not accomplish his objective at Bath? Did he not break Northern communications, in spite of the bad weather we faced on the march here?" He waited until the prolonged silence made them look up. They nodded reluctantly.

Robert's voice and face softened somewhat. "I know it's hell out here, men, but regaining control of northwestern Virginia is critically important. We have to be willing to campaign and advance when Yankee troops are all holed up for the winter. We have to take what we can, when we can. You are accomplishing something the Northern troops have not even *attempted*."

Slowly, the defeated looks on the men's faces began to fade. The bitterness was replaced by a look of pride in their accomplishments.

Robert pushed on. "Romney is waiting for us. It may be hell to get there, but get there we will. We made it this far when we thought it was impossible. We can make it there, too." He turned and walked away, leaving the men to talk it out on their own. He had done all he could do.

He was staring down at the frozen stream minutes later when a voice sounded at his shoulder.

"Lieutenant?"

Robert turned. "Yes, Hobbs?"

"Thank you for what you said back there. I guess we kinda lost sight of things for a while."

"It happens to everyone, Hobbs."

Hobbs hesitated. "I wish you could talk to the rest of the troops."

There was a troubled tone in his voice that caused Robert to go on alert. He looked at Hobbs sharply. "Why?"

Hobbs looked up with troubled eyes. "The troops are angry, sir. They really don't understand why they are being made to endure such torture. And they're sick. Too many of them can't even walk anymore. I saw two yesterday. They were barefoot."

"Barefoot!" Robert exclaimed.

"Yes, sir. Their shoes got burnt up one night when they were trying to keep their feet warm by the fire. I'm afraid they got a bad case of frostbite."

"Are they my men?"

"Oh no, sir," Hobbs said quickly. "Your men would have told you. They know you care." He paused. "They are two of Hatcher's men."

Robert nodded grimly. "I will have it taken care of."

He heard a call behind him. "Lieutenant Borden." Robert spun to meet the rider coming toward him. "Yes, Colonel?"

"How are the men in your command faring, Lieutenant?"

Robert frowned. "Not too well, sir. Many of them are very sick. All of them are exhausted and weakened from the cold."

The colonel nodded. "General Jackson has ordered six days of rest. The men need to be healthy again before we attempt to take Romney."

Robert smiled. "I'm sure my men will be happy to hear that, sir."

The colonel smiled. "No more happy then you, I imagine. I believe all of us could use a rest."

"You're right, sir."

The colonel started to turn his horse. "How does a hot bath sound, Lieutenant?"

"Like a dream, Colonel."

"Some dreams come to life," he said with a smile. "The general has ordered water to be heated so all of the troops can have a hot bath. I'll expect you to take care of your unit." He turned and rode away.

"A bath?" Hobbs said in disbelief. "You mean that for a few minutes I get to be warm?" He paused. "I take back everything I said about General Jackson. I guess he has a heart underneath there somewhere."

Robert turned and stared back down at the river. "I'll be over in a few minutes. Would you like to tell the men they have a week's reprieve?"

"Yes, sir!" Hobbs said, smiling. He saluted smartly, spun on his heel, and strode off.

Robert resumed staring at the river. The past day had been a repeat of the first torturous day of the march. It had left him no time to ponder what had happened the day before. He had heard of men, when they came close to death, being forced to reevaluate their whole life—who they were, what they had done with their time on Earth. He had always been too busy living to spend time reflecting. Until now. His experience with the wagon had changed all that.

He was happy his men would have a chance to rest and recover their strength and health. He was happiest, though, for a chance to spend some time thinking. He turned away from the river. His men all needed a bath, and he must take care of that first. A smile flitted on his lips. His bath would be last, but it would be welcome.

Ike Adams cursed the weather as he pushed along the muddy river leading to the bridge across the Potomac. It would be a long ride. He had been called to the plantation of Quincy Moore, who had lost thirty of his forty-five slaves. They had simply disappeared during a stormy night. The man was frantic to get them back before planting season started. Bankruptcy loomed before him if he didn't have a good crop this year.

Adams didn't usually take jobs so far away, but Moore had offered him a price he couldn't refuse. He felt a deep sense of satisfaction that his skills were in such demand. When he was first booted from Cromwell Plantation, he had wondered how he would survive. Now he was making more money than before. The value of slaves was shooting up as more and more of them escaped. So had the value of slave hunters. He had steadily raised his rates, but not once had he been turned away.

And for good reason. He produced results. Many of the slaves he went after got no more than ten or twenty miles from their plantations. Many disappeared having no idea where they were going, much less how to get there. They would bog down in woods or swamps, hungry and desperate for freedom, but with no idea of how to achieve it. To be sure, there were slaves he never recovered, but his percentages were good, so he continued to demand top pay.

A strange object in the river caught his eye. He pulled his horse to a stop and peered closer. "What the ...?" He jumped from his horse and moved close to the edge of the water.

"My God!" he exclaimed, stepping back and fighting to control the nausea in his stomach. "It's a man." He looked around to see if there was anyone else around, even though he knew better. This little-traveled road would most certainly be uninhabited in a winter storm like the one raging around him.

Adams searched until he found a long, sturdy stick. He braced himself against a set of tree roots and leaned far out over the water. He finally managed to get an end of the stick snagged on the man's clothing. Grunting with the effort, he hauled the water-logged, bloated corpse toward him. With a final grunt, he dragged the man up into a few inches of water.

Adams stood and stared at his catch. Never had he seen a man dead from drowning. Or was it a drowning? He frowned when he saw the dark brown stain spread across the front of the man's shirt. No matter. The man was dead. Nothing was going to change that. By the looks of things, he had been dead for quite some time. His facial features were swollen beyond any possibility of recognition, and his clothes hung in tatters on his body. The only thing still resembling clothing was his heavy wool coat.

Adams was tempted to push him back in the water and move on. There was nothing he could do for the man now. He grabbed the stick and prepared to send him back to his watery grave. At some point, the body would wash out into the ocean.

Then he hesitated, not sure why he felt compelled to investigate. Adams scowled and tossed the stick down. He was wasting valuable time, and he would continue to be cold and miserable until he got where he was going. He knelt down, grabbed one edge of the coat jacket, and pulled. The body bobbed a few inches closer. Struggling once again to control his nausea, Adams took off one of his gloves and reached into the man's pockets. He knew the effort to determine his identity was futile. Any papers would surely have been ruined by the water after all this time.

He was surprised when his fingers located a pouch of some kind. He pulled it out and discovered a leather pouch that was doubled over and secured with a snap. His fingers were already growing numb from the cold, but he managed to open it and pull out what was inside. His curiosity grew as he looked at the sheaf of papers it held. They were slightly damp, but the pouch had done an incredible job of protecting them. Adams pocketed the pouch and turned his attention to the papers.

A blast of snow made him close his eyes in defense. He moved quickly to the protection of a grove of trees standing on the bank. Then he held the papers close to examine them. Slave documents! Adams almost threw them away in disgust. Then his eyes narrowed. If this man had been traveling with slave documents, it meant his slaves had been with him. Had they killed him and pushed him in the river? Had they been stolen from him by overzealous abolitionists? The last idea wasn't impossible this close to the Northern border.

Adams looked more closely at the documents. He gasped when he saw the two names. Rose and Moses. The papers stated the two slaves were owned by a man named John Salem. It should have ended there, but Adams had a feeling about this that wouldn't go away. His friends told him he had a sixth sense like a hound dog, and it was screaming there was more to this than he knew.

His eyes narrowed as his earlier instinct somehow hardened into certainty, even though he had no solid evidence. He was sure he was looking at papers for Rose and Moses from Cromwell Plantation. His eyes glittered in anger as he thought of the giant black man he hated so much. His face hardened as he thought of Carrie Cromwell, all the hate in him surging to the surface. He cursed and slammed his fist into a tree. Yes, he was making more money, but the humiliation that burned in him at the very thought of Carrie Cromwell throwing him off her plantation had only deepened as time went on. He was determined to get even with her.

His mind traveled back to his encounter with Louisa Blackwell months earlier. She had suggested then that Thomas Cromwell would appreciate his services, but he had not followed up. A job had taken him north for over a month. Another job followed. He was making so much money hunting slaves, he had no desire to go groveling to Cromwell for a job. All he wanted was to get even with Carrie Cromwell. He was sure his day would come.

His eyes glistened as he stared at the documents in his hand. Rose and Moses were two of Thomas Cromwell's most valuable slaves. He knew, too, how close Rose and Carrie were. Surely they had not just disappeared. His lips twisted as he imagined Cromwell's displeasure at discovering his precious daughter had helped such a valuable investment disappear. Adams laughed shortly and stuffed the papers in his pocket. They would come in very handy. Cromwell would think he was approaching him out of concern and might even pay him handsomely for the information.

He had no real desire to hunt down Rose and Moses. He knew how brutally strong the young giant was and was sure the man would do anything to help the girl he loved. Moses had been ready to attack him that day in the quarters before Carrie had shown up with the gun. Adams still regretted his failure at having his way with Rose. She was beautiful, even if she was a slave.

Adams shook his head and moved to mount his horse. He would figure out the best plan of action. There would be a way to meet his objective. After all, hadn't the fortunes allowed him to find the body of John Salem, or whatever the man's real name was? Adams was quite sure he had found the body of a conductor for the Underground Railroad.

He put his foot in the stirrup and stopped, glancing back at the river. If he left the body there, maybe someone would find it and give it a proper burial. Smiling cruelly, he turned away from his horse and stalked back to the river. It took only a moment to grab his stick and push the body back into the water. He watched with satisfaction as the bloated corpse continued on its bobbing course down the frigid river. Then he mounted and continued on his way. He had work to do.

"Hey, Lieutenant! It looks like the sun may be trying to come out," Hobbs called from the front of the line.

Robert looked up hopefully. After six days of resting at Unger's Store, Jackson's troops were ready to head on to Romney. Or at least they were supposed to. The men's spirits had risen over the course of the days, but there were still many sick men in the brigades. If the weather held, they might make it the rest of the way. If not...

"Here's hoping for good weather," Robert called out. He mounted and gave the signal his men were waiting for. "Move out, men!"

Not all of Jackson's troops had the luxury of resting for six days. After a few days, Jackson had ordered troops back to Bath to keep the Union forces there distracted. He directed more of his troops south of Romney and sent cavalry units almost to the gates of the city. He had been slowed, but he refused to be paralyzed.

The weather held a few hours. Then another winter storm as ferocious as the earlier ones moved in over the mountains. Once again, the men battled bitter cold, sleet and snow. Before the end of the day, precious regained energy was completely spent. Sickness once more held many of the men in its grip. More than one man lay where he fell, unable to move any further.

Robert had his head bent against the storm when he heard a gunshot directly to his left. Startled, but not surprised, he looked up. It had become almost a common occurrence. Men, scrambling for footing on the slick surface, would fall, discharging their guns as they went down.

Hobbs appeared through the blanket of snow. "It's Clark, sir. He's been shot."

Robert followed Hobbs' shadowy form as he darted back to the left. Moments later, he came upon Clark's huddled form. The gunshot had not been deadly, but the blood spreading on the ground from his leg wound made it obvious Clark would not continue in this march. Robert almost envied him, until he saw the stark pain on the man's face.

"Stop the next ambulance wagon," Robert ordered. He motioned to two of the men watching. Carefully, they picked Clark up and carried him to the side of the road. Just a few minutes later a wagon came lumbering up.

Robert waved for it to stop and placed Clark inside, covering him as well as he could with a mound of blankets. He smiled down at the suffering man and tried to sound encouraging. "We'll get us into camp as soon as we can," he promised.

Clark nodded bravely, his eyes searching Robert's face for strength. Robert took his hand and pressed it. "You'll make it, Clark. God be with you." Then he remounted and continued on.

Once again, the day felt as if it would never end as the men struggled to maneuver horses and wagons over hills and across icy streams. The days of rest vanished from their minds as once more the grip of winter tried to rip life from their grasp.

The first good news came when they were huddled around the campfire that night. Union forces had pulled out of Romney three days earlier. The very idea of the Confederate troops marching toward them had caused them to lose heart and withdraw. Jackson, who had taken some cavalry troops and gone on ahead, had found a vacated city. Now he was waiting for his troops, his messenger said. The time was ripe to press on and destroy railroad bridges. *Send the men on.*

The next day was no better than the first. Men weakened by the conditions could make no headway against the storm. Robert urged his men on, gratified to see their valiant effort even in the face of almost insurmountable obstacles. He realized they were passing other units. Soon, he knew, Jackson's troops would be spread out for miles. Any offensive against them would be disastrous, but the men were giving all they had to give. One of the leading brigades that day made only four miles. Another managed to cover only five hundred yards. The torture seemed interminable.

They were only a few miles from Romney when Robert called his troops to a halt several nights later. They would enter the town the next day. For now they would get some much needed rest in a sheltered grove of trees he had found. They would need all their energy to push the last few miles uphill. They gathered wood for fire, and soon roaring flames sent sparks flying toward the sky. Robert watched his men get settled and then retreated to the edge of the grove to stare out over the pasture.

In spite of his hatred for the suffering he and his men were enduring, Robert could see beauty in the landscape. The snow-covered ground glowed a soft gray under the moonless sky, with the mountains rising all around. A glimmering ribbon of ice cut through the field, promising moisture when spring reclaimed the land. A sudden gust of wind caused a brief break in the clouds, and for just a moment, the moon shone down. Robert drew his breath in with appreciation as it threw sparkling diamonds onto the snow and caused the frozen stream to ripple gently. Just as quickly, it was gone. A few minutes later the wind picked up, and snow once more began to fall.

Robert stayed where he was. Being responsible for so many men... Having almost lost his life... Experiencing a loneliness he had never known existed... Having to witness so much suffering... All of it was transforming him. He could feel the changes, but he couldn't really describe them. He knew he was different and that God was somehow responsible. Maybe when all this was over he could make sense of it.

"Lieutenant."

Robert sighed and turned back toward the camp. He had a job to do.

Robert's men were among the first to arrive in Romney. All were disappointed in the bleak winter conditions of the little town that had passed back and forth between the military power of the North and South.

Hobbs spoke all their hearts as they stood on the outskirts of the town. "I don't reckon we'll find much comfort around this place."

Robert frowned. He knew Hobbs was right. Romney might be a city of strategic importance, but it possessed nothing else to make it desirable. He had envisioned indoor comfort for his men, but reality dictated setting up camp outdoors once again. He searched for a place that would offer them the most protection. There was not much to be found.

Hobbs appeared beside him. Robert smiled. His affection for the youth had grown stronger by the day. He found himself depending on his unfailing good cheer. To be sure, it had been stretched to the limits over the course of the campaign, but he always managed to find an encouraging word for his lieutenant. "Hello, Hobbs."

"Howdy, Lieutenant."

They stood side by side, staring silently at the scene before them.

"Kinda hard to figure why we fought so hard to get to this God-forsaken place."

Robert merely nodded. He couldn't think of anything to say.

"Mind if I go into town, sir?"

"Why?"

Hobbs shrugged. "I figure the Yankees might have left behind something that will cheer the men up. Since we're one of the first here, I thought maybe we could take a look."

Robert grinned. "Let's go see what we can find."

When they returned an hour later, they were bent double under the sacks over their backs. The men had already set up their tents, fires were blazing, and tough pieces of meat were being cooked.

"What you got there, Lieutenant?" one of the men called out.

In just moments, all of them crowded around. Robert nodded to Hobbs. It had been his idea. Let him make the announcement.

Hobbs had a broad smile on his face when he yelled out, "How about some dessert, men?" Blank stares met his announcement. "Those bags are full of cans of peaches and cream. And they're all ours!"

The men whooped and hollered as if they had been offered dessert at the finest Richmond restaurant. Robert heard laughter for the first time in a week as the men inhaled the treat.

"Looks like they're having a good time."

Robert looked up. He had not heard the horse approaching. "They are, Colonel."

"They deserve it," he said. "General Jackson wants to destroy bridges tomorrow. He will need three brigades to accomplish his plan. How many can you contribute?"

"All but three of my men can take part," Robert assured him. "There are some that are sick, but they seem to be getting stronger. Now that they've come this far, I know they won't want to miss out on the final blow."

"What's the frown for?" the colonel asked sharply.

"I don't think Jackson is going to get what he wants. The rest of the troops are in sad shape. This campaign has sickened and demoralized them. They may get here in time to take part, but I doubt they have anything left to give." He shook his head. "You should see them, Colonel. Many of the men are frozen so badly I doubt they will ever recover. I think many of them have gotten a rheumatism they will never get rid of. Fevers have turned men into skeletons. I'm afraid Jackson doesn't have much of an army left."

The colonel listened, frowned deeply, then saluted and rode away. Robert watched him go and turned back to his men.

Robert's prediction turned out to be true. General Jackson, by the time his troops had reached Romney, simply didn't have enough men capable of launching the offensive he had envisioned. The men had been too incapacitated by the brutal campaign.

But General Jackson had accomplished his original goal. In ten days, he had maneuvered the Federals out of Morgan County. He had broken railroad connections with the west and recovered all that portion of the country east of the Big Cacapon Bridge that his men had destroyed. He had forced the enemy out of Romney and frightened Federal troops farther west. He had destroyed supplies. Most importantly, he had driven out all thought of an offensive among Federal troops, who had definitely been put on the defensive.

Ike Adams, with longing in his heart, looked south toward Richmond. As each day passed, his desire to find Thomas Cromwell and start his plan of vengeance against his lovely daughter had grown in his mind until it almost consumed him. He would love to see the high and mighty Miss Cromwell brought down.

With a sigh he turned his mare, Ginger, to the North. It had become increasingly dangerous to break through Union lines in search of runaway slaves, but the price offered to him had pushed away his misgivings. He knew that by the time he found them, the slaves may have reached help. His presence alone would not be enough to turn them back. He reached behind his saddle and was comforted by the solid presence of his whip. A pat at his waist confirmed the presence of his two pistols, and his rifle rested in its case on the saddle.

Adams had exacted enough of an advance from the man to simply turn around and go home. If he wanted to, he could write later saying his search had been unsuccessful. No one would be the wiser. However, the lure of money was strong enough to turn his mare north. He would see what he could do. Thomas Cromwell would not leave Richmond anytime soon. And Adams would not be in Philadelphia for long.

Chapter Twenty-Eight

Carrie breathed a sigh of relief as the carriage pulled away from the plantation. She had been waiting for a break in the weather—one long enough to dry out the roads. She felt if she were on the plantation even one day longer, she would go crazy. The weather had been intolerable since the beginning of the year. Cold rain had kept her indoors for days at a time. She had read huge stacks of books and had made considerable progress through the medical texts, but the loneliness of no one to talk to was eating at her heart and spirit. As soon as the roads were passable, she had asked Sam to take her to Richmond.

Carrie snuggled deeper under the heavy load of lap rugs Sam had laid across her. It was typical February weather. The sun struggled to make itself felt, but the biting wind and the bone-gnawing cold reigned supreme. Stark, barren trees stood out in glaring relief against the blue sky. There were still patches of snow hiding in shadowed areas of the woods, but the rest had melted away, leaving brown grass to stretch before her. Carrie tugged her hat down a little further over her head and prepared to endure the rough road winter had designed.

"You all right back there, Miss Carrie?" Sam called. "This here road be a little rough."

"You will not hear one word of complaint from me," Carrie called back cheerfully.

Sam grinned at the sight of just her eyes peeking above the rugs. "I'm glad you're going to Richmond, Miss Carrie. It ain't natural for a young girl like you to stay cooped up all alone on that plantation. You need to be with other young folks."

Carrie couldn't have agreed more. The four walls of her house had begun to close in on her. She wanted to sit down and talk to someone about what was going on in the world. She wanted to tell someone what she was learning. But she was basically leaving the plantation to run on its own. She was handling everything now that Moses was gone. Not that she expected any trouble from her people, but there would be no one there if a serious need arose.

Yet, she knew she had to go. She was emotionally on edge and would be good for no one if she didn't take this opportunity to get away. She would be back in plenty of time to take care of the final preparations for spring planting. Once she had something she could throw all of her heart into again, she would be fine.

Carrie could feel the heaviness in the air as soon as they reached Richmond. The streets were as crowded as ever, but there seemed to be a pall covering the whole city. She heard very little laughter and saw few smiles. Tight groups of people wearing frowns and concerned expressions gathered on every corner and around every light post. Carrie stared at them. What had happened?

The last letter from her father had come a few weeks before. In it, he had told her of Jackson's successful campaign against Romney. Had the tide changed since then?

Carrie was anxious to get to the house. She resisted the urge to tell Sam to go faster, knowing he was doing the best he could. Finally, they inched their way down Broad Street and broke out of the traffic somewhat. She counted the streets impatiently and almost cheered when they reached Twenty-Sixth Street.

A raindrop splashed onto the rug covering her. Carrie looked up and groaned. She had been so deep in her thoughts, she had not even been aware another bank of dark clouds had swallowed the sun.

"Looks like you timed your trip just right, Miss Carrie."

"It certainly looks like it," Carrie agreed, "but what are you going to do? How are you going to get back to the plantation?"

Sam shrugged and cast a practiced eye at the sky. "That rain ain't gonna get too serious about things for a while. I reckon I got time to make it home 'fore the roads get too bad."

"You're going back tonight?" Carrie asked, surprised. "It will be dark before you get there, and the roads will be horrible." She shook her head. "I don't think that's such a good idea. You should stay at Father's."

Sam looked down at her with a smile. "Are you orderin' me to stay here, Carrie girl?"

"No," Carrie said quickly. "I just don't want anything to happen to you." She didn't know how to tell her faithful slave that she thought he was getting too old to endure such bad conditions anymore. She understood male pride—black or white.

Sam laughed. "Then don't you be worryin' none 'bout me. The sky is going to spit for a while, but these here clouds ain't moving very fast. I got me a plantation to look after. I reckon I'll be headin' on home sho 'nuff."

Carrie said nothing. She recognized that look in Sam's eyes. She knew he felt responsible for making things run smoothly while she was gone. "Thank you, Sam," she said softly as the carriage rolled to a halt.

Sam nodded, stepped lightly down, and picked up her two bags to carry inside.

Just then Thomas Cromwell strode out onto the porch. "Carrie! I was hoping you would come soon. I figured the last few days would be your best chance to beat the soggy road conditions." He reached down to envelop her in a big hug. "It's wonderful to see you, dear. Come inside where you can get warm." He turned to the old black man standing to the side. "It's good to see you, Sam. Thank you for bringing Carrie into the city. Is Charles still sick?"

Carrie thought quickly. She had counted on her father being at the Capitol when she arrived, so she wouldn't have to explain about Sam driving her. "No, Father," she said. "I asked Charles to stay behind to watch for Jewel's foal that is due any day. I thought that was most important." She was relieved when her father gave a pleased nod. At the same time, she felt that familiar nausea that came from lying so blatantly. It was becoming harder and harder to deceive this man she loved so much.

"So it's Jewel's time, is it? She was always one of my favorite mares. I hope all goes well."

"I'm sure it will," Carrie said, glad to know her story had been so easily accepted, yet heartsick at the non-questioning trust it represented. "She's very strong and healthy." She had wanted to surprise him with the news of the beautiful colt Jewel had dropped just the week before in the middle of a horrendous storm. Carrie had known the mare's time was soon, so she had gone out late at night to check on her. She had arrived just in time to witness the birth. Never would she forget that miracle. She was excited to tell her father. Now she would have to wait longer, and the story would have to be substantially different.

Carrie turned to exchange a conspiratorial look with Sam. He touched his hand to his hat. "I reckon I'll be on my way now, Miss Carrie." He moved to get in the carriage.

Carrie frowned. "You will do nothing of the sort," she said. "Not without something hot to drink and eat first. You've been sitting on that seat for over three hours. It won't take you long."

"Yessum, Miss Carrie," Sam said meekly.

Carrie wanted to laugh. She knew this show was for the benefit of her father, who stood on the porch listening. She watched as Sam climbed onto the carriage seat and drove around to the back of the house. Then Carrie turned and ran up to stand beside her father.

"It's wonderful to be here, Father," she said with a bright smile. She stepped back and looked him more fully in the face. She had not seen such a strained look since he had met her on the porch of the plantation house with the news that her mother was ill. "What's wrong?" she asked.

Thomas managed a weak smile. "Come inside, dear. We can talk in there." He paused. "Let's just say there is much going on in our country right now."

Carrie followed him into the house, grateful for the warmth reaching out to her. Fires blazed in every fireplace. She heard the back door open and close, and then the murmur of voices. She knew May would fix Sam something to eat.

Thomas moved forward to stir the fire, and Carrie studied him from the back. Every line of his body spoke of deep tension and fatigue. He had just turned from the fire when she heard the back door again and then the rattle of carriage wheels. Sam was obviously more concerned about the movement of this new storm than he had let on.

Thomas walked over to his chair and settled into it slowly. He reached for his pipe and began to tamp it.

Carrie could not stand the suspense one moment longer. "Why aren't you in the office, Father? Why are you home in the middle of the day? Are you sick?"

Thomas shook his head. "I didn't reach home until early this morning. The governor insisted I get some rest. I will head to the Capitol shortly."

"What has happened? The whole city seems to be covered with a blanket of gloom. I haven't seen you look this bad in a very long time."

Thomas tried to smile. "The South has taken some very hard hits, I'm afraid. The news from all directions seems to be nothing but bad."

"The last letter I got from you said the news was good. Jackson had taken Romney, and northwestern Virginia was once more in our control."

Thomas nodded. "I did write that, didn't I? Seems like ancient history," he mused with a frown. "I'm afraid our forces evacuated Romney a week or so ago. I did receive some good news, though. General Jackson has withdrawn his resignation."

Carrie stared at him. "Maybe you should start from the beginning."

Thomas managed a real smile this time. "I'm sorry, dear. You're right. I'll start from the beginning. Maybe it will help me make some sense out of it myself." He stared into the fire for a few moments. "Jackson did indeed occupy Romney, just as he planned. He left some of his men to hold that area, took some of his troops to Bath, and returned to Winchester himself."

Carrie had only one question at this point. Her father correctly interpreted the look on her face and saved her from having to ask.

"Robert returned with General Jackson to Winchester before he was sent back to Richmond. We spent several hours talking about the campaign."

"Robert is all right?" Carrie asked, managing to keep her voice casual.

Thomas nodded. "He and his men had a rough time of it, but they came through. There are a lot of men, though, who I fear will not fight again." He described the sickness and injuries that had plagued the winter campaign.

Carrie shuddered. She could imagine how the men must have suffered. She had tried to envision herself out in the mountains like that, but it had been impossible. She had been anxious about Robert ever since the night she had been so certain he was in danger. It was wonderful to know he was all right.

Thomas continued. "Jackson left General Loring and his men in Romney to hold it."

"What happened?"

Thomas shrugged. "Seems the general and his men didn't like the conditions there very much. Said they had suffered quite enough for one winter, and they saw no reason to hold Romney because they didn't see that it had any strategic value. They started a letter writing campaign. To make a long story short, Secretary of War Benjamin ordered Jackson to have them withdraw from Romney."

Carrie stared at him. She didn't pretend to fully understand military matters, but she knew something wasn't right about that. "Wasn't Benjamin's action a little unusual?"

Thomas laughed, the first genuine sign of amusement he had displayed since she had arrived. "Ever the diplomat, aren't you?" he asked. "Benjamin's actions were indeed unusual. He claims he was working under President Davis' orders. Anyway, General Jackson obeyed his orders and then promptly sent in his letter of resignation, explaining that with such interference in his command, he could not expect to be of much service in the field."

"What about Romney?"

Thomas' face hardened. "Federal forces occupied the city on February seventh. We also had troops south of Romney in Moorefield, but they were driven out three days ago. Yesterday, the Federals surprised our men at Bloomery Gap, capturing seventeen officers and three times as many men." He paused. "The Romney campaign is indeed over."

"So all those men suffered for nothing," Carrie said.

"It would seem so."

"And General Jackson?"

Thomas sighed. "His letter of resignation created quite an uproar. He has a strong support system. It took some powerful persuasion to change his mind, but a final plea that his resignation would harm the country finally swayed him. He withdrew it."

Carrie nodded. "I can understand why you are upset."

This time, Thomas' laugh held no mirth. "Oh, that's just the beginning of our troubles, my dear."

"What else?" Carrie asked, startled.

"I'm afraid Forts Henry and Donelson have fallen. The Tennessee River is now open to Union gunboats, and Nashville to the Union armies. Their loss is a crushing blow to the Confederacy."

Carrie listened, trying to analyze her own feelings. That her father was terribly distraught was obvious. She opened her mouth to comment, but he wasn't done.

"Roanoke Island has fallen to the Yankees as well. It was a humiliating defeat. Our men didn't stand a chance against the superior forces arrayed against them."

Carrie thought for a moment. "Wasn't that where Virginia's ex-Governor Wise was stationed?"

Thomas nodded. "He became quite ill before the attack, so he wasn't on the island when the Union struck." His face saddened. "I'm afraid his son was, though. He will not return to retake his position as editor of the *Enquirer*."

Carrie gasped. "He's dead?"

Thomas nodded gravely. "His funeral was several days ago at St. James Church. He is buried in Hollywood Cemetery."

Carrie was now certain of her feelings. She was furious at a war that was destroying so many of the nation's finest men. Slowly, she shook her head. How should she respond to her father? Thomas, however, didn't seem to need for her to say anything. He continued to talk.

"Roanoke Island was a serious loss. The Federals now have control of North Carolina's inland seas and the rivers that come into them. They have also been given a backdoor approach to Norfolk." His voice was grim.

"Why has all this happened? After Bull Run, I thought our troops were superior."

Thomas shrugged wearily. "The Union has not sat idle since then. They have worked endlessly to build up their forces so they would not face the same humiliation. I'm afraid the South became rather lazy after their easy victories. But it's more than that," he continued. "It's really a matter of a simple lack of resources. The Confederacy is just too big for us to defend adequately." He paused. "I think the South is getting the reality check that has been needed. Part of our problem is the expiration of so many short-term enlistments. We are being forced to reorganize under terribly difficult conditions."

"Because the South was sure it would be a very short war," Carrie stated.

Thomas nodded. "The only good that may come out of this—if it can happen in time—is what happened in the North after their early defeat. I believe the people of the South will draw new determination out of their humiliation and defeat. I believe they will discard their unthinking arrogance and prepare to see the war as it really is, not as it has been ignorantly imagined."

Carrie tried to introduce a lighter note. "Is there any good news in the midst of all this bad?"

Thomas frowned and thought for a moment. Then he shook his head. "You are sitting in my parlor. That is the only good news I can think of." His face softened. "I'm sorry to dump so much on you just as you have arrived."

"Nonsense," Carrie said immediately. "I felt isolated on the plantation. I've been dying to know what was going on in the rest of the world. I know now, however bad it may be." She smiled. "And I wanted to be with my father, whom I miss very much. I'm here," she said firmly. "I have the two things I wanted."

Thomas smiled affectionately, then jumped when the hall clock chimed. "I'm afraid we've talked longer than I thought. I must leave immediately to go to the Capitol." He glanced quickly out the window. "The rain seems to have stopped for a while. I think it will begin in earnest again tonight. I have secured another carriage so you will be free to roam the city, though I urge you to be very careful. If I thought it would do any good, I would order you to stay inside where you're safe." He smiled. "I trust Spencer, though. I will stop on my way to the Capitol to tell him you're in town. Would you like for me to send him up for you this afternoon?"

Carrie thought for a moment. "Tomorrow morning will be fine. A long hot bath sounds wonderful after the cold ride here. Then I'm going to bury myself in your newspapers and catch up on the world."

The sun filtered weakly through a hazy sky as Carrie stepped into the carriage. "Good morning, Spencer."

"Good morning, Miss Cromwell. Where to today?"

Today, she was going to visit Opal. Carrie had spent the day before just roaming the city. She had wanted to see for herself how the war was affecting Richmond. Her father had warned her that prices had risen, but she had not been prepared for what she had found. Many food items could simply not be found. Those that could had skyrocketed. Fancy dresses were non-existent. Clothing of any kind was ridiculously expensive.

Earlier that morning, she had attended church with her father, but he had gone back to the Capitol after lunch. She was on her own for the rest of the day. She gave Spencer the address and settled back against the seat.

She was deep in thought when she heard someone scream. "What was that?" she asked, as she sat up and looked around. A sudden movement to her right caught her attention. "Stop the carriage," she ordered.

"I don't reckon this is a good place to be right now," Spencer protested. "Your daddy told me to keep you safe."

"And I said to stop the carriage," she ordered. She leaned forward and tried to determine where the scream had come from.

As the carriage rolled to a halt, she heard a slurred, deep voice. "Now come on, little lady. Don't you know how to keep a soldier happy in this city?"

Carrie was horrified at what she saw. A burly soldier with a whiskered face and bloodshot eyes, obviously drunk, was holding tight to the hand of a struggling, well-dressed woman.

"Let me go!" she screamed again.

"I just need me some loving," the soldier protested. "Don't you ladies around here know how to do that?" He raised his hand and reached for the top of her dress.

"No!" The lady writhed violently in her attempt to break away.

Carrie gasped and looked around desperately for some help. There was no one in sight but other women and children. "Spencer, we have to do something," she cried.

"The police will probably be along soon, Miss Cromwell."

Carrie was furious at the casual tone in his voice. She whirled on him. "How would you feel if it was your wife?" she demanded.

"If it was a white soldier going after her, I don't reckon there would be a thing I could do but watch," he said bitterly.

Carrie jumped from the carriage. "Well, I don't intend to watch." She had no idea what she could do to stop the drunken soldier, but she began to run forward.

Suddenly, a large hand stopped her. "What you think you doing?" Spencer demanded.

Carrie wrenched away. "Someone has to do something," she snapped.

Spencer rolled his eyes, resignation on his face. "I'll stop that soldier, Miss Cromwell. Leastways, I'll try."

Another deep voice sounded behind him. "I'll help him, Miss Cromwell. You go back to your carriage."

Carrie spun around at the sound of her name. "Eddie! You're Eddie, aren't you? Opal's cousin?"

Eddie nodded and dashed off to join Spencer. The two men approached the struggling pair.

The soldier didn't even seem to notice that he was the center of attention. He was too drunk to care, anyway. Suddenly, he became aware of the two black men moving toward him. With no warning, he whipped a pistol out of his belt and began to wave it wildly in the air, all the while holding on to the still screaming woman.

Carrie thought of Rose the year before. She would give anything to have her rifle now. She looked around desperately, afraid the two men trying to help were going to be seriously hurt, possibly killed, yet, they couldn't walk away.

She jumped when a pistol shot exploded several feet behind her.

A policeman, even bigger than the inebriated soldier, rushed past her. "Take your hands off the lady, soldier boy," he yelled. The soldier, stunned by the sound of a pistol other than his own, had already dropped the lady's arm and was staring around stupidly. The policeman moved in quickly, secured his arms, and pocketed the pistol. "Seems to me you need some time in the city jail to cool off and dry out," he said.

He turned to the now weeping woman. "I'm sorry, ma'am. Did he hurt you?"

The lady shook her head, struggling for control.

Carrie rushed to her side. "Are you all right?" she asked anxiously. "What a horrible thing to happen. And here in the streets of Richmond in broad daylight."

The policeman turned to look at her. "Everyone in this city needs to be real careful, ma'am. We're trying our hardest to keep things under control, but things have gotten out of hand. Too much alcohol and too many guns around this place." He turned his prisoner roughly and marched away.

Carrie watched him go and turned back to the lady. "You must be terribly shaken. My carriage is here. Can I take you somewhere?"

The lady managed a shaky smile. "That is very kind. Where are you headed?"

"Wherever you are," Carrie responded.

That brought a genuine smile. "My name is Janie Winthrop, and yes, I would very much appreciate a ride. I saw you send the two men to try and help me. Thank you," she said, tears shining in her eyes again.

With those words, Carrie remembered Eddie. She looked around and saw him standing next to Spencer by the carriage. She took Janie's arm and led her over. "Thank you very much for trying to help."

Spencer nodded gravely. "You're welcome, Miss Cromwell," he said, and climbed back in the carriage.

Then Carrie turned to Eddie again. "It's wonderful to see you again, Eddie. How is everything?"

"Things be just fine, Miss Cromwell. It's good to see you again, too."

"We were headed to your house, Eddie. I was hoping to see Opal."

"You won't be finding Opal there just now, Miss Cromwell."

"Oh?" Was that a flicker of alarm in his eyes?

Eddie shook his head. "She and Fannie have gone visiting. They won't be home till later. I'll tell her you asked about her, though. I'm sure she would love to see you."

"She is doing well?" Why was she feeling uneasy? She couldn't shake the feeling that Eddie was hiding something, yet she didn't want to pry.

"Yes, ma'am. She be doing real well."

Carrie nodded. "Tell her I'll try again another time." She turned to Janie. "Now. Where is it you were going?"

Janie smiled. "I was on my way to visit a friend, but I seem to have lost any desire for that. I would really love to go home."

"Of course you would," Carrie said quickly. "Where is home?"

"I have a room in a house on Church Hill. Twenty-Second Street. Is it terribly out of your way?"

Carrie smiled. "You live only a few blocks from where I am visiting my father. My plans to visit a friend have ended, so I am going to head back home. It won't be out of the way at all."

Silence fell on the carriage as Spencer clucked to the horses. As they rolled forward, Carrie shuddered, wondering what would have happened to Janie if they had not happened along. True, it had been the policeman who had saved her, but she was sure Eddie and Spencer's presence had distracted the man from his immediate agenda. She took time now to study the woman across from her. Janie could not be more than twenty-two or twenty-three. Her slender, soft hands still shook in her lap, and her bright blue eyes were still slightly swollen. Brown hair, once carefully pulled back in a bun, was now mussed all over her head.

Janie reached up a hand and straightened her hat. Then she lifted her shoulders, and when she spoke, the tremor was gone from her voice. It was at once calm and slightly cheerful. "I am really most grateful for what you've done. There were other people around, but you were the only one to step forward to try to help. At first I felt angry toward the people who merely watched, but now I find I feel nothing but pity. I hope I never reach the place where I am so hardened that I could watch such a thing, even if it meant my own safety could be in jeopardy."

Carrie nodded. "I couldn't have lived with myself if I hadn't done something to help." She leaned forward. "Are you from Richmond, Miss Winthrop?"

"Please, call me Janie. I shall call you Carrie. Surely your helping to save me should move us beyond formalities." She waited for Carrie's nod, then continued.

"No, I'm not from Richmond. The war has brought me here from Raleigh, North Carolina."

"The war brought you here?"

Janie nodded. "I understood there was need of medical help here. I arrived just after the Battle of Bull Run, but I have chosen to stay. I am helping to prepare Chimborazo Hospital." She paused. "I am trusting my instincts that you are not another Southerner who believes a woman in a military hospital is a shameful thing because of the atrocities against our feminine delicacy that abound in such a setting."

Carrie smiled. She had known instantly this was a woman she could be friends with, and she had been right. "I think that's wonderful. I understand Dr. McCaw has big plans for the place." She and her father had discussed it just the night before.

"Yes, he does," Janie said enthusiastically. "He is a wonderful man. It is exciting to work with him." Again she paused, and then laughed merrily. "Not that I'm doing much of what I would call real nursing. The men who run the place seem to think the few women there can be best utilized cleaning and cooking. Matron Pember tells me I must be patient." Carrie looked at her blankly. "Matron Pember came to us from Georgia. She is the head matron in charge of one of the divisions. She keeps telling me it is going to be women who save the day for Confederate medical care. She believes that soon all the men will be on the battlefront. Then women will get the chance to show what they can do."

Since Carrie had not gotten far from home when the unpleasant incident had occurred, the carriage was already approaching Twenty-Second Street. She leaned forward impulsively. "I know you've had a harrowing experience, but I would love to have you join me for some tea. Would you care to?"

Janie's eyes lighted. "That would be lovely, Carrie. I really am feeling much better. I have learned one has to be tough to survive in Richmond now."

Carrie frowned. "It has not always been like this. There was a time when a lady was perfectly safe to roam the streets at will."

Spencer spoke up from the driver's seat. "That time ain't now, though, Miss Cromwell." He turned as the carriage rolled up in front of the house. "I'll be around back when Miss Winthrop be ready to go home. You just give me a call."

"Thank you, Spencer," Carrie said as she led the way up the walk and into the house.

There was no more talk until Micah had delivered hot tea and biscuits.

Then Janie turned to Carrie. "Did you know that black man who tried to help your driver?"

Carrie nodded. "He is the cousin by marriage of one of my father's slaves. I was on my way to visit her."

Janie looked at her quizzically, opened her mouth as if she wanted to say something, then shut it again.

Carrie smiled. If this was going to be a friendship worth having, and she sensed it was, she needed to be honest from the first. "Opal, Eddie's cousin, is not just my slave. She is a friend. I visit her whenever I'm in town."

Janie looked at her closely. "You are friends with your slaves?"

"My father's slaves," Carrie corrected. "I'm one of those evidently rare Southerners who believes slavery is wrong. I find my views make me extremely unpopular with some people, especially during these times."

"Yet, you are so open with me. Why?" Janie asked bluntly.

Carrie chose honesty again. "Because I sense you and I could be good friends. I'd just as soon be open from the start. If my beliefs repulse you, it could save us both a lot of time."

Janie laughed. "You're right. You and I are going to be good friends. I have found no one in this city as refreshingly honest as you. And, no, your beliefs hardly repulse me. I feel the same way you do. I, too, have lost friends because of my beliefs."

Carrie smiled in delight and moved forward to squeeze Janie's hand.

The rest of the afternoon passed in a haze of conversation and laughter, until finally, Janie looked at the clock.

"Oh my goodness, I really must be going. My landlady will think something horrible has happened." She paused. "I would love for you to come for tea tomorrow. Where I live is not as grand as this—I have only a room—but I would love for you to come."

"And I would love to do so," Carrie said, delighted.

She walked out to the carriage with her new friend, waved goodbye, and then returned to the porch. She smiled as she stared up at the darkening sky. "Thank you," she whispered. Her heart was light as she went inside. She had been so lonely for a friend. She knew she had found one.

Carrie was resting by the fire when the front door slammed open and her father strode in. She knew instantly something was wrong. "Father!" she exclaimed. "What is it?"

Thomas scowled and threw his hat into the nearest chair. "I want you here in Richmond, Carrie."

Carrie stuffed down her alarm and tried to be casual. "I *am* in Richmond," she said with a smile. Her father's scowl did not diminish.

"It's simply not safe for you on the plantation."

Carrie was confused. "What are you talking about?" She tried to keep her voice calm.

"I'm talking about the confirmed intelligence we received today. We have heard rumors that McClellan had plans to take Richmond, but there has been no action on his part. I had begun to believe the Union was going to focus their efforts elsewhere and leave us alone."

"You no longer believe that?"

Thomas shook his head. "Lincoln is getting impatient for action. There has begun to be a great deal of criticism leveled at his administration, as well as at McClellan, for doing nothing with the huge army sitting outside of

Washington. Our sources tell us something will have to happen soon."

"What does McClellan plan to do?" Carrie asked carefully. If she could keep him talking, she knew it would diffuse some of the stress exploding within him.

Thomas sighed and leaned back in his chair for the first time. "No one knows for sure, but reports say he is planning an offensive on the coast and then overland to Richmond." He frowned again. "That would take him right past the plantation, Carrie. I simply cannot allow you to return there."

Carrie struggled to control herself. She had to give her father time to calm down. As much as part of her yearned to be in Richmond, she also knew she had to return to Cromwell Plantation. It wasn't time yet. "No one knows for sure what he is going to do, do they?"

"No," Thomas admitted, "but I'm sure President Davis is going to order Johnston back to the vicinity of Richmond. We simply cannot lose the Capitol!"

Carrie hated conflict with her father when he was upset, but she knew she had to face this now, before he assumed she was in agreement with him. "No one knows for sure what the North is going to do. It could be nothing. It could be McClellan decides to attack from a different direction." She paused. "Regardless, no one can move an army that size without being detected. Am I right?"

Thomas nodded reluctantly, opening his mouth as if to interrupt, but Carrie pushed on. "The plantation is only three hours from the Capitol. In case of danger, you will be able to notify me." Her voice became firm. "I *am* returning to the plantation, Father. I'm sorry if you will worry about me, but I have a job to do. We have talked about this before. I am no longer a little girl. I promised you I would leave the plantation if things became too dangerous. So far there is only talk, but I will promise you again." She leaned forward, looked him in the eyes, and spoke softly but firmly. "I will leave the plantation if it becomes too dangerous. I promise."

Thomas sighed and shook his head. "I didn't really expect to have my way."

His look of resignation and agony tore at Carrie's heart, but she felt she was doing the only thing she could.

Carrie prepared to leave Richmond one week later. She had already told her father goodbye before he left for the office, and Janie had just arrived to see her off.

"You're really not afraid to be on the plantation by yourself?" Janie asked.

Carrie shrugged. "I try not to think about it. I just know I have to go back." She and Janie had talked it through already, and she knew Janie was just making conversation to avoid saying goodbye. Carrie stepped forward and gave her new friend a big hug. "Take good care of yourself." Then she stepped into the carriage.

Janie waved until she was out of sight.

Carrie could not remember a time when it had been so hard to return to the plantation. Janie was the first friend her age, other than Rose, who she felt truly understood and accepted her for all she was. She had shared with Janie her dream of being a doctor. Her friend had done nothing but encourage her ever since. She had told of her heartache with Robert. Janie had shared secrets as well. They had agreed to exchange letters, but still it wouldn't be the same. They had spent time together every day since they first met. She would miss Janie sorely.

Carrie shook her head and tried to force her thoughts back to the plantation. It would soon be time to start plowing and planting the fields. She had a job to do. She was determined to do it well.

Chapter Twenty-Nine

Pepper pot, right hot!
All hot! All hot!
Makee back strong!
Makee live long!
Come buy my pepper pot!

Rose smiled at the black woman standing on the sidewalk next to a cart with its kettle of stew. She remembered her amazement the first time she had seen street vendors hawking their wares. The tiny woman who stood on the corner of Washington Street, no matter what the weather, was one of her favorites. Often, she stopped to talk to her, but not today. Today she was in a hurry.

My hoss is blind and he's got no tail,
When he's put in prison I'll go his bail.
Yeddy go, sweet potatoes, oh!
Fif-en-ny bit a half peck!

Rose hurried past the vendor with his sweet potatoes as well. His leering looks made her nervous, anyway.

One look at the sky this morning had told her Philadelphia was going to have another winter storm. She was sure this winter was never going to end. By the first week of March in the South, the air would become warm with the promise of spring. Trees would sprout buds and the first crocuses would pop up from their winter hiding places. Here in Philadelphia, winter still held the city in its brutal grasp. She ducked her head against a blast of cold air and pressed on.

She reached the Quaker School for Females and gave a sigh of relief as she pushed inside. She pulled off her heavy coat, scarf and gloves, adding them to the assortment on the coat stand. Then she hurried into the classroom and took her usual seat in the front row.

Today more than any other, she wanted to be on time and close to the speaker.

"Good morning, Rose."

"Good morning, Alice." It had taken Rose quite some time to become comfortable using her teacher's first name. She had been taught to always use white people's titles when she spoke with them. Mr., Miss, and Mrs. were an integral part of her vocabulary. The Quaker custom of addressing people of all ages by their first names was foreign to her, but eventually it was becoming more comfortable. She appreciated the feeling of equality it offered her.

"Are you looking forward to our speaker today?"

"I certainly am. To actually talk to someone who has taught other blacks in the South... I have so many questions"

"Questions I'm sure she'll be more than happy to answer," Alice said with a smile.

The door opened and another group of students pushed their way in from the cold. Alice went to greet them while Rose opened the book she was now reading. The rest of the room faded away as she once again lost herself in the world of *Moby Dick*.

It was a sudden silence that caught her attention. She looked up and hurriedly put her book away. The guest speaker had arrived. Rose watched as the matronly, middle-aged woman made her way to the front of the room. She was rather unremarkable looking, except for her eyes, which shone with caring and warmth as bright as the sun. Rose liked her immediately.

Alice made the introductions. "Good morning, class. This is Marianne Lockins. I told you about her a few days ago. Until last week, she was in one of the contraband camps of Virginia working with the refugee slaves there. She has returned to accumulate books for her school and has graciously agreed to speak with us today." Alice stepped aside while Marianne took her place behind the simple podium.

Rose leaned forward, determined not to miss a single word. Her eyes were glued to the woman's face. You could tell a lot by looking at a person's face.

Marianne's voice was strong and surprisingly deep. "Good morning. Thank you for having me here today. I have indeed come from one of the contraband camps in Virginia. I can easily say it has been the most exciting time of my life. I hope when I'm done talking that some of you will decide to take what has been given you here and give it to others."

Rose could feel her heart rising to the challenge. She knew the camps were where she was supposed to be, but when? That was the answer she didn't yet know.

Marianne smiled and began her story. "The contraband camp is not my first experience teaching in the South. I have been a teacher for many years. The last ten have been spent in southeastern Virginia, near Roanoke. I loved my job, and I loved the people I worked with, the adults as well as the children. Alas, things changed drastically as the war drew nearer. Many people decided those from the North were there to brainwash and miseducate their children. People began to watch me suspiciously—even those I had known for years. As the tensions mounted, there was another campaign mounting to rid the South of all Northern teachers." She paused. "Even though they did not have qualified teachers in the South to take our places." A sad look crossed her face. "I stayed as long as I could. When I was certain my life was in danger because of intense feelings, I decided it was time to leave. I came north hoping to start over again."

Rose stared at her. She could not imagine anyone wanting to hurt this gentle-looking woman. She sighed. She knew reason often fell to the wayside when intense feelings were involved.

"I was in for quite a shock when I moved north as well. Because I had been a teacher in the South, I was suspected of disloyalties. I refused to belittle my previous students and friends. I believe the South has made grave errors in judgment. That does not mean I believe Southerners are bad people. There are people erring in grievous passions on both sides of this issue, I think." She paused again. "Anyway, I discovered before long there was no real place for me in the North, yet all I wanted to do was teach. I began to ask God what I was to do with the gifts he had given me. Not too long after, I heard about the contraband camps."

Rose resisted the urge to start asking questions. She had to let Marianne finish her story. Alice had promised her some time with the speaker afterward if Marianne could stay.

"Going to the contraband camps was a truly incredible experience. I have always abhorred the idea of slavery, but I think in the back of my mind I held the belief that blacks really were inferior to whites. I wasn't sure they could learn as well as whites." She laughed, a deep laugh that spread to her whole face. "It's rather embarrassing to admit that in a room full of very intelligent black students, but I feel I need to be honest with you. If any of you choose to go down there, I am afraid you will find it a rather prevalent attitude."

Rose found her liking of the woman increasing. Her refreshing honesty reminded her of Carrie and Aunt Abby.

"I have never seen such a thirst for knowledge as I found in those camps. That seems to be the first thing former slaves want. They want education. They want to read and write. They are eager to make something of themselves." She paused again, remembering. "My classes were full from the very beginning. Children came during the day, and even the youngest ones were hungry to learn. The adults came at night." She shook her head. "I have never seen such a desire to learn.

"And learn they have," she said. "I have come north to accumulate books, as the supplies I have are simply inadequate. Many of my students have already surpassed what I have to teach them with. I struggle to keep them challenged. They are truly remarkable." She looked down for a moment and then faced them again. "I realized quickly how unfounded my prejudices were. My students learn as quickly and well as any white people I have taught. Just like in a white school, there are students who learn faster than others, and ones who struggle to catch on. It has absolutely nothing to do with color."

Her voice grew more serious. "Why I am telling you this? Because some of the teachers going there from the North are not willing to reexamine their prejudices. They assume their students are going to be slow. So many of them are. Or they drop out. It has broken my heart to see what has happened in some of the classes when mine are going so well." She laughed. "I'm not trying to sound egotistical. I don't necessarily believe my teaching techniques are better. I think it is simply because I believe in my students. My parents taught me from a very early age to believe in the power of an individual to achieve."

Rose nodded her head as she listened. She had discovered the very same thing in teaching her students. They achieved because she believed they could. Her belief had transferred to them.

"I truly hope some of you will join me in the camps. The need is great, and I believe it will continue to get greater. The number of slaves increases every day. If indeed slavery is abolished in the South, the need will be phenomenal. There will literally be millions of people who have never had the benefit of education. You, more than anyone else, are qualified to teach your people. You know what it's like to have to push beyond people's prejudices to accomplish your dreams."

Marianne looked out over the classroom with a brilliant smile. "Are there any questions you would like to ask?"

Rose's hand was already in the air. "What does it take to be a good teacher, Marianne?"

Marianne smiled. "Well, of course it takes knowing how to teach, but I'd say that is only the beginning. You have to have a heart for what you're doing. I believe, to be a good teacher, you have to be passionate about it. Unfortunately, our country is full of women who have become teachers simply because there is nothing else for them to do. Teaching used to be the man's domain, but when our country discovered women would teach for much less pay, the number of women teachers increased tremendously. Now, with so many of our men at war, teaching has fallen almost entirely into the hands of women. That is both good and bad. Many women have become teachers who never should have, because it's more appealing than working in the mills or in the fields. Yet, their students suffer."

"Because they don't love to teach?" Rose asked.

"Yes, because they don't love to teach. You cannot impart a passion for learning if you yourself don't have both a passion for learning and a love for your students." She paused. "I don't want to be too hard on the women, though. Teaching is not only reading and writing."

"What do you mean?" Rose asked. She blushed and looked around, realizing she was giving no one else a chance to talk. The others didn't seem to mind, so she turned back around to hear the answer.

"Teachers have a rather difficult place in the community. Especially if they are young women. They are expected not only to teach, but to serve the community as well. The restrictions on them are very stern. For some reason, towns think that if a teacher has fun, it somehow keeps her from being a good teacher. I don't share those feelings, but they can be very difficult to fight."

"It's worth it, isn't it?" Rose asked anxiously.

"My goodness, yes," Marianne laughed. "I would do nothing else. There is nothing like watching the face of a child light up when they finally catch on to what you're teaching them."

Rose smiled. "I know," she said softly, more to herself than to anyone.

"You're Rose, aren't you?" Marianne asked with a smile.

Rose nodded.

"Alice has told me about you. About your desire to teach."

"It's all I want to do."

Alice stepped to the front then. "It's time for math class. Gather your books, and I will meet you in the other room." She turned to Rose. "You may stay here and talk with Marianne. You two have a lot in common."

Rose turned to Marianne as soon as the room was empty. "Thank you so much for coming today and telling us about the contraband camps."

"Did you know anything of them before?"

Rose nodded. "I intend to teach there."

"Would you like a place in my school? I would be pleased to have you join me," Marianne said sincerely.

Rose was startled. "Now?"

Marianne nodded. "Alice has told me about your plantation school. She says you are a very bright student, far above many here. You would be a wonderful addition to our school."

Rose flushed with pleasure but shook her head. "I can't go now."

"Why not?"

Rose struggled to explain. "It's not time yet. I know I will be teaching in the contraband camps, but there is still so much I want to learn. When I begin to help my people, I want to be as well-equipped as possible." She paused. "I believe my people will be free someday soon. I feel it in my bones. I agree with you they are going to need black teachers who can understand them because they know where they have come from—teachers who understand that their perceived laziness is merely an indication of being told what to do all their lives and being robbed of any personal initiative."

She stopped and looked Marianne straight in the eye. "I don't simply want to be a teacher, I want to be a leader for my people. I want to start schools that will make a difference." She paused, embarrassed at her own honesty. She had never told anyone the full scope of her dream before.

Marianne reached forward and took her hand. "I believe you will do that, Rose," she said. "You have a vision and a dream, and a willingness to work hard to make it come true. That combination can never be defeated." She looked at the clock and rose to her feet. "I have to speak at a luncheon in a few minutes. I'm afraid I must be going, but I will count on hearing from you when you're ready to come to the camps."

"You can indeed count on it, Marianne," Rose said.

Rose was walking as fast on the way home as she had on the way to school. She knew Moses wouldn't be home for a while, but being in the house waiting for him so that she could share her news was enough. Bursting through the door, she was startled to see him rise from the chair by the window. Obviously, he had been waiting for her.

"Moses! What in the world are you doing home this time of day? Did you lose your job?" She looked at him more closely. There was a huge grin on his face.

Moses shook his head. "Nope. I quit."

Rose stared at him. "What in the world did you do a thing like that for?" In spite of his obvious happiness, she felt a pang of uneasiness. "Did something bad happen?"

Moses laughed and stepped forward to take her hand. "Nothing happened. At least not anything bad. Come over by the window. I want to talk to you."

Rose followed him to the window and took a seat. "All right," she said. "I'm listening."

Moses gave her a brilliant smile. "I was accepted as a Union spy today," he said triumphantly.

Rose gasped and sank back against the pillows. She knew Moses wanted her to be excited, but the first thing that flashed through her mind was that they were going to be apart. "Why don't you tell me more about it," she managed.

"McClellan is finally going to make his move. I heard he met with Lincoln two days ago, and the pressure is on. The plan is to take Richmond. They figure if they can take the capital, the Confederacy will collapse. They are going to go in from the coast."

"Past the plantation," Rose murmured, frightened for Carrie.

Moses read her face. "I've thought of Carrie, too," he said with a troubled look. "I've taken a look at the map, though, and we don't seem to be going too awfully close to the plantation. It looks like we'll be north of it."

Rose nodded, but she was still troubled. "What will you be doing?"

Moses shrugged. "Whatever they tell me, I reckon. They need someone who knows the area and can get around without raising too much suspicion. Someone who can help them figure out the best way to get where they're going. I'll help anyway I can."

Rose had rarely seen him so excited. She knew how much he wanted to play a part in helping the Union win, and that he hoped it would mean the end to slavery. She also knew how much he wanted to return south to find his family. She took a deep breath and smiled. "When do you leave?"

Moses hesitated but held her gaze. "Tomorrow."

Rose felt as if she had been kicked in the stomach. "Tomorrow?" she whispered.

Moses nodded. "I know it's sudden, honey, but they are already beginning to pull together the troops. Now that the decision has been made, everything needs to move quickly."

Rose shook her head, too stunned to really comprehend what he was saying. "How many of you?"

"How many Union troops?"

"No," Rose answered. "How many black spies?"

Again Moses hesitated. "Just one. Me."

Rose stared at him. "You're going to be the only black man with all those white men?"

Moses nodded again, the excitement returning to his face. "I could be blazing the way for more blacks to follow. If I do a good job, if I can prove myself, maybe they'll let other blacks serve. There are thousands eager to enlist."

Rose struggled to push down the bile of fear rushing to her throat. "Let me get this straight. You are leaving tomorrow to be the only black spy with thousands of white men?"

Moses stood and walked over to her, then he lifted her from the chair and took her into his arms. "I'll be fine, Rose. You know I've got to do this."

"Yes, I know," Rose murmured into his broad chest. She wrapped her arms around him and began to sob.

Dinner that night was a somber affair. Aunt Abby had been as stunned as Rose when she arrived home and received the news. She had insisted on fixing a special dinner. Now, an hour later, Rose could hardly remember what she had eaten. Whatever it had been, it was sitting like a lead weight in the bottom of her stomach. Moses was still talking quietly to Aunt Abby when she excused herself and climbed up the stairs to their bedroom.

When she entered the room, all she could do was stare dully at the canopy bed. Soon, she would be sleeping alone. Soon, she would be spending all her nights wondering if Moses was dead or alive. She knelt beside the window and stared out at the swirling snowflakes dancing in the light of the gas lamps lining the street.

"Lettin' go of someone you love... Why girl, that be the hardest thing you ever have to do."

Rose lifted her head as her mama's words rang through her heart. It was as if her mama was right in the room with her. She could almost feel her wrinkled hand smoothing her hair as she talked.

"You gonna think 'bout him every day. You gonna miss him with an achin' every day. That's how you gonna keep him alive in your heart, girl."

"But Mama, what if I never see him again? What if something happens to him?" Rose moaned.

"Then you'll cry and go on livin'. But girl, you be borrowing trouble 'fore there be trouble to borrow. You done be lettin' that fear take over your heart again. What happened to your trust, chile? What happened to your trust?"

Rose bowed her head on the windowsill. What, indeed, had happened to her trust? How could she totally trust God one minute and wallow in fear the next?

"Trustin' done take a lifetime, Rose girl. Every time, it seems like you got to learn it again. But it gets to be some easier. You finally figure out that God does really love you. Then the trustin' get easier. God done already know how you feel. Let him take you through the hard times. He'll teach you to trust..."

Tears filled Rose's eyes when she finally looked up from the windowsill. A strange peace had entered her heart. Along with it came an understanding. Moses needed to leave secure in her love. Secure in her belief in him. "Thank you, Mama," she whispered.

She was ready for Moses when he finally entered the room. His eyes glowed when he saw her waiting on the bed for him. Not taking his eyes from her, he undressed and lowered himself on the bed beside her.

Rose gazed into his dark eyes for a long moment. "I love you, Moses." She kissed him as she whispered. "And I'm very proud of you." She allowed her fingers to trace a pattern on his muscular back, moving gently over the whip scars he had gained in his early years of slavery.

"Oh, Rose," he groaned. "I love you, too." He kissed her then, his tenderness quickly changing to passion.

It was a long time before they rolled over to face each other. Moses held both of her hands while they talked.

"I'm coming home to you, Rose. This war is a horrible thing, but we've just started new. We still have a lot of living to do. I'm coming home."

Rose nodded and put her finger to his lips. "I believe you, Moses. I know you have to do this thing. I'm proud of you. I believe you're going to open up the way for many more black men to follow." She paused. "One of the reasons I love you is because you're a leader. I'm sorry I let my fears get the best of me. I guess I'll always have to fight them."

She paused again.

"I don't want to lose you," she whispered. "You hold all my heart, you know."

Moses nodded. "And you hold all of mine", he said gently, leaning forward to kiss her again.

Rose never wanted this night to end. She returned his kiss and pressed her body close to his. Once again, they were lost in the passion of their love. If there were no more, at least they would have this one last night.

Chapter Thirty

Eddie had a worried look on his face when he strode in the door and threw a quick glance back over his shoulder as if he were afraid someone was watching him.

Fannie glanced up from her sewing and frowned. "Something wrong?"

Eddie shook his head. "I don't know. I guess I'm a little spooked. This city be making me more and more nervous."

Opal looked up from her own sewing to watch the exchange. Once again, she was trying to patch the only other dress she owned. For a brief moment, she longed for the plantation. Their clothes hadn't been fancy, but they were always in good condition. She was ashamed of the two dresses she owned now. Of course, things might be as scarce on the plantation as they were becoming in Richmond. She could have made herself a new dress if the material that could be found was not so exorbitant in price. She finished her last stitch, tied a knot, and broke the thread.

Fannie's face had grown more anxious. "Do you think they know what we're doing?" Her tone was furtive, and she kept her voice low, even though the windows in the house were closed, and no one was home but them.

Opal understood. You couldn't be too careful right now. Martial law had been declared in Richmond. It was impossible to enter the city without a pass. Alcohol and firearms had been outlawed. The city had become desperate to find a way to stop the lawlessness sweeping its streets. At first Opal had been glad. At least she was sleeping without sporadic gunfire jolting her from her bed all hours of the night. But it was the crackdown on Union sympathizers that had them all worried. People were being taken from their homes and put in jail for not avowing wholehearted loyalty to the Confederate cause.

Eddie shook his head. "I don't know how they could. We've been so careful, but I don't know." He sighed. "I can't get out of my head how that policeman watched me walk away after I stopped to help Spencer and Miss Carrie. I knowed I shouldn't have stopped, but I couldn't see Miss Carrie getting hurt." He shook his head firmly. "No sir, I couldn't see her getting hurt. I done the right thing."

"Of course you did," Opal said quickly. "That policeman couldn't have known anything. I think everybody is just nervous right now."

Fannie nodded, looking at Opal in gratitude. Opal knew her cousin lived in constant fear something was going to happen to one of them. Because of their activities, much information had been smuggled out to the Union authorities, but so far, it seemed the crackdowns were concentrated on white people.

Eddie took a quick glance at Fannie's face and tried to reassure her. "I'm sure there ain't nobody be knowing about what we're doing. I'm being extra careful, I guess. Anyway, we seem to keep getting by with things."

"Like not having Miss Carrie walk right into the middle of one of our meetings?" Fannie asked with a glimmer of her normal humor.

Opal laughed. "I would have so loved to see her, but not that Sunday. Not with the house full of people supposedly here for lunch. We wouldn't have gotten *any* planning done."

Eddie nodded. "I felt sorry for that little lady the soldier tried to have his way with, but I sure was glad I had a chance to tell Miss Carrie you wasn't at home."

Opal nodded. Seeing Carrie would have been wonderful, but what they were doing was much more important.

Fannie nodded, her face once more composed as she picked up the dress she was mending for Sadie. "I guess the good Lord done be looking after us."

Eddie dropped his voice low. "He'll get another chance tomorrow."

Fannie looked up sharply. "A delivery?"

Eddie nodded, his eyes bright with excitement. "Mrs. Hamilton done bribed one of those prison guards. I guess he needed the money real bad. Anyway, she says she has some information the Union will find real helpful."

"When?" Fannie asked.

Eddie shrugged. "I have to go downtown to one of the drops tomorrow morning sometime. They'll put the sign out when the way is clear."

Fannie merely nodded, but the worried look had returned to her face.

Opal searched for the other hole in her dress she wanted to mend, wondering how long they would be able to get away with what they were doing.

Just then the back door opened and shut quickly. The children had been told in no uncertain terms not to let any precious heat out of the house. Spring was on the way, but winter was still teasing them. Opal pulled her coat closer around her as a draft of cold air whirled past. Firewood had become scarce in the city, and there had been many days when there was no heat in the house at all.

"Mama, I'm hungry," nine-year-old Amber announced.

Fannie looked even more anxious as she got up and headed to the kitchen. Minutes later, Amber walked into the room holding a piece of cornbread.

Opal frowned at the pinched look on the little girl's face. There simply was not enough food to keep them all satisfied. At first, Opal had felt guilty for being another mouth to feed, but Eddie reminded her they would have even less than they did now without her paycheck to help.

Prices had skyrocketed, and the staple items could oftentimes not be found. The food from the garden had run out about a month or so ago. It would be several more months before the garden would produce again. Thin, watery soup and cornbread had become the mainstays of their diet. All of them were feeling it, but Opal felt worse for the children. She thought longingly of the stocked cellar and smokehouses of the plantation. What she wouldn't give to see the children well fed.

Opal waved goodbye to Fannie as she made the turn that would take her to the State Armory building where she worked. Fannie returned the wave and continued on her way to the Tredegar Iron Works perched on the banks of the James River.

Opal sighed when she entered the building. She didn't miss working in the tobacco fields, but she did miss being outdoors in the sunshine. Coming in to work at seven o'clock in the morning and not leaving until seven o'clock at night made it seem as if the whole world were shrouded in perpetual darkness—especially during the long winter she had just endured. At least now, with spring right around the corner, she could enjoy a little light while she walked to work.

She nodded pleasantly to the other women around her before she moved to her place on the sorting bench. The work of sorting shells was tedious, but at least it wasn't dangerous. Fannie's job of packing shells with gunpowder had already injured more than one careless worker.

"Howdy, Opal. You goin' to the meetin' at church tonight?"

Opal smiled at Mabel, the cheerful old woman who worked next to her. They had become friends during all the hours they worked side by side. "Why, I suppose I am," she said absently. Her mind was with Eddie, wherever he was. They had talked at home again this morning about how important the message was that he was trying to send on. She had been worried about the anxious look in his eyes. Was he not telling them something? Was there a reason for people to suspect him? Was he hiding something to keep Fannie from worrying?

The questions twirled in her brain as her fingers nimbly sorted the shells in front of her. As soon as one container was done, she rose to get another one, grateful for the brief respite to stretch her back and flex her hands. She smiled at the women who glanced up, then carried her new box back to her place and settled down to sort more shells. She was only on her second box of the ten she usually made it through before the day was over. She sighed heavily and let her thoughts carry her out of the Armory. It was going to be a long day.

She was on her fourth box when she heard a commotion at the door. Her supervisor, Mrs. Whiteside, strode into the room and looked around.

"Is there someone in here by the name of Opal?" she called.

Opal stared at her with a sick feeling in her stomach. Something was wrong.

"I say, is there an Opal in here?" she called again. "I was told I would find her here."

Opal stood slowly and walked over to her. "I'm Opal," she said, her voice trembling.

Mrs. Whiteside looked at her closely. "You got a cousin named Fannie?"

Opal nodded, her eyes wide with fear. She waited silently, too frightened to speak.

Mrs. Whiteside's rough face softened a little with compassion. "You're needed over at the Iron Works. Fannie is asking for you."

Opal finally found her voice. "Fannie...is she all right? Has something happened?"

"There has been an accident. An explosion. Fannie is asking for you," she said grimly.

Opal swayed, but Fannie needed her. At least she was alive. Her voice was firm when she spoke this time. "May I go right over?"

Her supervisor nodded, her voice strangely soft for one who was so hard and demanding. "You may take the rest of the day off." Then her voice became rough again. "Just today, though. I will expect you back here tomorrow."

Opal ran back to her place to grab her coat, squeezed the hand Mabel reached out, and ran from the room. Unmindful of what people thought, she ran all the way down the hill to the Iron Works. Her first look reassured her somewhat. All the buildings were still standing, and there were no flames. The explosion must not have been a bad one. Fannie could not be too seriously injured.

Then she remembered the look of compassionate pity on Mrs. Whiteside's face, and she ran faster.

She was gasping for breath when she broke through the door into the office of Fannie's building. A young lady behind the front desk looked up immediately.

"You're Opal?"

Opal nodded, her fears increasing as she saw the serious look on the lady's face.

"Come with me, please."

"What happened?" Opal pleaded.

"There was an explosion. Some of the gunpowder went off. We're still not sure why."

"How many people were hurt?"

"Just Fannie. She was carrying a box of shells to be stored."

Opal stopped in her tracks. "Fannie was carrying a box that exploded?" she whispered. The young lady kept walking. Opal stuffed down her feeling of horror and ran to catch up with her.

They rounded a bend, and Opal caught sight of a figure on the floor. With a moan, she dashed forward and knelt down next to her cousin.

"Fannie..." she said softly, trying to control the tears rolling down her face. Her cousin lay on the ground where she had fallen. Opal fought the nausea crowding her throat. She had to be strong. Fannie needed her.

At the sound of her name, Fannie managed to open her eyes a tiny bit, in spite of the swollen, charred condition of her face. She struggled to raise a hand, and Opal bit her lip to keep from crying out. Both of Fannie's hands were missing.

Opal groaned at the confused pain on her cousin's face. Choking back her sobs, she rested her hands on Fannie's shoulders. "I'm here, Fannie. I'm here." That was all she could think of to say. She knew there was nothing she could do. There was nothing anyone could do.

Fannie managed to nod. Her lips opened, and Opal leaned closer to hear what she was trying to say.

"My children... My children..." The words were slurred and gargled, but Opal understood. Fannie's lips continued to move, but nothing else would come out. Tears edged down her charred face as it twisted in agony.

Opal moved back far enough to gaze into Fannie's eyes. "I'll take care of your children, Fannie. I'll take care of them. I'll treat them like they were my own." Her voice broke as she choked back her sobs. "I promise you. I'll take care of your children."

A measure of peace settled over Fannie's face, and she opened her lips again. Opal could barely hear the words she struggled to say.

"Ed...Eddie... Love...him..." she managed.

Opal nodded. "I'll tell Eddie. I'll tell him you love him." She could no longer control the sobs racking her body. "I love you, Fannie. I love you!"

Fannie gave one last faint nod, and then her eyes closed. Moments later, Opal felt her go slack beneath her hands. She didn't know how long she knelt next to her cousin, sobbing hysterically, before she felt hands reach for her.

"It's me, Opal. Jamilla."

Opal gazed up, the words barely registering in her mind. Jamilla... Fannie's closest friend at the Works.

"She went quick, Opal. It's best this way. There would have been too much suffering."

Opal stared at her. She heard the words, but they weren't penetrating. Fannie... Fannie, her only family, was gone. One minute she had been laughing, waving at her. The next minute she was dead.

Eventually, Opal let Jamilla lead her back to the two-story home she had shared with her cousin. Numbness had begun to set in. Along with the numbness, was the realization she would have to be the one to tell Eddie and the children what had happened to their beautiful mother. Her grief thickened as she thought of the children.

"When is Daddy coming home, Opal?" Amber asked in a lost voice.

Opal shook her head, drawing the little girl closer. None of the children had left her side since she had gathered them together and broken the horrible news. Amber had refused to leave her lap all day. Susie was holding Carl close, soothing the little boy's broken cries.

Opal exchanged a long look with Susie. "I don't know, Amber. I'm sure he'll be home soon." Actually she wasn't sure of any such thing. Where was Eddie? He was always home by five o'clock in the evening. It had been dark for at least an hour. It had to be close to seven o'clock. Where was he?

Opal tried to swallow her fears. She had to be strong for the children. In the midst of their grief, they were looking to her for strength and comfort. She had to control her desire to scream out her own pain and anguish.

Little Carl had begun sobbing immediately when Opal had carefully told them of the accident. She had left out the details that would have haunted them the rest of their lives—the details she knew would never leave her mind. Carl simply knew his mama was never coming home again.

Amber had said not a word. She'd listened wide-eyed, and then walked quietly to Opal and snuggled close. The question about her daddy was the first words she had uttered.

Sadie had asked a few careful questions and then withdrawn into her own shell. Opal was most worried about her. Sadie's look of sorrow had gradually turned into a gaze of hardened defiance. What was she thinking?

Susie had cried when Opal told her. She had told Susie first, and they had clung together for a long time as Opal tried to answer her questions. There hadn't been many, but Opal expected more later. Then they had gone to find the rest of the children.

Outside, a slashing rain beat at the house. Opal shuddered and drew Amber closer to her side. She would have to get the children something to eat soon. She was sure no one would feel like eating, but they must keep their strength up.

Again, Opal gazed at the windows. *Come home, Eddie. The rain will hide your movements in the night. We need you, Eddie. Please come home*, she pleaded silently.

None of them heard the back door open. Opal almost screamed when she heard a noise and looked up to see a man standing in the doorway. She gasped and clutched Amber to her side. "Frank! What are you doing here? You scared me near to death."

Frank, a friend of Eddie's who had often been at their meetings, moved forward. "I'm sorry, Opal. I had to make sure no one saw me come in here."

Opal looked at him more closely. There was stark fear in his widened eyes. She turned to Susie. "Why don't you take the children in the kitchen and fix them a bite to eat?" She tried to keep her trembling voice casual. "Frank and I will join you in a minute."

Susie stared long and hard at Frank with knowing in her eyes. Then she rose and took Carl by the hand. "Come, everyone. We'll fix something hot." Woodenly, the children followed her.

Opal turned to Frank as soon as they were out of the room. "Eddie?" she whispered.

Frank frowned, his face a mixture of pain and worry. He shook his head. "I'm afraid Eddie won't be coming home, Opal."

"Why not?" she asked quietly, amazed at her own control.

"They been watching him, Opal. Somehow they got wind of what we was doing."

"The police?" Opal breathed.

Frank nodded. "They were waiting when he left the shop this morning. They took him to jail. Him and the owner of that shop."

Opal lowered her face in her hands. She heard a slight noise and looked up. Susie was standing in the doorway, staring at Frank with a hard, set face.

"How long?" Susie asked.

Frank started at the sound of her voice and shook his head. "I don't know. It could be a right long time. Once they put us niggers in jail, they ain't in no hurry to let us out." He looked around quickly. "Fannie. Where is Fannie? I need to tell her. I promised Eddie a long time ago I would be the one to tell Fannie if something happened."

Tears filled Opal's eyes. "I'm afraid you won't be telling Fannie, Frank."

Frank stared around. "Why not?"

"My mama is dead," Susie announced. "Killed in an explosion at the Works today." Tears filled her eyes, but her voice was even.

Frank shook his head in disbelief, tears filling his own eyes. "I'm sorry. I'm so sorry," he moaned.

Silence filled the room for several long minutes.

Frank looked up. "The children...? What is going to happen to the children?"

"I'm going to take care of them," Opal said firmly.

"But how?" Frank asked.

Up until that moment, Opal had no idea. Suddenly, the answer was there. Her voice was strong as she spoke. "I'm taking them back to the plantation. They will be safe there." The plan began to take shape in her mind as she spoke.

Then she thought of something. "Am I safe here for now? Are they coming for me, too?" Suddenly she was seized with a new fear. What if they came and put her in jail, too? Who would take care of the children? Would she have enough time to get them out of Richmond?

Frank shook his head. "I heard the men talking from where I was hiding in the shadows of some of the buildings. They are just after the men. Don't think the women can do much."

Any other time, Opal would have laughed. They had no idea how much women could do. Now, she was simply grateful. It would give her time to contact Carrie.

"Can you send someone to Cromwell Plantation with a message? Can they get back into the city?"

Frank nodded. "It's risky, but yes, there are still ways to get past the military blocks. I'll send someone tonight. The rain will help them."

Opal nodded and moved over to where she kept her paper and pen. Quickly, she wrote a letter, folded it, and handed it to Frank. "Thank you," she said.

Right now, she was under control, thinking clearly. Later, she knew she would grieve. Right now, she had four children to care for.

Chapter Thirty-One

Carrie stooped down and gathered up a handful of fresh dirt. She let it sift through her fingers slowly and fall to the ground as she looked out over the freshly plowed fields. Spring had finally returned to the South. Birds sang gloriously, and trees sported their new clothing in myriad shades of green. Limbs swayed in response to the warm wind bathing her body. Carrie gave a sigh of delight and knelt to gather up another handful of dirt.

She had loved to do it since she was just a little girl. She had claimed then it was like feeling God, because only God could put all the magic things in dirt to make plants grow. She still felt that way. Dark and soft to the touch, the fertile soil was ready to do its job. Planting would begin tomorrow. The largest part of her father's plantation would be replanted in tobacco and corn, but over three hundred acres would be planted in food crops.

Carrie knew it was a tremendous undertaking. Even with all of her father's original slaves, it would be an incredible amount of work to maintain and harvest the crops, not to mention transporting them to Richmond. The food crops were incredibly labor intensive. She would simply do the best she could with the slaves that remained. They had performed amazing feats so far, but without Moses to supervise them...

Carrie shook her head to push away any negative thoughts. Even if half the crops rotted from lack of care and harvest, she would have tried her best. And there was no real loss. Unless things changed dramatically with the war and the blockade, her crops of tobacco and corn weren't going anywhere either. They would simply rot in the barns or fields. She was determined to feed as many people as she could from the fields of Cromwell Plantation. If she could have managed it, she would have planted the whole plantation in food.

Carrie heard someone call her name and looked up expectantly.

Jubal ran up to her, panting from his dash down the road. "They be here, Miss Carrie!"

She had asked Jubal to come to the fields as soon as Opal arrived with the children. She knew they were to arrive in a day or so, but wasn't sure how much the rain-soaked roads would slow them down.

"Wonderful!" Carrie exclaimed. "Do they look well?" She wasn't sure why she was asking a twelve-year-old boy.

Jubal shrugged. "I reckon they look all right." His face broke forth in a huge grin. "There for sho be one that look mighty fine."

Carrie laughed. "Sadie caught your eye, did she?"

Jubal nodded. "That be her name? The one looks to be my age?"

Carrie nodded. "Yes, her name is Sadie. I believe she's thirteen."

Jubal continued to grin, his eyes shining brightly.

Carrie swung into her saddle. "Come on, Jubal. You can ride up here with me." She reached down to help him swing up behind her.

Jubal gasped, his eyes even wider than before. "You's gonna let me ride on Granite with you, Miss Carrie? Why, I ain't never been on a horse before."

"It's high time you started," she replied. "Put your foot in the stirrup here."

Jubal sprang to obey.

"Now swing up behind me." She reached down her hand and helped hoist the boy behind her. Then she urged Granite into an easy canter.

"Great Jehoshaphat!" Jubal breathed. He wrapped his arms around her tightly and made not another sound.

Opal and the children were standing in the clearing when Carrie rode up. She dismounted and helped Jubal swing down. He stared at Sadie for a moment and then ran off to brag to all his friends. Carrie moved quickly to where Opal was standing.

"Opal, it's so wonderful to see you." They embraced warmly. There was still sorrow pooled in her eyes, but she had a determined air about her. "I'm so sorry about Fannie," Carrie said. She knew how much Opal had loved her cousin. She also knew Fannie had been the only blood family Opal had left, other than Fannie's children.

Opal merely nodded and looked down at the kids for a moment. "Thank you so much for having us back on the plantation."

"It will always be your home if you need it," Carrie said simply. "At least while I'm here." She knelt down to put herself on level with the smaller children. "Hello," she said. "Welcome to Cromwell Plantation. I'm glad you're here. It's good to see you all again." Her heart twisted at the pain locked in their eyes and on their faces. She remembered so well their happy exuberance the last time she had seen them. She stood and reached out her hand to Susie. "I'm so sorry," she said. There were no other words.

Susie took her hand and gazed into her eyes for a long moment. She seemed to be trying to bring her emotions under control before she spoke. "Thank you for having us here. The children needed to get out of Richmond."

Carrie nodded and smiled. She looked at Opal again. "I am letting you and the children have Rose and Moses' cabin."

Opal nodded. "Sam told me on the way that Rose and Moses are gone. I will miss them, but I sure am glad they're free." She paused. "But putting us in their cabin... We don't have to have a place so grand. Any of the cabins will do."

"Good. Rose and Moses' will do the job just fine then." Carrie looked at Susie. "Could you please take the children into the cabin? We will bring your things in soon. I'd like a few minutes to talk to Opal." Susie nodded and took Carl by the hand. Sadie took Amber's hand and followed. Once they were inside, Carrie turned to Opal. "Did you have any trouble leaving the city?"

Opal shook her head. "I showed your letter to the guards, and they let me right by. That is, once they saw your last name, and I told them who your daddy was.

Seems like your daddy must be pretty important around there."

"I believe he is. It has helped me several times, too." She allowed herself a brief thought of Matthew. Was he still in prison? "Have you heard any more about Eddie?"

Opal shook her head again, and tears filled her eyes.

"I'm so sorry," Carrie said. "I have written a letter to my father asking him to find out whatever he can. I don't have much confidence he can do much, though. Nor, I am afraid, will he be very motivated once he discovers the charges are treason."

Opal nodded. "Thank you for at least trying," she said softly. "Your daddy knows I am back on the plantation?"

Carrie nodded. "I didn't say anything about the children. I didn't see a need. I simply told him you had been very ill and could no longer work at the Armory. I told him you would be of great use here once I had nursed you back to health." Lying to her father seemed to have become a habit.

She looked up to see Opal staring off into the distance. "Opal?"

Opal continued to stare, but she answered. "All that thinking about being free. All that work to try to help... I'm right back where I started from." She paused for a long moment. "Life seems kinda funny sometime, don't it?"

Carrie didn't know what to say. She knew what it was like to have big plans changed by life's circumstances in the blink of an eye. Something Sarah said came back to her. "Sarah told me once that you can't look on the surface of things. She said you had to search deep underneath and inside. She said it takes time to really see something for what it is." She paused for a moment, remembering. "She said that a lot of times the things we think are horrible really turn out for the best." She moved forward and slipped her arm around Opal's waist. "I guess we'll both have the chance to find out how the bad can turn out for the good."

Opal nodded. "Thank you, Miss Carrie." She squared her shoulders and lifted her head high. "I'd better go look after my children," she said, turning away.

Carrie watched her go. Opal would soon discover the food she had left in the cabin and the bunks Jupiter had built into the wall for the children. Warm blankets were folded on each one. It had been all she had time to do on such short notice. She remounted Granite, then trotted swiftly up the road.

Sam was waiting on the porch for her. "Your daddy sent back a letter."

"You saw my father?"

Sam shook his head. "I ran into the fella bringing it here. He gave it to me to deliver." He looked down. "Got one more here for you, too."

Carrie nodded and reached for the letters, her eyes brightening in excitement when she spotted Janie's name in the top corner. "May I have my lunch on the porch today, Sam?" She waited for his nod and walked over to the porch swing to read her letters. She turned to her father's first.

Dear Carrie,

It is with great anxiety that I write this letter. I have just been informed of a massive buildup of Union troops at Fort Monroe. There can be but one purpose for their presence. The North is finally ready to make its assault on Richmond. Their position will bring them in your direction unless they can be stopped. General Johnston has moved closer to Richmond and will be sent to stop them if indeed they make a move proving the capital is their objective. It is time for you to come to the city. I cannot bear to think of your life being in danger. I will expect a letter from you soon informing me of your plans.

I fear what will become of my glorious plantation if indeed the Union succeeds in their plans. I am enclosing a letter for Ike Adams. He is to be in charge of things until the time comes when it is safe for you to return. I have given him instructions to occupy the plantation as long as possible, but to flee if Union troops actually come there. I am sure the slaves are in no danger, though I fear I will lose all I have worked so hard to accomplish. The North seems to treat them very well. I have heard of whole plantations of slaves being carried behind lines and sent off to contraband camps. The Yankees will stop at nothing to destroy us. They will not succeed.

A bit of good news. Congressman Ely of New York, for several months a guest in our officers' prison, finally arranged an exchange of prisoners for several of the officers and the remaining two civilian prisoners. Matthew Justin is now a free man and on his way north. I had breakfast with him this morning before he left on the train. He is certainly a happy man, though a bit sad at having to leave his friends behind. He sends his fondest greetings and gratitude for all you did for him.

Matthew was free! Carrie leaned back against the swing and wiped away the tears of happiness rolling down her cheeks. How happy he must be. And how happy Aunt Abby would be to know he was free and safe. She picked up the letter and continued.

I know how dedicated you are to growing food for the city. I am sorry it has come to this, but I simply must insist you come to Richmond. It is the only way I will get any rest. I will look forward to hearing from you soon about the date of your arrival.

Much love,
Father

Carrie frowned and laid her father's letter aside. Then she reached for Janie's.

Dear Carrie,

How I miss you and long for your cheerful, steady presence. Panic seems to be spreading in the city as word has reached us about McClellan's movements. I am sure your father is keeping you abreast of the news.

The hospital has become even busier as General Johnston has sent hundreds of men here who are too ill to join him in the march to the coast to meet McClellan. Seldom have I seen such tired, sick and discouraged men. They break my heart on a daily basis, yet their gratefulness keeps me going. I see my own two brothers in every one of their faces.

Dr. McCaw continues to develop his plans for a massive hospital operation. We will soon have our own bakery and distillery. He has plans to add more tent wards when the many buildings here are full, as he expects them to be. He is in the process of purchasing cattle and goats to make sure the men are properly fed. I have told him of your mission to provide food for the city. He is hoping you will keep the hospital in mind.

I think of you daily. I admire your commitment to stay where you are, but I long to have you here where we can work side by side. The needs are great and, I fear, will do nothing but grow greater. Keep studying those books. The South is going to need your skills and abilities. They just don't know it yet!

With much affection,
Janie

Carrie folded the letter, leaned back against the swing, and stared out over the pastures once again turning a lush green. She merely nodded when Sam carried out her tray of food.

After a long time, she finally stood and walked to her father's office. She sat down at the desk, pulled out a sheet of paper, and began to write.

Dearest Father,
I received your letter today. I am so thrilled to know Matthew Justin is a free man. He must indeed be very happy.

As to the buildup of troops at Fort Monroe, I find I am not willing to allow the Union to scare me from my present course. The fields of Cromwell are too important to the feeding of Richmond. Tomorrow we begin to plant. Let the troops come. I do not think they will bother with Cromwell Plantation—not that I think they will even get this far. I have great confidence in General Johnston to stop them. He has proven himself at Bull Run.

Please do not worry about me. I have not forgotten my promise to you. I simply do not feel in danger. If the time comes, I will join you in Richmond.

With much love from your hardheaded daughter,
Carrie

With a sigh, Carrie folded the letter, slipped it in an envelope, and addressed it. She knew it would do little to alleviate her father's worry. She also knew she simply could not leave the plantation now. She had lost valuable planting time the summer before when she was called to Richmond during the Battle of Bull Run. She was not going to run to Richmond every time there was a threat. There was too much to do.

Janie's letter had been harder to resolve in her mind, and she knew her friend understood the conflict in her heart. Never had she thought she would be so torn by desires and loyalty.

Rose walked out of school and stopped to take a deep breath. Spring was finally making itself felt in Philadelphia. There were still mounds of snow hiding in shadows and cold alcoves, but there was a warm glow in the air, and the trees in the park were filled with buds ready to burst forth with new life. Rose lifted her face gratefully to the sun. She didn't miss being a slave, but she still missed the beauty and openness of the plantation.

The sound of a deep male voice caused her to look around quickly, but her face fell when she identified it. She couldn't help it. Everywhere she went, she looked for Moses. She daydreamed that someday he would sneak up behind her and grab her in a big hug. She knew her daydreams were ridiculous, but they kept her hopeful.

Moses had been gone for three weeks. The days weren't quite so bad. School, housework and Aunt Abby kept her busy. But the nights... The nights were endless. She missed him with a fierce aching that left her in tears when she crawled into bed and reached out for the empty place beside her, wondering what he was doing, if he was safe, if she would ever see him again.

Rose cleared her thoughts and started down the street. If she hurried, she could get home in time to have a special dinner fixed for Aunt Abby. Today, for the first time, she slowed when she came to the sweet potato man.

The street vendor watched her coming. "Why, if it ain't the pretty little lady! I got me some o' the best sweet taters you ever put in your mouth. Why don't you buy some, pretty lady?"

Rose cringed at the leering wheedle in his voice. He wasn't usually quite so bold. Only the idea of fixing Aunt Abby a sweet potato pie made her stop. She kept her face expressionless. "I'd like three sweet potatoes, please," she said coolly.

The street vendor leered again and closed his eye in a wink. "Well, listen to the pretty lady. She even talks pretty." He raised a hand to motion to someone, then abruptly turned away.

"What—"

Suddenly, she felt herself grabbed from behind. In moments, her arms were pinned to her side roughly, causing her to gasp in pain. She knew instantly this was no fulfillment of her daydream about Moses.

"Good job, Mitchell." It was the voice from her worst nightmare.

Ike Adams! Rose gasped and struggled to free herself. The pain that blazed through her body when he cruelly twisted one of her arms caused her to quit fighting. She looked around frantically. Her only friend, the pepper pot lady, had chosen this one day of the year to leave early.

The vendor shrugged and looked at Rose. "You should've been a little friendlier, pretty lady," he said in a flat tone. He turned to Adams. "Where's my money?"

Adams maintained his cruel grasp on her arm while he reached into his pocket and pulled out an envelope. With a laugh, he tossed it into the vendor's outstretched hand. "Like I said, good work."

Rose looked at the vendor in disbelief. "You sold out one of your own people?" she gasped.

The vendor never blinked an eye. Calmly, he counted the money in the envelope. Then he looked up. "Like I said, pretty lady, you should have been a little friendlier. It's hard times, you know. I got me a wife and kids to feed." He stuffed the money in his pocket. "It's just business," he said. He glared at Adams. "Get her out of here. You standin' round here is bad for business."

Adams laughed and pushed Rose in front of him. "Let's go, Rose."

The way he said her name made Rose cringe in fear and fury. Aunt Abby had a late meeting this afternoon. She wouldn't be anywhere near here. Frantically, she tried to figure some way to get free.

Adams seemed to read her mind. Twisting her arm so tightly she almost cried out in pain, he said roughly, "Don't even think about getting away. I could break your little arm in a flash. We're going somewhere to wait for that big husband of yours. I aim to present Mr. Cromwell with both his runaway slaves."

Rose thought quickly. Adams didn't know about Moses being gone.

"I left a little note on the door to that fancy nigger school you go to. I reckon they know where you're shacking up right now. They'll get a message to Moses."

Rose was relieved to find out he didn't know where she lived. At least Aunt Abby wouldn't be in any danger. "How did you find me?" she finally asked.

Adams' laugh made her insides tremble. "I got my ways, Rose. I can smell a runaway nigger a mile away. I got lucky with you, though," he admitted. "I wasn't even looking for you until I saw you walking to your school a couple of days ago. I've been following you ever since. I lost you yesterday when you climbed into that carriage. I decided I wasn't going to lose you again. Worked out my little deal with the sweet potato nigger then." He twisted her arm again and laughed when she gasped from the pain. "You were beginning to worry me today. That vendor nigger wasn't sure he could get you to stop. I was gonna have to figure out something else. Thank you for saving me the trouble."

Rose remained silent. He was telling her an awful lot. That must mean he was confident no one would be able to save her. She tried to bluff. "Moses will kill you when he finds you," she stated.

The laugh Adams gave this time chilled her to the bone. She felt him reach for something and then a sinister-looking pistol appeared in front of her face. "I sure hope he tries to. That will make killing *him* a little easier." He paused. "If this one don't stop him, I got two more to finish him off. I understand big niggers can be hard to kill."

Panic surged like bile into Rose's throat. She had to get away from this evil man, but how?

Adams continued. "I figure it will take Moses a little while to find you. I got a nice soft bed waiting for us. This time there ain't nobody to keep me from having my way. Even if you're a nigger woman, I figure you can keep a man happy. Carrie Cromwell ain't around to save you this time." He twisted her arm again.

Unmindful of the pain ripping through her body, Rose began to struggle violently. Let him break her arm. Let him break every bone in her body. She was not going to let him rape her. "Let...me...go!" she gasped.

Suddenly, miraculously, she felt herself break free from his grasp. Her dress ripped as he grabbed for her, but she was free! Without looking behind her, she began to run.

There was a loud curse, and she heard pounding footsteps behind her. Rose knew Adams would do everything possible to catch her. He had been thwarted too many times. Would he use the gun? Heart racing, she dashed through the crowds of people, hoping they would slow him down.

A boy emerged from an alley between two buildings. Too late, she saw the handle in his hands. There was no way to avoid the long cart that followed him. She crashed into it, moaning with pain as she crumpled to the sidewalk.

"Hey, lady!" the young boy exclaimed. "I didn't see you. You okay?"

Adams loomed over her. Rose stiffened as he pinned her arms against her body and pressed his cold gun to her neck.

"This ain't no lady, boy. She ain't nothing but a runaway slave. You did everyone around here a favor, and now you can keep moving on."

The boy looked at Adams uncertainly. Then he looked back at Rose. She begged him for help with her eyes, but realized there was nothing a young boy could do.

Adams twisted one of her arms cruelly and waved his pistol in the boy's direction. "I said to keep moving. My patience is running real short. Unless you want trouble, too, you better do what I say."

Rose watched as fear gripped the young boy's face. She was glad when he picked up his cart handle and turned to move on. She didn't want anyone else to be hurt.

Adams spun Rose around to face him. His face was red with fury. He stared at her for a long moment and pulled his hand back.

Rose's head snapped back as the slap connected with her face, but she remained silent. She would not give him the satisfaction of crying out.

"You and I need to reach an understanding, nigger girl," Adams snapped. He snarled and shoved her back into the cold, dark depths of the alley. He released her arm long enough to push her back against the building's cold bricks. He gripped both her arms and pressed his body against her. "You're making it harder on yourself, Rose. My loving tends to get a little rough when I'm angry," he sneered.

Rose stared at him and screamed again. "Let me go!"

Adams cursed loudly and raised his hand to slap her again. Rose shrank back against the bricks but met his evil gaze levelly. She was not afraid to die. She *was* afraid of living with what this man wanted to do to her.

"You heard the lady."

Rose gasped when a strong voice cracked in the alley.

"She said let her go."

The voice stopped Adams' hand. Cursing again, he whirled to face his newest tormentor.

"He has a gun," Rose cried.

In a flash, the tall, thin man peering into the alley shot his fist out and connected with Adams' jaw. Rose heard the sharp crack and watched as Adams, a surprised look on his narrow face, sank to the sidewalk and lay still.

Only then did the tall man turn to Rose. His voice was gentle. "I'm so sorry, Rose." He reached for her hand and helped her step over Adams' body and onto the sidewalk. "I've been trying to catch up to you. I saw you break away from this man a ways back. I'm afraid my months in prison have left me rather slow."

Rose stared at him, her breath coming in gasps. "You know me?" She didn't remember ever seeing the skinny man with the flowing red hair and beard.

He smiled. "You might not remember me anyway, but you certainly wouldn't with the way I look now. I'm Matthew Justin."

"Carrie and Robert's friend?" When she looked closer, she recognized him. His blue eyes were tired, but they still held the sparkle she remembered. And even the beard could not disguise the smile.

Matthew nodded, studying her. "Are you all right? Did this brute hurt you? " His tone was severe. "I'm sorry it took me so long to catch up."

Rose shook her head. "I'm all right," she managed. She knew her arms would be sore for days to come, and she was sure there would be a welt on her face, but it was nothing when she thought of what could have happened. She couldn't control the shudder that coursed through her.

Matthew looked at her closely. "Can you walk home?" When she nodded, he continued. "I'll meet you at Aunt Abby's."

"You know where I am staying?" Rose asked incredulously.

Matthew nodded. "Carrie told me."

Rose gazed at him in amazement and delight. "You've seen Carrie? Is she all right? Is she...?"

More questions would have poured from her mouth, but Matthew raised a hand to stop her. "We'll have plenty of time to talk later. Aunt Abby doesn't know I'm back. I was planning on surprising her tonight."

"Oh, she'll be so happy!"

Matthew nodded. "No happier than I," he said with a laugh. Then he sobered. "You go on ahead. I'm going to take care of this scum," he said in a voice like ice. He looked down at Adams' still body. "Adams and I are going to have a talk. By the time we're done, I don't think you'll need to worry about him bothering you again."

Rose had to know one thing. "Marse Cromwell... Did he send Adams after us?"

Matthew shook his head. "Thomas still doesn't know you're not both on the plantation." Just then Adams stirred and groaned. Matthew spoke more adamantly this time. "Go home, Rose. I'll be there as soon as I can."

Rose turned and flew down the sidewalk.

"Are you going to tell me what you're so fidgety about?" Aunt Abby finally demanded. "I've been watching you for the last hour, and you're about to drive me crazy with curiosity."

Rose struggled to think of something to say. She had so badly wanted to tell Aunt Abby about her encounter with Ike Adams, but doing so would have necessitated telling her about Matthew. And Matthew wanted to surprise her.

"Well?" Aunt Abby's expression was one of concern now. "Are you all right, Rose? Is something wrong?"

Rose opened her mouth, knowing she needed to say something, but just then the doorbell rang. She gasped with relief and jumped up. "I'll get it," she said, but as she approached the door, she suddenly slowed. What if Adams had gotten the best of Matthew? What if it was Ike Adams on the other side of the door? Fear grabbed her for a moment until she realized how silly it was. A weasel like Ike Adams was no match for Matthew Justin. She smiled and reached forward to open the door.

"Who in the world is it?" Aunt Abby demanded from just behind her. "It's too late for callers."

Rose jerked the door open.

"Is it too late for this caller?" Matthew called teasingly.

Aunt Abby stared at him for a moment as if he were a ghost and then gave a glad cry. She leapt forward and fell into his arms. "Matthew! Matthew Justin! You're home!" Tears rolled down her face as she sobbed joyously.

Rose wiped at her own tears as she witnessed the jubilant reunion.

Matthew made no attempt to hide his own as well. Finally, laughing, he moved Aunt Abby back into the hallway and pushed the door shut behind him. He smiled down at Rose. "Thank you for keeping my secret."

Aunt Abby spoke through her tears. "You knew he was here?" she asked Rose. "How?"

Rose hesitated.

Matthew answered for her. "I helped her with a little run-in with Ike Adams today."

Aunt Abby frowned. "Ike Adams?" Her voice sharpened. "Isn't he the old overseer from Carrie's plantation?"

Rose nodded mutely.

Aunt Abby took a deep breath and stepped back from Matthew. "Why don't we go into the parlor? I'd say we all have a lot of talking to do."

"I'd say you're right," Matthew agreed with a smile.

It was past midnight when Rose wearily climbed the stairs to her room. Matthew and Aunt Abby were still talking. Aunt Abby's laughter pealed through the house again. The sound made Rose happy, but her own aching for Moses had deepened. She had longed all night to hear another knock on the door so she could open it to find Moses standing on the stoop.

She stared out the window for a long time. Matthew had assured her Adams would no longer be a threat. She had questioned him about what happened, but his face had merely grown grim when he said, "Ike Adams is basically a selfish man. He will always look out for himself first. I convinced him it would not be healthy for him to mess with either you or Moses."

That was all he would say. His calm assurance had comforted her, but she couldn't help peering out the window to see if Adams' wiry form was outside lurking behind a bush, his beady eyes watching them.

Finally, she turned away from the window and retreated to her bed. She couldn't help the tears that engulfed her as she longed for Moses' strength to shield her. Her body still ached from her struggle today. When the tears had run their course, she lay in bed quietly, thinking of all they had talked about tonight. She was so glad to know Carrie was doing well. She had eagerly absorbed everything Matthew had told her.

She could hardly believe it when Matthew told her Carrie's father still believed she and Moses were still on the plantation, along with Ike Adams. He had evidently accepted Carrie's explanation that she could not send Moses to the city last October because he was needed on the plantation to prepare for this year's food crops. How long could she get away with what she was doing?

His voice had broken when he said, "Carrie Cromwell made my stay in prison bearable. Her visits and gifts were like a light in the darkness. The food she had Opal bring me was sometimes all that gave us the hope to keep going. We knew there was at least one person who cared about what was going on behind those walls."

Aunt Abby had listened with tears in her eyes. "What now, Matthew?" she asked.

Matthew shrugged. "I will keep doing what I was doing. I have my old job back on the paper. This war has just barely begun. I will have my work cut out for me, to try to make sense to the reading public of what is happening in our country. "

Rose latched onto what he had said. She would continue to work hard, to prepare, so that, when her time was ready, she would be able, by education and caring, to make sense out of the world to the scores of blacks who would be suddenly free.

Chapter Thirty-Two

Moses gazed around him in awe as he marched toward the Alexandrian docks. His mind traveled back to the little rowboats he and Rose had traveled in during their escape. He had been told that hundreds of vessels of every imaginable kind were arriving at the wharves of the historic little brick town that had marked the head of deep-water navigation on the Potomac since colonial days. Nothing they had said prepared him for the sight that met him when they rounded the last curve.

"A sight to behold, isn't it?"

Moses nodded as he turned to his new friend, James. "It sure is. What are all those things? Other than boats," he added quickly. "That much I can figure out myself." He had already found himself the brunt of many jokes and hateful jibes the last few weeks. He was learning to be very careful what he said. He had discovered the Northern white was much like the Southern white.

James smiled easily. "That one there is a Philadelphia ferryboat." He pointed to one with a huge wheel. "That one is a Long Island Sound side-wheeler. Over there is a Hudson River excursion boat." His voice grew more excited. "The real big one is a transatlantic passage." He continued on to point out schooners, barges and canal boats. "I hear there are going to be almost three hundred of them making trips back and forth until the whole army has been moved."

Moses stared around him, fascinated. "I reckon it takes a lot to move over a hundred thousand men."

James nodded. "Not to mention all the animals, supplies and food."

Moses turned to look at him. "How come you know so much about boats?"

James shrugged, his eyes lighting with excitement. "I've loved boats since I was just a little boy fishing off the Maine coast. My father captained his own boat for a while. He taught me most of what I know. After this crazy war is over, I hope to own my own fishing fleet. I had just saved enough money to buy my own boat when the war started."

Moses nodded. He knew about thwarted dreams.

"Hey! Look at the big nigger," someone yelled off to his right. "Didn't anybody tell him the Union Army doesn't need dumb niggers?" Raucous laughter followed his statement.

Moses continued to stare straight ahead. It would do no good to respond. He had already been in a few fights. His brute strength had easily triumphed each time, but he wasn't here to fight. He had finally decided the best course was to ignore whatever was said to him. Violence was no way to fight prejudice. He would let his actions speak for themselves.

"I'm sorry, Moses," James said sympathetically.

Moses shrugged. "I can't let ignorance bother me. I'll spend my whole life being bothered if I do. I aim to prove myself." He smiled at James. "At least not everyone around here is ignorant."

He had met James a few days after he joined McClellan's army. James was as big as he was—just as big, and just as powerful. The two had talked for hours and become close friends. Most of the soldiers left Moses alone now. They had no desire to take on the two of them. Moses had made a few other friends, but none he liked as well as James.

In front of them, men marched up ship gangplanks in steady procession. Moses watched, once again in awe, as steam derricks hoisted wagons, guns and supplies aboard. Even artillery horses were hoisted aboard in slings. Nothing during his years on the plantation had prepared him for such innovations. He was quickly realizing the world was much more complex and fascinating than he had ever imagined.

Everywhere there was laughter and cheering. McClellan's army was happy to be free of their winter quarters, and warm weather had lifted their spirits even more. Flags flew from many of the ships, making the event seem more like a pleasure excursion than the transporting of an army looking for the enemy. Bands played and ships' whistles shrieked.

Moses held his head high as he marched with the rest of the men up the plank. He was fulfilling his dream of having a role, no matter how small, in the efforts of the Union Army. He would soon be back in the South that had stolen his freedom and robbed him of his family. His mind traveled back to one of the first conversations he had with a sympathetic officer.

"You need to be careful, Moses. The efforts to return runaway slaves have increased even more since you left. The slave hunters and militia will stop at nothing. If they find out you're working with the Union, they will kill you," he said bluntly. "There have already been hangings."

Moses had nodded solemnly. "I'll be careful."

He had been thinking about the officer's words ever since. He wasn't afraid, but neither would he be careless. He thought about Rose. Then he thought about his mama and sisters. There was too much at stake.

With a shriek of the whistle, the boat Moses was on drew away from the dock and headed toward the open sea. Moses hung against the railing, drinking in all he could. Up ahead, he saw some smaller boats moving swiftly down the river.

James saw the direction he was looking. "Navy gunboats," he said. "They're going to prowl the Virginia shoreline looking for Rebel raiders that might try to attack the boats."

Moses grinned. "Do they really think the Confederates have anything that could come after so many ships?" The idea seemed preposterous to him as he watched the impressive display of strength.

James nodded grimly. "They *know* they do." When Moses shot a questioning look at him, he continued. "Did you not hear about the *Merrimack*?"

Moses shook his head.

"It's ironic, really. The *Merrimack* was one of the most powerful warships the Union ever built. When Virginia seceded, the navy tried to get the boat out, but Commandant McCauley was convinced there was no way to fight off the Confederates. So the old guy had the naval yard torched and sunk all the ships."

"The *Merrimack* wasn't sunk?"

"Oh, yes," James laughed. "They sunk it all right. Then the Rebels came in right behind them and raised it again. She's not really the *Merrimack* anymore. They renamed her the *Virginian.* Anyway," he continued, "I've been told they completely remodeled the ship into something that doesn't look like any ship that has ever floated. They wrapped that boat all up in iron. They say nothing can do her harm."

"You reckon that's true?" Moses tried to picture what James was describing.

James shrugged. "Evidently. A few weeks ago, the *Merrimack* attacked the Federal blockading squadron in Hampton Roads. The monster destroyed two of our ships and drove two more ashore. I heard someone say the cannon shot fired at her glanced off like pebble stones."

Moses whistled and looked out to sea. What awaited them out there?

It wasn't long before he could not have cared less. Once they struck the ocean, the swells of six to seven feet made life miserable for a great number of them. His own stomach had started turning flips.

James merely grinned. "I didn't know black men could turn green," he teased. "There isn't anything to do but ride it out. You'll feel like dying, but it will get better."

Moses hung onto his words all the time he was leaning over the water, his insides heaving violently. He had never been so sick in his life. The only thing giving him any comfort was that scores of other men hung over the railings with him as the putrid stench of vomit filled the air.

It was two full days before he cared enough to notice what was going on around him. He had half a day to enjoy his new seaworthiness before they caught their first glimpse of Fort Monroe. There were still men too sick to move from their bunks, but most crowded eagerly around the railings to catch sight of their destination.

Fort Monroe was the largest coastal fortress in America. The enormous hexagonal masonry work was a whole third of a mile across.

As Moses craned to see the fort, James appeared at his side. "That fort was finished about fifteen years ago. It's sitting right on the tip of the Virginia Peninsula. I've heard the guns in that place are really something."

"Why do we still have it if it's in Virginia?" Moses asked. He was realizing more and more that he had a lot to learn.

James smiled. "The fort was too strongly defended for the Rebels to even try to take it."

Moses nodded and continued to stare. The harbor looked much like the one they had left two days earlier. Boats bobbed everywhere, mixing with the navy warships stationed there. "What's that thing?"

James smiled again. "You mean that little boat that looks like a Yankee cheese box on a raft? That's the *Monitor*. Some say she looks like a tin can on a shingle. She was built when the Union Navy discovered what the Rebels had done with the *Merrimack*."

"Can the *Monitor* take on the *Merrimack*?"

James nodded. "They did just that a couple of weeks ago. The *Monitor* was sent down to avenge Union honor. I hear they battled to a draw. Neither did much damage to the other. Just a bunch of shot and cannon bouncing off metal." He shrugged. "One thing is for sure. The day of wooden warships is over for good. They don't have a wooden nickel's chance of standing against the ironclads."

Moses nodded and continued to stare at the scene unfolding before him. Suddenly, an order was shouted to the men. They would not disembark tonight. There was simply no place for them to dock. There was grumbling and complaining, but soon the men decided to make the best of it. Cheers rang out all around when men from one of the New York regiments hauled out a barrel of whiskey they had smuggled aboard at Alexandria.

Moses watched the men crowd around the whiskey barrel and went in search of a quiet place. He knew what alcohol could do to men. Weaving through bodies, he made his way to the front of the ship and found a secluded place to watch the activity on shore.

That's where they found him. He was lost in thought, thinking about Rose, when he heard them shout his name.

"Moses! Oh, Moses!" One man stumbled against some of the rigging and let out a curse. "Come on out, nigger boy. We want to talk to you."

Moses edged closer to the bow and looked around for a weapon. A stout stick was all he could find. He gripped it tightly and turned to face the three men approaching him. All of them were reeling drunk. He didn't think he would have trouble handling them, but he was sick to death of the hatred he saw surrounding him.

"Well, here's the nigger boy!" The largest and drunkest soldier turned to his two companions. "You know boys, this nigger must be pretty special to get to be a part of us. What do you think makes him so special?"

One of the men laughed coarsely. "Maybe he's gonna lead us to all the nigger girls along the way who will make us happy. I hear tell those women make fine lovers."

Moses' face flushed with anger and he gripped his stick tighter. His muscles coiled as the men drew closer.

Suddenly, James appeared with two other men beside him. James reached forward and grabbed the drunk man. Without speaking, he turned and dragged the thrashing figure across the deck of the boat. The other two men grabbed the remaining troublemakers. They quickly brought the drunks to a door leading below, opened it, and tossed them down the stairs unceremoniously. Then they slammed the door shut.

James joined Moses in the bow. "Sorry, Moses. We knew they were looking for trouble tonight. I guess they're a little anxious about what is coming."

Moses heaved a sigh of relief. He was tired of fighting. He turned his head to look out over the ocean again. Would he always have to battle misunderstanding and prejudice? Would the darkness of men's hearts and the stark injustice of the slavery system that had brought his people to these shores haunt him for the rest of his life? His own heart was heavy within him as he stared out at the gentle swells catching the last rays of the setting sun.

Something Sarah had once told him seemed to float to him on the waves. *"You be a leader, Moses. Bein' a leader can be a right lonely thin' at times. You gets to fight for all them people 'round you that be too scared or too lazy to fight for themselves. Bein' a leader means you got to stand up to folks when other folks be lyin' down. Bein' a leader means you got to blaze a trail where there ain't one. Ain't nothin' lonelier than goin' somewhere on yo' own."* She had reached forward and taken his hand. *"But you remember this, boy. Ain't nothin' better than bein' a leader. Ain't nothin' better than knowin' somethin' you done has made life better for folks. It's what makes you hold your head high. It's what makes your heart keep beatin'. It's what makes life worth livin'. You can't be a leader and pretend you're not."*

Moses felt stronger as Sarah's words filled his heart. Being a leader was indeed lonely. But Sarah had been right. There was no other way to live. There was no other way he wanted to live.

Early the next morning, Moses moved onto land with the troops. He was glad to leave the bobbing ship and put his feet on solid ground. As soon as they landed, the order was given to march. Moses looked around as they moved quickly through the hastily laid out camps on the outskirts of the fort. Their marching brought them to the outskirts of Hampton. Moses stared at the forest of charred chimneys lining the skyline. "What happened here? Was there a battle?"

"Hardly!" James snorted. "Magruder, the Confederate general running the show around here, heard the North was planning on turning Hampton into a settlement for runaway slaves."

"He burned his own city?" Moses asked in disbelief.

James shrugged. "I think the guy is nuts. He decided he could not bear to see the city suffer such desecration, so he burned it to the ground."

Moses stared at the devastation in front of him. Once more, he was reminded of the passions running unrestrained in the country. It also drove home to him how careful he must be. Passions that could wreak such destruction would not hesitate to kill him if his Union loyalties were discovered.

Chapter Thirty-Three

Robert had been in Richmond almost a week before he was able to break away from his duties to have dinner with Thomas Cromwell. He could feel the anxiety and fear pulsating in the air as he rode his horse through the streets. It felt like a living thing he could reach out and touch. The city, once so gaily defiant, was now afraid. He shook his head grimly as he pushed his horse through the crowds and moved as quickly as he could down Broad Street. The beauty of a glorious spring day was wasted on everyone he saw. The drawn lines in their faces and the trouble in their eyes said tragedy was about to fall.

"Robert! It's good to see you. Come in," Thomas said when Micah announced his arrival.

Robert knew Thomas had not brought him here for small talk. There were too many serious situations brewing in their country.

Thomas turned to him as soon as he sat down. "I'm so glad you were able to come. I have been longing to talk to you. I spend hours talking to politicians, but I have found myself needing the cold logic of a military officer to balance things out."

"I'm not sure I'm going to be able to make you feel much better," Robert replied.

Thomas shook his head. "That's not what I want. I'm not looking for good-hearted fantasy. I simply want to hear things from your perspective."

Robert nodded. "Where do you want me to start?"

"With Johnston's withdrawal from Manassas. Was it really as chaotic as I have heard?"

Robert grimaced. "I'm afraid so," he said. "Oh, Johnston tried, but he had a lot of things working against him. He discovered early, after Davis' orders to bring the army closer to Richmond, that security had been breached. There was no telling who in the Union might know of what he had been told to do, or what they would do to stop it. Davis wanted him to bring all the artillery with him, but the spring rain made the roads impassable for heavy weapons. To top it all off, the railroad was unable to remove the massive amount of supplies and goods they had stockpiled around Manassas in the last eight months."

"I understand the commissary department had rather outdone itself."

Robert nodded. "That would be one way to put it. There were over three million pounds of subsistence stores to be moved. Not to mention all the soldiers' baggage."

"Did every soldier really have a trunk to move?"

"Including Johnston himself," Robert affirmed. "When the call was given to withdraw, there were still tons of supplies that had not been moved. Johnston got word of unusual activity among the Union troops on the Potomac. He was afraid his worst fears had been realized—someone had tipped off the Union to his evacuation. Whatever couldn't be carried away, was destroyed."

Thomas closed his eyes and groaned. "A very serious loss."

"Yes, a very serious loss." Robert allowed himself a small smile. "It was the best smelling withdrawal of any army in the world, though, I bet."

"What in the world do you mean?"

"You are aware of the meat-curing plant that was fifteen miles behind the lines?"

Thomas nodded. "Of course. It was the largest in the South. It had over two million pounds of bacon and salted meat."

Robert smiled. "The cavalry rear guard torched the depots and the plant when the last columns passed. The smell of frying bacon followed us for twenty miles." He would never forget the blue and yellow flames curling up from the huge piles of meat set aflame, but he was also aware of the tremendous loss to the army.

Thomas chuckled briefly, but his mind was intent on other things. "Johnston sent you ahead?"

"Yes. I was sent on to Richmond to help with the fortifications of the city here once again. Lee was still not certain what the buildup of troops at Fort Monroe meant. He wasn't sure which direction McClellan was headed."

"It's certainly obvious now," Thomas exclaimed.

For a few minutes, both men were silent with their thoughts. McClellan had made his intentions clear when his one hundred thousand-man army had marched away from Fort Monroe and advanced on Yorktown. Richmond was his target. The cry of *On to Richmond* was once more being acted upon.

Finally Thomas shook his head. "What I can't figure out—even though I thank God for it daily—is why McClellan is stalling at Yorktown. Magruder has a mere twenty thousand men to combat his one hundred thousand. What in the world is he waiting for?"

This time Robert's chuckle was genuine. "I think our man Magruder is playing a game with McClellan. I think he should consider the theater when this war is over."

Thomas stared at him blankly. "Would you like to explain that?"

"Magruder is well known for his ability to make things seem to be much more than they are. Some reports of his actions have come back to us here. Some of his units have been split into two parts. He has kept them traveling twenty-four hours a day, instructing them to show themselves in different places all along the line. I'm sure the poor men are exhausted, but it has worked. I'm convinced McClellan believes he is facing a much bigger army than he actually is. He is known to be extremely cautious. Magruder is counting on that."

"Until we can get reinforcements to him."

Robert nodded, suddenly grim again. "Not that I'm sure how much good it will do. We simply don't have enough troops to stop McClellan when he determines to move forward. Johnston's additional troops may enable us to slow him down, but I don't think we can stop him. He is simply too powerful, even though he doesn't seem to know it yet."

"The longer we can keep him from knowing it, the better," Thomas replied. "The government is doing all it can to get you the manpower you need."

"The Conscription Act?" Robert asked.

Thomas nodded. "Congress passed the legislation last week. It conscripts every man between the ages of eighteen and thirty-five. There are exceptions, of course, but we should see the numbers rise immediately."

Robert was glad there was more manpower on the way, but he had to ask the question on his mind. "How does that sit with the rights of each state to determine their own destiny and defense?" He was aware of President Davis' efforts to honor that principle.

When Thomas spoke, his face was as grim as his words. "Idealism does not always have its way. Without an adequate force to defend it, there will be no Confederate States to worry about their rights. You know as well as I do that the picture for us right now is bleak."

Robert did indeed know. With the fall of Shiloh ten days before, the Confederacy had for all intents and purposes lost the middle Mississippi. The coast of North Carolina was sealed from the sea, and all the major South Carolina ports were either occupied or blockaded. Now there was a force of one hundred thousand Yankee soldiers moving toward Richmond.

Robert's next question was one that had been bothering him for weeks. "Have you called Carrie to the city, Thomas?" He had had countless nightmares of Carrie being alone on the plantation when Union troops came through. He was not telling Thomas how sure he was that Johnston could not stop McClellan. Hope was sometimes all that kept people going.

Thomas scowled. "You know my daughter," he said helplessly. "Of course I wrote her right away when McClellan started building up his troops at Fort Monroe. She wrote back telling me she was too busy planting crops to come to Richmond, and besides, she had confidence in Johnston to control things."

Robert frowned. "I see." He wasn't sure what to say. He did indeed know Thomas' strong-willed daughter. He also knew if it were up to him, he probably would have ridden out, thrown her across his saddle, and returned her to Richmond. He almost laughed at his own thoughts. They sounded noble, but he knew how impossible Carrie was to move once she set her mind on something.

Thomas read his face. "I don't know what to do. I can tell you think I should force her to return. Don't think I haven't considered it."

Robert smiled reluctantly. "Yes, I did think that. I also reached the same conclusion you did." He paused. "Have you sent her more letters?"

"One a day," Thomas said wearily. "I haven't heard any more from her. Not even her regular letters. Of course, everything in the city is disrupted with the current crisis. I have no way of knowing if she has actually received my correspondence."

Robert frowned again. "I wonder if she realizes her crops may end up feeding the Union Army as they pass through on the way to Richmond," he muttered.

Thomas shrugged. "She is convinced she has a job to do. She promised me she would leave the plantation if it became too dangerous for her to remain, but she is so isolated she may not realize the danger until it is too late." He shook his head. "I will go get her myself if the need arises."

Robert shook his head. "I will make sure Carrie gets off the plantation if it comes to that, Thomas." He paused for a moment, and then leaned forward to ask, "Does she know the secret?"

Thomas shook his head morosely. "I should have told her. I had planned to, even, but for some reason I never did. I was convinced she would come to Richmond if I asked her to. I learned the secret when my father wanted me to. Not until he died did I find the letter he wrote me shortly before. He had kept the secret since after his father died. He wanted the secret kept until I was gone, as well. Carrie knows there is a letter in the safe. I put it there after Abigail died. She also knows she is not to open it until I'm gone. I'm confident she will heed my wishes."

Robert realized once more how desperately troubled Thomas must have been that day to reveal the secret to him. Not that his knowledge was doing anyone any good, least of all Carrie. He was too far away.

A sudden roar from the city grabbed their attention. They jumped up and strode to the porch. From Thomas' house, they had a commanding view of the city. They could see Broad Street, which resembled nothing more than a dark, moving mass. The cheers and yells of citizens created the roar floating up to them.

Robert watched for a moment. "Eight thousand of Johnston's men were scheduled to pass through the city today. They are marching as fast as they can to join up with the rest of his troops."

Thomas nodded. "Here's hoping they can do some good."

Robert continued watching for a moment before turning to his host. "Will a great many people leave the city?"

Thomas shrugged. "People with money will. There are already a lot who have left to visit relatives in the country and in North Carolina. Richmond seems to be losing its popularity," he said.

"Will you leave?"

"Never." Thomas proclaimed. "I have cast my lot with Virginia and Richmond. The capital must not fall."

Robert stared into his eyes and then turned to look at the troops moving down Broad Street. He knew how tired these men were. He knew how discouraged and disheartened they were. Would they be able to stand against McClellan's far superior force? He had said little to offer Thomas hope.

Both men stared down at the city as blackness swirled through the streets, seeking to invade every crevice and every heart. The country had carelessly allowed the dark clouds to descend. But darkness is never content with where it is. It always seeks to expand—to control everything and everyone within its ever-growing reach.

Robert was deep in thought as he rode down Broad Street. Johnston's troops had passed, but the street was still full of the throngs of people who had come to watch and cheer on the troops. He had replayed every word of his conversation with Thomas in his mind more than once.

Slowly, Robert became aware someone was calling his name. He thought of ignoring the female voice. He was not in the mood for small talk.

"Robert Borden!"

This time the voice was much closer. Robert sighed and turned around. His lips tightened as he spotted Louisa Blackwell moving through the crowd toward him. This girl meant nothing but trouble. He well remembered her catty remarks about Carrie when he had run into her at the dance the year before.

Somehow he managed to force a pleasant smile to his lips. "Hello, Miss Blackwell." He made no move to dismount.

Louisa smiled up at him brightly. "Why, Lieutenant Borden. It's so wonderful to see you. I thought surely you must be on the front somewhere guarding our honor. What a wonderful surprise to find you right here in the city."

Robert nodded pleasantly. "Duty deems I be here for a while." He offered no more explanation.

Louisa continued to beam up at him. "I find myself in somewhat the same situation. My poor daddy couldn't bear to think of harm coming to me on the plantation, so he insisted I come to live in Richmond with one of my aunts. I have been here for two months now. It looks as though I will be here in the capital until all this is finally over and we can return to our homes. I don't think I have ever been so busy. My days are spent rolling bandages and knitting things to keep our soldiers warm in cold weather. It is wonderful to be able to help."

Robert looked at her carefully. She sounded sincere. Maybe the war was helping her grow up. She would never be his type, but he couldn't help feeling the guy who married her would be happier if some of her selfishness was dispersed. Her next words dispelled his hopes.

"I do hope those boys who marched through today will do their job. I really don't understand why they are taking so long to end this dreadful conflict. It really is quite inconvenient to do without so many things, and the prices have simply become ridiculous," she said petulantly. "Honestly, it's time for our soldiers to quit playing around and take this war seriously."

Robert frowned as he thought of the suffering his men endured during the Romney campaign and of the pain he had seen so many men suffer. Somehow he managed to keep his voice even. "I can assure you, Miss Blackwell, the men are eager to end your inconveniences. They are also eager to regain their lives," he added in a hard tone. "I promise you each one of them is taking this war very seriously."

Louisa seemed to realize she had gone too far. She reached out a gloved hand and laid it lightly on his horse's saddle. "I'm sure you're right, Lieutenant," she said to appease him, as she flashed a brilliant smile. "Will I see you at the starvation dance for the officers at the Fielders' mansion tonight?" Her voice became coy. "I hear they are going to allow the officers to nominate a queen. Maybe you would like the opportunity to follow your heart instead of your convictions..." She looked up at him and allowed her lashes to droop becomingly over her eyes.

Robert struggled to control his laughter. He also fought to stuff down his anger that Louisa would so subtly snub Carrie, who was placing herself in grave danger because of her commitment to what she believed in. She might be acting foolishly, but she was acting out of the greatness of her heart. He stared down at Louisa for a long moment and decided to indeed follow his heart instead of his convictions about the proper way to treat a lady. He wasn't sure Louisa fit in the category of a lady anyway.

He smiled pleasantly and said in a cheerful tone, "I'm usually one to follow my heart, Miss Blackwell. I'm afraid my vote tonight would do no one any good. Carrie Cromwell is too far away to be aware of it." He stared down into Louisa's furious eyes and pressed his mount forward. He felt her eyes boring into him. The knowledge filled him with a deep satisfaction.

Chapter Thirty-Four

Thomas was white-faced as he strode up the sidewalk and onto his porch, where he stopped for a moment and turned to face east. As he stared out over the city, he tried to penetrate the surrounding woods with his anxious eyes. He felt as if there were hostile enemies viewing the city already. Frustration rose up in him as he tried, in his mind, to see Cromwell Plantation—to know if Carrie was safe.

He raised a clenched fist and slammed it against the porch column, completely ignoring the pain that shot through him. Not knowing was about to drive him crazy.

"You haven't heard from her yet?"

Startled, Thomas spun around to look at Robert who had just strode out on the porch.

"I got here a little while ago," Robert said. "I've been waiting inside."

Thomas shook his head heavily. "No. I haven't heard from her yet."

"You are aware of the news from the front?" Robert asked grimly.

"That we have not only lost Yorktown, but now Williamsburg has fallen as well?" Thomas asked. "Yes, I know." His face twisted in agony. "Why does Carrie not come? Why not at least send a letter? Does she not know I am losing my mind with worry?" He groaned. "Is it not bad enough that I could be watching the death of all I have ever held dear? Must I lose her as well?" Once again he raised his fist, but then let it fall to his side. The agony welling up in him was too familiar. He had lost Abigail. He couldn't lose Carrie, too.

Robert moved forward and gripped his shoulder. "We don't know yet why Carrie hasn't returned your letters. You said yourself she might never have received them."

"Why doesn't she write me then?" Thomas cried. He quickly answered his own question. "I know. I know. The mail may not be coming through here either. I've thought of that. But why hasn't she come? It is impossible not to wonder if she hasn't come because something has already happened to her." Once again he could feel his emotions building to a bursting point. "And here I sit in Richmond, while my daughter could be hurt or captured by those damn Yankees trying to destroy my home."

Thomas knew he was becoming unreasonable, but he couldn't seem to control it. The last weeks of strain and crisis had driven him almost to the breaking point. The worry over Carrie was about to send him catapulting over the edge.

Robert turned away to look over the city.

Thomas was torturing the young man with his thoughts, but he wasn't saying anything Robert hadn't already thought about himself. When Robert finally turned back, the agonized look on his face told Thomas he was right.

"I would like to tell you Carrie is going to be fine," Robert said in a troubled voice. "The facts say something very different. McClellan's army will soon begin to move from Williamsburg. I believe their route will take them east of your plantation, but already soldiers are scouting far to each side of the line in search of food for the army. They are raiding and marauding every farm animal and crop they find along the way."

Thomas groaned. "I'm going to the Capitol to tell Governor Letcher I am leaving for the plantation. I cannot go one more day without doing something to know Carrie is all right."

Robert shook his head. "You can't do that. Richmond needs you too much right now. I have talked to General Lee about going myself, but he insists I must stay here in the city, even though he has much sympathy for my situation." He paused for a moment. "I have a plan, though."

Thomas heard the firm command in his voice and latched onto his last words. He knew Robert was right. He had too many responsibilities to be able to leave the city right now. It seared his soul to think he was making decisions for the whole that might end up sacrificing

Carrie, but so far he had seen no other course of action. "What is your plan?" he asked.

"I have spoken with one of my men. He is young, but I would trust him with my life. I have drawn him careful maps of the area leading out to the plantation. The area is new to him, but he is a crackerjack in the woods. General Lee has given me permission to send him out. He can leave this afternoon. That's why I'm here. To see if you agree with my plan."

Thomas listened carefully. "What is this man's name?"

"Warren Hobbs."

"The soldier whose life you saved?"

"Well, from Hobbs' viewpoint, at least," Robert replied modestly.

Thomas turned to look out over the city again. He would have preferred an older man go after his daughter. Hobbs was just seventeen years old. He knew, though, that the young lad was intensely loyal to Robert and would do anything for him. That kind of passion would serve him well in the task of breaching enemy lines. Finally, he nodded. "Send him," he said shortly.

Robert didn't wait for him to say more. He abruptly turned and strode down the steps. With one last look at Thomas, Robert vaulted onto his horse and cantered down the road.

Thomas watched him go. Then his head bent in wordless prayer. All he could do now was wait. Wait and pray.

Robert raced back to his quarters, scattering people before him as he flew through the streets. He took no heed and never thought of slowing down. His frustration had eaten at him for days. Now there was at least some action he could take. He would allow nothing to get in his way.

"Hobbs!" he called as he swung off his horse.

The youth was at his side in moments. He had obviously been watching for him. "Yes, Lieutenant!"

Robert looked him over closely. He was satisfied with what he saw. He had meant it when he said he would trust his life with Hobbs. "I want you to leave as soon as possible for Cromwell Plantation. I have a letter for Miss Cromwell. I'm sure it will convince her of the wisdom to return." He smiled slightly. "Of course, this lady isn't like many others." His voice turned grim. "If she refuses to return with you, I want you to stay with her."

"Yes, sir."

Robert looked at him and spoke directly. "Your odds of protecting her against raiding Yankee soldiers are not very good."

Hobbs grinned. "I reckon we've done a lot of things where the odds didn't look too good, Lieutenant. Don't you worry. I'll take care of your lady."

Robert opened his mouth to protest that Carrie wasn't his lady, then shut it. Any fool could tell he was in love with her. Why deny it? "Thank you, Hobbs," he said instead. "Good luck."

Hobbs saluted and spun on his heel. "I'll have her back here as soon as I can," he threw over his shoulder. He ran into one of the tents and moments later reappeared with a pack and his pistol strapped to his waist.

Robert handed him the reins of the horse he had chosen and watched until Hobbs rode out of view. He had done all he could do.

Hobbs came to a crossroads and stopped to carefully examine the map. He had already memorized it. Every detail was etched in his mind, but he didn't intend to take any chances. He knew how important this was to the lieutenant. Careful perusal of the map confirmed what he knew, so he turned right and headed further east. Rain had turned the roads to mud, but if he stayed to the side and out of the ruts created by the wagons, he could press on at a fairly good pace.

He knew that he would be on this particular road for several miles. He relaxed as the beauty of the day finally began to penetrate his senses. Already, plum trees and dogwoods carpeted the woods with their pink and white blossoms. Hobbs took a deep breath, trying to pretend he was back home in his mountains. If he tried really hard, maybe he could make himself believe he was heading out on a hunting trip with his dog, Bridger. Gosh, how he missed that dog!

A sharp crack in the woods jerked him back to the present. A penetrating look convinced him it had been nothing except the deer peering out at him, but he pushed all fantasies and daydreams out of his mind nonetheless. The next crack might reveal Union soldiers advancing on Richmond. Completely alert, he continued to push forward.

He would not much longer have the luxury of a road to ride on. The lieutenant had told him it would be too dangerous to stay out in the open. He would be open game for anyone who might want to try to stop him.

He noticed the white board house Robert had described to him. It stood in abandoned misery. Hobbs was sure the inhabitants had already fled to Richmond. He stared at it as he rode by. What would it see in the next few weeks? Would it still be standing to tell its story?

Riding more slowly now, Hobbs peered into the woods along the trail. He knew what he was looking for, but would he be able to find it? The massive oak Robert had described and penciled in on the map appeared in his view, but Hobbs still didn't see the trail Robert had told him about. He vaulted off his horse and carefully led the animal into the woods at a slight break. He was almost fifty feet in before he saw it, a faint glimmer of a trail that could only be followed in daylight unless you knew it well.

Hobbs frowned. A quick glance at the sun told him he probably would not be able to make it all the way to the plantation before it would be too dark for him to continue. He debated pressing on anyway, but knew that was a foolish idea. If he got lost in these strange woods, he would be of no help to anyone. He had maybe forty more minutes of light. He would get as far as possible and then he would stop and make camp. Tomorrow morning he would get up with the sun and keep going. It wouldn't take him long from there.

He kept his senses alert as he rode, constantly scanning the woods for movement that would indicate an enemy presence. He had to pick his way around fallen trees and logs, once almost losing the trail in the process. It was becoming more difficult to see in the waning light. Finally, Hobbs spotted a small clearing where he could spend the night. Just to the right was a small stream to water his horse.

He took care of his gelding, then reached into his saddle bag and pulled out some beef and hardtack. It would have to do. He grabbed his blanket and wished he could build a fire, but it would be a dead giveaway of his position. As the sun dropped, the air cooled tremendously, reminding him it was not yet summer. He found a log to huddle up against, then pulled the blanket around him. He was perfectly comfortable. He had spent days in the mountains of Virginia with less than this.

Hobbs had barely dozed off when crashing in the woods jolted him awake. His horse snorted and pulled back against his lead in protest. Hobbs was instantly on his feet, crouched and waiting. He pulled his pistol from his waist and cocked it. He wouldn't go down without a fight. His heart pounded as he waited for whatever was headed his way.

Moments later, a figure on horseback emerged from the darkness, obviously startled to see Hobbs crouched and waiting for him. The man swore and fumbled for his pistol.

"Touch that pistol and I'll put a hole through you, mister," Hobbs said in a sinister voice, glad for the darkness that would cover his youth. For now he was content to let the other man know he was armed.

The man swore again and raised his hands in the air. "Don't shoot," he said.

Hobbs examined the intruder. He was not dressed in Union blues. He also didn't have the appearance of being a Union spy. His accent clearly marked him as a Southerner, and he must be someone from around here if he was confident enough to follow this trail in the dark. "Who are you?" Hobbs demanded.

"My name is Adams," the man replied. Slowly, he lowered his hands. "You a Confederate soldier?"

"What's it to you?"

Adams didn't answer that question. Instead, he asked another one. "You from around here? Ain't many people who know this trail."

"Seeing as how you're at the end of my pistol, it seems I should be the one asking questions," Hobbs responded coolly. "What are you doing skulking through these woods at night?"

"Good God, man. You call that skulking? I was making enough noise to raise the dead. I sure didn't figure anyone to be on this trail. Everybody in this area already hightailed it for Richmond. Everybody with any sense, anyway. I'm on my way there myself."

Hobbs had to admit the man was probably telling the truth. He certainly hadn't been skulking. Anybody would have heard him coming.

Adams continued. "I just got back from a trip and found out my wife and kids already took off. I'm trying to find them."

He had interjected a caring tone in his voice that made Hobbs immediately suspicious. It was easy to tell it was fake, but that didn't necessarily mean anything. Not every man had a good relationship with his wife. Hobbs was pretty sure Adams was just trying to reach safety while he still could. He could have even left his wife behind.

"What kind of trip?" Hobbs still held the pistol on him.

"A slave hunting trip," Adams responded immediately. "Got back from risking my life in Philadelphia and found out I'm probably about to lose my home, too," he said bitterly.

Hobbs frowned. He had no use for slavery, and he certainly had no use for slave hunters, but it at least explained why a healthy male of conscription age was not wearing Confederate gray. Slave hunters were exempt from army service.

Slowly, Hobbs lowered his pistol. "They'll stop you at the city gates for a pass," he said abruptly.

Adams let out a fast sigh of relief and swung from his saddle. Now that he knew Hobbs was not going to shoot him, he seemed to have a lot of questions. "How close is the Union Army?"

"They've taken Williamsburg. They'll probably stay there a couple of days before they'll march on," Hobbs said grimly. "You've picked a good time to get out of here."

Adams nodded. Then his mind seemed to turn to more immediate problems. "How do I get a pass into the city...? What's your name, anyway?"

Hobbs saw no reason not to tell him. "Hobbs. And I don't know too much about passes. You'll have to ask at the blocks." He paused. "I'm sure they're going to allow refugees from the country in, but it might help if you know someone of influence."

Adams thought for a moment. "Do you know a fellow by the name of Thomas Cromwell?"

Hobbs hesitated. Something was telling him to be very cautious. This did not seem like the kind of man to be close to Thomas Cromwell. "Why?" he asked carefully.

"I know Cromwell. Used to be the overseer on his plantation. I'm sure he would vouch for me."

Hobbs looked at the man in the little light that was left. He didn't like the narrow lines of his face or the beady look in his eyes. Alarms were going off inside, and he knew to listen when that happened. Slave hunters had a reputation of being mean and brutal. He couldn't see Thomas Cromwell having a man like that as an overseer. "You say you used to be his overseer? What happened?"

"What's it matter to you?" Adams' voice tightened with anger.

Hobbs knew he had hit a sore point. He also knew he had no real reason to make it his business. "Just curious," he said casually. A thought suddenly struck him. Perhaps running into Adams had been a piece of luck. If he could get him to lead him to the plantation tonight, he would lessen his chances of anything happening to Miss Cromwell. He decided to ignore the alarms. He could forgive the man for being a slave hunter if Adams could get him to Cromwell Plantation sooner.

"You know the way from here to Cromwell Plantation?"

Now it was Adams' turn to study him closely. "Might. What's it to you?"

"That happens to be where I'm headed."

Adams peered at him. "What for?"

It was a fair question. Why would he be headed to Cromwell Plantation when everyone else in the area was running away? "I have orders to bring Carrie Cromwell back to the city. Her father is very worried about her. I understand she is growing huge crops of food on the plantation to help feed Richmond."

Once again Adams adopted his fake caring voice. "Carrie Cromwell is alone on Cromwell Plantation? She hasn't retreated to the city yet?"

Hobbs shook his head, wondering if he had said too much.

Adams was quiet for few minutes. Then he seemed to reach a decision. "I tell you what. I'm going to do you a big favor. Sure, I could lead you back to Cromwell Plantation, but it would take a lot longer for both of us to do it. I can make much faster time on my own." He paused. "Time is critical, Hobbs. I took to this trail because I saw Union soldiers scouting the road a ways back."

Hobbs listened, although he had no intention of going along with anything Adams might suggest. Lieutenant Borden had made Carrie Cromwell his responsibility, and he planned to finish his mission, but he was willing to hear Adams out. He had a feeling there was more going on here than he knew.

"You can go on back to the city," Adams continued. "I'm sure your skills are in demand there. You can tell them the Union soldiers are advancing. I'll get Miss

Cromwell and return to Richmond with her." He gave a sympathetic laugh. "I'm sure her father is worried sick. I know I would be if she was my daughter." He paused. "Let me guess. She has refused to leave the plantation. Carrie Cromwell can be very hard-headed."

In spite of his attempt to sound caring and sympathetic, Hobbs heard the edge of anger in the man's voice. He was certain now he had made a mistake in revealing his mission to Adams. The only thing to do was send him on his way and move on in the morning. He tried to keep his voice casual as he responded. "Thanks for your offer, Adams, but I reckon this job is mine. I started it, and I aim to finish it."

Adams scowled. "And what if staying here in the woods tonight means harm comes to Carrie Cromwell? Her father will never get over it, and he will certainly never forgive you."

Nor will the lieutenant, Hobbs thought. He would not be swayed, though. The lieutenant had trusted him, and Hobbs was not going to let him down. He took a deep breath and stared at the ground. "I reckon I'm gonna have to take that chance," he said.

When Hobbs looked up again, he was staring down the barrel of Adams' pistol. "And I don't reckon I'm going to *let* you take that chance. Carrie Cromwell is too important to me."

Hobbs shuddered at the hatred he heard in the man's voice and cursed himself for his stupidity in letting this happen. "What's your game, Adams?"

Adams merely shrugged. "Seeing as how you're the one at the end of *my* pistol now, I reckon I get to ask the questions," he said sarcastically. "But for your information, Miss Carrie Cromwell ain't nobody you should be risking your life for. She ain't nothing but a nigger lover. She and those Union fellows ought to get along just fine."

Hobbs stared at him. He had no idea what Carrie Cromwell had done to gain the enmity of this man, but whatever it was, he was quite sure Adams deserved it. He had seen men like him before—men so full of hatred and bitterness it poured out on everyone they came in contact with. He found himself hoping Adams' wife and kids truly were safe in Richmond, because he was quite sure they weren't safe with him.

As he stared down the barrel of Adams' gun, he tried to figure a way out of the mess he had placed himself in. Wrestling Adams for his gun was out of the question. He for sure wouldn't do Miss Cromwell any good if he was dead.

Adams read his mind. "You don't even need to think about getting away. It wouldn't hurt me none to put a bullet right between your eyes."

"Except if Yankee soldiers in the area hear you," Hobbs reminded him, thinking fast. "I don't reckon you'll be able to pass as a Yankee with that accent." When Adams scowled, he knew he had scored a point.

Adams sat silently for a moment, never removing his eyes from Hobbs. It was almost completely dark in the woods now. The glow from the moon rising on the horizon cast the only faint light there was. "I reckon you're right, boy. I reckon you're right."

Hobbs tried to duck as Adams raised his arm, but everything went black.

Chapter Thirty-Five

Adams stared down at Hobbs' still form, his lips curled in a hateful sneer. It had not taken him long to discover there was nothing but a kid on the other end of that pistol. Once he had thrown him off guard, it had been easy to take control.

Adams pondered his options. It was quite interesting to know Carrie Cromwell was on the plantation alone. He had thought about her briefly but was sure she would have followed the example of all her neighbors and fled to Richmond. He should have known better. His eyes narrowed as he realized there was probably no one in the house to afford her much protection. Her father was in Richmond, and Moses was in Philadelphia somewhere.

Adams cursed under his breath as he thought again of the beating Matthew Justin had inflicted on him. He had deemed it wise to leave Philadelphia for the time being, but it certainly didn't mean he had given up his mission. Money from Cromwell was no longer even a point to consider. He was out for vengeance, pure and simple. Vengeance against Carrie Cromwell. Against Moses and Rose. And now he had added Matthew Justin to his list.

It would be foolish to turn back to Cromwell Plantation, he decided. For some reason, Carrie must not be aware of the advancing troops. If she was, surely she would have left. From the talk he had heard today while he was hiding in the woods on the side of the road, the Union soldiers were wandering far afield in their search for food. It was only a matter of time before they found Cromwell. Still, they may decide not to harm the beautiful girl. They would frighten her, but Adams wanted more than that.

Maybe he should sneak back in the woods after all. He wasn't sure what he would do once he got there, but he would think of something. A snap in the woods startled him, bringing him to reality. If he turned around now, he was in danger of running into Union soldiers or spies. Hobbs had been right about one thing. His accent would reveal his identity immediately.

He made his decision. He would press on to Richmond. Hobbs would not be able to deliver his message, and Carrie Cromwell would be left to deal with things on her own. He smiled grimly in the dark, feeling somewhat satisfied. *Miss High and Mighty* liked to be in charge. She would soon discover it wasn't always so much fun.

Adams gave a hard laugh and stared down at Hobbs. He couldn't just leave him here like this. Hobbs would come to eventually, even though he was sure it would be a while. He had delivered the blow to his head with all his strength. With a thoughtful look, he leaned down close to the prostrate form. He was still breathing. What a shame. It would have made things much easier if the blow had killed him. Hobbs had been right about another thing. A shot would alert any Union soldiers in the area. He wasn't willing to take that chance, but how could he make sure Hobbs didn't reach Carrie to warn her?

An idea sprang to mind. He quickly stripped Hobbs of his clothes and then removed his own and tied them behind his saddle. He put Hobbs' uniform on. The fit was almost perfect. A Confederate uniform would certainly make it more difficult to reach Richmond if he was spotted by Union soldiers. On the other hand, he would have an easier time getting past the blocks without a pass. And Hobbs wouldn't be going very far with no clothes. He certainly wouldn't dare show up at Cromwell Plantation wearing nothing but his underclothes. He would look more than a little suspicious. Hobbs laughed as he gathered his reins and mounted.

He rode several yards and then realized he couldn't leave Hobbs' horse there. He cursed and turned back around. Another horse would add to the noise as he moved through the woods, but it couldn't be helped. He untied the lead line and led the horse behind him. He would lose the horse when he broke out onto the road.

Adams' face was scratched and bleeding from lashing limbs before he had gone little more than a mile. He thought of stopping many times, while cursing the necessity of continuing. He simply couldn't take the chance of traveling those roads in the daytime in a Confederate uniform. Hobbs had been lucky. Adams knew how close the Union soldiers really were.

Finally, he broke free from the woods and found himself on the road leading to Richmond. He dismounted quickly and tied Hobbs' horse to a nearby tree. Someone would find the horse soon. In the meantime, he would not be slowed by the added encumbrance.

Adams walked back to his horse and stood quietly, straining to hear any noise in the stillness. Thankfully, there was not a loud chorus of crickets and frogs tonight. They would have drowned out any warning sounds. Satisfied he was alone on the deserted road, he gathered up his reins and mounted. He would be in Richmond before dawn.

Adams was smiling as he turned Ginger in the direction of Richmond. Up ahead, he could see the white house that acted as a general store for people in this area. He could tell by its vacant air that the owners had followed the others fleeing for the capital. He toyed with the idea of stopping and helping himself to some food. He hadn't eaten since morning. Then he discarded the idea. He could eat when he reached the safety of Richmond.

He had just drawn even with the house when four men on horseback emerged from the shadows to confront him.

"Halt!" the lead rider commanded.

Adams cursed under his breath and stopped. There was no other choice. He would not make it past four men. He reached slowly for his pistol, certain the darkness would obscure his movement. A hand grabbed his shoulder from behind.

"I wouldn't do that if I were you, Rebel boy," an icy voice spoke into his ear.

Adams almost groaned aloud as his pistol was lifted from his waist. As the four men facing him edged closer, he could see they were all dressed in Union blues. He realized now the foolishness of dressing in Hobbs' uniform. He should have worn his own clothes until he'd gotten closer to Richmond. They would never believe he was not actually a Confederate soldier. His mind raced to figure a way out of his newest predicament.

"Who are you?" the lead soldier demanded.

"My name is Ike Adams," he responded immediately. There was no reason to antagonize these men any further.

"Whose unit are you with?" he snapped.

Adams shook his head. "I'm not a Confederate soldier," he said. He flushed angrily when derisive laughter met his statement. "Look," he said a little desperately. "If I were a soldier, do you really think I would be wandering around by myself in the dark?"

"Don't see anything to indicate you're just wandering around," their spokesman said caustically. "Looks to me like you're on the road to Richmond. What kind of information were you thinking about taking back to your commander?" he demanded. "Besides, I thought most of your army had retreated to cower in front of Richmond by now. This country cleared out pretty quick after we whipped you soundly yesterday."

Adams opted for honesty. "Look, I'm really not a Confederate soldier. I stole this uniform from a man a little while ago. I thought it would make it easier to get into Richmond."

One of the soldiers laughed. "That would be my next indicator you're really as stupid as I thought."

Adams gritted his teeth as the soldiers once more broke into laughter. He decided to play their game. "You're right. It was really stupid. I was being held at gunpoint by this soldier in the woods. When I finally got the best of him, I decided to help myself to his clothes."

"When did this supposed act occur?" the spokesman asked in an amused voice. He turned to the rest of the men. "You have to give this man credit for being entertaining. I'm sure the other boys in the prison camps will be glad to have him join them. We might as well let him entertain us for a while first, though. I don't reckon we have much else to do until it gets light. Can't find much food in the dark like this. We cleaned out this store already."

Adams' mind was racing as the spokesman turned back to him. He was coming up with a plan, but first he would answer the soldier's question. "It was less than thirty minutes ago. I was on my way through the woods when the Rebel got me."

One of the men bent over almost double from laughter. "You're right, Captain. This man will provide great entertainment. He actually expects us to believe he came through those woods. Why, they're so thick, no one could make their way through them at night. This guy is hallucinating."

Adams fought to keep his voice calm. "It's impossible unless you know the trails around here." He paused. "Unless you know the trails that will lead you to the plantations that will provide you with the food you need." His voice was pregnant with meaning. Adams knew he had finally gotten the captain's attention when the man quit smiling and leaned forward to stare at him. He had no delusions he had convinced him, but at least the captain was listening.

He decided to press the advantage while it at least swayed in his direction. "Look, Captain. I want to go to Richmond. You don't believe me, but I'm really not a Confederate soldier."

Another soldier spoke up this time. "What's a healthy man like you doing not serving in the army? No wonder you Rebels can't field an army that can stop us," he said boastfully.

Adams shrugged. "I'm a plantation overseer. I'm exempt from conscription." He saw no reason he had to tell the complete truth. For all he knew, these Yankee soldiers were nigger lovers. He wasn't about to tell them he was a slave hunter. He turned back to the captain. "Like I said, I want to go to Richmond. You want to get food to feed your army. I know just the place for you." He paused, waiting to see if his words were having any effect.

"I'm listening," the captain said coldly.

Adams resisted the urge to smile. At least he was making progress. "Cromwell Plantation ain't too far from here. The plantation owner's daughter is all by herself. Her father is an official in the Virginia government. Carrie Cromwell's been growing massive crops of produce to help feed the city. If you need food for your army, that's the place you should go." He finished and waited quietly.

"Why are you telling me all this?" the captain demanded.

"Let's just say Carrie Cromwell and I aren't great friends, and I want to get to Richmond. It's really very simple."

"Survival of the fittest?" the captain asked.

Adams shrugged but didn't say anything else.

"He could be telling the truth," one of the soldiers said thoughtfully. "Seems to me I remember hearing about a man named Cromwell who's been working with Governor Letcher. He's supposed to own one of the biggest plantations around these parts."

Adams nodded. "That's Cromwell all right." He thought of something else. Men were men, whether Yankee or Rebel. "I guess you guys been traveling a long time, ain't you?" He paused but didn't wait for an answer. "I reckon you boys will never find a woman as pretty as Carrie Cromwell. She and I might not see eye to eye right now, but I can tell you she makes a mighty fine lover..." He allowed his voice to trail off suggestively.

"We are not here to enjoy women," the captain responded angrily.

"You may not be, Captain," one soldier protested, "but that don't mean the rest of us can't enjoy a little fun. Adams is right. We been without a woman for a right long time. We could make the colonel real happy if we came back with a lot of food. Ain't no reason we can't have a little fun while we get it."

"I will have no such actions by people under my command," the captain insisted, more weakly this time.

Adams smiled to himself. The captain couldn't be everywhere at once. Adams was fairly certain one of the soldiers would get what they wanted. At the very least, they would rough Carrie up and scare her to death. He could obtain much satisfaction from thoughts like that.

Another of the soldiers spoke up. "Hey, Captain. We got this soldier's gun. He ain't gonna hurt nobody. And what's he gonna tell people when he gets back to Richmond? That the Union Army is close? They know that. That's why this country is so darned empty. We haven't seen a soul for miles." He laughed easily. "I think this scumbag is telling the truth. I say we head for Cromwell Plantation and reap the benefits." He paused. "All of them."

A chorus of laughter and cheers erupted, and Adams sagged in his saddle with relief. He couldn't relax yet, though. There was no telling what the captain would decide. He might head for Cromwell and make him go along. Or, now that he had his information, he could shoot him. He held his breath while the captain made up his mind.

Finally, the captain nodded. "How do we get to Cromwell?" he asked abruptly.

Adams answered quickly. "Go down this road five miles until you get to the next fork. Take a left and go another three miles. You will see a set of brick pillars on your left. The road leading to their house is almost two miles long. You won't have any trouble finding it." He tried not to sound too eager, but the sardonic grin on the captain's face told him he had failed.

"You're a lucky man, Adams," the captain said coldly. "You caught me in a good mood. Frankly, I have no use for men like you, either Yankee or Rebel. You're the kind that would sell out your own mother if you thought it would do you any good."

Adams clenched his fist in anger as the captain continued to stare at him.

"I'm going to let you go because I hate having to deal with scum, but you better get going fast. I might change my mind any minute." He turned to his men. "We've wasted enough time with this man. I promised the colonel food. Food he will get."

The captain touched his hand to his hat, then spurred his horse and galloped off down the road. His men, whooping with delight, followed him.

Adams took a deep breath and tried to steady his trembling limbs. Once more, he had managed to save himself with his wits. Pride began to salve his wounded ego. The Union soldiers may have amused themselves at his expense, but in the end he had won. He was free, and Carrie Cromwell was soon going to have more trouble than she had ever imagined. He smiled with deep satisfaction.

The moon emerged from behind a bank of clouds, and the darkness was suddenly illuminated.

"I wouldn't smile so quick if I were you, Adams," a deadly serious voice spoke from the bushes to his left.

Adams jumped and peered around him. Had one of the soldiers stayed behind? He was sure they had all ridden away. He reached quickly for his waist and then remembered they had taken his gun. Before he had time to move, a large figure stepped from the bushes and grabbed his horse's bridle.

"Moses," Adams breathed in shocked amazement. Fury blazed through his body. "What are you doing around here?" he hissed.

Moses reached up and hauled Adams from the saddle. Adams fell heavily, once again wondering if this night was ever going to end. This one had been nothing but trouble for him from the minute he laid eyes on him. Somehow he would have to kill him and end his troubles.

Moses glared down at him. "I ought to kill you and rid the world of you. The captain was right. You aren't anything but scum." His eyes glittered with rage.

Adams scowled up at him. "You ain't one to be talking, boy. You ain't nothing but a good-for-nothing runaway." He battled the fear threatening to choke him.

Moses shrugged, going suddenly silent as he stared at him.

Adams broke out into a heavy sweat. He knew what kind of damage a brute the size of Moses could do. Then realization hit him. "You're a spy for the Union, ain't you?" He gave an abrupt laugh. "Won't that make you even more popular around here? Not only are you a runaway, you're a Union spy to boot." He laughed again. "I reckon your neck will be stuck in a noose any time now."

Moses' eyes blazed, and he took a step forward.

Adams shut up, but he could tell the mention of a noose had unnerved the giant man. He looked for a gun but didn't see one. "Let me guess. Those Union boys won't give you a gun. At least they're smart enough to know not to put a gun in a nigger's hand."

Moses' hand clamped on his shoulder and drew him up close to his face. "Shut up, Adams. If I had my way, I'd kill you with my bare hands right now. You know I could do it."

Adams shut up. The viselike grip on his shoulder verified what Moses was saying, but the question remained. Why didn't he?

Moses shook his head. "I decided one thing in the last few months—that I wasn't going to lower myself to the same level as scum like you."

Adams watched him. Moses must not know what he had done to Rose, or he was sure the giant would not hesitate to kill him instantly.

"Take off your clothes, Adams," Moses ordered.

"What? Ain't no way I'm taking off my clothes," Adams sputtered.

"It doesn't seem to bother you that some Confederate soldier is knocked out with no clothes on somewhere. I figure it will do you some good to find out how it feels." His voice sharpened. "Hurry up, Adams. I'm running out of time and patience."

Adams stared at him but refused to move. There was no way he was going to follow the orders of a runaway slave. His eyes sharpened. "You thinking you're going to go help your Miss Cromwell out of the nice mess she is about to land in. Don't waste your time. Something tells me your captain won't be happy if you interfere with his plans. Them soldiers looking forward to a little loving ain't gonna be too happy with you either."

The look in Moses' eyes told him he had gone too far. Pain exploded in his head as Moses' fist slammed into his face. He felt the pain shoot through every part of his body before darkness claimed him.

Moses stared down at the prostrate body and took deep breaths to regain control. Every part of him screamed to finish off the man. He knew the world would be better off without him. If he had a gun... He shook his head as the idea rose appealingly. The sound of a gun would alert the rest of his unit, and he couldn't take that chance. He couldn't believe they hadn't returned to find him yet. They might not even be aware he was missing.

Moses leaned over the still body. A few powerful blows to the head would accomplish the same thing. He stood up and stepped back as reason was slowly returning. He had meant it when he said he didn't want to stoop to the same level as Adams. He simply couldn't bring himself to kill a man in cold blood.

Reality returned with his reason. He had to figure out a way to get to Carrie. He had known all day how close they were to the plantation and had nurtured a futile hope that the men would march right past, not turning off the main road. But a hundred thousand men were a lot to feed. Scouts were raiding every plantation and farm in the area. When it became obvious that all the residents of the area had fled, he had comforted himself with the knowledge that while Cromwell Plantation might suffer damage, Carrie would be fine.

Adams' betrayal of Carrie's would-be rescuer had alerted Moses to the truth, but what to do with Adams? Moses made up his mind and sprang into action.

He quickly undressed Adams then reached inside his saddle bag for a length of rope. His hands flashed as he bound Adams tightly. If someone found him, fine. If not, well, the man would have gotten what was coming to him. One thing was for sure, he would not have a chance to interfere with Moses' plans. He picked up Adams' limp form and carried it several yards back into the woods. Then, as an afterthought, he ripped off his shirttail and stuffed it in Adams' mouth.

Moses looked around and noticed, with deep satisfaction, that a thick fog was rolling into the area. At least it would slow the rest of the men down. As fast as he could, he tied Adams' clothes behind his saddle and leapt onto his horse. Now if he could just make it in time.

Chapter Thirty-Six

Carrie stood on the porch and watched as a heavy fog crept in to blanket the plantation. Right now it was low to the ground, but soon it would thicken and make travel impossible. Would it slow down the Union troops? Did an army travel at night? Frustration welled up in her as she struggled to know what to do. There had been no letters from her father since the one telling her of McClellan's arrival at Fort Monroe. She had stayed so busy, it was easy to convince herself all was well. The Confederate Army must have indeed been able to push them back.

As she had watched the fields explode with new growth, she worked harder to plant even more. It had been enough to keep her mind occupied. She had decided to stagger the planting times. That way crops would mature all the way through to the end of fall. She had felt good about her decision to stay on the plantation.

Now she wasn't so sure. The pounding sounds of guns and artillery from the direction of Williamsburg two days ago had both startled and frightened her. The slaves were absolutely terrified. She was doing everything she could to keep them calm. She carried a weight of responsibility for them now that often threatened to overwhelm her.

The roar of guns had erupted early that first morning and continued long into the afternoon. A steady rain and gray skies had done nothing but increase the sense of foreboding that crept over her as she listened. When the day ended and the guns were silent, she was left with nothing but questions. Who had won? Were there Union soldiers on their way to Richmond? What about Cromwell Plantation?

Somehow, she made it through the long day that followed. Now, another had come and almost gone, and she was no closer to knowing what to do. Her mind screamed at her to leave immediately. In spite of the fact she hadn't heard from her father, she knew he must be worried sick. She had no idea whether she was in actual danger or not, but every nerve in her screamed she was.

Her heart told her to stay. She had a job to do, but this time it was much more important than raising food. The slaves on Cromwell looked to her for care and protection. Sam had been right. The ones who had chosen to stay were those in need of the security and safety the plantation offered. The battle sounds had sent them into a state of panic. How could she go away and leave them?

"You out here, Miss Carrie?"

Carrie turned and smiled weakly at Opal. "Yes, I'm here. Come on out and join me." Opal and the children had moved into the house a few weeks ago. They had been fine down in the quarters, but Carrie finally admitted she was lonely and asked Opal to join her. Having the children around was indeed a blessing. They were gradually emerging from the shock of losing both their parents and were beginning to take an interest in life again.

Susie, especially, was a joy. The sixteen-year-old reminded her so much of Rose. When she wasn't taking care of household chores, Carrie could find her in the library. She devoured everything she could get her hands on.

"What you thinking about, Miss Carrie?"

Carrie shrugged. "I don't know what to do," she said helplessly.

A stern voice sounded behind her. "You need to be gettin' yo'self to Richmond, Miss Carrie. I don't reckon it be too safe for you 'round here right now." Sam moved toward them from the yard.

"You scared me to death, Sam," Carrie gasped. "What in the world are you doing sneaking around in the yard?"

"I ain't sneakin'," he protested. "I'm watchin'. Ain't no soldiers gonna get past me iffen I got somethin' to do 'bout it."

Carrie smiled in spite of herself. She could not imagine her elderly friend being able to do much to stop determined soldiers. "You really think they'll come here, Sam?"

"I don't reckon I be knowin' much more than you, Miss Carrie. Ain't no way of knowin' who won that battle we heard, but I figure if the North done won, they's gonna be headed this way."

"Are you scared?" Carrie asked.

Sam shook his head. "Not for me I'm not. It's you I be scared for." He paused. "Them Union soldiers ain't got a fight with me. It's you they got a fight with. I heard enough to figure them soldiers ain't gonna do nothing to us slaves. But to you...?" His voice trailed off.

Carrie's heart beat faster. Suddenly every fog-shrouded tree became a Union soldier. She peered around, wondering if she was being watched even now. "What do you think I should do, Sam?"

"You know what you should do, Miss Carrie. You ought to let me take you into Richmond as fast as I can."

"But what about the plantation?" Carrie protested.

Sam snorted. "You ain't goin' to be runnin' no plantation if the Yankees take it over, no how. And what you think we's gonna do? I ain't plannin' on goin' nowhere. I reckon I can help take care of this place. Once I get you to Richmond, I'll turn 'round and come straight back. "

Carrie shook her head. "But what about all the crops?" she cried desperately. "I can't just leave." She tried to stuff down the bile of fear rising in her throat.

Sam stepped forward and took her by the shoulders. "Now, you listen to me, Carrie girl," he said sternly. "There be some thin's in life you can't be controllin'. No matter how you be used to doin' that. I reckon this be one o' them times. You done worked harder than any one person I ever seen. You done poured all yo'self into this plantation and growin' food. But sometimes there be thin's you can't control. This be one o' those times," he repeated. "And besides," he continued, "you already done come up with the worst end to this here story. Who's to say you won't be comin' back? Maybe it was the South who won that battle we heard. You might get yo'self to Richmond and find out you get to come right back."

Carrie latched onto his last words. "Maybe it *was* the South who won the battle. Maybe I should wait a little longer to see what happens."

Sam shook his head in frustration. "You ain't seein' thin's clear, girl. Even if it was the South who won that battle, it still means there be a lot of Northern soldiers not too far from here. What's to stop them from sneakin' up here, by land, or by water? The river ain't too far, and it sure would be hard to watch all of it."

Carrie's heart sank. She knew Sam was right. She nodded slowly. "I promised my father I would leave the plantation if things became too dangerous. I guess that time has come."

"Now you finally talkin' some sense, girl."

Carrie turned and stared out at the fog-shrouded fields. "We'll leave at first light. It's too dangerous to try it in this fog."

"That be the best," Sam agreed. "You got work to do around here, anyhow."

Carrie stared at him. "What kind of work, Sam?"

"Ain't there some thin's here you would hate to never have again?" he asked.

Carrie's eyes filled with tears. She had never allowed herself to think that Cromwell Plantation might actually be lost. Sam's quiet question brought the reality blasting home. She took a deep breath and willed herself to stay calm. "You're right," she said.

Sam nodded. "I'll get you a bag you can take with you. Fit whatever you can in that bag. Me and Opal will hide whatever else you find. I reckon that's the best we be able to do."

Carrie stared at him again before she swung around once more to probe the woods with her eyes. Then she turned and disappeared into the house.

"Goldarn, Captain!" one of the soldiers yelled. "How we gonna find Cromwell Plantation? I can't even find my hand in front of my face."

"My horse doesn't even want to move," another complained. "There's no way we're going to find the fork in the road that guy told us about."

There was a brief silence, and then the captain barked, "Halt! You're right. We'll stay here for the night. When the sun comes up and we can see our way, we'll continue on."

Moses, riding quietly behind them, smiled as they reached the conclusion he had known they would. Only someone very familiar with the area would have any idea where they were going. It had not taken him long to catch up with them once he disposed of Adams. He had been following them, several hundred feet back, for the last two miles.

"Hey, Captain. Where's Moses?" James yelled.

The smile faded from his face. He had known they would miss him sometime. He pulled his horse to a halt, dismounted quickly, and led his horse into the bush. The noise of the men would cover any sound he made. In the brief silence, Moses could imagine them all craning their necks to peer around.

"I don't remember seeing him since we left that little store," the soldier named Albert said in a bewildered tone.

Moses listened carefully. Most of the men riding with Captain Jones had given him no trouble. They had actually seemed grateful for his knowledge of the area and the ease with which he took them from place to place. He was the only one who knew he had steered a wide berth around Cromwell Plantation.

A rough voice floated back to him. "I told you we couldn't trust that nigger!"

Moses frowned. It was Clyde, one of the soldiers who had almost accosted him on the boat. The burly, rough soldier seemed to have no recollection of his actions that night, had even pleaded drunken innocence when other soldiers told him, but Moses had known all along what his real feelings were. He had very deliberately avoided him. Now Clyde's voice shot back to him.

"I bet that nigger is up to no good. I say we send someone back to find out what he's up to."

James laughed. "You want to volunteer, Clyde? I bet you would never even find that store. You'd probably walk right into a batch of Rebel soldiers. Isn't nobody going to find nothing in this fog. It's as thick as pea soup. I don't think any of us have to worry about Moses, except to wonder if something happened to him." His voice thickened with worry. "Maybe that Adams fellow had some backup we never knew about. Something tells me that man wouldn't be too fond of our friend Moses."

Captain Jones spoke then. "You're right, James. Moses can be trusted. Something must have happened." His voice sharpened. "Why didn't someone tell me before that he was missing?"

A chorus of protests rose immediately. James' was the only voice that floated to Moses clearly. "Finding Adams caught us all off guard, Captain. When you took off, we weren't really thinking. We just followed you. We all assumed we were all here."

Moses smiled in the darkness. It was always helpful to listen to people talk about you when they didn't know you were around. Sometimes it was the only way to know what folks were really thinking. It felt good to know Captain Jones trusted him. Of course, he wouldn't trust him for long if he knew what he was up to. His smile disappeared.

Captain Jones spoke again. "There's nothing we can do now. James is right. No one could find their way through this fog. We can't do anything about any of this until we can see. We leave here at the crack of dawn. Cromwell Plantation is our top priority. Then we'll find out what happened to Moses." He paused. "He'll probably show up any time now, anyway. He knows this area like the back of his hand."

Clyde laughed. "I don't know why any of you are worried about that nigger. He's probably gone hunting for a woman to love."

Moses' face flushed with anger as he remembered Clyde's exuberant response to Adams' suggestion about Carrie. His fists clenched as he thought about Carrie under the control of this ignorant man. He was dedicated to the cause of the Union, but his dedication and loyalty to Carrie came first. He would do anything to keep her from harm, even kill a Union soldier if it was necessary. If his plan worked, though, he wouldn't have to.

Moses thought carefully as he blocked out the rest of the conversation floating down toward him. He was going to have to leave his horse behind. It would be hard to make his way through the woods on foot, but his horse would never make it past the soldiers. They would take potshots at any strange noise they heard in the woods, shooting first and asking questions later.

Moses led the horse a little further back in the woods, moving as quietly as possible. Finally, he was convinced it would not be seen by the men the next morning. He quickly removed the saddle and bridle, then tied the mare loosely to a branch. He knew the rope would work itself free, but hopefully not until dawn. He planned on being back before that happened, but if he wasn't, it wouldn't be left to starve or die from thirst. He tested the rope one more time, turned, and slipped into the fog.

All Moses knew to do was head southwest toward the river. He knew there was no trail in this area. He would have to navigate through the dark, fog-shrouded woods. The going would be slow, but surely he could make it before dawn. If he was calculating right, his southwesterly course should deposit him on the road that led to the Cromwell drive. It would be an easy run from there to the main house. He would alert Carrie to the danger and help her avoid the patrol. She should have enough time to make it to Richmond. He would accompany her as far as possible.

Four hours later, Moses was still pushing his way through the woods. Frustration was close to choking him. Spring storms had brought down many large trees. The fog made it impossible to tell what direction he was headed once he had gone around them. He lost track of the number of times he had stumbled and fallen. Once, his head had struck a rock, and he lay there dazed for long minutes. Finally, he had pushed himself to his feet and kept going. He had to reach Carrie in time.

He held aside a huge clump of bushes and stumbled out onto a road. Anxiously, he looked around. Where was he? The curves in the road before and behind him looked like any of a million on a road like this. Moses ground his teeth in frustration. He realized suddenly that the heaviness of the night air was pushing the fog down, compressing it closer to the ground. He looked up and gasped. He could almost make out specks in the sky. He dashed over to a huge oak and swung onto the lowest limb. Climbing nimbly, he was soon high enough to break out from the fog. A quick glance gave him a bearing on the North Star. He breathed a prayer of thanks and swung down. At least he knew what direction to go.

He jumped down and began to run. He had wasted valuable time in the woods, and if the fog was compressing, Captain Jones may choose to move on before dawn. Moses knew how anxious the captain was to find food and report back.

Moses gasped when he rounded a curve and saw an abandoned little cabin on the left of the road. He was barely a mile from where Captain Jones and his men were camped. His four hours of wandering in the woods had taken him largely in circles. Moses gritted his teeth and lengthened his stride. He could still make it.

Moses was gasping for breath when he finally came to the brick pillars that marked the entrance to Cromwell Plantation. He realized his floundering in the woods necessitated a change in plans. He might possibly reach Carrie before the soldiers did, but how was she going to slip past them? He glanced at the horizon and saw the first glimmer of light reaching out for him. The fog was now lying close to the ground, a thick cover that would allow men on horseback to ride unhindered. For all he knew, his comrades were right behind him.

The sound of horses far down the road confirmed his worst fears. He never even hesitated as he dashed past the pillars and continued down the road away from the plantation. He would have to go in another way. He knew his way through the woods leading to the quarters like the back of his hand. Thank goodness it was a shorter distance than the drive. But once he broke out into the quarters, would he be able to find the quickest way to the river? It was Carrie's only hope now.

As he ran, he searched for that familiar spot in the road that would lead into the woods. When he found it, he turned into the trees and continued to run down the trail unwinding before him. His lungs burned as he gasped for air, but he didn't slow down. The vision of Carrie's face kept him going. Rose's face appeared before him as well.

Save her, Moses! Save her!

Moses ran faster. He barely even turned his head as he flashed past the clearing where Rose had taught her little school, but the spirits of those who had defied the shackles on their souls leapt up to encourage him. Their courage gave him the strength to continue.

The first of the quarters' cabins appeared through a crack in the woods. Praying no one was awake and aware of what was going on, Moses flashed into the clearing, raced along the edge of the woods, and in just moments disappeared again down a narrow trail leading to the river

Could he find it? Was he crazy to think he could actually find something he had never laid eyes on? What if it wasn't even there? Moses ran on. All he could do was try. Visions of soldiers tramping up on Carrie's porch—of Clyde demanding his entertainment—drove him on.

Finally, he broke out onto the river trail. He struggled to remember everything he had heard Marse Cromwell say that day. His run slowed to a deliberate walk, his sides heaving heavily as he peered into the bank. Would he be able to find it?

Chapter Thirty-Seven

Carrie sat by her window, staring out into the early morning darkness. She hadn't slept a wink all night. Tossing and turning in her bed had only exhausted her more and had creased deep wrinkles in the dress she hadn't bothered taking off. Finally, she had given up the effort and risen to sit by the window, watching as the thick fog settled down to hug the earth. She alternated now between staring at the myriad of twinkling stars above her and the dark border of trees facing her. She was watching the stars for courage and strength, but watching the woods was necessary if she wanted to stay ahead of the enemy.

Her heart had grown heavy with grief during the long night. She grieved the necessity to flee her home, yet it was much more than that. The knowledge that hurt the worst was the stark realization of what her country had come to. Americans forced to flee from those they had once stood side by side with. The dark clouds that had settled over men in power now engulfed the entire country. Very few were able to see beyond their passions or to feel beyond their hatred and anger—to think beyond what was important to them. The clouds of passion had closed off men to themselves and shrouded the best of men's hearts.

Carrie, during the long reaches of the night, clearly realized it might soon be over. If the Union Army truly was advancing on Richmond, the glorious Confederacy might be breathing its last breath. A country split apart by civil war might be reunited, yet only in a physical sense. Carrie knew that even if the South acquiesced defeat to a more powerful military force, the passions that had ignited this war would continue. What would happen with the fury that was raging unchecked? It could not be put in a bottle and corked. It could not be legislated away. It could not be swept under a rug.

Carrie sighed deeply and stood to take a final look around her room. The sun would be coming up soon. She had promised Sam she would leave then. The glow of the moon dipping low on the horizon was all that illuminated her room, but it was enough. Her dear bed, a gift from her loving father. The dresser with her mother's silver brush set arranged perfectly. The bookcase holding her medical texts. The vanity whose drawers held the letters from Aunt Abby.

There was so much Carrie wanted to take with her. In the end, she had chosen to leave it all behind. She had hidden some of her father's valuable papers, but that was all. It seemed disloyal to all that held her heart to choose which of these things were most precious. None of it would ever be able to be replaced if it was lost. Its physical counterpart might be found, but the memories that made it special would no longer be there. Yet, it was more than even that. To take things with her meant she was leaving with the idea she might not be able to return. She was simply unwilling to acknowledge that. To do so would be to give up hope.

Carrie had also acknowledged the stirrings of excitement in her heart. Yes, she grieved leaving the plantation, but leaving also meant it could now be her time to be in Richmond—to see what could become of her dream of being a doctor. She had done all she could to fulfill her responsibilities on the plantation. Was it really coming to a close, or was it all a false scare? Would it be safe to return to the plantation in a few days? Maybe the South *had* won the battle she had heard and she could return to raise food.

Finally, Carrie turned to the mirror. It, of all her belongings, would have been the one thing she would have chosen to take. Of course it was impossible. It would take two strong men even to move it. She walked over to stare into it. More than ever, she needed the courage and strength it represented. There was just enough light to send her reflection wavering back to her. She frowned when she saw her wide eyes and pinched face.

She sank down on the chair in front of it, cupped her head in her hand, and tried once more to lose herself in its depths. Did it have any secrets to tell her before she had to walk away, possibly never to see into it again? She knew she should be leaving, but she couldn't tear herself away.

"Miss Carrie..." Sam added a soft knock to the calling of her name. "It be time for us to be goin'."

Carrie nodded but didn't move. "In a minute, Sam," she called softly.

Sam stood silently by her door for several minutes and then moved away. She could imagine the impatient look on his face. She knew she needed to go, yet the mirror seemed to be holding her. Was it her imagination, or was it calling to her? She stared into its depths until she felt as if her eyes were going to cross. Finally, in frustration, she pushed away from it. She had spent her whole life trying to understand its secrets. Maybe it wasn't possible. Maybe that was its greatest secret—the fact that there was no secret. It was really only a beautiful mirror.

Carrie immediately regretted her thoughts. She gazed once more into its depths. "Keep your secrets. Maybe one day I will understand," she said softly.

She turned and grabbed the bag on her bed. Her packing job had been hasty. Thankfully, she had plenty of clothes at her father's house. She looked around once more, took a deep breath, and reached for the door knob.

A sudden clatter of heavy boots caused her to freeze, her heart racing. Was she too late? She flew to her window and peered around the curtains. Her heart sank at the sight of four Union soldiers mounting the steps. She looked around wildly, but she knew the answer already. There was no escape. The only way out of the house was through the ground level.

"Open up in there!" a voice shouted, as a steady banging began on the front door.

Carrie quickly calculated the distance from her window to the tree outside, but she discarded the idea. Even if she made the jump, which was doubtful, there would be no way to get past the soldiers.

"Open the door or we'll bust it down!" came another shouted command.

Carrie could hear Sam's measured footsteps across the floor. She could imagine the fear he was feeling. Not for himself, but for her. She was sure he was berating himself for not getting her away sooner. Carrie groaned as she heard the door slam open.

"Can I help you soldier boys with something?" she heard Sam ask calmly.

"You bet you can, old man," a new voice said sternly. "We're looking for Miss Carrie Cromwell."

Carrie's heart sank further. How had they known she was still here? She was sure Sam had hoped to distract them and give them what they wanted so they would leave. But they were here for her!

Sam's voice was still calm. "Ain't nobody on this here plantation but slaves. Miss Carrie done left some days ago. Same as everyone else 'round here."

"You're lying," a voice said. "Where is Miss Cromwell?"

Sam continued on calmly. "Like I said, Miss Cromwell ain't here."

"Get out of my way, old man. We'll find her ourselves."

Carrie imagined Sam pulling himself up erectly. "I don't reckon you boys got any reason to be in this house."

"Look, old man, I ain't got nothing against you, but I don't know why in the world you want to protect someone who chained you in slavery. Not that it matters. I just want you out of my way."

"I be right sorry—" Sam began again. He never finished his words.

Tears rolled down Carrie's face as she heard Sam moan and drop to the floor below with a thud. That's when she began to move toward the door. She could not allow her friends to be hurt in her defense.

A shrill voice below stopped her. "What are you doing picking on an old man for? Didn't he tell you Miss Cromwell isn't here?" Opal's voice was loud and strident. "You ain't got no business in this house."

Carrie groaned again as she imagined Opal receiving the same treatment as Sam. With a determined tilt to her chin, she reached for the door. She was going to put a stop to this.

She had barely laid her hand on the doorknob when she felt herself grabbed from behind. She opened her mouth to scream, but a hand clapped across it and muffled her scream to a low moan.

"*Shh*, Carrie. We have to get out of here."

Carrie gasped and spun, her eyes bugging out of her face. "Moses?" she whispered. She could think of nothing else to say. Stunned, she wondered how he had suddenly appeared behind her. Her eyes traveled over his shoulder to a gaping hole in the wall.

A clatter of boots on the stairs broke into her shocked senses. Moses grabbed her hand and pulled her quickly toward the hole in her wall. Then they were inside. Moses reached out and pulled a handle. Instantly, they were shrouded in darkness. Carrie remained frozen beside him. They listened as footsteps pounded along the corridor of the second story. Doors were flung open one by one.

"This is the last room, Captain. I reckon we're going to find our little lady cowering in here. Too bad we had to be a little rough on that other woman to get here."

Carrie gasped as she wondered if Opal was all right. Moses squeezed her hand in warning.

She heard the door to her room fling open. The stout wood crashed against the wall and heavy footsteps approached within feet of where they were standing, barely breathing. If the situation had not been so serious, Carrie might have smiled at the imagined looks of frustration on their faces.

There was a brief silence and then, "Captain! She isn't in here."

Carrie could hear another set of footsteps approaching. "Are you sure? Look everywhere. That old man was protecting someone. She has to be here."

Carrie continued to hold her breath as her wardrobe was flung open. She could hear clothes being ripped from hangers and hooks. She heard someone drop to the floor, evidently looking under the bed. There was a long silence and then a heavy stream of curses filled the air.

"How in the world could she have known we were coming?" one man asked.

Another long silence was his only answer.

A commanding voice broke the silence. "I want this house completely searched. The lady herself is not so important. What I want to know is how she found out we were coming. *That* I would like very much to know." He paused. "Once we have found her, we will spread out and look for food. Empty the root cellar, the smoke houses, everything! When those are clean, we'll take what we can of the crops. There won't be a lot, but there may be some early crops that are producing. We can bring back help with wagons to get more."

Carrie stiffened in protest, but Moses pressed her shoulder in warning. She knew any noise would be fatal. There was a heavy clomp as the soldiers moved out of the room.

When they were all gone, Carrie turned to Moses. Now that they were alone, questions screamed through her mind, but again he pressed her shoulder.

"That girl didn't disappear into thin air," a heavy voice growled.

Carrie froze as she realized not all of the soldiers were gone.

"I aim to find her," the voice continued. "Adams sure got my appetite up for some real loving. I don't care what the captain said. There ain't no reason we can't have a little fun in the middle of all this."

"I don't think the captain will be any too happy if you try anything," another voice warned.

"To blazes with him! I almost got killed a couple of days ago when we had to fight them Rebels. If I'm gonna die any day, I might as well die with some loving. Adams seemed pretty sure this little lady would make us a good lover. I aim to find out!"

Carrie cringed against Moses as she felt his muscles tighten in fury.

The other voice continued thoughtfully. "How do you figure that lady found out we were coming? It doesn't seem possible."

There was a brief silence, and then the voice Carrie had quickly learned to fear broke it. "I been doing me some thinking. Ain't Moses a spy for us because he knows this area so well?"

"I reckon."

"Did you notice how he took us to all the other plantations and farms but steered us away from this one? This looks to be a right big place. He must have known about it."

The other voice was a little more thoughtful. "What are you driving at, Clyde?"

The answer was quick and hard. "I think our spy might have come from this plantation. Maybe he has a little more loyalty to his Rebel owners than he's been letting on. We ain't seen him since last night. Maybe he took off to come warn her."

"But he ain't in this house," the other voice protested, "and that old man downstairs wouldn't have made us rough him up if he weren't protecting somebody."

"I thought about that, too. Still, there is something more to this than we can see. I aim to figure out what it is. I aim to ask that old man some questions." With that final statement, there was a sound of clomping boots and then silence.

Only then did Moses lean over to whisper in her ear. "Don't say a word. Just follow me."

Carrie heard a scrape and then a match flared, its brightness almost blinding her after the pitch black darkness. She watched, amazed, as Moses lit a candle and held it high. She stared around her. They were in a tunnel. Now that her fear was beginning to abate, she was consumed with curiosity. The hole in the wall had appeared behind her mirror. She had a thousand questions, but they would have to wait. Moses was making his way slowly down the passageway, and she had no choice but to follow him.

The candle cast flickering shadows against the solid brick walls of the tunnel. They went about thirty feet straight ahead until they reached a solidly built wooden staircase. They descended, and Carrie knew they must be on the first floor of the house. She could hear yelling and talking as the men searched. As they moved along quietly, they came even with what must be her father's library.

Moses stopped abruptly when he heard the captain's voice, but he didn't blow out the candle. Carrie knew he was afraid their footsteps would be detected, though she was sure the solid brick flooring was absorbing any sound. Her fascination with the surprise tunnel was so complete she almost missed what the captain said.

"The girl doesn't seem to be here, but I have a feeling she hasn't gone far. I want you to put one of the men on watch for her, and the rest of you can gather food. We've wasted enough time here."

"Yes, sir!"

The next sound they heard was disappearing footsteps. Moses let his breath out, and they moved on until they came to another set of stairs and descended into a lower part of the tunnel. Carrie knew they must be parallel to the basement. The air was heavier and carried a lot more moisture. She reached out to touch Moses, but he shook his head and continued on. She knew he was not willing to talk until they were farther from the house.

Just then he stopped and held up his hand. Without saying anything, he pointed to the outline of a door in the wall. Carrie leaned forward to gaze at the barely visible door, its looped handle resting almost solid against the bricks. It must lead into a part of the basement. She tried to ascertain where they were. The closest she could figure, they were almost directly under the kitchen. Suddenly, she remembered the wall of shelves holding all the herbs she had bottled. Was there a door hidden in those shelves? They had been there for as long as she could remember.

Her amazement grew as they continued along. Never in her wildest dreams would she have imagined her house held such a secret. How had Moses known about it? That intrigued her almost more than the tunnel.

They made several more turns before Moses finally came to a stop. I think it's okay to talk now."

Carrie could do no more than stare at him. The reality of the situation hit her, and tears flooded her eyes. When Moses opened his arms, she walked into them. A moment later, sniffing back her tears, she stepped away. She wouldn't waste their precious time crying. She took a deep breath and looked up at him. "You know I have a thousand questions. Why don't you start talking?"

Moses nodded. "I will, but let's get out of this tunnel. I'm not sure how long my candle is going to last. We don't want to be stuck in the dark."

Carrie nodded. She gazed around her as they walked. The tunnel was circular and tall enough for even Moses to walk straight. Who had built this thing? How long had it been here? *Why* was it here?

Her mind flashed back to the house. How were Sam and Opal? What about the children? All she could do was pray the Union soldiers wouldn't hurt them. She hoped Sam was right that they didn't have a fight with the slaves. Other concerns crowded in, though. What would the slaves do if they had no food? How would they survive with her not there to run things? Impatiently, she shoved the thoughts from her mind. There was nothing she could do about them now.

They broke out of the tunnel, and Carrie stared at the gentle lapping swells of the James River just feet from where she stood. Moses waved her over to sit on a rock right next to the entrance. There was no chance anyone would sneak up on them. The entrance commanded a view of the river bank a hundred feet or more in either direction. The entrance itself was well concealed with a heavy growth of brush.

Carrie gazed at Moses. She wasn't sure which question to ask first. "I got your letter from Aunt Abby. I'm so glad you made it safely."

Moses nodded. "I could take all morning to tell you about that trip. I reckon it will have to wait for another time."

Carrie couldn't miss the anxious look on Moses' face. She knew it had to be more than worry for her safety. She remembered the last conversation she had heard between the soldiers in her bedroom. The one called

Clyde, he'd talked about Moses. She's almost forgotten it in her amazement over the tunnel. "You're a Union spy?"

Moses nodded. "I told you I would find a way to help the Union." He answered Carrie's next question before she asked it. "Rose is doing fine. She's in school and helping Aunt Abby around the house."

Carrie was glad to know her friend was okay, but her mind quickly moved on. "If you don't reconnect with the rest of the men soon, you will be in danger."

Moses nodded again. "It's not me I'm so worried about. I can figure out a story to keep them at least guessing. It's Sam and the rest I'm worried about. That man Clyde can cause a lot of trouble." He shook his head. "First we got to get you out of here safely, though."

Carrie had to know one thing. "How in the world did you know about the tunnel, Moses?"

Moses shrugged. "I was listening when I shouldn't have been listening," he said with a small smile. "I've found out it can come in handy sometimes. Your father took Robert up to your bedroom one day when your mama was real sick. I was taking up a bucket of ice to you. I wasn't even sure myself why I snuck down that day to listen to them. I knew he would beat me within an inch of my life if he found me, but for some reason I had to go." His heavy brow creased. "I heard your father tell Robert the mirror was the entrance to a tunnel that ran all the way to the river. That your great-granddaddy had put it in to be ready for Indian attacks."

"But why didn't Father ever tell me?" Carrie cried.

Moses shrugged. "I reckon you'll have to ask him that. Anyway, I heard a scraping noise and knew the entrance must be opening. Then I heard your father say sometimes the handle sticks on the outside."

"There's a handle on my mirror?" Carrie asked in amazement.

"Evidently. Anyway, next he said the handle on the inside always worked."

"But why did he tell Robert?"

"Because he knows Robert loves you. He figured he would be the one to take care of you if he couldn't," Moses said.

Carrie's eyes filled with tears. How wonderful that would be. Then she shook her head. Dreaming was useless. Especially now.

Moses continued on. "I was hoping to get to you last night." Briefly, he explained his floundering in the woods. "When I realized I wasn't going to make it on time to get you out through the house, everything your daddy said came pouring back."

Carrie looked around where they were sitting. "How in the world did you know how to find the entrance?"

"I didn't," Moses said with a grin. "All I knew was that it broke out onto the river."

"But Moses," Carrie protested "the river bank goes a long way. How in the world did you find it?" She looked back over her shoulder and saw absolutely no evidence of a tunnel entrance. She jumped up and walked over for a closer look. If you looked closely you could see a slight break in the brush. She pushed it aside and could barely see the outline of a wooden door. She shook her head in amazement. "How—"

Moses' voice sounded over her shoulder. "Let's say I agree with Sarah about the power of prayer. I ain't never prayed so hard in all my life. I was walking along, knowing that with every second that passed you were in more and more danger. All of a sudden, it was like that pile of brush there was calling my name. I didn't even ask questions for once. I just walked over and there it was."

Carrie stared up at him. She didn't know what to say. At some point all of this would sink it, but right now it was hard to believe she wasn't living a dream. A single gunshot in the distance jerked her back to hard reality. "Sam! Opal..." she breathed. She squared her shoulders. "I can't leave them, Moses. I have to go back."

Moses took her by the shoulders and swung her around to face him. "You're not doing any such thing, Carrie Cromwell. I don't reckon God showed me that tunnel to make sure you were free, only to have you turn around and walk right back into the middle of trouble." His voice was stern.

Carrie gazed at him. As much as she hated to admit it, she knew he was right. Her eyes filled with tears. "What if they hurt them?"

Moses shook his head. "I don't think they'll hurt anybody. They might scare them, but it wouldn't do them any good to hurt them. They'll probably need their help getting all the food."

Carrie groaned again. "How in the world are they going to survive when the soldiers leave and all the food is gone?"

"They'll manage," Moses said. "And if I know the captain, he won't take it all. He's a good man. Hates slavery. He's not going to leave them to starve. They'll plant again, Carrie. They'll be fine."

Carrie wasn't sure she believed him, but believe it or not, she was forced to accept she could not do anything to help them right now. "What next?" she finally asked with a small smile.

"We've got to get you to Richmond. *How* is the question."

Carrie stared out over the water. "I probably wouldn't make it on foot. It sounds like there are a lot of troops in the area."

Moses nodded. "We can walk back together to find my horse, but I'm not at all certain she is still there." His voice was troubled.

Carrie thought hard. "They will take all our horses, won't they?" She could hardly bear to think of Granite in Union hands.

Moses nodded. "Most likely," he said regretfully.

"Today?"

Moses looked thoughtful. "Probably not today. They are more interested in food. They'll bring men back to gather the food, and then they'll probably help themselves to the animals. Most of the other plantations had turned them loose. We found them wandering in the woods."

"Everyone else is gone?"

"Sure looks like it."

Carrie shook her head. "Why didn't Father let me know?" She pushed such futile thoughts out of her mind. She must deal with the present. She was quiet for several minutes as she thought. Now that some of the terror had passed, she was able to think more clearly. Obviously God wanted her out of here, or he wouldn't have allowed Moses to find the tunnel. She just had to figure out what came next.

"You think this tunnel leads to the barn?" she asked.

"I wondered the same thing. I don't know for sure, but it would make sense. Animals were just as important then as they are now." He paused. "Why?"

"Granite is in the barn. With any luck they won't let him out. It's obvious how valuable he is." The plan took shape rapidly as she talked. "I'm going to wait here until it's dark. Then I'm going to figure out a way to get to the barn. When I do, Granite and I are going to clear out of here."

"You're going to ride right past Union soldiers?" Moses demanded. "Are you crazy?"

Carrie shrugged, her courage returning. "I know parts of this plantation no one else does. With any luck I'll make it."

"And if you don't?"

Carrie smiled up at Moses' tense face. "What if you hadn't been able to find the tunnel?"

"But I did."

"Exactly. But not because of anything you did. God showed you that tunnel. I guess he can help me get out of here, too." Her voice and mind were calm now.

"What if it doesn't work?" Moses protested.

"You got any better ideas?" Carrie asked.

Moses shook his head. "Let's go look for that tunnel to the stables." He turned to head back inside.

Carrie reached out her hand and stopped him. "I'll find it. You have to get back."

Moses' eyes flashed. "I'm not going to do any such thing. I aim to stay with you until I know you're safe."

Carrie's voice was firm. "That's ridiculous, Moses, and you know it. You've done all you can for me now." She took his rough hand and smiled up at him. "You risked your life for me. Thank you," she said softly.

"It was the least I could do," Moses growled.

"So now we're even," Carrie said. "If you don't get back to those soldiers, everything you have worked for is going to be lost. Sitting with me all day, holding my hand, is not going to change whether I make it or not." She made her voice stern, even though her own doubts had begun to crowd out some of her confidence.

Moses sighed. "There is a stack of candles inside the door. Make sure you take plenty with you."

"I will," Carrie promised. She looked up at him intently. "When you get back north, tell Rose I love her and miss her. Aunt Abby, too. Tell them I believe we will be together when this horrible war is over." She paused. "I would like to think I can come back to the plantation, but my heart is saying my job here is done for now. I have a feeling I will be in Richmond for the rest of the war with my father."

Moses looked troubled. "That may not be for long, Carrie." He filled her in on the actions of McClellan's army. "Richmond is their next target."

Carrie nodded. "I'll face that when I have to," she said firmly. "First, I have to get there." She stretched up and kissed Moses on his strong cheek. "I love you, Moses. Thank you for everything." She stepped back. "You have to go," she said urgently.

Moses looked down at her for several long moments and pulled her close in a warm embrace. "Be careful, Carrie," he said in a broken whisper. Then he turned and began to run along the river bank.

Carrie watched him until he was out of sight. She wiped at the tears rolling down her face, then turned and disappeared into the tunnel.

Chapter Thirty-Eight

As soon as Carrie entered the tunnel she noticed the box of candles and matches Moses had talked about. She picked a candle up and stared at in wonder. Who had put it there? Her father? Her grandfather? Her great-grandfather? She struck a match, lit her candle, and stuck a huge handful of them in her dress pocket. Thank goodness she had not undressed for bed last night. Her present situation would be even more ridiculous.

She reached behind her and pulled the door to the tunnel firmly shut. Once it was closed, not even a shred of light seeped around the edges to reveal its presence. Whoever built this tunnel had been a master craftsman. Carrie stared at it for a long moment, wondering at the skill and labor it had taken to build what she had walked through this morning. She still could not believe she had never known of its existence. Had her mother known? She and her father would have much to talk about when she reached Richmond.

That thought was enough to pull her back to the present. First she had to discover if there was a tunnel that led to the barn. If there wasn't, she would find another way to sneak there once it was dark. She had already decided she would not leave Granite. Besides, he was probably her only way out of here. She stood still and tried to envision where the barn was from the end of the tunnel. All the many twists and turns had made her lose all sense of direction. She wasn't even sure where the tunnel had come out on the river. The only thing she was sure of was that the door would be off the right side. She would begin there.

Carrie raised the candle high so it would cast the greatest amount of light. She began to creep down the passage, her eyes glued to the wall for anything that would reveal the presence of another tunnel. An hour later she was startled when she heard a muffled shout above her head. She moved to extinguish her candle and realized how silly she was being. No one could possibly know she was down here.

She realized she was once more under the house. Part of her longed to stay and see what she could discover, but the realistic side of her said she needed to concentrate on nothing but finding the door to the stable—if one existed. Only then could she think of something else. She turned around and began to retrace her steps, moving even more slowly this time.

She had gone barely a hundred yards when she stopped suddenly. She held the candle closer to the wall and peered at it intently. Was that a faint outline in the bricks? She knelt down to get a better look, and ran her hands lightly over the wall. She could just barely discern a crack in the bricks, but where was the handle? She rocked back on her heels and stared at it, then ran her hands along the outline again. There was simply no handle. Suddenly, she felt one of the bricks shift slightly under her hand. Carrie held her breath while she shook the brick until it came loose in her hand. She laid it aside and leaned closer, holding the candle to the hole.

"The handle," she breathed triumphantly. "My great-grandfather was a genius," she whispered.

Carrie stood and pulled at the metal handle. The door opened slowly but easily. There was no way of knowing if this tunnel led to the stable, but there was only one way to find out. She lit another candle, stepped into the gaping hole, and pressed on.

The tunnel made three turns and ended abruptly. Carrie stared at the ladder set into the wall in front of her. Where did it lead? What was on the other side of the door above her head? For all she knew she could walk right into a group of Union soldiers. How could she determine where she was?

"I believe that's one of the finest horses I've ever seen."

Carrie gasped and shrank back as a voice sounded just above her head. She recognized the captain's voice immediately.

"Looks like a slab of granite, Captain. A mighty fine slab of granite."

Carrie didn't recognize the second voice, but she was relieved to know it wasn't the fellow named Clyde. She didn't want him anywhere near her horse.

The unidentified voice continued. "You would look mighty fine riding that horse, Captain. Since Miss Carrie Cromwell wasn't here to greet you, I reckon she would want to extend some of that famous Southern hospitality and give you her horse."

Carrie clinched her teeth to keep from crying out.

The captain's voice, when he answered, was amused. "I think you're right, James. It would be a shame to let a fine animal like this go to waste. I want you to tell the other men the barn is off-limits. Tomorrow afternoon, once we're done cleaning this place out, this beautiful Thoroughbred will carry me away from here."

"You'll be the envy of everyone," James said.

"I'm afraid you may be right. Here's hoping I can hold onto this animal when some of our many generals lay eyes on him."

The captain laughed, and Carrie heard him slap something.

"Well, old man, you take it easy in here. We'll clear out of here tomorrow."

Not if I have anything to say about it, Carrie thought to herself. She unclenched her fists as the footsteps above her faded away. She had discovered valuable information. The men were indeed planning on spending a night there, and the barn would supposedly be empty of soldiers. So far everything was going her way. Carrie forced herself to breathe evenly and considered her options.

By her best calculations it must be around ten o'clock in the morning. She had decided she wouldn't make her move until almost midnight. By then, most of the soldiers should be sleeping, and she would be able to catch any guards by surprise. That left fourteen hours to fill. Confident now no one could hear her when she was in the tunnel, she decided to move back into the house and see if she could determine what was going on.

She turned and retraced her steps until she reached the main tunnel and carefully used the brick that had concealed the handle to prop the heavy door open. She didn't want to have to repeat her initial search. Pulling against it firmly, she satisfied herself it was secure and then set off toward the house.

Her stomach growled loudly, but Carrie shook her head and pressed on. She would just have to be hungry until she reached Richmond. It was a small price to pay for her freedom.

She was even with what she knew was her father's office when she finally heard voices. Carrie strained to hear what was being said. Whoever it was, the voices were very low. She had to press her head almost into the bricks before she could make out the quiet words.

"Where in the world you figure Miss Carrie got off to?"

Carrie clapped her hand over her mouth to keep from crying out in delight. It was Sam! They must not have hurt him too badly. She could imagine the perplexed look on his kindly face and the worry darkening his eyes. He had taken seriously his job of caring for her. She longed to reveal her presence but knew she couldn't.

"It's like that girl disappeared into thin air," Opal said.

Tears filled Carrie's eyes as she realized both her friends were safe. The soldiers must have put them in the office while they searched the house. Sam's next words confirmed her suspicions.

"I sure wish I could get up there in her room and look for myself. Must be somethin' magic up there that took her away. I heard her in that room myself, not two minutes 'fore them soldiers came stomping up on the porch."

Carrie smiled. It had indeed been magic. All these years she had known deep in her heart that the beautiful mirror held secrets, but never in her wildest imagination had she envisioned the secret she discovered. Gratitude toward her great-grandparents rose in her like a wave. She knew there had been no more Indian attacks after they had completed the house. The tunnel had simply been there for years, a hidden extension of the house. When it was needed, it was there, patiently waiting to be put to use.

"I believe Miss Carrie is okay, Sam. We may never know how, but somehow that girl got away. Why, she's probably riding into Richmond right now."

Carrie smiled and sunk down against the wall. In spite of everything, she was suddenly very tired. Two nights of no sleep and the anxiety of the last few days had caught up with her. She leaned her head against the wall and closed her eyes. She would rest here, close to her friends. If anything else happened to them, she would know about it.

The sharp slamming of a door jolted her awake. Heart pounding, she realized she must have slept, but for how long? What time was it? Her immediate thought was to follow the tunnel back to the river so she could look outside and determine the time of day. A sudden voice held her where she was.

"I say we bring him in here, Captain. If he really is from around here, these slaves will know him."

Carrie leaned forward anxiously as Clyde's voice erupted on the other side of the wall.

"You're making too much out of this, Clyde," the captain protested. "Moses explained what happened. Adams had someone with him when we stopped him. They were hiding in the woods. Moses was still in the store gathering food when we took off. When he came out, the two men jumped him and tied him up."

"Adams wasn't big enough to even faze our nigger giant," Clyde said coldly.

"Two men surprising him could certainly pull it off. You saw how scratched and cut he was. I believe he's telling the truth. Besides, if he really helped the Cromwell girl escape—which I believe is completely ludicrous—what in the world would he be doing back here?"

"I don't know," Clyde admitted, "but I got me a feeling, Captain, and it ain't gonna hurt none to bring him in here. The old ones might be able to pull off faking like they never seen him, but these kids sure can't."

Carrie breathed a sigh of relief. Moses had returned to his unit and made up a story like he said he would. She was confident in Sam and Opal's ability to reveal nothing, but Clyde was right about one thing. Any of the other children in the quarters would have been a dead giveaway. They all worshipped Moses. But Fannie's kids had never laid eyes on him. Barely breathing, she pressed herself against the wall and waited.

Soon she heard heavy footsteps approaching again. "Have any of you ever seen this man before?" the captain asked sharply.

"Don't know as how I'd be havin' a reason to know a Yankee nigger, Captain," Sam drawled.

Carrie almost laughed out loud as she pictured his wide-eyed innocence.

"This man isn't a Yankee," the captain snapped. "He's from around here."

There was a slight pause. "Nope. Don't reckon as how I've ever seen him 'fore."

"What about you, woman?"

"I ain't never laid eyes on him neither," Opal said easily. "Is that man really a Yankee soldier?"

"Let's say he helps us with information we need around here," the captain responded.

Clyde spoke up then. "Ask the children," he said impatiently.

"I've been watching the children," the captain responded. "I'd have known in an instant if they knew Moses. Nope, Clyde, this time you're barking up the wrong tree." There was a slight pause. "Moses, I'm sorry. Everyone is a little tense right now."

"I understand, Captain," Moses responded calmly. "What would you like me to do now?"

"How about staying in here? Maybe *you* can get these slaves to talk. I think they know more than they're saying. Try to convince them we mean them no harm. Maybe they can be of some use to us."

"I'll see what I can do, Captain," Moses responded.

Carrie almost dissolved into laughter. The drama unfolding on the other side of the wall was better than any she had read in a book. She yearned to reveal her presence.

She stayed completely still during the long silence that followed. She knew Moses was waiting until he was sure no one was lurking around to hear his conversation with Sam and Opal. She smiled as she imagined the looks of delight on their faces at seeing their old friend.

Carrie strained to hear, but they were talking so lowly she could only catch snatches.

"Carrie is safe..."

"How...?

"Just know she's safe..."

"You really ...?

"Yes...spy."

Carrie ground her teeth in frustration at not being able to hear the conversation.

"Took me hours..." Moses said.

Carrie remembered she still had no idea what time it was. It could be night for all she knew. How long had she slept? She would have to go back out to the river to be sure. Tears were in her eyes when she turned away. She didn't know when she would see her friends again. Being on the other side of the wall, while frustrating, had also been a comfort.

She held the candle high again and moved down the tunnel. She hurried past the turn that led to the stable, and within minutes she was once more at the entrance to the river. She reached eagerly for the door handle and then froze. Though the thick door muffled it, she was certain she heard voices. She knelt and pressed her ear to the crack.

Was that the slap of oars on water? Were the voices so muffled because they were out on the water, not directly overhead or beside her? Carrie waited for what seemed like forever. It had been a long while since she had heard anything. Finally, she could stand it no longer.

She held her breath as she cracked the door open and listened. Nothing. Bolder now, she swung the door open wide enough for her to step through. The thickness of the brush should offer her enough protection. Again, only silence. Confident now, she stepped out onto the bank.

A faraway yell caused her to jerk her head around in time to see a large boat slip around the curve of the river.

Carrie stared. Was that what she had heard? Was a Union boat moving in to make an assault on the city?

The sun was almost resting on the horizon. She had slept longer than she thought, but she still had several hours before she could make her escape. She watched as the sun slipped down, kissing the river one final time before it bid adieu. Sitting down on a rock to think, she watched as night slowly claimed its dominion over the world. She was sure now that her father had tried to contact her. He would have known of the danger advancing toward her, but something must have gone wrong. He must be frantic.

Stars were twinkling in the sky when Carrie stood and walked back into the tunnel. She had decided to spend the last few hours under the barn. That way she would know if anyone came or went. Maybe it would give her some idea of how heavily guarded the plantation was. It took her only a few minutes to reach the same spot she discovered earlier. She stood still and listened carefully. She didn't hear voices, but that didn't mean anything. There could be one soldier on guard with no one to talk to.

Carrie soon realized she had no way to keep track of the amount of time passing. Then she remembered her first candle had burned for about an hour before going out—or at least what seemed to be about an hour. This crude method would at least give her an idea. As close as she could figure, it had been about eight o'clock when she reentered the tunnel. That meant four candles would take her close to midnight.

Carrie sank down on the floor and leaned her head back against the wall. Thankfully her nap had refreshed her. She would not have to worry about falling asleep. She would continue to map out her strategy while she waited.

Carrie looked thoughtfully at the remaining candle she had stuck into the dirt on the floor. It had only an inch left to burn. It was time for her to make her move. The only sound she heard since she settled down to wait was an occasional whinny from Granite, inquiring as to why she still had not come to let him out. The familiar sound comforted her.

She moved over to the ladder and tested it one more time. It looked sturdy, but if it came dislodged, she would never be able to reach the door over her head. She was still uncertain where it led, but her instincts told her it would open up into the tack room. Hitching her dress up around her, Carrie began to climb quietly. She knew the candle she had left burning would extinguish itself soon.

Carrie reached the top of the ladder. Her heart pounded as she pressed her hand against the door. It was heavy, but it moved easily enough. Keeping a tight hold on it so that it wouldn't fall back and make a loud noise, she carefully stepped up and out into utter darkness. Now she was sure she was in the tack room. As she waited for her eyes to adjust, praying no one could hear her racing heart, she could barely make out the saddles and bridles lining the walls. Moving ever so cautiously, she eased the door back down. Never in all the years she had spent in this tack room had she guessed the secret that lay beneath her feet.

She stood completely still and listened carefully. There was not a sound. Then, moving with the certainty of familiarity, Carrie eased over to the large trunk pushed against the wall. She almost groaned at the creaking noise when she opened it. She waited quietly again. Had anyone heard the noise? Convinced there was no one close by, she reached into the trunk and pulled out a pair of her father's riding pants, a shirt and a jacket. She held them close to her face and breathed in. The smell of her father gave her a feeling of courage. Just a little while longer and she would be safe in Richmond with him.

Her jaw tightened when she realized how much she had to overcome still. Moving fast now, she undressed and tossed her skirts aside in a heap. She slipped into her father's clothes, rolling up the pants and the sleeves to make sure they wouldn't hamper her movement. She wished she had a mirror. She was quite sure that no matter how she looked, she would rather dress this way all the time. The freedom of movement she felt in her father's clothes was wonderful.

Determined to make her move soon, Carrie stashed her dress in the trunk and groped around until she found a hat. She had unbraided her hair while she was waiting below. Now she quickly piled it on top of her head and pulled the cap down snugly. She was hoping to pass for a man in the dark. She had thought it all through carefully.

Carrie crept toward the door, then pressed her ear against it. She knew there might be someone standing on the other side, but there was only one way to find out. She took a deep breath, pushed the door open, and eased out into the aisle. The time for being careful had passed. Speed was all that mattered now.

Leaving the tack room door open, Carrie flew down the aisle and slipped the latch to Granite's stall. His joyous whinny was exactly what she had expected. Saddling him was out of the question. She could not afford either the noise or the time. She would have to ride bareback.

"What was that?" she heard a voice mutter from just outside the door.

Quick as a flash, she slipped the bridle into Granite's willing mouth, grabbed a handful of mane and leapt onto his back. She leaned forward and yelled into his ear, "Run!"

Granite bolted out of his stall door and was flying when he hit the stable entrance. The man who had jumped up to investigate fell back, yelling and cursing.

Carrie leaned low over Granite's neck and held tightly to his mane with one hand. She had never fallen off her horse, and now was certainly not the time to start.

"Stop!" a man screamed behind her. She heard the crack of a rifle. Carrie leaned even lower and urged Granite on. More rifle shots rang out behind her. She heard the whistle as one flew by her head. Granite seemed to skim the ground as he raced across the pasture. Carrie knew they were clearly visible in the moonlight. Had she not spent hours watching Granite graze on moonlit nights? She was also quite certain not one of those men had a horse that could catch Granite with such a head start.

All of a sudden, her body rocked forward with a sharp jolt. She cried out and grabbed onto Granite's mane more tightly as pain exploded in her right shoulder. One of the bullets had hit its mark. Gritting her teeth against the pain, she crouched down closer to her horse's neck and willed herself not to think about the fire burning in her body. She had no choice but to press on.

Shots still rang out, but they were more distant now. Carrie would have relaxed a little if she hadn't known what was ahead. This escape through the pasture meant there was no gate to exit through. She had never jumped without a saddle, and even then no more than two feet. The fence racing up on them was five feet tall. Carrie gripped Granite's mane tighter and prayed she would make it.

Granite never hesitated. One minute he was flying across the ground, the next moment he was soaring through the air. Carrie shouted with exhilaration as he landed smoothly on the other side and continued to run. Never had she experienced such a thrill. For a moment, the pain of her shoulder faded away. She had always suspected riding would be much more fun dressed like a man. Now she was certain of it.

Her exhilaration lasted only a moment. She was quite sure the captain would send his men after her. She had enough of a head start to make it to the hidden trail, but only if she pressed on. She slowed Granite to a fast trot and scanned the woods along the road until she found the landmark she was looking for. She eased Granite into the woods and pulled him to a stop no more than a hundred feet later, wrapping her arms around his neck, and talking to him quietly. Warm blood ran down her back, soaking her father's shirt. She had to do something to staunch it, but not yet.

Minutes later, she heard what she was waiting for. Rapid hoofbeats were faint at first, but became louder as they drew close. Carrie held her breath as she waited for them to pass. Only then would she press on.

The horses stopped. "We couldn't have just lost her like that," she heard the captain growl in a frustrated voice.

"Didn't look like no girl on that horse," one soldier protested. "Whoever raced off on that devil looked like a man. Sure as heck rode like one."

"I don't care what it looked like," the captain snapped. "I caught a good look at them as they raced across the pasture. There isn't a man in this country shaped like that. No, men, we've been outwitted by a woman."

Carrie grinned to herself in the darkness as she stroked Granite's neck and willed him to stand still.

"What do we do now, Captain? Keep on looking?"

"I'm afraid our efforts would be futile. You heard what Adams told us. There are trails through these woods that nobody but locals know about." He paused, then continued bitterly. "For all I know, she's listening to us right now."

"Want us to shoot some bullets into the woods?" one voice called cheerfully.

Carrie stiffened and wondered if she should risk revealing her position by allowing Granite his head in a dash through the woods.

"Don't waste the bullets, men. We don't really need Miss Carrie Cromwell. It was her horse I wanted. If she is in there, you could risk shooting that fine animal. I don't want that. She outwitted us this time. We won't always win the game." His voice was amused. "That was one of the finest pieces of riding I ever witnessed. I still can't believe she jumped that fence. And bareback! Good Lord."

Carrie grinned again. She had a feeling in different circumstances she would have liked the captain.

"Let's go, men. Carrie Cromwell has her horse, but we have her plantation, her slaves and all her crops. We haven't done too badly."

Carrie's grin disappeared as the triumph of her daring escape evaporated. The captain was right. They hadn't done too badly.

It took only minutes for her to be assured she was alone once more. Only then did she slip her father's shirt off and rip off a large piece. Granite stood quietly. Carrie gritted her teeth as she wrapped the heavy cloth around her neck and under her armpit. She pulled tightly, wincing at the pain, until she was sure there was sufficient pressure to staunch her shoulder's bleeding. She shook her head to push away her lightheadedness and pressed her lips together in determination.

She gave Granite his head, knowing he would follow the trail they had entered on. She would be in Richmond by morning.

Chapter Thirty-Nine

Carrie moved slowly but steadily all night. Only twice had she been forced to emerge from the protection of the woods to travel on main roads, and then only for a few minutes before she ducked back onto another hidden trail. She had gradually relaxed as she rode along. She had not heard anything other than animals and had not encountered another living being. She would be in Richmond in a couple of hours, just as the sun was coming up.

A crashing in the bushes alerted her, and Granite snorted and threw his head up in protest. "Easy," Carrie whispered quietly. Granite planted his feet and refused to budge another inch, his eyes riveted on the clump of bushes in front of them. Carrie stared wide-eyed at the bushes. What was there? She knew it was something, or someone, but it was too dark to see anything.

She summoned her courage and spoke sharply. "Who goes there?" She tried to make her voice deep.

"I'm a Confederate soldier, ma'am," a voice came back to her. "You ain't got no reason to be afraid."

Whoever he was, he surely didn't sound dangerous. "What are you doing out here?"

"Trying to figure out how to get to Cromwell Plantation, ma'am." The voice grew a little more hopeful. "It's real important I get there, ma'am. Can you tell me how far it is? I kind of got turned around."

"Why do you need to get to Cromwell Plantation?" Carrie demanded. Maybe this was another trick of some kind. Her heart started beating rapidly again as she imagined a Yankee soldier laughing derisively and striding out of the bushes once she had revealed her true identity. "And why are you hiding in those bushes?"

There was a slight hesitation and then he spoke again. "Can't really come out of these bushes, ma'am. I'm right embarrassed to say so, but I'm afraid I... I only...

Well, you see, ma'am... I only got underwear on," he finally blurted out.

"What?" Carrie exclaimed. "Why ever for?" Her confusion deepened. Why in the world was a Confederate soldier roaming around in the woods with only his underwear?

"I had a run-in with a good for nothing slave hunter," he said bitterly. "He knocked me out and stole my uniform and my horse." He paused. "When I came to, I guess I was still a little fuzzy. Somehow I got all turned around." His voice grew a little desperate. "I got to get to Cromwell Plantation. It's real important."

"Why?" Carrie asked. Her heart was telling her she could trust whoever was in the bushes. He sounded young and very vulnerable.

"My lieutenant sent me on a mission. That's really all I can tell you."

Carrie had a sudden wild thought. "Might that be Lieutenant Robert Borden?"

There was a sudden rustling in the bushes. Then a shocked voice. "You know my lieutenant, ma'am?"

"I might. Just who am I speaking to?"

"My name is Warren Hobbs."

Carrie almost laughed aloud with relief. "Hobbs! Is that really you? I thought your voice sounded strangely familiar." There was another shocked silence. She could imagine Hobbs' frustration at his need to stay hidden in the bushes.

"Do I know you, ma'am?" came the careful reply.

Carrie was impressed with his caution. He wasn't going to give away anything unless he had to. This time she did laugh aloud. "This is Carrie Cromwell, Hobbs. I met you when you were wounded after the battle."

She heard a gasp and then saw the shadowy outline of a face staring through the bushes. "You're all right! I've been worrying myself sick that I wasn't going to make it to the plantation on time. The lieutenant would have never forgiven me."

Carrie smiled to herself. "Hobbs, wait right here. I'm going back to get some clothes for you. I passed a little house not too far back. I'm sure there was no one there."

"You think there are clothes there, ma'am?" Hobbs' voice was almost pathetically hopeful.

"I'm going to find out," Carrie said.

"Are you sure it's safe, ma'am?"

"I'll be fine," she assured him. "I'll be back soon."

She wasn't nearly as sure as she sounded as she turned around to retrace her steps. Granite bobbed his head in protest of the change in direction. He, too, knew there could be danger lurking behind them, but she really had no choice. She couldn't leave Hobbs standing in the woods with nothing on, and he certainly couldn't show up in Richmond like that.

Her heart was pounding as she approached the deserted little house. She stopped and listened for several long minutes before she dismounted, gritting her teeth against the pain in her shoulder, and edged quietly toward the house. Her hand trembled as she reached for the doorknob, and the door opened easily under her touch. Fighting to control her desire to turn and run, she slipped into the tiny room and stood motionless, trying to steady her breathing.

Willing her eyes to adjust to the darkness, Carrie gazed around the room. Right next to where she was standing she thought she detected the outline of a coat or something on the wall. She reached out and encountered the rough feeling of wool. She grabbed whatever it was and pulled it toward her. It was indeed a coat. More groping produced a pair of pants and what seemed to be a shirt. Carrie clutched them under her good arm and left the house. She pulled Granite next to the porch so she could mount, knowing her shoulder wouldn't allow her to swing up. Moments later, he was trotting down the trail. He, too, was eager to make up for lost time.

When Carrie came even with where she thought they had been before, she called softly, "Hobbs?"

"I'm right here, Miss Cromwell. I was afraid you might not be able to find me again."

Carrie spoke quickly. "I have some clothes for you. I'm going to throw them down and ride several yards ahead. Let me know when you're dressed."

"Thank you, ma'am," came the fervent reply.

Carrie waited, staring into the darkness and fretting at the delay. She felt better riding under the protective covering of night.

"I'm here, Miss Cromwell, and I got to tell you, I don't know that I've ever been this embarrassed. I was supposed to be rescuing you. Now here you are rescuing me." Hobbs' voice was deeply chagrined.

Carrie felt a deep sympathy for him. She remembered his devotion to Robert. She was sure he had jumped at the chance to do something for his lieutenant. Then she remembered what he had said earlier about the man who had jumped him. "You said your attacker was a slave hunter?"

"Yes, ma'am. The fool even told me his name before he attacked me. A fellow by the name of Adams."

Carrie's lips thinned. "I take it he didn't want you to reach the plantation."

"No, ma'am. He wanted me to turn back and let him go on to the plantation to warn you. When I refused, he let me have it."

Carrie flushed with anger. Once she told her father this story he could not possibly be angry with her for throwing Adams off the plantation. A small smile replaced the anger. "I guess it's true that God knows how to turn the bad things to good, Hobbs."

"Huh?"

"Never mind," Carrie said briskly. "How do the clothes fit?"

"Well, let's just say there's plenty of room in here."

Carrie's laughter rang through the woods. It was good not to be alone anymore. The woods weren't nearly so scary with someone else there, but the need to reach Richmond was still critical.

Hobbs stepped forward. "If you'll give me a hand up, I can swing up beside you."

Carrie hesitated, once more aware of the pain raging in her shoulder. "I'm afraid I can't do that, Hobbs." Now that the newest excitement was dying down, she found it harder to hide the pain in her voice.

"Are you okay, Miss Cromwell?" Hobbs asked.

"I was shot during my escape."

"Shot?!" Hobbs cried in a horrified voice.

Carrie tried to sound matter-of-fact. "It's nothing that can't be taken care of when we reach Richmond. We just have to get there." She paused and thought for a moment. "I guess we'll have to backtrack to that little house again. You can use the porch to get on behind me."

Hobbs followed her to the house, and within minutes, they were once more on their way toward safety.

Carrie was less than a mile from Richmond when the last trail dumped her out onto the main road. She hated to ride even that far in the open, but she saw no other choice. "Where are the military blocks, Hobbs?" she asked.

He peered over her shoulder, careful to stay far enough back not to touch her. "Not too much further," he replied. "I'm afraid we may have a hard time getting past them."

"We'll get past them." She had come too far to be stopped by a roadblock. The pain in her shoulder was becoming unbearable. The long night had taken its toll. Speaking softly, she urged Granite into a canter. She still imagined that pursuing Union soldiers could break from the woods at any moment.

"Halt!" A harried-looking soldier stepped out in front of them, his rifle drawn.

Carrie pulled Granite to a stop.

The soldier looked at both of them curiously. "I need to see your pass, please."

Carrie stared at him but noticed he wasn't really looking at her. He seemed to be studying Hobbs instead. He didn't seem to be alarmed, however. It was more as if he were trying to keep from laughing.

"I don't have a pass," she said.

He frowned and was immediately all attention. "I'm afraid I can't let you enter the city, ma'am," he said. He stared at her, as if he had just been shocked into reality. "You're a woman?" he asked incredulously.

"I'm afraid so, soldier," Carrie replied, "and I have just escaped from my plantation, which is even now being raided by Union soldiers. I really don't care to continue sitting here. I would like to go to my father's house."

The soldier continued to stare at her. She realized how ludicrous she must look in her father's clothes. Finally he shook his head. "I'll have to get the lieutenant." He turned crisply and walked away to a small building set to the side.

Carrie's wild hope that the lieutenant might turn out to be Robert was dashed as soon as a short, portly man hurried from the building. He stared in the direction the guard was pointing and then ambled over. "May I help you?" His tone wasn't quite as courteous as the guard's.

"I understand from your guard that a pass is needed to get into the city. I don't have one. How do I go about procuring one, Lieutenant?"

"Why do you want into Richmond, ma'am?"

Carrie flushed at the patronizing tone in the officer's voice. She was tired, hurt and running very low on patience. "See here, officer. I know we look a little unusual, but our circumstances have been a little unusual. My name is Carrie Cromwell. My father, Thomas Cromwell, works with Governor Letcher. Until yesterday morning, I was running my father's plantation. It now happens to be in the hands of Union soldiers." She didn't wait to find out if he believed her or not. "The man behind me is one of your own soldiers. Lieutenant Borden sent him out to escort me back from the plantation. He was attacked on the way and barely escaped with his life." She paused. "Now, may I please enter the city?"

The lieutenant shook his head. "I'm not saying I don't believe your story, ma'am, but things are pretty tense around here right now. Our jails are filling up with people not too loyal to the Confederate cause. I'm going to have to do some checking to verify your story."

"Check all you want, Lieutenant," Carrie said quietly. "My father lives at 318 Twenty-Sixth Street. His office is in the Capitol Building if you don't find him at home."

Hobbs spoke up then. "All you have to do is go get Lieutenant Borden. He will be able to identify us."

The lieutenant smirked. "Lieutenant Borden is a very busy man right now. Or did you two not know there is a war going on?"

Carrie flushed with anger, but she managed to bite her tongue. It would do no good to antagonize the man any further. He had a thankless job. "We will wait while you verify our stories," she said.

The lieutenant nodded sharply and turned away. Carrie was overwhelmed with exhaustion. She had had very little sleep for three days and no food for the last thirty-six hours. "Let's get off, Hobbs. We can sit over on those rocks while we wait." She felt Hobbs slide off behind her and then followed suit, thankful for Hobbs' supporting arms to ease the pain of her shoulder. Every muscle ached from riding so many hours bareback. When she looked at Hobbs, however, she momentarily forgot everything else.

"Hobbs!" she cried. She bent almost double from laughter, mindless of the pain.

"I realized quite a ways back that I must make a very interesting looking fellow," Hobbs finally admitted.

Carrie nodded. Hobbs could easily pass for a clown. The pants were purple and hopelessly huge. If he weren't holding them, they would have slid right down. The red shirt was almost as bright as the kelly green coat that was at least four sizes too big on his lanky form. Everything had gaping holes. There must have been a large rat population in the old house. Carrie tried to control the twitching of her lips but failed miserably.

Hobbs smiled reluctantly, then looked down and managed a chuckle. In moments, they were both laughing uproariously. Carrie grabbed her sides as the laughter released the tension and pain that had been building to a crescendo.

"What seems to be the problem here?" she heard a commanding voice ask.

Carrie gasped and spun around.

"These two people claim to know you," the lieutenant said in an exasperated voice. "I'm sorry to bother you."

Robert nodded and walked over closer to where Carrie and Hobbs were waiting. Suddenly his eyes narrowed. "Hobbs?" he asked. He took a step closer. "Carrie?"

Carrie pulled her hat off and allowed her long black waves to tumble down her back. "I reckon it is, Lieutenant," she said with a grin. To her chagrin, she began to cry.

Robert held his arms out, and she walked into them, forgetting for a moment the bullet lodged in her shoulder. When he grabbed her to him, she cried out in pain before fainting.

An Invitation

Before you read the last chapter of On To Richmond, I would like to invite you to join my mailing list so that you are never left wondering what is going to happen next. ☺

Join my Email list so you can:

- Receive notice of all new books & audio releases.
- Be a part of my Launch celebrations. I give away lots of Free gifts! ☺
- Read my weekly blog while you're waiting for a new book.
- Be part of The Bregdan Chronicles Family!
- Learn about all the other books I write.

Just go to www.BregdanChronicles.net and fill out the form.

I look forward to having you become part of The Bregdan Chronicles Family!

Blessings,
Ginny Dye

Chapter Forty

May 15, 1862

Carrie fought her way back to consciousness mindful of the voices flowing around her. Vaguely she became aware of something soft surrounding her. As the voices continued, she could identify them. Her father's concerned voice was the loudest. Then Robert's deep tones answered him. Finally a female voice joined in. It was Janie. Carrie had a dim memory of falling into Robert's arms. How had she gotten here? Where was here?

She forced her eyes open, blinking against the light as she fought the dizziness that still threatened to overwhelm her. A cold cloth was laid on her head and another used to gently wipe her face.

"I think she's coming around," Janie said softly.

The cool cloths helped. Carrie was finally able to make the spinning shapes stand still. "Where am I?"

Her father stepped forward. "You're home, Carrie. In your bedroom."

"The plantation?" Carrie murmured, still confused.

"No, dear. You're with me in Richmond."

Carrie frowned at the anguished pain in his voice. "I'm okay, Father."

Thomas managed a cracked laugh. "You're going to be, my hard-headed, wonderful daughter. You're going to be."

Robert stepped forward then. "Do you remember fainting?"

"A little."

Robert smiled. "You didn't warn me you were carrying a bullet in your shoulder before I hugged you. I have to admit you scared me to death. I thought it was my hug that made you faint."

Carrie managed a weak smile and reached her hand out to touch Robert's. Robert grasped hers and gazed down at her tenderly. Then she turned to look at Janie.

"We got all the bullet," Janie assured her. "When Hobbs told us about your brave escape, I went straight to Dr. McCaw. He was happy to take care of it." Her voice grew stern. "He also said you are to take it easy for a few days. He has become quite aware of your independent spirit. He said he would not be responsible if you insist on being foolish."

Carrie's laugh this time was genuine. "Lying in bed seems like a welcome idea right now. I'll try not to cause anyone any more trouble."

Thomas laid his hand on her forehead tenderly. "You will never be trouble, Carrie. I'm glad you're okay. I've been sick with worry."

Carrie gazed at the deep lines on his face and knew he was telling the truth. Her heart saddened at the knowledge of the pain he had been forced to endure. "I'm sorry, Father."

Thomas shook his head. "There is nothing to be sorry for. Hobbs explained the situation to us. I'm very proud of you, dear. I can lose the plantation and survive. I could not survive losing you," he said roughly. He made no attempt to hide the tears in his eyes.

"Granite?"

"He's fine, Carrie," Robert said. "Well-fed and watered. He's trying to figure out what he's doing in the stable behind your father's house. I think he's making friends with the carriage horse. It will do his highness good to mingle with the common class," he said with a grin.

He turned to Janie. "Why don't we leave Carrie and her father alone for a few minutes?" He looked at Carrie then and added, "May I come back in to see you? Will you feel like it?"

Carrie nodded. "I would like that."

Carrie and Thomas sat quietly for several minutes, content to merely look at each other and know they were together again. Carrie's head was becoming clearer.

"Father, I need to talk to you about something." She had made her decision during the long night. The deception she had carried on for so long may have been necessary, but she could not now live with her father without telling him the truth. She would not let her fear of his reaction torment her any longer. It was time for truth.

Thomas frowned. "You sound very serious, Carrie. Can't this wait until later?"

Carrie shook her head and took a deep breath. "I have been lying to you, Father. I can't do it any longer."

Thomas looked at her closely as he sat down in the chair next to her bed. "Tell me about it," he invited.

Carrie poured the whole story out. About Adams attempting to rape Rose and how she had subsequently thrown him off the plantation. How Moses and Rose had helped run the plantation. How she had helped them and others escape, and simply turned her back when others left. She told him everything, holding nothing back. Finally she drew to an end.

"I understand you will probably be very angry. I have hated every minute of this deception. I know what I have done has hurt you. For that I am very sorry, but—"

"But you have acted according to your beliefs," Thomas finished for her.

Carrie nodded, unsure of how to take her father's words. She had watched the full range of emotions explode over his face while she talked. Disbelief. Anger. Sympathy. A struggle to understand. Sorrow.

Thomas reached out for her hand. "Lying to me was wrong, Carrie, but," he added in a firm voice, "I would have done the same thing if I had been in your place." He paused. "You know I don't agree with your position. I can, however, appreciate your commitment to your belief." He stopped again. "What you have done has cost me greatly, yet, I know now that it would probably have come to pass anyway. Slaves are running away everywhere. Other slaves are being set free by the Union soldiers, many escorted to freedom." His voice became bitter. "I was going to lose everything I've worked for one way or another."

Carrie watched him quietly, uncertain of what to say. "I'm sorry," she murmured.

Thomas squeezed her hand. "What is done is done. I'm sure we'll have more to talk about, but for now, knowing you are safe and here with me is simply enough. I forgive you because I love you. We will deal with our differences because we love each other. That's what counts."

Carrie smiled through the tears rolling down her face. "I love you," she said. A huge burden had been lifted. Their love would survive their differences.

"And I love you," Thomas replied. He leaned forward to kiss her forehead, then stepped back. "I believe there is a lieutenant who wants to talk with you."

Carrie wiped at her tears as her father left the room.

Within moments, Robert was striding into the room, a broad but tentative smile on his face. "You sure you have energy left, Carrie? I can come back later."

"I want you to stay."

Robert leaned forward to kiss her forehead. "Are you okay?"

Carrie nodded. "It's nice to know there is not still metal lodged in my body." When Robert's face darkened, she knew he was thinking about what she had gone through. She reached for his hand. "I'm going to be fine," she promised.

Robert nodded and gazed down at her for a long moment. Carrie stared back into his dark eyes. The air seemed to pulse around her.

"I love you, Carrie Cromwell," Robert said roughly.

Carrie nodded. "I love you, too, Robert Borden." It was the truth. In spite of everything, she couldn't deny what her heart was feeling.

Robert leaned forward to kiss her forehead again and then pulled a chair close to the bed. "I have something to tell you."

Carrie watched him quietly.

"I found God."

Carrie held her breath and waited for him to go on.

Robert glanced at her and then continued. "I think I have, anyway. All I know is that God showed me He loves me." He described the incident with the wagon.

"What day was that?" Carrie asked.

Robert frowned. "It was January seventh" he said.

"That was the day I prayed for you," Carrie said in wonder. She told him what had happened.

Robert smiled. "I would like to tell you I've changed how I feel about slavery. I can't say I have. I'm trying to release the hatred in my heart, but I still feel it is our destiny to control the slaves." He paused. "I can be nothing but honest with you."

Carrie listened. She was learning to trust God. She was also learning his timing was nothing like her own. If she and Robert were meant to share a life together, God would work things out. In the meantime, she would try to trust him with her future by choosing to live fully in the present. And living fully in the present meant loving Robert.

"You know I love you," Robert went on. "You know I want to marry you. But let's not talk of marriage until this war is over. I want us to be together, not separated by one endless battle after another."

Carrie nodded. "Let's take one day at a time. We'll face the question of our future when it is time to face it. In the meantime, do I have to be content with mere kisses on the forehead, Lieutenant?"

His response silenced her for long moments.

Carrie stood side by side with her father and Janie as the grounds surrounding City Hall filled with desperate, determined citizens. Even as the crowd grew, they could hear Federal guns pounding the batteries at Drewry's Bluff, just south of the city on the James. Large numbers of elite Richmonders had abandoned their city. President Davis' wife had joined that number. The general spirit of the city was one of doom, yet still a glimmer of hope flickered in the darkness.

Governor Letcher had called volunteers to join companies of citizens for the city's defense. The response was immediate and tremendous. Richmond might fall, but it would not go down without a fight. If the military fell, there would yet be citizens willing to put their lives on the line for their beloved city—their beloved capital.

Mayor Mayo appeared beside the governor. He raised his hands to get the crowd's attention. Finally, he was able to speak.

"Before God and Heaven, I will say to one and all, that, if they want the mayor to surrender the city, they must get some other mayor. So help me God, I'll never do it!"

For one significant moment, the cheers of the beleaguered city drowned out the booming of guns. Richmond was not dead yet.

~ *To Be Continued...*

Available Now!
www.DiscoverTheBregdanChronicles.com

*Would you be so kind as to leave a Review on Amazon?
I love hearing from my readers! Just go to
Amazon.com, put **On To Richmond** into the Search box,
click to read the Reviews, and you'll be able to leave one
of your own!*

Thank you!

<u>The Bregdan Principle</u>

Every life that has been lived until today is a part of the woven braid of life.

It takes every person's story to create history.

Your life will help determine the course of history.

You may think you don't have much of an impact.

You do.

Every action you take will reflect in someone else's life.

Someone else's decisions.

Someone else's future.

Both good and bad.

The Bregdan Chronicles

Storm Clouds Rolling In
1860 – 1861

On To Richmond
1861 – 1862

Spring Will Come
1862 – 1863

Dark Chaos
1863 – 1864

The Long Last Night
1864 – 1865

Carried Forward By Hope
April – December 1865

Glimmers of Change
December – August 1866

Shifted By The Winds
August – December 1866

***Many more coming... Go to
DiscoverTheBregdanChronicles.com to see how
many are available now!***

<u>Other Books by Ginny Dye</u>

<u>Pepper Crest High Series</u> - Teen Fiction

Time For A Second Change
It's Really A Matter of Trust
A Lost & Found Friend
Time For A Change of Heart

<u>When I Dream Series</u> – Children's Bedtime Stories

When I Dream, I Dream of Horses
When I Dream, I Dream of Puppies
When I Dream, I Dream of Snow
When I Dream, I Dream of Kittens
When I Dream, I Dream of Elephants
When I Dream, I Dream of the Ocean

<u>Fly To Your Dreams Series</u> – Allegorical Fantasy

Dream Dragon
Born To Fly
Little Heart

101+ Ways to Promote Your Business Opportunity

All titles by Ginny Dye
<u>www.AVoiceInTheWorld.com</u>

Author Biography

Who am I? Just a normal person who happens to love to write. If I could do it all anonymously, I would. In fact, I did the first go round. I wrote under a pen name. On the off chance I would ever become famous - I didn't want to be! I don't like the limelight. I don't like living in a fishbowl. I especially don't like thinking I have to look good everywhere I go, just in case someone recognizes me! I finally decided none of that matters. If you don't like me in overalls and a baseball cap, too bad. If you don't like my haircut or think I should do something different than what I'm doing, too bad. I'll write books that you will hopefully like, and we'll both let that be enough! :) Fair?

But let's see what you might want to know. I spent many years as a Wanderer. My dream when I graduated from college was to experience the United States. I grew up in the South. There are many things I love about it but I wanted to live in other places. So I did. I moved 42 times, traveled extensively in 49 of the 50 states, and had more experiences than I will ever be able to recount. The only state I haven't been in is Alaska, simply because I refuse to visit such a vast, fabulous place until I have at least a month. Along the way I had glorious adventures. I've canoed through the Everglade Swamps, snorkeled in the Florida Keys and windsurfed in the Gulf of Mexico. I've white-water rafted down the New River and Bungee jumped in the Wisconsin Dells. I've visited every National Park (in the off-season when there is more freedom!) and many of the State Parks. I've hiked thousands of miles of mountain trails and biked through Arizona deserts. I've canoed and biked through Upstate New York and Vermont, and polished off as much lobster as possible on the Maine Coast.

I had a glorious time and never thought I would find a place that would hold me until I came to the Pacific Northwest. I'd been here less than 2 weeks, and I knew I would never leave. My heart is so at home here with the towering firs, sparkling waters, soaring mountains and rocky beaches. I love the eagles & whales. In 5 minutes I can be hiking on 150 miles of trails in the mountains around my home, or gliding across the lake in my rowing shell. I love it!

Have you figured out I'm kind of an outdoors gal? If it can be done outdoors, I love it! Hiking, biking, windsurfing, rock-climbing, roller-blading, snow-shoeing, skiing, rowing, canoeing, softball, tennis... the list could go on and on. I love to have fun and I love to stretch my body. This should give you a pretty good idea of what I do in my free time.

When I'm not writing or playing, I'm building I Am A Voice In The World - a fabulous organization I founded in 2001 - along with 60 amazing people who poured their lives into creating resources to empower people to make a difference with their lives.

What else? I love to read, cook, sit for hours in solitude on my mountain, and also hang out with friends. I love barbeques and block parties. Basically - I just love LIFE!

I'm so glad you're part of my world!

Ginny

Join my Email List so you can:

- Receive notice of all new books
- Be a part of my Launch Celebrations. I give away lots of Free gifts!
- Read my weekly BLOG while you're waiting for a new book.
- Be part of The Bregdan Chronicles Family!
- Learn about all the other books I write.

Just go to www.BregdanChronicles.net and fill out the form.